Villa Rubein, and Ot

John Galsworthy

Alpha Editions

This edition published in 2024

ISBN : 9789362996749

Design and Setting By
Alpha Editions
www.alphaedis.com
Email - info@alphaedis.com

As per information held with us this book is in Public Domain. This book is a reproduction of an important historical work. Alpha Editions uses the best technology to reproduce historical work in the same manner it was first published to preserve its original nature. Any marks or number seen are left intentionally to preserve its true form.

Contents

PREFACE .... - 1 -
VILLA RUBEIN .... - 5 -
I .... - 7 -
II .... - 12 -
III .... - 18 -
IV .... - 22 -
V .... - 26 -
VI .... - 33 -
VII .... - 39 -
VIII .... - 44 -
IX .... - 50 -
X .... - 55 -
XI .... - 59 -
XII .... - 62 -
XIII .... - 67 -
XIV .... - 71 -
XV .... - 73 -
XVI .... - 76 -
XVII .... - 79 -
XVIII .... - 83 -
XIX .... - 90 -
XX .... - 96 -
XXI .... - 100 -
XXII .... - 105 -
XXIII .... - 107 -
XXIV .... - 110 -

XXV	- 113 -
XXVI	- 116 -
XXVII	- 119 -
XXVIII	- 123 -
XXIX	- 127 -
A MAN OF DEVON	- 131 -
I	- 133 -
II	- 137 -
III	- 140 -
IV	- 147 -
V	- 154 -
VI	- 162 -
VII	- 165 -
VIII	- 168 -
A KNIGHT	- 171 -
I	- 173 -
II	- 177 -
III	- 182 -
IV	- 186 -
V	- 189 -
VI	- 192 -
VII	- 195 -
VIII	- 198 -
SALVATION OF A FORSYTE	- 203 -
I	- 205 -
II	- 209 -
III	- 213 -
IV	- 216 -

V	- 219 -
VI	- 221 -
VII	- 223 -
VIII	- 226 -
IX	- 228 -
X	- 231 -
XI	- 233 -
XII	- 235 -
THE SILENCE	- 239 -
I	- 241 -
II	- 245 -
III	- 248 -
IV	- 251 -
V	- 254 -
VI	- 258 -

PREFACE

Writing not long ago to my oldest literary friend, I expressed in a moment of heedless sentiment the wish that we might have again one of our talks of long-past days, over the purposes and methods of our art. And my friend, wiser than I, as he has always been, replied with this doubting phrase "Could we recapture the zest of that old time?"

I would not like to believe that our faith in the value of imaginative art has diminished, that we think it less worth while to struggle for glimpses of truth and for the words which may pass them on to other eyes; or that we can no longer discern the star we tried to follow; but I do fear, with him, that half a lifetime of endeavour has dulled the exuberance which kept one up till morning discussing the ways and means of aesthetic achievement. We have discovered, perhaps with a certain finality, that by no talk can a writer add a cubit to his stature, or change the temperament which moulds and colours the vision of life he sets before the few who will pause to look at it. And so— the rest is silence, and what of work we may still do will be done in that dogged muteness which is the lot of advancing years.

Other times, other men and modes, but not other truth. Truth, though essentially relative, like Einstein's theory, will never lose its ever-new and unique quality-perfect proportion; for Truth, to the human consciousness at least, is but that vitally just relation of part to whole which is the very condition of life itself. And the task before the imaginative writer, whether at the end of the last century or all these aeons later, is the presentation of a vision which to eye and ear and mind has the implicit proportions of Truth.

I confess to have always looked for a certain flavour in the writings of others, and craved it for my own, believing that all true vision is so coloured by the temperament of the seer, as to have not only the just proportions but the essential novelty of a living thing for, after all, no two living things are alike. A work of fiction should carry the hall mark of its author as surely as a Goya, a Daumier, a Velasquez, and a Mathew Maris, should be the unmistakable creations of those masters. This is not to speak of tricks and manners which lend themselves to that facile elf, the caricaturist, but of a certain individual way of seeing and feeling. A young poet once said of another and more popular poet: "Oh! yes, but be cuts no ice." And, when one came to think of it, he did not; a certain flabbiness of spirit, a lack of temperament, an absence, perhaps, of the ironic, or passionate, view, insubstantiated his work; it had no edge—just a felicity which passed for distinction with the crowd.

Let me not be understood to imply that a novel should be a sort of sandwich, in which the author's mood or philosophy is the slice of ham. One's demand is for a far more subtle impregnation of flavour; just that, for instance, which makes De Maupassant a more poignant and fascinating writer than his master Flaubert, Dickens and Thackeray more living and permanent than George Eliot or Trollope. It once fell to my lot to be the preliminary critic of a book on painting, designed to prove that the artist's sole function was the impersonal elucidation of the truths of nature. I was regretfully compelled to observe that there were no such things as the truths of Nature, for the purposes of art, apart from the individual vision of the artist. Seer and thing seen, inextricably involved one with the other, form the texture of any masterpiece; and I, at least, demand therefrom a distinct impression of temperament. I never saw, in the flesh, either De Maupassant or Tchekov—those masters of such different methods entirely devoid of didacticism—but their work leaves on me a strangely potent sense of personality. Such subtle intermingling of seer with thing seen is the outcome only of long and intricate brooding, a process not too favoured by modern life, yet without which we achieve little but a fluent chaos of clever insignificant impressions, a kind of glorified journalism, holding much the same relation to the deeply-impregnated work of Turgenev, Hardy, and Conrad, as a film bears to a play.

Speaking for myself, with the immodesty required of one who hazards an introduction to his own work, I was writing fiction for five years before I could master even its primary technique, much less achieve that union of seer with thing seen, which perhaps begins to show itself a little in this volume—binding up the scanty harvests of 1899, 1900, and 1901—especially in the tales: "A Knight," and "Salvation of a Forsyte." Men, women, trees, and works of fiction—very tiny are the seeds from which they spring. I used really to see the "Knight"—in 1896, was it?—sitting in the "Place" in front of the Casino at Monte Carlo; and because his dried-up elegance, his burnt straw hat, quiet courtesy of attitude, and big dog, used to fascinate and intrigue me, I began to imagine his life so as to answer my own questions and to satisfy, I suppose, the mood I was in. I never spoke to him, I never saw him again. His real story, no doubt, was as different from that which I wove around his figure as night from day.

As for Swithin, wild horses will not drag from me confession of where and when I first saw the prototype which became enlarged to his bulky stature. I owe Swithin much, for he first released the satirist in me, and is, moreover, the only one of my characters whom I killed before I gave him life, for it is in "The Man of Property" that Swithin Forsyte more memorably lives.

Ranging beyond this volume, I cannot recollect writing the first words of "The Island Pharisees"—but it would be about August, 1901. Like all the stories in "Villa Rubein," and, indeed, most of my tales, the book originated in the curiosity, philosophic reflections, and unphilosophic emotions roused in me by some single figure in real life. In this case it was Ferrand, whose real name, of course, was not Ferrand, and who died in some "sacred institution" many years ago of a consumption brought on by the conditions of his wandering life. If not "a beloved," he was a true vagabond, and I first met him in the Champs Elysees, just as in "The Pigeon" he describes his meeting with Wellwyn. Though drawn very much from life, he did not in the end turn out very like the Ferrand of real life—the figures of fiction soon diverge from their prototypes.

The first draft of "The Island Pharisees" was buried in a drawer; when retrieved the other day, after nineteen years, it disclosed a picaresque string of anecdotes told by Ferrand in the first person. These two-thirds of a book were laid to rest by Edward Garnett's dictum that its author was not sufficiently within Ferrand's skin; and, struggling heavily with laziness and pride, he started afresh in the skin of Shelton. Three times he wrote that novel, and then it was long in finding the eye of Sydney Pawling, who accepted it for Heinemann's in 1904. That was a period of ferment and transition with me, a kind of long awakening to the home truths of social existence and national character. The liquor bubbled too furiously for clear bottling. And the book, after all, became but an introduction to all those following novels which depict—somewhat satirically—the various sections of English "Society" with a more or less capital "S."

Looking back on the long-stretched-out body of one's work, it is interesting to mark the endless duel fought within a man between the emotional and critical sides of his nature, first one, then the other, getting the upper hand, and too seldom fusing till the result has the mellowness of full achievement. One can even tell the nature of one's readers, by their preference for the work which reveals more of this side than of that. My early work was certainly more emotional than critical. But from 1901 came nine years when the critical was, in the main, holding sway. From 1910 to 1918 the emotional again struggled for the upper hand; and from that time on there seems to have been something of a "dead beat." So the conflict goes, by what mysterious tides promoted, I know not.

An author must ever wish to discover a hapless member of the Public who, never yet having read a word of his writing, would submit to the ordeal of reading him right through from beginning to end. Probably the effect could only be judged through an autopsy, but in the remote case of survival, it would interest one so profoundly to see the differences, if any, produced in that reader's character or outlook over life. This, however, is a consummation which will remain devoutly to be wished, for there is a limit to human complaisance. One will never know the exact measure of one's infecting power; or whether, indeed, one is not just a long soporific.

A writer they say, should not favouritize among his creations; but then a writer should not do so many things that he does. This writer, certainly, confesses to having favourites, and of his novels so far he likes best: The Forsyte Series; "The Country House"; "Fraternity"; "The Dark Flower"; and "Five Tales"; believing these to be the works which most fully achieve fusion of seer with thing seen, most subtly disclose the individuality of their author, and best reveal such of truth as has been vouchsafed to him. JOHN GALSWORTHY.

VILLA RUBEIN

I

Walking along the river wall at Botzen, Edmund Dawney said to Alois Harz: "Would you care to know the family at that pink house, Villa Rubein?"

Harz answered with a smile:

"Perhaps."

"Come with me then this afternoon."

They had stopped before an old house with a blind, deserted look, that stood by itself on the wall; Harz pushed the door open.

"Come in, you don't want breakfast yet. I'm going to paint the river to-day."

He ran up the bare broad stairs, and Dawney followed leisurely, his thumbs hooked in the armholes of his waistcoat, and his head thrown back.

In the attic which filled the whole top story, Harz had pulled a canvas to the window. He was a young man of middle height, square shouldered, active, with an angular face, high cheek-bones, and a strong, sharp chin. His eyes were piercing and steel-blue, his eyebrows very flexible, nose long and thin with a high bridge; and his dark, unparted hair fitted him like a cap. His clothes looked as if he never gave them a second thought.

This room, which served for studio, bedroom, and sitting-room, was bare and dusty. Below the window the river in spring flood rushed down the valley, a stream, of molten bronze. Harz dodged before the canvas like a fencer finding his distance; Dawney took his seat on a packingcase.

"The snows have gone with a rush this year," he drawled. "The Talfer comes down brown, the Eisack comes down blue; they flow into the Etsch and make it green; a parable of the Spring for you, my painter."

Harz mixed his colours.

"I've no time for parables," he said, "no time for anything. If I could be guaranteed to live to ninety-nine, like Titian—he had a chance. Look at that poor fellow who was killed the other day! All that struggle, and then—just at the turn!"

He spoke English with a foreign accent; his voice was rather harsh, but his smile very kindly.

Dawney lit a cigarette.

"You painters," he said, "are better off than most of us. You can strike out your own line. Now if I choose to treat a case out of the ordinary way and the patient dies, I'm ruined."

"My dear Doctor—if I don't paint what the public likes, I starve; all the same I'm going to paint in my own way; in the end I shall come out on top."

"It pays to work in the groove, my friend, until you've made your name; after that—do what you like, they'll lick your boots all the same."

"Ah, you don't love your work."

Dawney answered slowly: "Never so happy as when my hands are full. But I want to make money, to get known, to have a good time, good cigars, good wine. I hate discomfort. No, my boy, I must work it on the usual lines; I don't like it, but I must lump it. One starts in life with some notion of the ideal—it's gone by the board with me. I've got to shove along until I've made my name, and then, my little man—then—"

"Then you'll be soft!"

"You pay dearly for that first period!"

"Take my chance of that; there's no other way."

"Make one!"

"Humph!"

Harz poised his brush, as though it were a spear:

"A man must do the best in him. If he has to suffer—let him!"

Dawney stretched his large soft body; a calculating look had come into his eyes.

"You're a tough little man!" he said.

"I've had to be tough."

Dawney rose; tobacco smoke was wreathed round his unruffled hair.

"Touching Villa Rubein," he said, "shall I call for you? It's a mixed household, English mostly—very decent people."

"No, thank you. I shall be painting all day. Haven't time to know the sort of people who expect one to change one's clothes."

"As you like; ta-to!" And, puffing out his chest, Dawney vanished through a blanket looped across the doorway.

Harz set a pot of coffee on a spirit-lamp, and cut himself some bread. Through the window the freshness of the morning came; the scent of sap and blossom and young leaves; the scent of earth, and the mountains freed from winter; the new flights and songs of birds; all the odorous, enchanted, restless Spring.

There suddenly appeared through the doorway a white rough-haired terrier dog, black-marked about the face, with shaggy tan eyebrows. He sniffed at Harz, showed the whites round his eyes, and uttered a sharp bark. A young voice called:

"Scruff! Thou naughty dog!" Light footsteps were heard on the stairs; from the distance a thin, high voice called:

"Greta! You mustn't go up there!"

A little girl of twelve, with long fair hair under a wide-brimmed hat, slipped in.

Her blue eyes opened wide, her face flushed up. That face was not regular; its cheek-bones were rather prominent, the nose was flattish; there was about it an air, innocent, reflecting, quizzical, shy.

"Oh!" she said.

Harz smiled: "Good-morning! This your dog?"

She did not answer, but looked at him with soft bewilderment; then running to the dog seized him by the collar.

"Scr-ruff! Thou naughty dog—the baddest dog!" The ends of her hair fell about him; she looked up at Harz, who said:

"Not at all! Let me give him some bread."

"Oh no! You must not—I will beat him—and tell him he is bad; then he shall not do such things again. Now he is sulky; he looks so always when he is sulky. Is this your home?"

"For the present; I am a visitor."

"But I think you are of this country, because you speak like it."

"Certainly, I am a Tyroler."

"I have to talk English this morning, but I do not like it very much—because, also I am half Austrian, and I like it best; but my sister, Christian, is all English. Here is Miss Naylor; she shall be very angry with me."

And pointing to the entrance with a rosy-tipped forefinger, she again looked ruefully at Harz.

There came into the room with a walk like the hopping of a bird an elderly, small lady, in a grey serge dress, with narrow bands of claret-coloured velveteen; a large gold cross dangled from a steel chain on her chest; she nervously twisted her hands, clad in black kid gloves, rather white about the seams.

Her hair was prematurely grey; her quick eyes brown; her mouth twisted at one corner; she held her face, kind-looking, but long and narrow, rather to one side, and wore on it a look of apology. Her quick sentences sounded as if she kept them on strings, and wanted to draw them back as soon as she had let them forth.

"Greta, how can, you do such things? I don't know what your father would say! I am sure I don't know how to—so extraordinary—"

"Please!" said Harz.

"You must come at once—so very sorry—so awkward!" They were standing in a ring: Harz with his eyebrows working up and down; the little lady fidgeting her parasol; Greta, flushed and pouting, her eyes all dewy, twisting an end of fair hair round her finger.

"Oh, look!" The coffee had boiled over. Little brown streams trickled spluttering from the pan; the dog, with ears laid back and tail tucked in, went scurrying round the room. A feeling of fellowship fell on them at once.

"Along the wall is our favourite walk, and Scruff—so awkward, so unfortunate—we did not think any one lived here—the shutters are cracked, the paint is peeling off so dreadfully. Have you been long in Botzen? Two months? Fancy! You are not English? You are Tyrolese? But you speak English so well—there for seven years? Really? So fortunate!—It is Greta's day for English."

Miss Naylor's eyes darted bewildered glances at the roof where the crossing of the beams made such deep shadows; at the litter of brushes, tools, knives, and colours on a table made out of packing-cases; at the big window, innocent of glass, and flush with the floor, whence dangled a bit of rusty chain—relic of the time when the place had been a store-loft; her eyes were hastily averted from an unfinished figure of the nude.

Greta, with feet crossed, sat on a coloured blanket, dabbling her finger in a little pool of coffee, and gazing up at Harz. And he thought: 'I should like to paint her like that. "A forget-me-not."

He took out his chalks to make a sketch of her.

"Shall you show me?" cried out Greta, scrambling to her feet.

"'Will,' Greta—'will'. how often must I tell you? I think we should be going—it is very late—your father—so very kind of you, but I think we should be going. Scruff!" Miss Naylor gave the floor two taps. The terrier backed into a plaster cast which came down on his tail, and sent him flying through the doorway. Greta followed swiftly, crying:

"Ach! poor Scrufee!"

Miss Naylor crossed the room; bowing, she murmured an apology, and also disappeared.

Harz was left alone, his guests were gone; the little girl with the fair hair and the eyes like forget-me-nots, the little lady with kindly gestures and bird-like walk, the terrier. He looked round him; the room seemed very empty. Gnawing his moustache, he muttered at the fallen cast.

Then taking up his brush, stood before his picture, smiling and frowning. Soon he had forgotten it all in his work.

II

It was early morning four days later, and Harz was loitering homewards. The shadows of the clouds passing across the vines were vanishing over the jumbled roofs and green-topped spires of the town. A strong sweet wind was blowing from the mountains, there was a stir in the branches of the trees, and flakes of the late blossom were drifting down. Amongst the soft green pods of a kind of poplar chafers buzzed, and numbers of their little brown bodies were strewn on the path.

He passed a bench where a girl sat sketching. A puff of wind whirled her drawing to the ground; Harz ran to pick it up. She took it from him with a bow; but, as he turned away, she tore the sketch across.

"Ah!" he said; "why did you do that?"

This girl, who stood with a bit of the torn sketch in either hand, was slight and straight; and her face earnest and serene. She gazed at Harz with large, clear, greenish eyes; her lips and chin were defiant, her forehead tranquil.

"I don't like it."

"Will you let me look at it? I am a painter."

"It isn't worth looking at, but—if you wish—"

He put the two halves of the sketch together.

"You see!" she said at last; "I told you."

Harz did not answer, still looking at the sketch. The girl frowned.

Harz asked her suddenly:

"Why do you paint?"

She coloured, and said:

"Show me what is wrong."

"I cannot show you what is wrong, there is nothing wrong—but why do you paint?"

"I don't understand."

Harz shrugged his shoulders.

"You've no business to do that," said the girl in a hurt voice; "I want to know."

"Your heart is not in it," said Harz.

She looked at him, startled; her eyes had grown thoughtful.

"I suppose that is it. There are so many other things—"

"There should be nothing else," said Harz.

She broke in: "I don't want always to be thinking of myself. Suppose—"

"Ah! When you begin supposing!"

The girl confronted him; she had torn the sketch again.

"You mean that if it does not matter enough, one had better not do it at all. I don't know if you are right—I think you are."

There was the sound of a nervous cough, and Harz saw behind him his three visitors—Miss Naylor offering him her hand; Greta, flushed, with a bunch of wild flowers, staring intently in his face; and the terrier, sniffing at his trousers.

Miss Naylor broke an awkward silence.

"We wondered if you would still be here, Christian. I am sorry to interrupt you—I was not aware that you knew Mr. Herr—"

"Harz is my name—we were just talking"

"About my sketch. Oh, Greta, you do tickle! Will you come and have breakfast with us to-day, Herr Harz? It's our turn, you know."

Harz, glancing at his dusty clothes, excused himself.

But Greta in a pleading voice said: "Oh! do come! Scruff likes you. It is so dull when there is nobody for breakfast but ourselves."

Miss Naylor's mouth began to twist. Harz hurriedly broke in:

"Thank you. I will come with pleasure; you don't mind my being dirty?"

"Oh no! we do not mind; then we shall none of us wash, and afterwards I shall show you my rabbits."

Miss Naylor, moving from foot to foot, like a bird on its perch, exclaimed:

"I hope you won't regret it, not a very good meal—the girls are so impulsive—such informal invitation; we shall be very glad."

But Greta pulled softly at her sister's sleeve, and Christian, gathering her things, led the way.

Harz followed in amazement; nothing of this kind had come into his life before. He kept shyly glancing at the girls; and, noting the speculative innocence in Greta's eyes, he smiled. They soon came to two great poplar-trees, which stood, like sentinels, one on either side of an unweeded gravel walk leading through lilac bushes to a house painted dull pink, with green-shuttered windows, and a roof of greenish slate. Over the door in faded crimson letters were written the words, "Villa Rubein."

"That is to the stables," said Greta, pointing down a path, where some pigeons were sunning themselves on a wall. "Uncle Nic keeps his horses there: Countess and Cuckoo—his horses begin with C, because of Chris—they are quite beautiful. He says he could drive them to Kingdom-Come and they would not turn their hair. Bow, and say 'Good-morning' to our house!"

Harz bowed.

"Father said all strangers should, and I think it brings good luck." From the doorstep she looked round at Harz, then ran into the house.

A broad, thick-set man, with stiff, brushed-up hair, a short, brown, bushy beard parted at the chin, a fresh complexion, and blue glasses across a thick nose, came out, and called in a bluff voice:

"Ha! my good dears, kiss me quick—prrt! How goes it then this morning? A good walk, hein?" The sound of many loud rapid kisses followed.

"Ha, Fraulein, good!" He became aware of Harz's figure standing in the doorway: "Und der Herr?"

Miss Naylor hurriedly explained.

"Good! An artist! Kommen Sie herein, I am delight. You will breakfast? I too—yes, yes, my dears—I too breakfast with you this morning. I have the hunter's appetite."

Harz, looking at him keenly, perceived him to be of middle height and age, stout, dressed in a loose holland jacket, a very white, starched shirt, and blue silk sash; that he looked particularly clean, had an air of belonging to Society, and exhaled a really fine aroma of excellent cigars and the best hairdresser's essences.

The room they entered was long and rather bare; there was a huge map on the wall, and below it a pair of globes on crooked supports, resembling two inflated frogs erect on their hind legs. In one corner was a cottage piano, close to a writing-table heaped with books and papers; this nook, sacred to Christian, was foreign to the rest of the room, which was arranged with supernatural neatness. A table was laid for breakfast, and the sun-warmed air came in through French windows.

The meal went merrily; Herr Paul von Morawitz was never in such spirits as at table. Words streamed from him. Conversing with Harz, he talked of Art as who should say: "One does not claim to be a connoisseur—pas si bete—still, one has a little knowledge, que diable!" He recommended him a man in the town who sold cigars that were "not so very bad." He consumed porridge, ate an omelette; and bending across to Greta gave her a sounding kiss, muttering: "Kiss me quick!"—an expression he had picked up in a London music-hall, long ago, and considered chic. He asked his daughters' plans, and held out porridge to the terrier, who refused it with a sniff.

"Well," he said suddenly, looking at Miss Naylor, "here is a gentleman who has not even heard our names!"

The little lady began her introductions in a breathless voice.

"Good!" Herr Paul said, puffing out his lips: "Now we know each other!" and, brushing up the ends of his moustaches, he carried off Harz into another room, decorated with pipe-racks, prints of dancing-girls, spittoons, easy-chairs well-seasoned by cigar smoke, French novels, and newspapers.

The household at Villa Rubein was indeed of a mixed and curious nature. Cut on both floors by corridors, the Villa was divided into four divisions; each of which had its separate inhabitants, an arrangement which had come about in the following way:

When old Nicholas Treffry died, his estate, on the boundary of Cornwall, had been sold and divided up among his three surviving children—Nicholas, who was much the eldest, a partner in the well-known firm of Forsyte and Treffry, teamen, of the Strand; Constance, married to a man called Decie; and Margaret, at her father's death engaged to the curate of the parish, John Devorell, who shortly afterwards became its rector. By his marriage with Margaret Treffry the rector had one child called Christian. Soon after this he came into some property, and died, leaving it unfettered to his widow. Three years went by, and when the child was six years old, Mrs. Devorell, still young and pretty, came to live in London with her brother Nicholas. It was there that she met Paul von Morawitz—the last of an old Czech family, who had lived for many hundred years on their estates near Budweiss. Paul had been left an orphan at the age of ten, and without a solitary ancestral acre. Instead of acres, he inherited the faith that nothing was too good for a von Morawitz. In later years his savoir faire enabled him to laugh at faith, but it stayed quietly with him all the same. The absence of acres was of no great consequence, for through his mother, the daughter of a banker in Vienna, he came into a well-nursed fortune. It befitted a von Morawitz that he should go into the Cavalry, but, unshaped for soldiering, he soon left the Service; some said he had a difference with his Colonel over the quality of food provided during some manoeuvres; others that he had retired because his chargers did not fit his legs, which were, indeed, rather round.

He had an admirable appetite for pleasure; a man-about-town's life suited him. He went his genial, unreflecting, costly way in Vienna, Paris, London. He loved exclusively those towns, and boasted that he was as much at home in one as in another. He combined exuberant vitality with fastidiousness of palate, and devoted both to the acquisition of a special taste in women, weeds, and wines; above all he was blessed with a remarkable digestion. He was thirty when he met Mrs. Devorell; and she married him because he was so very different from anybody she had ever seen. People more dissimilar were never mated. To Paul—accustomed to stage doors—freshness, serene tranquillity, and obvious purity were the baits; he had run through more than half his fortune, too, and the fact that she had money was possibly not overlooked. Be that as it may, he was fond of her; his heart was soft, he developed a domestic side.

Greta was born to them after a year of marriage. The instinct of the "freeman" was, however, not dead in Paul; he became a gambler. He lost the remainder of his fortune without being greatly disturbed. When he began to lose his wife's fortune too things naturally became more difficult. Not too much remained when Nicholas Treffry stepped in, and caused his sister to settle what was left on her daughters, after providing a life-interest for herself and Paul. Losing his supplies, the good man had given up his cards. But the instinct of the "freeman" was still living in his breast; he took to drink. He was never grossly drunk, and rarely very sober. His wife sorrowed over this new passion; her health, already much enfeebled, soon broke down. The doctors sent her to the Tyrol. She seemed to benefit by this, and settled down at Botzen. The following year, when Greta was just ten, she died. It was a shock to Paul. He gave up excessive drinking; became a constant smoker, and lent full rein to his natural domesticity. He was fond of both the girls, but did not at all understand them; Greta, his own daughter, was his favourite. Villa Rubein remained their home; it was cheap and roomy. Money, since Paul became housekeeper to himself, was scarce.

About this time Mrs. Decie, his wife's sister, whose husband had died in the East, returned to England; Paul invited her to come and live with them. She had her own rooms, her own servant; the arrangement suited Paul—it was economically sound, and there was some one always there to take care of the girls. In truth he began to feel the instinct of the "freeman" rising again within him; it was pleasant to run over to Vienna now and then; to play piquet at a Club in Gries, of which he was the shining light; in a word, to go "on the tiles" a little. One could not always mourn—even if a woman were an angel; moreover, his digestion was as good as ever.

The fourth quarter of this Villa was occupied by Nicholas Treffry, whose annual sojourn out of England perpetually surprised himself. Between him and his young niece, Christian, there existed, however, a rare sympathy; one of those affections between the young and old, which, mysteriously born like everything in life, seems the only end and aim to both, till another feeling comes into the younger heart.

Since a long and dangerous illness, he had been ordered to avoid the English winter, and at the commencement of each spring he would appear at Botzen, driving his own horses by easy stages from the Italian Riviera, where he spent the coldest months. He always stayed till June before going back to his London Club, and during all that time he let no day pass without growling at foreigners, their habits, food, drink, and raiment, with a kind of big dog's growling that did nobody any harm. The illness had broken him very much; he was seventy, but looked more. He had a servant, a Luganese, named Dominique, devoted to him. Nicholas Treffry had found him overworked in an hotel, and had engaged him with the caution: "Look—here, Dominique! I swear!" To which Dominique, dark of feature, saturnine and ironical, had only replied: "Tres biens, M'sieur!"

III

Harz and his host sat in leather chairs; Herr Paul's square back was wedged into a cushion, his round legs crossed. Both were smoking, and they eyed each other furtively, as men of different stamp do when first thrown together. The young artist found his host extremely new and disconcerting; in his presence he felt both shy and awkward. Herr Paul, on the other hand, very much at ease, was thinking indolently:

'Good-looking young fellow—comes of the people, I expect, not at all the manner of the world; wonder what he talks about.'

Presently noticing that Harz was looking at a photograph, he said: "Ah! yes! that was a woman! They are not to be found in these days. She could dance, the little Coralie! Did you ever see such arms? Confess that she is beautiful, hein?"

"She has individuality," said Harz. "A fine type!"

Herr Paul blew out a cloud of smoke.

"Yes," he murmured, "she was fine all over!" He had dropped his eyeglasses, and his full brown eyes, with little crow's-feet at the corners, wandered from his visitor to his cigar.

'He'd be like a Satyr if he wasn't too clean,' thought Harz. 'Put vine leaves in his hair, paint him asleep, with his hands crossed, so!'

"When I am told a person has individuality," Herr Paul was saying in a rich and husky voice, "I generally expect boots that bulge, an umbrella of improper colour; I expect a creature of 'bad form' as they say in England; who will shave some days and some days will not shave; who sometimes smells of India-rubber, and sometimes does not smell, which is discouraging!"

"You do not approve of individuality?" said Harz shortly.

"Not if it means doing, and thinking, as those who know better do not do, or think."

"And who are those who know better?"

"Ah! my dear, you are asking me a riddle? Well, then—Society, men of birth, men of recognised position, men above eccentricity, in a word, of reputation."

Harz looked at him fixedly. "Men who haven't the courage of their own ideas, not even the courage to smell of India-rubber; men who have no desires, and so can spend all their time making themselves flat!"

Herr Paul drew out a red silk handkerchief and wiped his beard. "I assure you, my dear," he said, "it is easier to be flat; it is more respectable to be flat. Himmel! why not, then, be flat?"

"Like any common fellow?"

"Certes; like any common fellow—like me, par exemple!" Herr Paul waved his hand. When he exercised unusual tact, he always made use of a French expression.

Harz flushed. Herr Paul followed up his victory. "Come, come!" he said. "Pass me my men of repute! que diable! we are not anarchists."

"Are you sure?" said Harz.

Herr Paul twisted his moustache. "I beg your pardon," he said slowly. But at this moment the door was opened; a rumbling voice remarked: "Morning, Paul. Who's your visitor?" Harz saw a tall, bulky figure in the doorway.

"Come in," called out Herr Paul. "Let me present to you a new acquaintance, an artist: Herr Harz—Mr. Nicholas Treffry. Psumm bumm! All this introducing is dry work." And going to the sideboard he poured out three glasses of a light, foaming beer.

Mr. Treffry waved it from him: "Not for me," he said: "Wish I could! They won't let me look at it." And walking over, to the window with a heavy tread, which trembled like his voice, he sat down. There was something in his gait like the movements of an elephant's hind legs. He was very tall (it was said, with the customary exaggeration of family tradition, that there never had been a male Treffry under six feet in height), but now he stooped, and had grown stout. There was something at once vast and unobtrusive about his personality.

He wore a loose brown velvet jacket, and waistcoat, cut to show a soft frilled shirt and narrow black ribbon tie; a thin gold chain was looped round his neck and fastened to his fob. His heavy cheeks had folds in them like those in a bloodhound's face. He wore big, drooping, yellow-grey moustaches, which he had a habit of sucking, and a goatee beard. He had long loose ears that might almost have been said to gap. On his head there was a soft black hat, large in the brim and low in the crown. His grey eyes, heavy-lidded, twinkled under their bushy brows with a queer, kind cynicism. As a young man he had sown many a wild oat; but he had also worked and made money in business; he had, in fact, burned the candle at both ends; but he had never been unready to do his fellows a good turn. He had a passion for driving, and his reckless method of pursuing this art had caused him to be nicknamed: "The notorious Treffry."

Once, when he was driving tandem down a hill with a loose rein, the friend beside him had said: "For all the good you're doing with those reins, Treffry, you might as well throw them on the horses' necks."

"Just so," Treffry had answered. At the bottom of the hill they had gone over a wall into a potato patch. Treffry had broken several ribs; his friend had gone unharmed.

He was a great sufferer now, but, constitutionally averse to being pitied, he had a disconcerting way of humming, and this, together with the shake in his voice, and his frequent use of peculiar phrases, made the understanding of his speech depend at times on intuition rather than intelligence.

The clock began to strike eleven. Harz muttered an excuse, shook hands with his host, and bowing to his new acquaintance, went away. He caught a glimpse of Greta's face against the window, and waved his hand to her. In the road he came on Dawney, who was turning in between the poplars, with thumbs as usual hooked in the armholes of his waistcoat.

"Hallo!" the latter said.

"Doctor!" Harz answered slyly; "the Fates outwitted me, it seems."

"Serve you right," said Dawney, "for your confounded egoism! Wait here till I come out, I shan't be many minutes."

But Harz went on his way. A cart drawn by cream-coloured oxen was passing slowly towards the bridge. In front of the brushwood piled on it two peasant girls were sitting with their feet on a mat of grass—the picture of contentment.

"I'm wasting my time!" he thought. "I've done next to nothing in two months. Better get back to London! That girl will never make a painter!" She would never make a painter, but there was something in her that he could not dismiss so rapidly. She was not exactly beautiful, but she was sympathetic. The brow was pleasing, with dark-brown hair softly turned back, and eyes so straight and shining. The two sisters were very different! The little one was innocent, yet mysterious; the elder seemed as clear as crystal!

He had entered the town, where the arcaded streets exuded their peculiar pungent smell of cows and leather, wood-smoke, wine-casks, and drains. The sound of rapid wheels over the stones made him turn his head. A carriage drawn by red-roan horses was passing at a great pace. People stared at it, standing still, and looking alarmed. It swung from side to side and vanished round a corner. Harz saw Mr. Nicholas Treffry in a long, whitish dust-coat; his Italian servant, perched behind, was holding to the seat-rail, with a nervous grin on his dark face.

'Certainly,' Harz thought, 'there's no getting away from these people this morning—they are everywhere.'

In his studio he began to sort his sketches, wash his brushes, and drag out things he had accumulated during his two months' stay. He even began to fold his blanket door. But suddenly he stopped. Those two girls! Why not try? What a picture! The two heads, the sky, and leaves! Begin to-morrow! Against that window—no, better at the Villa! Call the picture—Spring...!

IV

The wind, stirring among trees and bushes, flung the young leaves skywards. The trembling of their silver linings was like the joyful flutter of a heart at good news. It was one of those Spring mornings when everything seems full of a sweet restlessness—soft clouds chasing fast across the sky; soft scents floating forth and dying; the notes of birds, now shrill and sweet, now hushed in silences; all nature striving for something, nothing at peace.

Villa Rubein withstood the influence of the day, and wore its usual look of rest and isolation. Harz sent in his card, and asked to see "der Herr." The servant, a grey-eyed, clever-looking Swiss with no hair on his face, came back saying:

"Der Herr, mein Herr, is in the Garden gone." Harz followed him.

Herr Paul, a small white flannel cap on his head, gloves on his hands, and glasses on his nose, was watering a rosebush, and humming the serenade from Faust.

This aspect of the house was very different from the other. The sun fell on it, and over a veranda creepers clung and scrambled in long scrolls. There was a lawn, with freshly mown grass; flower-beds were laid out, and at the end of an avenue of young acacias stood an arbour covered with wisteria.

In the east, mountain peaks—fingers of snow—glittered above the mist. A grave simplicity lay on that scene, on the roofs and spires, the valleys and the dreamy hillsides, with their yellow scars and purple bloom, and white cascades, like tails of grey horses swishing in the wind.

Herr Paul held out his hand: "What can we do for you?" he said.

"I have to beg a favour," replied Harz. "I wish to paint your daughters. I will bring the canvas here—they shall have no trouble. I would paint them in the garden when they have nothing else to do."

Herr Paul looked at him dubiously—ever since the previous day he had been thinking: 'Queer bird, that painter—thinks himself the devil of a swell! Looks a determined fellow too!' Now—staring in the painter's face—it seemed to him, on the whole, best if some one else refused this permission.

"With all the pleasure, my dear sir," he said. "Come, let us ask these two young ladies!" and putting down his hose, he led the way towards the arbour, thinking: 'You'll be disappointed, my young conqueror, or I'm mistaken.'

Miss Naylor and the girls were sitting in the shade, reading La Fontaine's fables. Greta, with one eye on her governess, was stealthily cutting a pig out of orange peel.

"Ah! my dear dears!" began Herr Paul, who in the presence of Miss Naylor always paraded his English. "Here is our friend, who has a very flattering request to make; he would paint you, yes—both together, alfresco, in the air, in the sunshine, with the birds, the little birds!"

Greta, gazing at Harz, gushed deep pink, and furtively showed him her pig.

Christian said: "Paint us? Oh no!"

She saw Harz looking at her, and added, slowly: "If you really wish it, I suppose we could!" then dropped her eyes.

"Ah!" said Herr Paul raising his brows till his glasses fell from his nose: "And what says Gretchen? Does she want to be handed up to posterities a little peacock along with the other little birds?"

Greta, who had continued staring at the painter, said: "Of—course—I—want—to—be."

"Prrt!" said Herr Paul, looking at Miss Naylor. The little lady indeed opened her mouth wide, but all that came forth was a tiny squeak, as sometimes happens when one is anxious to say something, and has not arranged beforehand what it shall be.

The affair seemed ended; Harz heaved a sigh of satisfaction. But Herr Paul had still a card to play.

"There is your Aunt," he said; "there are things to be considered—one must certainly inquire—so, we shall see." Kissing Greta loudly on both cheeks, he went towards the house.

"What makes you want to paint us?" Christian asked, as soon as he was gone.

"I think it very wrong," Miss Naylor blurted out.

"Why?" said Harz, frowning.

"Greta is so young—there are lessons—it is such a waste of time!"

His eyebrows twitched: "Ah! You think so!"

"I don't see why it is a waste of time," said Christian quietly; "there are lots of hours when we sit here and do nothing."

"And it is very dull," put in Greta, with a pout.

"You are rude, Greta," said Miss Naylor in a little rage, pursing her lips, and taking up her knitting.

"I think it seems always rude to speak the truth," said Greta. Miss Naylor looked at her in that concentrated manner with which she was in the habit of expressing displeasure.

But at this moment a servant came, and said that Mrs. Decie would be glad to see Herr Harz. The painter made them a stiff bow, and followed the servant to the house. Miss Naylor and the two girls watched his progress with apprehensive eyes; it was clear that he had been offended.

Crossing the veranda, and passing through an open window hung with silk curtains, Hart entered a cool dark room. This was Mrs. Decie's sanctum, where she conducted correspondence, received her visitors, read the latest literature, and sometimes, when she had bad headaches, lay for hours on the sofa, with a fan, and her eyes closed. There was a scent of sandalwood, a suggestion of the East, a kind of mystery, in here, as if things like chairs and tables were not really what they seemed, but something much less commonplace.

The visitor looked twice, to be quite sure of anything; there were many plants, bead curtains, and a deal of silverwork and china.

Mrs. Decie came forward in the slightly rustling silk which—whether in or out of fashion—always accompanied her. A tall woman, over fifty, she moved as if she had been tied together at the knees. Her face was long, with broad brows, from which her sandy-grey hair was severely waved back; she had pale eyes, and a perpetual, pale, enigmatic smile. Her complexion had been ruined by long residence in India, and might unkindly have been called fawn-coloured. She came close to Harz, keeping her eyes on his, with her head bent slightly forward.

"We are so pleased to know you," she said, speaking in a voice which had lost all ring. "It is charming to find some one in these parts who can help us to remember that there is such a thing as Art. We had Mr. C—-here last autumn, such a charming fellow. He was so interested in the native customs and dresses. You are a subject painter, too, I think? Won't you sit down?"

She went on for some time, introducing painters' names, asking questions, skating round the edge of what was personal. And the young man stood before her with a curious little smile fixed on his lips. 'She wants to know whether I'm worth powder and shot,' he thought.

"You wish to paint my nieces?" Mrs. Decie said at last, leaning back on her settee.

"I wish to have that honour," Harz answered with a bow.

"And what sort of picture did you think of?"

"That," said Harz, "is in the future. I couldn't tell you." And he thought: 'Will she ask me if I get my tints in Paris, like the woman Tramper told me of?'

The perpetual pale smile on Mrs. Decie's face seemed to invite his confidence, yet to warn him that his words would be sucked in somewhere behind those broad fine brows, and carefully sorted. Mrs. Decie, indeed, was thinking: 'Interesting young man, regular Bohemian—no harm in that at his age; something Napoleonic in his face; probably has no dress clothes. Yes, should like to see more of him!' She had a fine eye for points of celebrity; his name was unfamiliar, would probably have been scouted by that famous artist Mr. C——, but she felt her instinct urging her on to know him. She was, to do her justice, one of those "lion" finders who seek the animal for pleasure, not for the glory it brings them; she had the courage of her instincts—lion-entities were indispensable to her, but she trusted to divination to secure them; nobody could foist a "lion" on her.

"It will be very nice. You will stay and have some lunch? The arrangements here are rather odd. Such a mixed household—but there is always lunch at two o'clock for any one who likes, and we all dine at seven. You would have your sittings in the afternoons, perhaps? I should so like to see your sketches. You are using the old house on the wall for studio; that is so original of you!"

Harz would not stay to lunch, but asked if he might begin work that afternoon; he left a little suffocated by the sandalwood and sympathy of this sphinx-like woman.

Walking home along the river wall, with the singing of the larks and thrushes, the rush of waters, the humming of the chafers in his ears, he felt that he would make something fine of this subject. Before his eyes the faces of the two girls continually started up, framed by the sky, with young leaves guttering against their cheeks.

V

Three days had passed since Harz began his picture, when early in the morning, Greta came from Villa Rubein along the river dyke and sat down on a bench from which the old house on the wall was visible. She had not been there long before Harz came out.

"I did not knock," said Greta, "because you would not have heard, and it is so early, so I have been waiting for you a quarter of an hour."

Selecting a rosebud, from some flowers in her hand, she handed it to him. "That is my first rosebud this year," she said; "it is for you because you are painting me. To-day I am thirteen, Herr Harz; there is not to be a sitting, because it is my birthday; but, instead, we are all going to Meran to see the play of Andreas Hofer. You are to come too, please; I am here to tell you, and the others shall be here directly."

Harz bowed: "And who are the others?"

"Christian, and Dr. Edmund, Miss Naylor, and Cousin Teresa. Her husband is ill, so she is sad, but to-day she is going to forget that. It is not good to be always sad, is it, Herr Harz?"

He laughed: "You could not be."

Greta answered gravely: "Oh yes, I could. I too am often sad. You are making fun. You are not to make fun to-day, because it is my birthday. Do you think growing up is nice, Herr Harz?"

"No, Fraulein Greta, it is better to have all the time before you."

They walked on side by side.

"I think," said Greta, "you are very much afraid of losing time. Chris says that time is nothing."

"Time is everything," responded Harz.

"She says that time is nothing, and thought is everything," Greta murmured, rubbing a rose against her cheek, "but I think you cannot have a thought unless you have the time to think it in. There are the others! Look!"

A cluster of sunshades on the bridge glowed for a moment and was lost in shadow.

"Come," said Harz, "let's join them!"

At Meran, under Schloss Tirol, people were streaming across the meadows into the open theatre. Here were tall fellows in mountain dress, with leather breeches, bare knees, and hats with eagles' feathers; here were fruit-sellers, burghers and their wives, mountebanks, actors, and every kind of visitor. The audience, packed into an enclosure of high boards, sweltered under the burning sun. Cousin Teresa, tall and thin, with hard, red cheeks, shaded her pleasant eyes with her hand.

The play began. It depicted the rising in the Tyrol of 1809: the village life, dances and yodelling; murmurings and exhortations, the warning beat of drums; then the gathering, with flintlocks, pitchforks, knives; the battle and victory; the homecoming, and festival. Then the second gathering, the roar of cannon; betrayal, capture, death. The impassive figure of the patriot Andreas Hofer always in front, black-bearded, leathern-girdled, under the blue sky, against a screen of mountains.

Harz and Christian sat behind the others. He seemed so intent on the play that she did not speak, but watched his face, rigid with a kind of cold excitement; he seemed to be transported by the life passing before them. Something of his feeling seized on her; when the play was over she too was trembling. In pushing their way out they became separated from the others.

"There's a short cut to the station here," said Christian; "let's go this way."

The path rose a little; a narrow stream crept alongside the meadow, and the hedge was spangled with wild roses. Christian kept glancing shyly at the painter. Since their meeting on the river wall her thoughts had never been at rest. This stranger, with his keen face, insistent eyes, and ceaseless energy, had roused a strange feeling in her; his words had put shape to something in her not yet expressed. She stood aside at a stile to make way for some peasant boys, dusty and rough-haired, who sang and whistled as they went by.

"I was like those boys once," said Harz.

Christian turned to him quickly. "Ah! that was why you felt the play, so much."

"It's my country up there. I was born amongst the mountains. I looked after the cows, and slept in hay-cocks, and cut the trees in winter. They used to call me a 'black sheep,' a 'loafer' in my village."

"Why?"

"Ah! why? I worked as hard as any of them. But I wanted to get away. Do you think I could have stayed there all my life?"

Christian's eyes grew eager.

"If people don't understand what it is you want to do, they always call you a loafer!" muttered Harz.

"But you did what you meant to do in spite of them," Christian said.

For herself it was so hard to finish or decide. When in the old days she told Greta stories, the latter, whose instinct was always for the definite, would say: "And what came at the end, Chris? Do finish it this morning!" but Christian never could. Her thoughts were deep, vague, dreamy, invaded by both sides of every question. Whatever she did, her needlework, her verse-making, her painting, all had its charm; but it was not always what it was intended for at the beginning. Nicholas Treffry had once said of her: "When Chris starts out to make a hat, it may turn out an altar-cloth, but you may bet it won't be a hat." It was her instinct to look for what things meant; and this took more than all her time. She knew herself better than most girls of nineteen, but it was her reason that had informed her, not her feelings. In her sheltered life, her heart had never been ruffled except by rare fits of passion—"tantrums" old Nicholas Treffry dubbed them—at what seemed to her mean or unjust.

"If I were a man," she said, "and going to be great, I should have wanted to begin at the very bottom as you did."

"Yes," said Harz quickly, "one should be able to feel everything."

She did not notice how simply he assumed that he was going to be great. He went on, a smile twisting his mouth unpleasantly beneath its dark moustache—"Not many people think like you! It's a crime not to have been born a gentleman."

"That's a sneer," said Christian; "I didn't think you would have sneered!"

"It is true. What is the use of pretending that it isn't?"

"It may be true, but it is finer not to say it!"

"By Heavens!" said Harz, striking one hand into the other, "if more truth were spoken there would not be so many shams."

Christian looked down at him from her seat on the stile.

"You are right all the same, Fraulein Christian," he added suddenly; "that's a very little business. Work is what matters, and trying to see the beauty in the world."

Christian's face changed. She understood, well enough, this craving after beauty. Slipping down from the stile, she drew a slow deep breath.

"Yes!" she said. Neither spoke for some time, then Harz said shyly:

"If you and Fraulein Greta would ever like to come and see my studio, I should be so happy. I would try and clean it up for you!"

"I should like to come. I could learn something. I want to learn."

They were both silent till the path joined the road.

"We must be in front of the others; it's nice to be in front—let's dawdle. I forgot—you never dawdle, Herr Harz."

"After a big fit of work, I can dawdle against any one; then I get another fit of work—it's like appetite."

"I'm always dawdling," answered Christian.

By the roadside a peasant woman screwed up her sun-dried face, saying in a low voice: "Please, gracious lady, help me to lift this basket!"

Christian stooped, but before she could raise it, Harz hoisted it up on his back.

"All right," he nodded; "this good lady doesn't mind."

The woman, looking very much ashamed, walked along by Christian; she kept rubbing her brown hands together, and saying: "Gracious lady, I would not have wished. It is heavy, but I would not have wished."

"I'm sure he'd rather carry it," said Christian.

They had not gone far along the road, however, before the others passed them in a carriage, and at the strange sight Miss Naylor could be seen pursing her lips; Cousin Teresa nodding pleasantly; a smile on Dawney's face; and beside him Greta, very demure. Harz began to laugh.

"What are you laughing at?" asked Christian.

"You English are so funny. You mustn't do this here, you mustn't do that there, it's like sitting in a field of nettles. If I were to walk with you without my coat, that little lady would fall off her seat." His laugh infected Christian; they reached the station feeling that they knew each other better.

The sun had dipped behind the mountains when the little train steamed down the valley. All were subdued, and Greta, with a nodding head, slept fitfully. Christian, in her corner, was looking out of the window, and Harz kept studying her profile.

He tried to see her eyes. He had remarked indeed that, whatever their expression, the brows, arched and rather wide apart, gave them a peculiar look of understanding. He thought of his picture. There was nothing in her face to seize on, it was too sympathetic, too much like light. Yet her chin was firm, almost obstinate.

The train stopped with a jerk; she looked round at him. It was as though she had said: "You are my friend."

At Villa Rubein, Herr Paul had killed the fatted calf for Greta's Fest. When the whole party were assembled, he alone remained standing; and waving his arm above the cloth, cried: "My dears! Your happiness! There are good things here—Come!" And with a sly look, the air of a conjurer producing rabbits, he whipped the cover off the soup tureen:

"Soup-turtle, fat, green fat!" He smacked his lips.

No servants were allowed, because, as Greta said to Harz:

"It is that we are to be glad this evening."

Geniality radiated from Herr Paul's countenance, mellow as a bowl of wine. He toasted everybody, exhorting them to pleasure.

Harz passed a cracker secretly behind Greta's head, and Miss Naylor, moved by a mysterious impulse, pulled it with a sort of gleeful horror; it exploded, and Greta sprang off her chair. Scruff, seeing this, appeared suddenly on the sideboard with his forelegs in a plate of soup; without moving them, he turned his head, and appeared to accuse the company of his false position. It was the signal for shrieks of laughter. Scruff made no attempt to free his forelegs; but sniffed the soup, and finding that nothing happened, began to lap it.

"Take him out! Oh! take him out!" wailed Greta, "he shall be ill!"

"Allons! Mon cher!" cried Herr Paul, "c'est magnifique, mais, vous savez, ce nest guere la guerre!" Scruff, with a wild spring, leaped past him to the ground.

"Ah!" cried Miss Naylor, "the carpet!" Fresh moans of mirth shook the table; for having tasted the wine of laughter, all wanted as much more as they could get. When Scruff and his traces were effaced, Herr Paul took a ladle in his hand.

"I have a toast," he said, waving it for silence; "a toast we will drink all together from our hearts; the toast of my little daughter, who to-day has thirteen years become; and there is also in our hearts," he continued, putting down the ladle and suddenly becoming grave, "the thought of one who is not today with us to see this joyful occasion; to her, too, in this our happiness we turn our hearts and glasses because it is her joy that we should yet be joyful. I drink to my little daughter; may God her shadow bless!"

All stood up, clinking their glasses, and drank: then, in the hush that followed, Greta, according to custom, began to sing a German carol; at the end of the fourth line she stopped, abashed.

Heir Paul blew his nose loudly, and, taking up a cap that had fallen from a cracker, put it on.

Every one followed his example, Miss Naylor attaining the distinction of a pair of donkey's ears, which she wore, after another glass of wine, with an air of sacrificing to the public good.

At the end of supper came the moment for the offering of gifts. Herr Paul had tied a handkerchief over Greta's eyes, and one by one they brought her presents. Greta, under forfeit of a kiss, was bound to tell the giver by the feel of the gift. Her swift, supple little hands explored noiselessly; and in every case she guessed right.

Dawney's present, a kitten, made a scene by clawing at her hair.

"That is Dr. Edmund's," she cried at once. Christian saw that Harz had disappeared, but suddenly he came back breathless, and took his place at the end of the rank of givers.

Advancing on tiptoe, he put his present into Greta's hands. It was a small bronze copy of a Donatello statue.

"Oh, Herr Harz!" cried Greta; "I saw it in the studio that day. It stood on the table, and it is lovely."

Mrs. Decie, thrusting her pale eyes close to it, murmured: "Charming!"

Mr. Treffry took it in his fingers.

"Rum little toad! Cost a pot of money, I expect!" He eyed Harz doubtfully.

They went into the next room now, and Herr Paul, taking Greta's bandage, transferred it to his own eyes.

"Take care—take care, all!" he cried; "I am a devil of a catcher," and, feeling the air cautiously, he moved forward like a bear about to hug. He caught no one. Christian and Greta whisked under his arms and left him grasping at the air. Mrs. Decie slipped past with astonishing agility. Mr. Treffry, smoking his cigar, and barricaded in a corner, jeered: "Bravo, Paul! The active beggar! Can't he run! Go it, Greta!"

At last Herr Paul caught Cousin Teresa, who, fattened against the wall, lost her head, and stood uttering tiny shrieks.

Suddenly Mrs. Decie started playing The Blue Danube. Herr Paul dropped the handkerchief, twisted his moustache up fiercely, glared round the room, and seizing Greta by the waist, began dancing furiously, bobbing up and down like a cork in lumpy water. Cousin Teresa followed suit with Miss Naylor, both very solemn, and dancing quite different steps. Harz, went up to Christian.

"I can't dance," he said, "that is, I have only danced once, but—if you would try with me!"

She put her hand on his arm, and they began. She danced, light as a feather, eyes shining, feet flying, her body bent a little forward. It was not a great success at first, but as soon as the time had got into Harz's feet, they went swinging on when all the rest had stopped. Sometimes one couple or another slipped through the window to dance on the veranda, and came whirling in again. The lamplight glowed on the girls' white dresses; on Herr Paul's perspiring face. He constituted in himself a perfect orgy, and when the music stopped flung himself, full length, on the sofa gasping out:

"My God! But, my God!"

Suddenly Christian felt Harz cling to her arm.

Glowing and panting she looked at him.

"Giddy!" he murmured: "I dance so badly; but I'll soon learn."

Greta clapped her hands: "Every evening we will dance, every evening we will dance."

Harz looked at Christian; the colour had deepened in her face.

"I'll show you how they dance in my village, feet upon the ceiling!" And running to Dawney, he said:

"Hold me here! Lift me—so! Now, on—two," he tried to swing his feet above his head, but, with an "Ouch!" from Dawney, they collapsed, and sat abruptly on the floor. This untimely event brought the evening to an end. Dawney left, escorting Cousin Teresa, and Harz strode home humming The Blue Danube, still feeling Christian's waist against his arm.

In their room the two girls sat long at the window to cool themselves before undressing.

"Ah!" sighed Greta, "this is the happiest birthday I have had."

Cristian too thought: 'I have never been so happy in my life as I have been to-day. I should like every day to be like this!' And she leant out into the night, to let the air cool her cheeks.

VI

"Chris!" said Greta some days after this, "Miss Naylor danced last evening; I think she shall have a headache to-day. There is my French and my history this morning."

"Well, I can take them."

"That is nice; then we can talk. I am sorry about the headache. I shall give her some of my Eau de Cologne."

Miss Naylor's headaches after dancing were things on which to calculate. The girls carried their books into the arbour; it was a showery day, and they had to run for shelter through the raindrops and sunlight.

"The French first, Chris!" Greta liked her French, in which she was not far inferior to Christian; the lesson therefore proceeded in an admirable fashion. After one hour exactly by her watch (Mr. Treffry's birthday present loved and admired at least once every hour) Greta rose.

"Chris, I have not fed my rabbits."

"Be quick! there's not much time for history."

Greta vanished. Christian watched the bright water dripping from the roof; her lips were parted in a smile. She was thinking of something Harz had said the night before. A discussion having been started as to whether average opinion did, or did not, safeguard Society, Harz, after sitting silent, had burst out: "I think one man in earnest is better than twenty half-hearted men who follow tamely; in the end he does Society most good."

Dawney had answered: "If you had your way there would be no Society."

"I hate Society because it lives upon the weak."

"Bah!" Herr Paul chimed in; "the weak goes to the wall; that is as certain as that you and I are here."

"Let them fall against the wall," cried Harz; "don't push them there...."

Greta reappeared, walking pensively in the rain.

"Bino," she said, sighing, "has eaten too much. I remember now, I did feed them before. Must we do the history, Chris?"

"Of course!"

Greta opened her book, and put a finger in the page. "Herr Harz is very kind to me," she said. "Yesterday he brought a bird which had come into his studio with a hurt wing; he brought it very gently in his handkerchief—he is very kind, the bird was not even frightened of him. You did not know about that, Chris?"

Chris flushed a little, and said in a hurt voice

"I don't see what it has to—do with me."

"No," assented Greta.

Christian's colour deepened. "Go on with your history, Greta."

"Only," pursued Greta, "that he always tells you all about things, Chris."

"He doesn't! How can you say that!"

"I think he does, and it is because you do not make him angry. It is very easy to make him angry; you have only to think differently, and he shall be angry at once."

"You are a little cat!" said Christian; "it isn't true, at all. He hates shams, and can't bear meanness; and it is mean to cover up dislikes and pretend that you agree with people."

"Papa says that he thinks too much about himself."

"Father!" began Christian hotly; biting her lips she stopped, and turned her wrathful eyes on Greta.

"You do not always show your dislikes, Chris."

"I? What has that to do with it? Because one is a coward that doesn't make it any better, does it?"

"I think that he has a great many dislikes," murmured Greta.

"I wish you would attend to your own faults, and not pry into other people's," and pushing the book aside, Christian gazed in front of her.

Some minutes passed, then Greta leaning over, rubbed a cheek against her shoulder.

"I am very sorry, Chris—I only wanted to be talking. Shall I read some history?"

"Yes," said Christian coldly.

"Are you angry with me, Chris?"

There was no answer. The lingering raindrops pattered down on the roof. Greta pulled at her sister's sleeve.

"Look, Chris!" she said. "There is Herr Harz!"

Christian looked up, dropped her eyes again, and said: "Will you go on with the history, Greta?"

Greta sighed.

"Yes, I will—but, oh! Chris, there is the luncheon gong!" and she meekly closed the book.

During the following weeks there was a "sitting" nearly every afternoon. Miss Naylor usually attended them; the little lady was, to a certain extent, carried past objection. She had begun to take an interest in the picture, and to watch the process out of the corner of her eye; in the depths of her dear mind, however, she never quite got used to the vanity and waste of time; her lips would move and her knitting-needles click in suppressed remonstrances.

What Harz did fast he did best; if he had leisure he "saw too much," loving his work so passionately that he could never tell exactly when to stop. He hated to lay things aside, always thinking: "I can get it better." Greta was finished, but with Christian, try as he would, he was not satisfied; from day to day her face seemed to him to change, as if her soul were growing.

There were things too in her eyes that he could neither read nor reproduce.

Dawney would often stroll out to them after his daily visit, and lying on the grass, his arms crossed behind his head, and a big cigar between his lips, would gently banter everybody. Tea came at five o'clock, and then Mrs. Decie appeared armed with a magazine or novel, for she was proud of her literary knowledge. The sitting was suspended; Harz, with a cigarette, would move between the table and the picture, drinking his tea, putting a touch in here and there; he never sat down till it was all over for the day. During these "rests" there was talk, usually ending in discussion. Mrs. Decie was happiest in conversations of a literary order, making frequent use of such expressions as: "After all, it produces an illusion—does anything else matter?" "Rather a poseur, is he not?" "A question, that, of temperament," or "A matter of the definition of words"; and other charming generalities, which sound well, and seem to go far, and are pleasingly irrefutable. Sometimes the discussion turned on Art—on points of colour or technique; whether realism was quite justified; and should we be pre-Raphaelites? When these discussions started, Christian's eyes would grow bigger and clearer, with a sort of shining reasonableness; as though they were trying to see into the depths. And Harz would stare at them. But the look in those eyes eluded him, as if they had no more meaning than Mrs. Decie's, which, with their pale, watchful smile, always seemed saying: "Come, let us take a little intellectual exercise."

Greta, pulling Scruff's ears, would gaze up at the speakers; when the talk was over, she always shook herself. But if no one came to the "sittings," there would sometimes be very earnest, quick talk, sometimes long silences.

One day Christian said: "What is your religion?"

Harz finished the touch he was putting on the canvas, before he answered: "Roman Catholic, I suppose; I was baptised in that Church."

"I didn't mean that. Do you believe in a future life?"

"Christian," murmured Greta, who was plaiting blades of grass, "shall always want to know what people think about a future life; that is so funny!"

"How can I tell?" said Harz; "I've never really thought of it—never had the time."

"How can you help thinking?" Christian said: "I have to—it seems to me so awful that we might come to an end."

She closed her book, and it slipped off her lap. She went on: "There must be a future life, we're so incomplete. What's the good of your work, for instance? What's the use of developing if you have to stop?"

"I don't know," answered Harz. "I don't much care. All I know is, I've got to work."

"But why?"

"For happiness—the real happiness is fighting—the rest is nothing. If you have finished a thing, does it ever satisfy you? You look forward to the next thing at once; to wait is wretched!"

Christian clasped her hands behind her neck; sunlight flickered through the leaves on to the bosom of her dress.

"Ah! Stay like that!" cried Harz.

She let her eyes rest on his face, swinging her foot a little.

"You work because you must; but that's not enough. Why do you feel you must? I want to know what's behind. When I was travelling with Aunt Constance the winter before last we often talked—I've heard her discuss it with her friends. She says we move in circles till we reach Nirvana. But last winter I found I couldn't talk to her; it seemed as if she never really meant anything. Then I started reading—Kant and Hegel—"

"Ah!" put in Harz, "if they would teach me to draw better, or to see a new colour in a flower, or an expression in a face, I would read them all."

Christian leaned forward: "It must be right to get as near truth as possible; every step gained is something. You believe in truth; truth is the same as beauty—that was what you said—you try to paint the truth, you always see the beauty. But how can we know truth, unless we know what is at the root of it?"

"I—think," murmured Greta, sotto voce, "you see one way—and he sees another—because—you are not one person."

"Of course!" said Christian impatiently, "but why—"

A sound of humming interrupted her.

Nicholas Treffry was coming from the house, holding the Times in one hand, and a huge meerschaum pipe in the other.

"Aha!" he said to Harz: "how goes the picture?" and he lowered himself into a chair.

"Better to-day, Uncle?" said Christian softly.

Mr. Treffry growled. "Confounded humbugs, doctors!" he said. "Your father used to swear by them; why, his doctor killed him—made him drink such a lot of stuff!"

"Why then do you have a doctor, Uncle Nic?" asked Greta.

Mr. Treffry looked at her; his eyes twinkled. "I don't know, my dear. If they get half a chance, they won't let go of you!"

There had been a gentle breeze all day, but now it had died away; not a leaf quivered, not a blade of grass was stirring; from the house were heard faint sounds as of some one playing on a pipe. A blackbird came hopping down the path.

"When you were a boy, did you go after birds' nests, Uncle Nic?" Greta whispered.

"I believe you, Greta." The blackbird hopped into the shrubbery.

"You frightened him, Uncle Nic! Papa says that at Schloss Konig, where he lived when he was young, he would always be after jackdaws' nests."

"Gammon, Greta. Your father never took a jackdaw's nest, his legs are much too round!"

"Are you fond of birds, Uncle Nic?"

"Ask me another, Greta! Well, I s'pose so."

"Then why did you go bird-nesting? I think it is cruel"

Mr. Treffry coughed behind his paper: "There you have me, Greta," he remarked.

Harz began to gather his brushes: "Thank you," he said, "that's all I can do to-day."

"Can I look?" Mr. Treffry inquired.

"Certainly!"

Uncle Nic got up slowly, and stood in front of the picture. "When it's for sale," he said at last, "I'll buy it."

Harz bowed; but for some reason he felt annoyed, as if he had been asked to part with something personal.

"I thank you," he said. A gong sounded.

"You'll stay and have a snack with us?" said Mr. Treffry; "the doctor's stopping." Gathering up his paper, he moved off to the house with his hand on Greta's shoulder, the terrier running in front. Harz and Christian were left alone. He was scraping his palette, and she was sitting with her elbows resting on her knees; between them, a gleam of sunlight dyed the path golden. It was evening already; the bushes and the flowers, after the day's heat, were breathing out perfume; the birds had started their evensong.

"Are you tired of sitting for your portrait, Fraulein Christian?"

Christian shook her head.

"I shall get something into it that everybody does not see—something behind the surface, that will last."

Christian said slowly: "That's like a challenge. You were right when you said fighting is happiness—for yourself, but not for me. I'm a coward. I hate to hurt people, I like them to like me. If you had to do anything that would make them hate you, you would do it all the same, if it helped your work; that's fine—it's what I can't do. It's—it's everything. Do you like Uncle Nic?"

The young painter looked towards the house, where under the veranda old Nicholas Treffry was still in sight; a smile came on his lips.

"If I were the finest painter in the world, he wouldn't think anything of me for it, I'm afraid; but if I could show him handfuls of big cheques for bad pictures I had painted, he would respect me."

She smiled, and said: "I love him."

"Then I shall like him," Harz answered simply.

She put her hand out, and her fingers met his. "We shall be late," she said, glowing, and catching up her book: "I'm always late!"

VII

There was one other guest at dinner, a well-groomed person with pale, fattish face, dark eyes, and hair thin on the temples, whose clothes had a military cut. He looked like a man fond of ease, who had gone out of his groove, and collided with life. Herr Paul introduced him as Count Mario Sarelli.

Two hanging lamps with crimson shades threw a rosy light over the table, where, in the centre stood a silver basket, full of irises. Through the open windows the garden was all clusters of black foliage in the dying light. Moths fluttered round the lamps; Greta, following them with her eyes, gave quite audible sighs of pleasure when they escaped. Both girls wore white, and Harz, who sat opposite Christian, kept looking at her, and wondering why he had not painted her in that dress.

Mrs. Decie understood the art of dining—the dinner, ordered by Herr Paul, was admirable; the servants silent as their shadows; there was always a hum of conversation.

Sarelli, who sat on her right hand, seemed to partake of little except olives, which he dipped into a glass of sherry. He turned his black, solemn eyes silently from face to face, now and then asking the meaning of an English word. After a discussion on modern Rome, it was debated whether or no a criminal could be told by the expression of his face.

"Crime," said Mrs. Decie, passing her hand across her brow—"crime is but the hallmark of strong individuality."

Miss Naylor, gushing rather pink, stammered: "A great crime must show itself—a murder. Why, of course!"

"If that were so," said Dawney, "we should only have to look about us—no more detectives."

Miss Naylor rejoined with slight severity: "I cannot conceive that such a thing can pass the human face by, leaving no impression!"

Harz said abruptly: "There are worse things than murder."

"Ah! par exemple!" said Sarelli.

There was a slight stir all round the table.

"Verry good," cried out Herr Paul, "a vot' sante, cher."

Miss Naylor shivered, as if some one had put a penny down her back; and Mrs. Decie, leaning towards Harz, smiled like one who has made a pet dog do a trick. Christian alone was motionless, looking thoughtfully at Harz.

"I saw a man tried for murder once," he said, "a murder for revenge; I watched the judge, and I thought all the time: 'I'd rather be that murderer than you; I've never seen a meaner face; you crawl through life; you're not a criminal, simply because you haven't the courage.'"

In the dubious silence following the painter's speech, Mr. Treffry could distinctly be heard humming. Then Sarelli said: "What do you say to anarchists, who are not men, but savage beasts, whom I would tear to pieces!"

"As to that," Harz answered defiantly, "it maybe wise to hang them, but then there are so many other men that it would be wise to hang."

"How can we tell what they went through; what their lives were?" murmured Christian.

Miss Naylor, who had been rolling a pellet of bread, concealed it hastily. "They are—always given a chance to—repent—I believe," she said.

"For what they are about to receive," drawled Dawney.

Mrs. Decie signalled with her fan: "We are trying to express the inexpressible—shall we go into the garden?"

All rose; Harz stood by the window, and in passing, Christian looked at him.

He sat down again with a sudden sense of loss. There was no white figure opposite now. Raising his eyes he met Sarelli's. The Italian was regarding him with a curious stare.

Herr Paul began retailing a piece of scandal he had heard that afternoon.

"Shocking affair!" he said; "I could never have believed it of her! B——is quite beside himself. Yesterday there was a row, it seems!"

"There has been one every day for months," muttered Dawney.

"But to leave without a word, and go no one knows where! B——is 'viveur' no doubt, mais, mon Dieu, que voulez vous? She was always a poor, pale thing. Why! when my——" he flourished his cigar; "I was not always——what I should have been——one lives in a world of flesh and blood——we are not all angels——que diable! But this is a very vulgar business. She goes off; leaves everything——without a word; and B——is very fond of her. These things are not done!" the starched bosom of his shirt seemed swollen by indignation.

Mr. Treffry, with a heavy hand on the table, eyed him sideways. Dawney said slowly:

"B——is a beast; I'm sorry for the poor woman; but what can she do alone?"

"There is, no doubt, a man," put in Sarelli.

Herr Paul muttered: "Who knows?"

"What is B——going to do?" said Dawney.

"Ah!" said Herr Paul. "He is fond of her. He is a chap of resolution, he will get her back. He told me: 'Well, you know, I shall follow her wherever she goes till she comes back.' He will do it, he is a determined chap; he will follow her wherever she goes."

Mr. Treffry drank his wine off at a gulp, and sucked his moustache in sharply.

"She was a fool to marry him," said Dawney; "they haven't a point in common; she hates him like poison, and she's the better of the two. But it doesn't pay a woman to run off like that. B——had better hurry up, though. What do you think, sir?" he said to Mr. Treffry.

"Eh?" said Mr. Treffry; "how should I know? Ask Paul there, he's one of your moral men, or Count Sarelli."

The latter said impassively: "If I cared for her I should very likely kill her— if not—" he shrugged his shoulders.

Harz, who was watching, was reminded of his other words at dinner, "wild beasts whom I would tear to pieces." He looked with interest at this quiet man who said these extremely ferocious things, and thought: 'I should like to paint that fellow.'

Herr Paul twirled his wine-glass in his fingers. "There are family ties," he said, "there is society, there is decency; a wife should be with her husband. B—— will do quite right. He must go after her; she will not perhaps come back at first; he will follow her; she will begin to think, 'I am helpless—I am ridiculous!' A woman is soon beaten. They will return. She is once more with her husband—Society will forgive, it will be all right."

"By Jove, Paul," growled Mr. Treffry, "wonderful power of argument!"

"A wife is a wife," pursued Herr Paul; "a man has a right to her society."

"What do you say to that, sir?" asked Dawney.

Mr. Treffry tugged at his beard: "Make a woman live with you, if she don't want to? I call it low."

"But, my dear," exclaimed Herr Paul, "how should you know? You have not been married."

"No, thank the Lord!" Mr. Treffry replied.

"But looking at the question broadly, sir," said Dawney; "if a husband always lets his wife do as she likes, how would the thing work out? What becomes of the marriage tie?"

"The marriage tie," growled Mr. Treffry, "is the biggest thing there is! But, by Jove, Doctor, I'm a Dutchman if hunting women ever helped the marriage tie!"

"I am not thinking of myself," Herr Paul cried out, "I think of the community. There are rights."

"A decent community never yet asked a man to tread on his self-respect. If I get my fingers skinned over my marriage, which I undertake at my own risk, what's the community to do with it? D'you think I'm going to whine to it to put the plaster on? As to rights, it'd be a deuced sight better for us all if there wasn't such a fuss about 'em. Leave that to women! I don't give a tinker's damn for men who talk about their rights in such matters."

Sarelli rose. "But your honour," he said, "there is your honour!"

Mr. Treffry stared at him.

"Honour! If huntin' women's your idea of honour, well—it isn't mine."

"Then you'd forgive her, sir, whatever happened," Dawney said.

"Forgiveness is another thing. I leave that to your sanctimonious beggars. But, hunt a woman! Hang it, sir, I'm not a cad!" and bringing his hand down with a rattle, he added: "This is a subject that don't bear talking of."

Sarelli fell back in his seat, twirling his moustaches fiercely. Harz, who had risen, looked at Christian's empty place.

'If I were married!' he thought suddenly.

Herr Paul, with a somewhat vinous glare, still muttered, "But your duty to the family!"

Harz slipped through the window. The moon was like a wonderful white lantern in the purple sky; there was but a smoulder of stars. Beneath the softness of the air was the iciness of the snow; it made him want to run and leap. A sleepy beetle dropped on its back; he turned it over and watched it scurry across the grass.

Someone was playing Schumann's Kinderscenen. Harz stood still to listen. The notes came twining, weaving round his thoughts; the whole night seemed full of girlish voices, of hopes and fancies, soaring away to mountain heights—invisible, yet present. Between the stems of the acacia-trees he could see the flicker of white dresses, where Christian and Greta were walking arm in arm. He went towards them; the blood flushed up in his face, he felt almost surfeited by some sweet emotion. Then, in sudden horror, he stood still. He was in love! With nothing done with everything before him! He was going to bow down to a face! The flicker of the dresses was no longer visible. He would not be fettered, he would stamp it out! He turned away; but with each step, something seemed to jab at his heart.

Round the corner of the house, in the shadow of the wall, Dominique, the Luganese, in embroidered slippers, was smoking a long cherry-wood pipe, leaning against a tree—Mephistopheles in evening clothes. Harz went up to him.

"Lend me a pencil, Dominique."

"Bien, M'sieu."

Resting a card against the tree Harz wrote to Mrs. Decie: "Forgive me, I am obliged to go away. In a few days I shall hope to return, and finish the picture of your nieces."

He sent Dominique for his hat. During the man's absence he was on the point of tearing up the card and going back into the house.

When the Luganese returned he thrust the card into his hand, and walked out between the tall poplars, waiting, like ragged ghosts, silver with moonlight.

VIII

Harz walked away along the road. A dog was howling. The sound seemed too appropriate. He put his fingers to his ears, but the lugubrious noise passed those barriers, and made its way into his heart. Was there nothing that would put an end to this emotion? It was no better in the old house on the wall; he spent the night tramping up and down.

Just before daybreak he slipped out with a knapsack, taking the road towards Meran.

He had not quite passed through Gries when he overtook a man walking in the middle of the road and leaving a trail of cigar smoke behind him.

"Ah! my friend," the smoker said, "you walk early; are you going my way?"

It was Count Sarelli. The raw light had imparted a grey tinge to his pale face, the growth of his beard showed black already beneath the skin; his thumbs were hooked in the pockets of a closely buttoned coat, he gesticulated with his fingers.

"You are making a journey?" he said, nodding at the knapsack. "You are early—I am late; our friend has admirable kummel—I have drunk too much. You have not been to bed, I think? If there is no sleep in one's bed it is no good going to look for it. You find that? It is better to drink kummel...! Pardon! You are doing the right thing: get away! Get away as fast as possible! Don't wait, and let it catch you!"

Harz stared at him amazed.

"Pardon!" Sarelli said again, raising his hat, "that girl—the white girl—I saw. You do well to get away!" he swayed a little as he walked. "That old fellow—what is his name-Trrreffr-ry! What ideas of honour!" He mumbled: "Honour is an abstraction! If a man is not true to an abstraction, he is a low type; but wait a minute!"

He put his hand to his side as though in pain.

The hedges were brightening with a faint pinky glow; there was no sound on the long, deserted road, but that of their footsteps; suddenly a bird commenced to chirp, another answered—the world seemed full of these little voices.

Sarelli stopped.

"That white girl," he said, speaking with rapidity. "Yes! You do well! get away! Don't let it catch you! I waited, it caught me—what happened? Everything horrible—and now—kummel!" Laughing a thick laugh, he gave a twirl to his moustache, and swaggered on.

"I was a fine fellow—nothing too big for Mario Sarelli; the regiment looked to me. Then she came—with her eyes and her white dress, always white, like this one; the little mole on her chin, her hands for ever moving—their touch as warm as sunbeams. Then, no longer Sarelli this, and that! The little house close to the ramparts! Two arms, two eyes, and nothing here," he tapped his breast, "but flames that made ashes quickly—in her, like this ash—!" he flicked the white flake off his cigar. "It's droll! You agree, hein? Some day I shall go back and kill her. In the meantime—kummel!"

He stopped at a house close to the road, and stood still, his teeth bared in a grin.

"But I bore you," he said. His cigar, flung down, sputtered forth its sparks on the road in front of Harz. "I live here—good-morning! You are a man for work—your honour is your Art! I know, and you are young! The man who loves flesh better than his honour is a low type—I am a low type. I! Mario Sarelli, a low type! I love flesh better than my honour!"

He remained swaying at the gate with the grin fixed on his face; then staggered up the steps, and banged the door. But before Harz had walked on, he again appeared, beckoning, in the doorway. Obeying an impulse, Harz went in.

"We will make a night of it," said Sarelli; "wine, brandy, kummel? I am virtuous—kummel it must be for me!"

He sat down at a piano, and began to touch the keys. Harz poured out some wine. Sarelli nodded.

"You begin with that? Allegro—piu—presto!

"Wine—brandy—kummel!" he quickened the time of the tune: "it is not too long a passage, and this"—he took his hands off the keys—"comes after."

Harz smiled.

"Some men do not kill themselves," he said.

Sarelli, who was bending and swaying to the music of a tarantella, broke off, and letting his eyes rest on the painter, began playing Schumann's Kinderscenen. Harz leaped to his feet.

"Stop that!" he cried.

"It pricks you?" said Sarelli suavely; "what do you think of this?" he played again, crouching over the piano, and making the notes sound like the crying of a wounded animal.

"For me!" he said, swinging round, and rising.

"Your health! And so you don't believe in suicide, but in murder? The custom is the other way; but you don't believe in customs? Customs are only for Society?" He drank a glass of kummel. "You do not love Society?"

Harz looked at him intently; he did not want to quarrel.

"I am not too fond of other people's thoughts," he said at last; "I prefer to think my own."

"And is Society never right? That poor Society!"

"Society! What is Society—a few men in good coats? What has it done for me?"

Sarelli bit the end off a cigar.

"Ah!" he said; "now we are coming to it. It is good to be an artist, a fine bantam of an artist; where other men have their dis-ci-pline, he has his, what shall we say—his mound of roses?"

The painter started to his feet.

"Yes," said Sarelli, with a hiccough, "you are a fine fellow!"

"And you are drunk!" cried Harz.

"A little drunk—not much, not enough to matter!"

Harz broke into laughter. It was crazy to stay there listening to this mad fellow. What had brought him in? He moved towards the door.

"Ah!" said Sarelli, "but it is no good going to bed—let us talk. I have a lot to say—it is pleasant to talk to anarchists at times."

Full daylight was already coming through the chinks of the shutters.

"You are all anarchists, you painters, you writing fellows. You live by playing ball with facts. Images—nothing solid—hein? You're all for new things too, to tickle your nerves. No discipline! True anarchists, every one of you!"

Harz poured out another glass of wine and drank it off. The man's feverish excitement was catching.

"Only fools," he replied, "take things for granted. As for discipline, what do you aristocrats, or bourgeois know of discipline? Have you ever been hungry? Have you ever had your soul down on its back?"

"Soul on its back? That is good!"

"A man's no use," cried Harz, "if he's always thinking of what others think; he must stand on his own legs."

"He must not then consider other people?"

"Not from cowardice anyway."

Sarelli drank.

"What would you do," he said, striking his chest, "if you had a devil-here? Would you go to bed?"

A sort of pity seized on Harz. He wanted to say something that would be consoling but could find no words; and suddenly he felt disgusted. What link was there between him and this man; between his love and this man's love?

"Harz!" muttered Sarelli; "Harz means 'tar,' hein? Your family is not an old one?"

Harz glared, and said: "My father is a peasant."

Sarelli lifted the kummel bottle and emptied it into his glass, with a steady hand.

"You're honest—and we both have devils. I forgot; I brought you in to see a picture!"

He threw wide the shutters; the windows were already open, and a rush of air came in.

"Ah!" he said, sniffing, "smells of the earth, nicht wahr, Herr Artist? You should know—it belongs to your father.... Come, here's my picture; a Correggio! What do you think of it?"

"It is a copy."

"You think?"

"I know."

"Then you have given me the lie, Signor," and drawing out his handkerchief Sarelli flicked it in the painter's face.

Harz turned white.

"Duelling is a good custom!" said Sarelli. "I shall have the honour to teach you just this one, unless you are afraid. Here are pistols—this room is twenty feet across at least, twenty feet is no bad distance."

And pulling out a drawer he took two pistols from a case, and put them on the table.

"The light is good—but perhaps you are afraid."

"Give me one!" shouted the infuriated painter; "and go to the devil for a fool."

"One moment!" Sarelli murmured: "I will load them, they are more useful loaded."

Harz leaned out of the window; his head was in a whirl. 'What on earth is happening?' he thought. 'He's mad—or I am! Confound him! I'm not going to be killed!' He turned and went towards the table. Sarelli's head was sunk on his arms, he was asleep. Harz methodically took up the pistols, and put them back into the drawer. A sound made him turn his head; there stood a tall, strong young woman in a loose gown caught together on her chest. Her grey eyes glanced from the painter to the bottles, from the bottles to the pistol-case. A simple reasoning, which struck Harz as comic.

"It is often like this," she said in the country patois; "der Herr must not be frightened."

Lifting the motionless Sarelli as if he were a baby, she laid him on a couch.

"Ah!" she said, sitting down and resting her elbow on the table; "he will not wake!"

Harz bowed to her; her patient figure, in spite of its youth and strength, seemed to him pathetic. Taking up his knapsack, he went out.

The smoke of cottages rose straight; wisps of mist were wandering about the valley, and the songs of birds dropping like blessings. All over the grass the spiders had spun a sea of threads that bent and quivered to the pressure of the air, like fairy tight-ropes.

All that day he tramped.

Blacksmiths, tall stout men with knotted muscles, sleepy eyes, and great fair beards, came out of their forges to stretch and wipe their brows, and stare at him.

Teams of white oxen, waiting to be harnessed, lashed their tails against their flanks, moving their heads slowly from side to side in the heat. Old women at chalet doors blinked and knitted.

The white houses, with gaping caves of storage under the roofs, the red church spire, the clinking of hammers in the forges, the slow stamping of oxen-all spoke of sleepy toil, without ideas or ambition. Harz knew it all too well; like the earth's odour, it belonged to him, as Sarelli had said.

Towards sunset coming to a copse of larches, he sat down to rest. It was very still, but for the tinkle of cowbells, and, from somewhere in the distance, the sound of dropping logs.

Two barefooted little boys came from the wood, marching earnestly along, and looking at Harz as if he were a monster. Once past him, they began to run.

'At their age,' he thought, 'I should have done the same.' A hundred memories rushed into his mind.

He looked down at the village straggling below—white houses with russet tiles and crowns of smoke, vineyards where the young leaves were beginning to unfold, the red-capped spire, a thread of bubbling stream, an old stone cross. He had been fourteen years struggling up from all this; and now just as he had breathing space, and the time to give himself wholly to his work—this weakness was upon him! Better, a thousand times, to give her up!

In a house or two lights began to wink; the scent of wood smoke reached him, the distant chimes of bells, the burring of a stream.

IX

Next day his one thought was to get back to work. He arrived at the studio in the afternoon, and, laying in provisions, barricaded the lower door. For three days he did not go out; on the fourth day he went to Villa Rubein....

Schloss Runkelstein—grey, blind, strengthless—still keeps the valley. The windows which once, like eyes, watched men and horses creeping through the snow, braved the splutter of guns and the gleam of torches, are now holes for the birds to nest in. Tangled creepers have spread to the very summits of the walls. In the keep, instead of grim men in armour, there is a wooden board recording the history of the castle and instructing visitors on the subject of refreshments. Only at night, when the cold moon blanches everything, the castle stands like the grim ghost of its old self, high above the river.

After a long morning's sitting the girls had started forth with Harz and Dawney to spend the afternoon at the ruin; Miss Naylor, kept at home by headache, watched them depart with words of caution against sunstroke, stinging nettles, and strange dogs.

Since the painter's return Christian and he had hardly spoken to each other. Below the battlement on which they sat, in a railed gallery with little tables, Dawney and Greta were playing dominoes, two soldiers drinking beer, and at the top of a flight of stairs the Custodian's wife sewing at a garment. Christian said suddenly: "I thought we were friends."

"Well, Fraulein Christian, aren't we?"

"You went away without a word; friends don't do that."

Harz bit his lips.

"I don't think you care," she went on with a sort of desperate haste, "whether you hurt people or not. You have been here all this time without even going to see your father and mother."

"Do you think they would want to see me?"

Christian looked up.

"It's all been so soft for you," he said bitterly; "you don't understand."

He turned his head away, and then burst out: "I'm proud to come straight from the soil—I wouldn't have it otherwise; but they are of 'the people,' everything is narrow with them—they only understand what they can see and touch."

"I'm sorry I spoke like that," said Christian softly; "you've never told me about yourself."

There was something just a little cruel in the way the painter looked at her, then seeming to feel compunction, he said quickly: "I always hated—the peasant life—I wanted to get away into the world; I had a feeling in here—I wanted—I don't know what I wanted! I did run away at last to a house-painter at Meran. The priest wrote me a letter from my father—they threw me off; that's all."

Christian's eyes were very bright, her lips moved, like the lips of a child listening to a story.

"Go on," she said.

"I stayed at Meran two years, till I'd learnt all I could there, then a brother of my mother's helped me to get to Vienna; I was lucky enough to find work with a man who used to decorate churches. We went about the country together. Once when he was ill I painted the roof of a church entirely by myself; I lay on my back on the scaffold boards all day for a week—I was proud of that roof." He paused.

"When did you begin painting pictures?"

"A friend asked me why I didn't try for the Academie. That started me going to the night schools; I worked every minute—I had to get my living as well, of course, so I worked at night.

"Then when the examination came, I thought I could do nothing—it was just as if I had never had a brush or pencil in my hand. But the second day a professor in passing me said, 'Good! Quite good!' That gave me courage. I was sure I had failed though; but I was second out of sixty."

Christian nodded.

"To work in the schools after that I had to give up my business, of course. There was only one teacher who ever taught me anything; the others all seemed fools. This man would come and rub out what you'd done with his sleeve. I used to cry with rage—but I told him I could only learn from him, and he was so astonished that he got me into his class."

"But how did you live without money?" asked Christian.

His face burned with a dark flush. "I don't know how I lived; you must have been through these things to know, you would never understand."

"But I want to understand, please."

"What do you want me to tell you? How I went twice a week to eat free dinners! How I took charity! How I was hungry! There was a rich cousin of my mother's—I used to go to him. I didn't like it. But if you're starving in the winter."

Christian put out her hand.

"I used to borrow apronsful of coals from other students who were as poor—but I never went to the rich students."

The flush had died out of his face.

"That sort of thing makes you hate the world! You work till you stagger; you're cold and hungry; you see rich people in their carriages, wrapped in furs, and all the time you want to do something great. You pray for a chance, any chance; nothing comes to the poor! It makes you hate the world."

Christian's eyes filled with tears. He went on:

"But I wasn't the only one in that condition; we used to meet. Garin, a Russian with a brown beard and patches of cheek showing through, and yellow teeth, who always looked hungry. Paunitz, who came from sympathy! He had fat cheeks and little eyes, and a big gold chain—the swine! And little Misek. It was in his room we met, with the paper peeling off the walls, and two doors with cracks in them, so that there was always a draught. We used to sit on his bed, and pull the dirty blankets over us for warmth; and smoke—tobacco was the last thing we ever went without. Over the bed was a Virgin and Child—Misek was a very devout Catholic; but one day when he had had no dinner and a dealer had kept his picture without paying him, he took the image and threw it on the floor before our eyes; it broke, and he trampled on the bits. Lendorf was another, a heavy fellow who was always puffing out his white cheeks and smiting himself, and saying: 'Cursed society!' And Schonborn, an aristocrat who had quarrelled with his family. He was the poorest of us all; but only he and I would ever have dared to do anything—they all knew that!"

Christian listened with awe. "Do you mean?" she said, "do you mean, that you—?"

"You see! you're afraid of me at once. It's impossible even for you to understand. It only makes you afraid. A hungry man living on charity, sick with rage and shame, is a wolf even to you!"

Christian looked straight into his eyes.

"That's not true. If I can't understand, I can feel. Would you be the same now if it were to come again?"

"Yes, it drives me mad even now to think of people fatted with prosperity, sneering and holding up their hands at poor devils who have suffered ten times more than the most those soft animals could bear. I'm older; I've lived—I know things can't be put right by violence—nothing will put things right, but that doesn't stop my feeling."

"Did you do anything? You must tell me all now."

"We talked—we were always talking."

"No, tell me everything!"

Unconsciously she claimed, and he seemed unconsciously to admit her right to this knowledge.

"There's not much to tell. One day we began talking in low voices—Garin began it; he had been in some affair in Russia. We took an oath; after that we never raised our voices. We had a plan. It was all new to me, and I hated the whole thing—but I was always hungry, or sick from taking charity, and I would have done anything. They knew that; they used to look at me and Schonborn; we knew that no one else had any courage. He and I were great friends, but we never talked of that; we tried to keep our minds away from the thought of it. If we had a good day and were not so hungry, it seemed unnatural; but when the day had not been good—then it seemed natural enough. I wasn't afraid, but I used to wake up in the night; I hated the oath we had taken, I hated every one of those fellows; the thing was not what I was made for, it wasn't my work, it wasn't my nature, it was forced on me—I hated it, but sometimes I was like a madman."

"Yes, yes," she murmured.

"All this time I was working at the Academie, and learning all I could.... One evening that we met, Paunitz was not there. Misek was telling us how the thing had been arranged. Schonborn and I looked at each other—it was warm—perhaps we were not hungry—it was springtime, too, and in the Spring it's different. There is something."

Christian nodded.

"While we were talking there came a knock at the door. Lendorf put his eye to the keyhole, and made a sign. The police were there. Nobody said anything, but Misek crawled under the bed; we all followed; and the knocking grew louder and louder. In the wall at the back of the bed was a little door into an empty cellar. We crept through. There was a trap-door behind some cases, where they used to roll barrels in. We crawled through that into the back street. We went different ways."

He paused, and Christian gasped.

"I thought I would get my money, but there was a policeman before my door. They had us finely. It was Paunitz; if I met him even now I should wring his neck. I swore I wouldn't be caught, but I had no idea where to go. Then I thought of a little Italian barber who used to shave me when I had money for a shave; I knew he would help. He belonged to some Italian Society; he often talked to me, under his breath, of course. I went to him. He was shaving himself before going to a ball. I told him what had happened; it was funny to see him put his back against the door. He was very frightened, understanding this sort of thing better than I did—for I was only twenty then. He shaved my head and moustache and put me on a fair wig. Then he brought me macaroni, and some meat, to eat. He gave me a big fair moustache, and a cap, and hid the moustache in the lining. He brought me a cloak of his own, and four gulden. All the time he was extremely frightened, and kept listening, and saying: 'Eat!'

"When I had done, he just said: 'Go away, I refuse to know anything more of you.'

"I thanked him and went out. I walked about all that night; for I couldn't think of anything to do or anywhere to go. In the morning I slept on a seat in one of the squares. Then I thought I would go to the Gallerien; and I spent the whole day looking at the pictures. When the Galleries were shut I was very tired, so I went into a cafe, and had some beer. When I came out I sat on the same seat in the Square. I meant to wait till dark and then walk out of the city and take the train at some little station, but while I was sitting there I went to sleep. A policeman woke me. He had my wig in his hand.

"'Why do you wear a wig?' he said.

"I answered: 'Because I am bald.'

"'No,' he said, 'you're not bald, you've been shaved. I can feel the hair coming.'

"He put his finger on my head. I felt reckless and laughed.

"'Ah!' he said, 'you'll come with me and explain all this; your nose and eyes are looked for.'

"I went with him quietly to the police-station...."

Harz seemed carried away by his story. His quick dark face worked, his steel-grey eyes stared as though he were again passing through all these long-past emotions.

The hot sun struck down; Christian drew herself together, sitting with her hands clasped round her knees.

X

"I didn't care by then what came of it. I didn't even think what I was going to say. He led me down a passage to a room with bars across the windows and long seats, and maps on the walls. We sat and waited. He kept his eye on me all the time; and I saw no hope. Presently the Inspector came. 'Bring him in here,' he said; I remember feeling I could kill him for ordering me about! We went into the next room. It had a large clock, a writing-table, and a window, without bars, looking on a courtyard. Long policemen's coats and caps were hanging from some pegs. The Inspector told me to take off my cap. I took it off, wig and all. He asked me who I was, but I refused to answer. Just then there was a loud sound of voices in the room we had come from. The Inspector told the policeman to look after me, and went to see what it was. I could hear him talking. He called out: 'Come here, Becker!' I stood very quiet, and Becker went towards the door. I heard the Inspector say: 'Go and find Schwartz, I will see after this fellow.' The policeman went, and the Inspector stood with his back to me in the half-open door, and began again to talk to the man in the other room. Once or twice he looked round at me, but I stood quiet all the time. They began to disagree, and their voices got angry. The Inspector moved a little into the other room. 'Now!' I thought, and slipped off my cloak. I hooked off a policeman's coat and cap, and put them on. My heart beat till I felt sick. I went on tiptoe to the window. There was no one outside, but at the entrance a man was holding some horses. I opened the window a little and held my breath. I heard the Inspector say: 'I will report you for impertinence!' and slipped through the window. The coat came down nearly to my heels, and the cap over my eyes. I walked up to the man with the horses, and said: 'Good-evening.' One of the horses had begun to kick, and he only grunted at me. I got into a passing tram; it was five minutes to the West Bahnhof; I got out there. There was a train starting; they were shouting 'Einsteigen!' I ran. The collector tried to stop me. I shouted: 'Business—important!' He let me by. I jumped into a carriage. The train started."

He paused, and Christian heaved a sigh.

Harz went on, twisting a twig of ivy in his hands: "There was another man in the carriage reading a paper. Presently I said to him, 'Where do we stop first?' 'St. Polten.' Then I knew it was the Munich express—St. Polten, Amstetten, Linz, and Salzburg—four stops before the frontier. The man put down his paper and looked at me; he had a big fair moustache and rather shabby clothes. His looking at me disturbed me, for I thought every minute he would say: 'You're no policeman!' And suddenly it came into my mind that if they looked for me in this train, it would be as a policeman!—they would know, of course, at the station that a policeman had run past at the last minute. I wanted to get rid of the coat and cap, but the man was there, and I didn't like to move out of the carriage for other people to notice. So I sat on. We came to St. Polten at last. The man in my carriage took his bag, got out, and left his paper on the seat. We started again; I breathed at last, and as soon as I could took the cap and coat and threw them out into the darkness. I thought: 'I shall get across the frontier now.' I took my own cap out and found the moustache Luigi gave me; rubbed my clothes as clean as possible; stuck on the moustache, and with some little ends of chalk in my pocket made my eyebrows light; then drew some lines in my face to make it older, and pulled my cap well down above my wig. I did it pretty well—I was quite like the man who had got out. I sat in his corner, took up his newspaper, and waited for Amstetten. It seemed a tremendous time before we got there. From behind my paper I could see five or six policemen on the platform, one quite close. He opened the door, looked at me, and walked through the carriage into the corridor. I took some tobacco and rolled up a cigarette, but it shook, Harz lifted the ivy twig, like this. In a minute the conductor and two more policemen came. 'He was here,' said the conductor, 'with this gentleman.' One of them looked at me, and asked: 'Have you seen a policeman travelling on this train?' 'Yes,' I said. 'Where?' 'He got out at St. Polten.' The policeman asked the conductor: 'Did you see him get out there?' The conductor shook his head. I said: 'He got out as the train was moving.' 'Ah!' said the policeman, 'what was he like?' 'Rather short, and no moustache. Why?' 'Did you notice anything unusual?' 'No,' I said, 'only that he wore coloured trousers. What's the matter?' One policeman said to the other: 'That's our man! Send a telegram to St. Polten; he has more than an hour's start.' He asked me where I was going. I told him: 'Linz.' 'Ah!' he said, 'you'll have to give evidence; your name and address please?' 'Josef Reinhardt, 17 Donau Strasse.' He wrote it down. The conductor said: 'We are late, can we start?' They shut the door. I heard them say to the conductor: 'Search again at Linz, and report to the Inspector there.' They hurried on to the platform, and we started. At first I thought I would get out as soon as the train had left the station. Then, that I should be too far from the frontier; better to go on to Linz and take my chance there. I sat still and tried not to think.

"After a long time, we began to run more slowly. I put my head out and could see in the distance a ring of lights hanging in the blackness. I loosened the carriage door and waited for the train to run slower still; I didn't mean to go into Linz like a rat into a trap. At last I could wait no longer; I opened the door, jumped and fell into some bushes. I was not much hurt, but bruised, and the breath knocked out of me. As soon as I could, I crawled out. It was very dark. I felt heavy and sore, and for some time went stumbling in and out amongst trees. Presently I came to a clear space; on one side I could see the town's shape drawn in lighted lamps, and on the other a dark mass, which I think was forest; in the distance too was a thin chain of lights. I thought:

'They must be the lights of a bridge.' Just then the moon came out, and I could see the river shining below. It was cold and damp, and I walked quickly. At last I came out on a road, past houses and barking dogs, down to the river bank; there I sat against a shed and went to sleep. I woke very stiff. It was darker than before; the moon was gone. I could just see the river. I stumbled on, to get through the town before dawn. It was all black shapes-houses and sheds, and the smell of the river, the smell of rotting hay, apples, tar, mud, fish; and here and there on a wharf a lantern. I stumbled over casks and ropes and boxes; I saw I should never get clear—the dawn had begun already on the other side. Some men came from a house behind me. I bent, and crept behind some barrels. They passed along the wharf; they seemed to drop into the river. I heard one of them say: 'Passau before night.' I stood up and saw they had walked on board a steamer which was lying head up-stream, with some barges in tow. There was a plank laid to the steamer, and a lantern at the other end. I could hear the fellows moving below deck, getting up steam. I ran across the plank and crept to the end of the steamer. I meant to go with them to Passau! The rope which towed the barges was nearly taut; and I knew if I could get on to the barges I should be safe. I climbed down on this rope and crawled along. I was desperate, I knew they'd soon be coming up, and it was getting light. I thought I should fall into the water several times, but I got to the barge at last. It was laden with straw. There was nobody on board. I was hungry and thirsty—I looked for something to eat; there was nothing but the ashes of a fire and a man's coat. I crept into the straw. Soon a boat brought men, one for each barge, and there were sounds of steam. As soon as we began moving through the water, I fell asleep. When I woke we were creeping through a heavy mist. I made a little hole in the straw and saw the bargeman. He was sitting by a fire at the barge's edge, so that the sparks and smoke blew away over the water. He ate and drank with both hands, and funny enough he looked in the mist, like a big bird flapping its wings; there was a good smell of coffee, and I sneezed. How the fellow started! But presently he took a pitchfork and prodded the straw. Then I stood up. I couldn't help laughing, he was so surprised—a huge, dark man, with a great black beard. I pointed to the fire and said 'Give me some, brother!' He pulled me out of the straw; I was so stiff, I couldn't move. I sat by the fire, and ate black bread and turnips, and drank coffee; while he stood by, watching me and muttering. I couldn't understand him well—he spoke a dialect from Hungary. He asked me: How I got there—who I was—where I was from? I looked up in his face, and he looked down at me, sucking his pipe. He was a big man, he lived alone on the river, and I was tired of telling lies, so I told him the whole thing. When I had done he just grunted. I can see him now standing over me, with the mist hanging in his beard, and his great naked arms. He drew me some water, and I washed and showed him my wig and moustache, and threw them overboard. All that day we lay out on the barge in the mist, with our feet to the fire, smoking; now and then he would spit into the ashes and mutter into his beard. I shall never forget that day. The steamer was like a monster with fiery nostrils, and the other barges were dumb creatures with eyes, where the fires were; we couldn't see the bank, but now and then a bluff and high trees, or a castle, showed in the mist. If I had only had paint and canvas that day!" He sighed.

"It was early Spring, and the river was in flood; they were going to Regensburg to unload there, take fresh cargo, and back to Linz. As soon as the mist began to clear, the bargeman hid me in the straw. At Passau was the frontier; they lay there for the night, but nothing happened, and I slept in the straw. The next day I lay out on the barge deck; there was no mist, but I was free—the sun shone gold on the straw and the green sacking; the water seemed to dance, and I laughed—I laughed all the time, and the barge man laughed with me. A fine fellow he was! At Regensburg I helped them to unload; for more than a week we worked; they nicknamed me baldhead, and when it was all over I gave the money I earned for the unloading to the big bargeman. We kissed each other at parting. I had still three of the gulden that Luigi gave me, and I went to a house-painter and got work with him. For six months I stayed there to save money; then I wrote to my mother's cousin in Vienna, and told him I was going to London. He gave me an introduction to some friends there. I went to Hamburg, and from there to London in a cargo steamer, and I've never been back till now."

XI

After a minute's silence Christian said in a startled voice: "They could arrest you then!"

Harz laughed.

"If they knew; but it's seven years ago."

"Why did you come here, when it's so dangerous?"

"I had been working too hard, I wanted to see my country—after seven years, and when it's forbidden! But I'm ready to go back now." He looked down at her, frowning.

"Had you a hard time in London, too?"

"Harder, at first—I couldn't speak the language. In my profession it's hard work to get recognised, it's hard work to make a living. There are too many whose interest it is to keep you down—I shan't forget them."

"But every one is not like that?"

"No; there are fine fellows, too. I shan't forget them either. I can sell my pictures now; I'm no longer weak, and I promise you I shan't forget. If in the future I have power, and I shall have power—I shan't forget."

A shower of fine gravel came rattling on the wall. Dawney was standing below them with an amused expression on his upturned face.

"Are you going to stay there all night?" he asked. "Greta and I have bored each other."

"We're coming," called Christian hastily.

On the way back neither spoke a word, but when they reached the Villa, Harz took her hand, and said: "Fraulein Christian, I can't do any more with your picture. I shan't touch it again after this."

She made no answer, but they looked at each other, and both seemed to ask, to entreat, something more; then her eyes fell. He dropped her hand, and saying, "Good-night," ran after Dawney.

In the corridor, Dominique, carrying a dish of fruit, met the sisters; he informed them that Miss Naylor had retired to bed; that Herr Paul would not be home to dinner; his master was dining in his room; dinner would be served for Mrs. Decie and the two young ladies in a quarter of an hour: "And the fish is good to-night; little trouts! try them, Signorina!" He moved on quickly, softly, like a cat, the tails of his dress-coat flapping, and the heels of his white socks gleaming.

Christian ran upstairs. She flew about her room, feeling that if she once stood still it would all crystallise in hard painful thought, which motion alone kept away. She washed, changed her dress and shoes, and ran down to her uncle's room. Mr. Treffry had just finished dinner, pushed the little table back, and was sitting in his chair, with his glasses on his nose, reading the Tines. Christian touched his forehead with her lips.

"Glad to see you, Chris. Your stepfather's out to dinner, and I can't stand your aunt when she's in one of her talking moods—bit of a humbug, Chris, between ourselves; eh, isn't she?" His eyes twinkled.

Christian smiled. There was a curious happy restlessness in her that would not let her keep still.

"Picture finished?" Mr. Treffry asked suddenly, taking up the paper with a crackle. "Don't go and fall in love with the painter, Chris."

Christian was still enough now.

'Why not?' she thought. 'What should you know about him? Isn't he good enough for me?' A gong sounded.

"There's your dinner," Mr. Treffry remarked.

With sudden contrition she bent and kissed him.

But when she had left the room Mr. Treffry put down the Times and stared at the door, humming to himself, and thoughtfully fingering his chin.

Christian could not eat; she sat, indifferent to the hoverings of Dominique, tormented by uneasy fear and longings. She answered Mrs. Decie at random. Greta kept stealing looks at her from under her lashes.

"Decided characters are charming, don't you think so, Christian?" Mrs. Decie said, thrusting her chin a little forward, and modelling the words. "That is why I like Mr. Harz so much; such an immense advantage for a man to know his mind. You have only to look at that young man to see that he knows what he wants, and means to have it."

Christian pushed her plate away. Greta, flushing, said abruptly: "Doctor Edmund is not a decided character, I think. This afternoon he said: 'Shall I have some beer-yes, I shall—no, I shall not'. then he ordered the beer, so, when it came, he gave it to the soldiers."

Mrs. Decie turned her enigmatic smile from one girl to the other.

When dinner was over they went into her room. Greta stole at once to the piano, where her long hair fell almost to the keys; silently she sat there fingering the notes, smiling to herself, and looking at her aunt, who was reading Pater's essays. Christian too had taken up a book, but soon put it down—of several pages she had not understood a word. She went into the garden and wandered about the lawn, clasping her hands behind her head. The air was heavy; very distant thunder trembled among the mountains, flashes of summer lightning played over the trees; and two great moths were hovering about a rosebush. Christian watched their soft uncertain rushes. Going to the little summer-house she flung herself down on a seat, and pressed her hands to her heart.

There was a strange and sudden aching there. Was he going from her? If so, what would be left? How little and how narrow seemed the outlook of her life—with the world waiting for her, the world of beauty, effort, self-sacrifice, fidelity! It was as though a flash of that summer lightning had fled by, singeing her, taking from her all powers of flight, burning off her wings, as off one of those pale hovering moths. Tears started up, and trickled down her face. 'Blind!' she thought; 'how could I have been so blind?'

Some one came down the path.

"Who's there?" she cried.

Harz stood in the doorway.

"Why did you come out?" he said. "Ah! why did you come out?" He caught her hand; Christian tried to draw it from him, and to turn her eyes away, but she could not. He flung himself down on his knees, and cried: "I love you!"

In a rapture of soft terror Christian bent her forehead down to his hand.

"What are you doing?" she heard him say. "Is it possible that you love me?" and she felt his kisses on her hair.

"My sweet! it will be so hard for you; you are so little, so little, and so weak." Clasping his hand closer to her face, she murmured: "I don't care."

There was a long, soft silence, that seemed to last for ever. Suddenly she threw her arms round his neck and kissed him.

"Whatever comes!" she whispered, and gathering her dress, escaped from him into the darkness.

XII

Christian woke next morning with a smile. In her attitudes, her voice, her eyes, there was a happy and sweet seriousness, as if she were hugging some holy thought. After breakfast she took a book and sat in the open window, whence she could see the poplar-trees guarding the entrance. There was a breeze; the roses close by kept nodding to her; the cathedral bells were in full chime; bees hummed above the lavender; and in the sky soft clouds were floating like huge, white birds.

The sounds of Miss Naylor's staccato dictation travelled across the room, and Greta's sighs as she took it down, one eye on her paper, one eye on Scruff, who lay with a black ear flapped across his paw, and his tan eyebrows quivering. He was in disgrace, for Dominique, coming on him unawares, had seen him "say his prayers" before a pudding, and take the pudding for reward.

Christian put her book down gently, and slipped through the window. Harz was coming in from the road. "I am all yours!" she whispered. His fingers closed on hers, and he went into the house.

She slipped back, took up her book, and waited. It seemed long before he came out, but when he did he waved her back, and hurried on; she had a glimpse of his face, white to the lips. Feeling faint and sick, she flew to her stepfather's room.

Herr Paul was standing in a corner with the utterly disturbed appearance of an easy-going man, visited by the unexpected. His fine shirt-front was crumpled as if his breast had heaved too suddenly under strong emotion; his smoked eyeglasses dangled down his back; his fingers were embedded in his beard. He was fixing his eye on a spot in the floor as though he expected it to explode and blow them to fragments. In another corner Mrs. Decie, with half-closed eyes, was running her finger-tips across her brow.

"What have you said to him?" cried Christian.

Herr Paul regarded her with glassy eyes.

"Mein Gott!" he said. "Your aunt and I!"

"What have you said to him?" repeated Christian.

"The impudence! An anarchist! A beggar!"

"Paul!" murmured Mrs. Decie.

"The outlaw! The fellow!" Herr Paul began to stride about the room.

Quivering from head to foot, Christian cried: "How dared you?" and ran from the room, pushing aside Miss Naylor and Greta, who stood blanched and frightened in the doorway.

Herr Paul stopped in his tramp, and, still with his eyes fixed on the floor, growled:

"A fine thing-hein? What's coming? Will you please tell me? An anarchist—a beggar!"

"Paul!" murmured Mrs. Decie.

"Paul! Paul! And you!" he pointed to Miss Naylor—"Two women with eyes!—hein!"

"There is nothing to be gained by violence," Mrs. Decie murmured, passing her handkerchief across her lips. Miss Naylor, whose thin brown cheeks had flushed, advanced towards him.

"I hope you do not—" she said; "I am sure there was nothing that I could have prevented—I should be glad if that were understood." And, turning with some dignity, the little lady went away, closing the door behind her.

"You hear!" Herr Paul said, violently sarcastic: "nothing she could have prevented! Enfin! Will you please tell me what I am to do?"

"Men of the world"—whose philosophy is a creature of circumstance and accepted things—find any deviation from the path of their convictions dangerous, shocking, and an intolerable bore. Herr Paul had spent his life laughing at convictions; the matter had but to touch him personally, and the tap of laughter was turned off. That any one to whom he was the lawful guardian should marry other than a well-groomed man, properly endowed with goods, properly selected, was beyond expression horrid. From his point of view he had great excuse for horror; and he was naturally unable to judge whether he had excuse for horror from other points of view. His amazement had in it a spice of the pathetic; he was like a child in the presence of a thing that he absolutely could not understand. The interview had left him with a sense of insecurity which he felt to be particularly unfair.

The door was again opened, and Greta flew in, her cheeks flushed, her hair floating behind her, and tears streaming down her cheeks.

"Papa!" she cried, "you have been cruel to Chris. The door is locked; I can hear her crying—why have you been cruel?" Without waiting to be answered, she flew out again.

Herr Paul seized his hair with both his hands: "Good! Very good! My own child, please! What next then?"

Mrs. Decie rose from her chair languidly. "My head is very bad," she said, shading her eyes and speaking in low tones: "It is no use making a fuss—nothing can come of this—he has not a penny. Christian will have nothing till you die, which will not be for a long time yet, if you can but avoid an apoplectic fit!"

At these last words Herr Paul gave a start of real disgust. "Hum!" he muttered; it was as if the world were bent on being brutal to him. Mrs. Decie continued:

"If I know anything of this young man, he will not come here again, after the words you have spoken. As for Christian—you had better talk to Nicholas. I am going to lie down."

Herr Paul nervously fingered the shirt-collar round his stout, short neck.

"Nicholas! Certainly—a good idea. Quelle diable d'afaire!"

'French!' thought Mrs. Decie; 'we shall soon have peace. Poor Christian! I'm sorry! After all, these things are a matter of time and opportunity.' This consoled her a good deal.

But for Christian the hours were a long nightmare of grief and shame, fear and anger. Would he forgive? Would he be true to her? Or would he go away without a word? Since yesterday it was as if she had stepped into another world, and lost it again. In place of that new feeling, intoxicating as wine, what was coming? What bitter; dreadful ending?

A rude entrance this into the life of facts, and primitive emotions!

She let Greta into her room after a time, for the child had begun sobbing; but she would not talk, and sat hour after hour at the window with the air fanning her face, and the pain in her eyes turned to the sky and trees. After one or two attempts at consolation, Greta sank on the floor, and remained there, humbly gazing at her sister in a silence only broken when Christian cleared her throat of tears, and by the song of birds in the garden. In the afternoon she slipped away and did not come back again.

After his interview with Mr. Treffry, Herr Paul took a bath, perfumed himself with precision, and caused it to be clearly understood that, under circumstances such as these, a man's house was not suited for a pig to live in. He shortly afterwards went out to the Kurhaus, and had not returned by dinner-time.

Christian came down for dinner. There were crimson spots in her cheeks, dark circles round her eyes; she behaved, however, as though nothing had happened. Miss Naylor, affected by the kindness of her heart and the shock her system had sustained, rolled a number of bread pills, looking at each as it came, with an air of surprise, and concealing it with difficulty. Mr. Treffry was coughing, and when he talked his voice seemed to rumble even more than usual. Greta was dumb, trying to catch Christian's eye; Mrs. Decie alone seemed at ease. After dinner Mr. Treffry went off to his room, leaning heavily on Christian's shoulder. As he sank into his chair, he said to her:

"Pull yourself together, my dear!" Christian did not answer him.

Outside his room Greta caught her by the sleeve.

"Look!" she whispered, thrusting a piece of paper into Christian's hand. "It is to me from Dr. Edmund, but you must read it."

Christian opened the note, which ran as follows:

"MY PHILOSOPHER AND FRIEND,—I received your note, and went to our friend's studio; he was not in, but half an hour ago I stumbled on him in the Platz. He is not quite himself; has had a touch of the sun—nothing serious: I took him to my hotel, where he is in bed. If he will stay there he will be all right in a day or two. In any case he shall not elude my clutches for the present.

"My warm respects to Mistress Christian.—Yours in friendship and philosophy,

"EDMUND DAWNEY."

Christian read and re-read this note, then turned to Greta.

"What did you say to Dr. Dawney?"

Greta took back the piece of paper, and replied: "I said:

"'DEAR DR. EDMUND,—We are anxious about Herr Harz. We think he is perhaps not very well to-day. We (I and Christian) should like to know. You can tell us. Please shall you? GRETA.'

"That is what I said."

Christian dropped her eyes. "What made you write?"

Greta gazed at her mournfully: "I thought—O Chris! come into the garden. I am so hot, and it is so dull without you!"

Christian bent her head forward and rubbed her cheek against Greta's, then without another word ran upstairs and locked herself into her room. The child stood listening; hearing the key turn in the lock, she sank down on the bottom step and took Scruff in her arms.

Half an hour later Miss Naylor, carrying a candle, found her there fast asleep, with her head resting on the terrier's back, and tear stains on her cheeks....

Mrs. Decie presently came out, also carrying a candle, and went to her brother's room. She stood before his chair, with folded hands.

"Nicholas, what is to be done?"

Mr. Treffry was pouring whisky into a glass.

"Damn it, Con!" he answered; "how should I know?"

"There's something in Christian that makes interference dangerous. I know very well that I've no influence with her at all."

"You're right there, Con," Mr. Treffry replied.

Mrs. Decie's pale eyes, fastened on his face, forced him to look up.

"I wish you would leave off drinking whisky and attend to me. Paul is an element—"

"Paul," Mr. Treffry growled, "is an ass!"

"Paul," pursued Mrs. Decie, "is an element of danger in the situation; any ill-timed opposition of his might drive her to I don't know what. Christian is gentle, she is 'sympathetic' as they say; but thwart her, and she is as obstinate as...."

"You or I! Leave her alone!"

"I understand her character, but I confess that I am at a loss what to do."

"Do nothing!" He drank again.

Mrs. Decie took up the candle.

"Men!" she said with a mysterious intonation; shrugging her shoulders, she walked out.

Mr. Treffry put down his glass.

'Understand?' he thought; 'no, you don't, and I don't. Who understands a young girl? Vapourings, dreams, moonshine I.... What does she see in this painter fellow? I wonder!' He breathed heavily. 'By heavens! I wouldn't have had this happen for a hundred thousand pounds!'

XIII

For many hours after Dawney had taken him to his hotel, Harz was prostrate with stunning pains in the head and neck. He had been all day without food, exposed to burning sun, suffering violent emotion. Movement of any sort caused him such agony that he could only lie in stupor, counting the spots dancing before, his eyes. Dawney did everything for him, and Harz resented in a listless way the intent scrutiny of the doctor's calm, black eyes.

Towards the end of the second day he was able to get up; Dawney found him sitting on the bed in shirt and trousers.

"My son," he said, "you had better tell me what the trouble is—it will do your stubborn carcase good."

"I must go back to work," said Harz.

"Work!" said Dawney deliberately: "you couldn't, if you tried."

"I must."

"My dear fellow, you couldn't tell one colour from another."

"I must be doing something; I can't sit here and think."

Dawney hooked his thumbs into his waistcoat: "You won't see the sun for three days yet, if I can help it."

Harz got up.

"I'm going to my studio to-morrow," he said. "I promise not to go out. I must be where I can see my work. If I can't paint, I can draw; I can feel my brushes, move my things about. I shall go mad if I do nothing."

Dawney took his arm, and walked him up and down.

"I'll let you go," he said, "but give me a chance! It's as much to me to put you straight as it is to you to paint a decent picture. Now go to bed; I'll have a carriage for you to-morrow morning."

Harz sat down on the bed again, and for a long time stayed without moving, his eyes fixed on the floor. The sight of him, so desperate and miserable, hurt the young doctor.

"Can you get to bed by yourself?" he asked at last.

Harz nodded.

"Then, good-night, old chap!" and Dawney left the room.

He took his hat and turned towards the Villa. Between the poplars he stopped to think. The farther trees were fret-worked black against the lingering gold of the sunset; a huge moth, attracted by the tip of his cigar, came fluttering in his face. The music of a concertina rose and fell, like the sighing of some disillusioned spirit. Dawney stood for several minutes staring at the house.

He was shown to Mrs. Decie's room. She was holding a magazine before her eyes, and received him with as much relief as philosophy permitted.

"You are the very person I wanted to see," she said.

He noticed that the magazine she held was uncut.

"You are a young man," pursued Mrs. Decie, "but as my doctor I have a right to your discretion."

Dawney smiled; the features of his broad, clean-shaven face looked ridiculously small on such occasions, but his eyes retained their air of calculation.

"That is so," he answered.

"It is about this unfortunate affair. I understand that Mr. Harz is with you. I want you to use your influence to dissuade him from attempting to see my niece."

"Influence!" said Dawney; "you know Harz!"

Mrs. Decie's voice hardened.

"Everybody," she said, "has his weak points. This young man is open to approach from at least two quarters—his pride is one, his work an other. I am seldom wrong in gauging character; these are his vital spots, and they are of the essence of this matter. I'm sorry for him, of course—but at his age, and living a man's life, these things—" Her smile was extra pale. "I wish you could give me something for my head. It's foolish to worry. Nerves of course! But I can't help it! You know my opinion, Dr. Dawney. That young man will go far if he remains unfettered; he will make a name. You will be doing him a great service if you could show him the affair as it really is—a drag on him, and quite unworthy of his pride! Do help me! You are just the man to do it!"

Dawney threw up his head as if to shake off this impeachment; the curve of his chin thus displayed was imposing in its fulness; altogether he was imposing, having an air of capability.

She struck him, indeed, as really scared; it was as if her mask of smile had become awry, and failed to cover her emotion; and he was puzzled, thinking, 'I wouldn't have believed she had it in her....' "It's not an easy business," he said; "I'll think it over."

"Thank you!" murmured Mrs. Decie. "You are most kind."

Passing the schoolroom, he looked in through the open door. Christian was sitting there. The sight of her face shocked him, it was so white, so resolutely dumb. A book lay on her knees; she was not reading, but staring before her. He thought suddenly: 'Poor thing! If I don't say something to her, I shall be a brute!'

"Miss Devorell," he said: "You can reckon on him."

Christian tried to speak, but her lips trembled so that nothing came forth.

"Good-night," said Dawney, and walked out....

Three days later Harz was sitting in the window of his studio. It was the first day he had found it possible to work, and now, tired out, he stared through the dusk at the slowly lengthening shadows of the rafters. A solitary mosquito hummed, and two house sparrows, who had built beneath the roof, chirruped sleepily. Swallows darted by the window, dipping their blue wings towards the quiet water; a hush had stolen over everything. He fell asleep.

He woke, with a dim impression of some near presence. In the pale glimmer from innumerable stars, the room was full of shadowy shapes. He lit his lantern. The flame darted forth, bickered, then slowly lit up the great room.

"Who's there?"

A rustling seemed to answer. He peered about, went to the doorway, and drew the curtain. A woman's cloaked figure shrank against the wall. Her face was buried in her hands; her arms, from which the cloak fell back, were alone visible.

"Christian?"

She ran past him, and when he had put the lantern down, was standing at the window. She turned quickly to him. "Take me away from here! Let me come with you!"

"Do you mean it?"

"You said you wouldn't give me up!"

"You know what you are doing?"

She made a motion of assent.

"But you don't grasp what this means. Things to bear that you know nothing of—hunger perhaps! Think, even hunger! And your people won't forgive—you'll lose everything."

She shook her head.

"I must choose—it's one thing or the other. I can't give you up! I should be afraid!"

"But, dear; how can you come with me? We can't be married here."

"I am giving my life to you."

"You are too good for me," said Harz. "The life you're going into—may be dark, like that!" he pointed to the window.

A sound of footsteps broke the hush. They could see a figure on the path below. It stopped, seemed to consider, vanished. They heard the sounds of groping hands, of a creaking door, of uncertain feet on the stairs.

Harz seized her hand.

"Quick!" he whispered; "behind this canvas!"

Christian was trembling violently. She drew her hood across her face. The heavy breathing and ejaculations of the visitor were now plainly audible.

"He's there! Quick! Hide!"

She shook her head.

With a thrill at his heart, Harz kissed her, then walked towards the entrance. The curtain was pulled aside.

XIV

It was Herr Paul, holding a cigar in one hand, his hat in the other, and breathing hard.

"Pardon!" he said huskily, "your stairs are steep, and dark! mais en, fin! nous voila! I have ventured to come for a talk." His glance fell on the cloaked figure in the shadow.

"Pardon! A thousand pardons! I had no idea! I beg you to forgive this indiscretion! I may take it you resign pretensions then? You have a lady here—I have nothing more to say; I only beg a million pardons for intruding. A thousand times forgive me! Good-night!"

He bowed and turned to go. Christian stepped forward, and let the hood fall from her head.

"It's I!"

Herr Paul pirouetted.

"Good God!" he stammered, dropping cigar and hat. "Good God!"

The lantern flared suddenly, revealing his crimson, shaking cheeks.

"You came here, at night! You, the daughter of my wife!" His eyes wandered with a dull glare round the room.

"Take care!" cried Harz: "If you say a word against her——"

The two men stared at each other's eyes. And without warning, the lantern flickered and went out. Christian drew the cloak round her again. Herr Paul's voice broke the silence; he had recovered his self-possession.

"Ah! ah!" he said: "Darkness! Tant mieux! The right thing for what we have to say. Since we do not esteem each other, it is well not to see too much."

"Just so," said Harz.

Christian had come close to them. Her pale face and great shining eyes could just be seen through the gloom.

Herr Paul waved his arm; the gesture was impressive, annihilating.

"This is a matter, I believe, between two men," he said, addressing Harz. "Let us come to the point. I will do you the credit to suppose that you have a marriage in view. You know, perhaps, that Miss Devorell has no money till I die?"

"Yes."

"And I am passably young! You have money, then?"

"No."

"In that case, you would propose to live on air?"

"No, to work; it has been done before."

"It is calculated to increase hunger! You are prepared to take Miss Devorell, a young lady accustomed to luxury, into places like—this!" he peered about him, "into places that smell of paint, into the milieu of 'the people,' into the society of Bohemians—who knows? of anarchists, perhaps?"

Harz clenched his hands: "I will answer no more questions."

"In that event, we reach the ultimatum," said Herr Paul. "Listen, Herr Outlaw! If you have not left the country by noon to-morrow, you shall be introduced to the police!"

Christian uttered a cry. For a minute in the gloom the only sound heard was the short, hard breathing of the two men.

Suddenly Harz cried: "You coward, I defy you!"

"Coward!" Herr Paul repeated. "That is indeed the last word. Look to yourself, my friend!"

Stooping and fumbling on the floor, he picked up his hat. Christian had already vanished; the sound of her hurrying footsteps was distinctly audible at the top of the dark stairs. Herr Paul stood still a minute.

"Look to yourself, my dear friend!" he said in a thick voice, groping for the wall. Planting his hat askew on his head, he began slowly to descend the stairs.

XV

Nicholas Treffry sat reading the paper in his room by the light of a lamp with a green shade; on his sound foot the terrier Scruff was asleep and snoring lightly—the dog habitually came down when Greta was in bed, and remained till Mr. Treffry, always the latest member of the household, retired to rest.

Through the long window a little river of light shone out on the veranda tiles, and, flowing past, cut the garden in two.

There was the sound of hurried footsteps, a rustling of draperies; Christian, running through the window, stood before him.

Mr. Treffry dropped his paper, such a fury of passion and alarm shone in the girl's eyes.

"Chris! What is it?"

"Hateful!"

"Chris!"

"Oh! Uncle! He's insulted, threatened! And I love his little finger more than all the world!"

Her passionate voice trembled, her eyes were shining.

Mr. Treffry's profound discomfort found vent in the gruff words: "Sit down!"

"I'll never speak to Father again! Oh! Uncle! I love him!"

Quiet in the extremity of his disturbance, Mr. Treffry leaned forward in his chair, rested his big hands on its arms, and stared at her.

Chris! Here was a woman he did not know! His lips moved under the heavy droop of his moustache. The girl's face had suddenly grown white. She sank down on her knees, and laid her cheek against his hand. He felt it wet; and a lump rose in his throat. Drawing his hand away, he stared at it, and wiped it with his sleeve.

"Don't cry!" he said.

She seized it again and clung to it; that clutch seemed to fill him with sudden rage.

"What's the matter? How the devil can I do anything if you don't tell me?"

She looked up at him. The distress of the last days, the passion and fear of the last hour, the tide of that new life of the spirit and the flesh, stirring within her, flowed out in a stream of words.

When she had finished, there was so dead a silence that the fluttering of a moth round the lamp could be heard plainly.

Mr. Treffry raised himself, crossed the room, and touched the bell. "Tell the groom," he said to Dominique, "to put the horses to, and have 'em round at once; bring my old boots; we drive all night...."

His bent figure looked huge, body and legs outlined by light, head and shoulders towering into shadow. "He shall have a run for his money!" he said. His eyes stared down sombrely at his niece. "It's more than he deserves!—it's more than you deserve, Chris. Sit down there and write to him; tell him to put himself entirely in my hands." He turned his back on her, and went into his bedroom.

Christian rose, and sat down at the writing-table. A whisper startled her. It came from Dominique, who was holding out a pair of boots.

"M'mselle Chris, what is this?—to run about all night?" But Christian did not answer.

"M'mselle Chris, are you ill?" Then seeing her face, he slipped away again.

She finished her letter and went out to the carriage. Mr. Treffry was seated under the hood.

"Shan't want you," he called out to the groom, "Get up, Dominique."

Christian thrust her letter into his hand. "Give him that," she said, clinging to his arm with sudden terror. "Oh! Uncle! do take care!"

"Chris, if I do this for you—" They looked wistfully at one another. Then, shaking his head, Mr. Treffry gathered up the reins.

"Don't fret, my dear, don't fret! Whoa, mare!"

The carriage with a jerk plunged forward into darkness, curved with a crunch of wheels, and vanished, swinging between the black tree-pillars at the entrance....

Christian stood, straining to catch the failing sound of the hoofs.

Down the passage came a flutter of white garments; soft limbs were twined about her, some ends of hair fell on her face.

"What is it, Chris? Where have you been? Where is Uncle Nic going? Tell me!"

Christian tore herself away. "I don't know," she cried, "I know nothing!"

Greta stroked her face. "Poor Chris!" she murmured. Her bare feet gleamed, her hair shone gold against her nightdress. "Come to bed, poor Chris!"

Christian laughed. "You little white moth! Feel how hot I am! You'll burn your wings!"

XVI

Harz had lain down, fully dressed. He was no longer angry, but felt that he would rather die than yield. Presently he heard footsteps coming up the stairs.

"M'sieu!"

It was the voice of Dominique, whose face, illumined by a match, wore an expression of ironical disgust.

"My master," he said, "makes you his compliments; he says there is no time to waste. You are to please come and drive with him!"

"Your master is very kind. Tell him I'm in bed."

"Ah, M'sieu," said Dominique, grimacing, "I must not go back with such an answer. If you would not come, I was to give you this."

Harz broke the seal and read Christian's letter.

"I will come," he said.

A clock was striking as they went out through the gate. From within the dark cave of the phaeton hood Mr. Treffry said gruffly: "Come along, sir!"

Harz flung his knapsack in, and followed.

His companion's figure swayed, the whiplash slid softly along the flank of the off horse, and, as the carriage rattled forward, Mr. Treffry called out, as if by afterthought: "Hallo, Dominique!" Dominque's voice, shaken and ironical, answered from behind: "M'v'la, M'sieu!"

In the long street of silent houses, men sitting in the lighted cafes turned with glasses at their lips to stare after the carriage. The narrow river of the sky spread suddenly to a vast, limpid ocean tremulous with stars. They had turned into the road for Italy.

Mr. Treffry took a pull at his horses. "Whoa, mare! Dogged does it!" and the near horse, throwing up her head, whinnied; a fleck of foam drifted into Harz's face.

The painter had come on impulse; because Christian had told him to, not of his own free will. He was angry with himself, wounded in self-esteem, for having allowed any one to render him this service. The smooth swift movement through velvet blackness splashed on either hand with the flying lamp-light; the strong sweet air blowing in his face-air that had kissed the tops of mountains and stolen their spirit; the snort and snuffle of the horses, and crisp rattling of their hoofs—all this soon roused in him another feeling. He looked at Mr. Treffry's profile, with its tufted chin; at the grey road adventuring in darkness; at the purple mass of mountains piled above it. All seemed utterly unreal.

As if suddenly aware that he had a neighbour, Mr. Treffry turned his head. "We shall do better than this presently," he said, "bit of a slope coming. Haven't had 'em out for three days. Whoa-mare! Steady!"

"Why are you taking this trouble for me?" asked Harz.

"I'm an old chap, Mr. Harz, and an old chap may do a stupid thing once in a while!"

"You are very good," said Harz, "but I want no favours."

Mr. Treffry stared at him.

"Just so," he said drily, "but you see there's my niece to be thought of. Look here! We're not at the frontier yet, Mr. Harz, by forty miles; it's long odds we don't get there—so, don't spoil sport!" He pointed to the left.

Harz caught the glint of steel. They were already crossing the railway. The sigh of the telegraph wires fluttered above them.

"Hear 'em," said Mr. Treffry, "but if we get away up the mountains, we'll do yet!" They had begun to rise, the speed slackened. Mr. Treffry rummaged out a flask.

"Not bad stuff, Mr. Harz—try it. You won't? Mother's milk! Fine night, eh?" Below them the valley was lit by webs of milky mist like the glimmer of dew on grass.

These two men sitting side by side—unlike in face, age, stature, thought, and life—began to feel drawn towards each other, as if, in the rolling of the wheels, the snorting of the horses, the huge dark space, the huge uncertainty, they had found something they could enjoy in common. The steam from the horses' flanks and nostrils enveloped them with an odour as of glue.

"You smoke, Mr. Harz?"

Harz took the proffered weed, and lighted it from the glowing tip of Mr. Treffry's cigar, by light of which his head and hat looked like some giant mushroom. Suddenly the wheels jolted on a rubble of loose stones; the carriage was swung sideways. The scared horses, straining asunder, leaped forward, and sped downwards, in the darkness.

Past rocks, trees, dwellings, past a lighted house that gleamed and vanished. With a clink and clatter, a flirt of dust and pebbles, and the side lamps throwing out a frisky orange blink, the carriage dashed down, sinking and rising like a boat crossing billows. The world seemed to rock and sway; to dance up, and be flung flat again. Only the stars stood still.

Mr. Treffry, putting on the brake, muttered apologetically: "A little out o'hand!"

Suddenly with a headlong dive, the carriage swayed as if it would fly in pieces, slithered along, and with a jerk steadied itself. Harz lifted his voice in a shout of pure excitement. Mr. Treffry let out a short shaky howl, and from behind there rose a wail. But the hill was over and the startled horses were cantering with a free, smooth motion. Mr. Treffry and Harz looked at each other.

XVII

Mr. Treffry said with a sort of laugh: "Near go, eh? You drive? No? That's a pity! Broken most of my bones at the game—nothing like it!" Each felt a kind of admiration for the other that he had not felt before. Presently Mr. Treffry began: "Look here, Mr. Harz, my niece is a slip of a thing, with all a young girl's notions! What have you got to give her, eh? Yourself? That's surely not enough; mind this—six months after marriage we all turn out much the same—a selfish lot! Not to mention this anarchist affair!

"You're not of her blood, nor of her way of life, nor anything—it's taking chances—and—" his hand came down on the young man's knee, "I'm fond of her, you see."

"If you were in my place," said Harz, "would you give her up?"

Mr. Treffry groaned. "Lord knows!"

"Men have made themselves before now. For those who don't believe in failure, there's no such thing. Suppose she does suffer a little? Will it do her any harm? Fair weather love is no good."

Mr. Treffry sighed.

"Brave words, sir! You'll pardon me if I'm too old to understand 'em when they're used about my niece."

He pulled the horses up, and peered into the darkness. "We're going through this bit quietly; if they lose track of us here so much the better. Dominique! put out the lamps. Soho, my beauties!" The horses paced forward at a walk the muffled beat of their hoofs in the dust hardly broke the hush. Mr. Treffry pointed to the left: "It'll be another thirty-five miles to the frontier."

They passed the whitewashed houses, and village church with its sentinel cypress-trees. A frog was croaking in a runlet; there was a faint spicy scent of lemons. But nothing stirred.

It was wood now on either side, the high pines, breathing their fragrance out into the darkness, and, like ghosts amongst them, the silver stems of birch-trees.

Mr. Treffry said gruffly: "You won't give her up? Her happiness means a lot to me."

"To you!" said Harz: "to him! And I am nothing! Do you think I don't care for her happiness? Is it a crime for me to love her?"

"Almost, Mr. Harz—considering...."

"Considering that I've no money! Always money!"

To this sneer Mr. Treffry made no answer, clucking to his horses.

"My niece was born and bred a lady," he said at last. "I ask you plainly What position have you got to give her?"

"If she marries me," said Harz, "she comes into my world. You think that I'm a common...."

Mr. Treffry shook his head: "Answer my question, young man."

But the painter did not answer it, and silence fell.

A light breeze had sprung up; the whispering in the trees, the rolling of the wheels in this night progress, the pine-drugged air, sent Harz to sleep. When he woke it was to the same tune, varied by Mr. Treffry's uneasy snoring; the reins were hanging loose, and, peering out, he saw Dominique shuffling along at the horses' heads. He joined him, and, one on each side, they plodded up and up. A haze had begun to bathe the trees, the stars burnt dim, the air was colder. Mr. Treffry woke coughing. It was like some long nightmare, this interminable experience of muffled sounds and shapes, of perpetual motion, conceived, and carried out in darkness. But suddenly the day broke. Heralded by the snuffle of the horses, light began glimmering over a chaos of lines and shadows, pale as mother-o'-pearl. The stars faded, and in a smouldering zigzag the dawn fled along the mountain tops, flinging out little isles of cloud. From a lake, curled in a hollow like a patch of smoke, came the cry of a water-bird. A cuckoo started a soft mocking; and close to the carriage a lark flew up. Beasts and men alike stood still, drinking in the air—sweet with snows and dew, and vibrating faintly with the running of the water and the rustling of the leaves.

The night had played sad tricks with Mr. Nicholas Treffry; his hat was grey with dust; his cheeks brownish-purple, there were heavy pouches beneath his eyes, which stared painfully.

"We'll call a halt," he said, "and give the gees their grub, poor things. Can you find some water, Mr. Harz? There's a rubber bucket in behind."

"Can't get about myself this morning; make that lazy fellow of mine stir his stumps."

Harz saw that he had drawn off one of his boots, and stretched the foot out on a cushion.

"You're not fit to go farther," he said; "you're ill."

"Ill!" replied Mr. Treffry; "not a bit of it!"

Harz looked at him, then catching up the bucket, made off in search of water. When he came back the horses were feeding from an india-rubber trough slung to the pole; they stretched their heads towards the bucket, pushing aside each other's noses.

The flame in the east had died, but the tops of the larches were bathed in a gentle radiance; and the peaks ahead were like amber. Everywhere were threads of water, threads of snow, and little threads of dewy green, glistening like gossamer.

Mr. Treffry called out: "Give me your arm, Mr. Harz; I'd like to shake the reefs out of me. When one comes to stand over at the knees, it's no such easy matter, eh?" He groaned as he put his foot down, and gripped the young man's shoulder as in a vise. Presently he lowered himself on to a stone.

"'All over now!' as Chris would say when she was little; nasty temper she had too—kick and scream on the floor! Never lasted long though.... 'Kiss her! take her up! show her the pictures!' Amazing fond of pictures Chris was!" He looked dubiously at Harz; then took a long pull at his flask. "What would the doctor say? Whisky at four in the morning! Well! Thank the Lord Doctors aren't always with us." Sitting on the stone, with one hand pressed against his side, and the other tilting up the flask, he was grey from head to foot.

Harz had dropped on to another stone. He, too, was worn out by the excitement and fatigue, coming so soon after his illness. His head was whirling, and the next thing he remembered was a tree walking at him, turning round, yellow from the roots up; everything seemed yellow, even his own feet. Somebody opposite to him was jumping up and down, a grey bear—with a hat—Mr. Treffry! He cried: "Ha-alloo!" And the figure seemed to fall and disappear....

When Harz came to himself a hand was pouring liquor into his mouth, and a wet cloth was muffled round his brows; a noise of humming and hoofs seemed familiar. Mr. Treffry loomed up alongside, smoking a cigar; he was muttering: "A low trick, Paul—bit of my mind!" Then, as if a curtain had been snatched aside, the vision before Harz cleared again. The carriage was winding between uneven, black-eaved houses, past doorways from which goats and cows were coming out, with bells on their necks. Black-eyed boys, and here and there a drowsy man with a long, cherry-stemmed pipe between his teeth, stood aside to stare.

Mr. Treffry seemed to have taken a new lease of strength; like an angry old dog, he stared from side to side. "My bone!" he seemed to say: "let's see who's going to touch it!"

The last house vanished, glowing in the early sunshine, and the carriage with its trail of dust became entombed once more in the gloom of tall trees, along a road that cleft a wilderness of mossgrown rocks, and dewy stems, through which the sun had not yet driven paths.

Dominique came round to them, bearing appearance of one who has seen better days, and a pot of coffee brewed on a spirit lamp. Breakfast—he said—was served!

The ears of the horses were twitching with fatigue. Mr. Treffry said sadly: "If I can see this through, you can. Get on, my beauties!"

As soon as the sun struck through the trees, Mr. Treffry's strength ebbed again. He seemed to suffer greatly; but did not complain. They had reached the pass at last, and the unchecked sunlight was streaming down with a blinding glare.

"Jump up!" Mr. Treffry cried out. "We'll make a finish of it!" and he gave the reins a jerk. The horses flung up their heads, and the bleak pass with its circling crown of jagged peaks soon slipped away.

Between the houses on the very top, they passed at a slow trot; and soon began slanting down the other side. Mr. Treffry brought them to a halt where a mule track joined the road.

"That's all I can do for you; you'd better leave me here," he said. "Keep this track down to the river—go south—you'll be in Italy in a couple of hours. Get rail at Feltre. Money? Yes? Well!" He held out his hand; Harz gripped it.

"Give her up, eh?"

Harz shook his head.

"No? Then it's 'pull devil, pull baker,' between us. Good-bye, and good luck to you!" And mustering his strength for a last attempt at dignity, Mr. Treffry gathered up the reins.

Harz watched his figure huddled again beneath the hood. The carriage moved slowly away.

XVIII

At Villa Rubein people went about, avoiding each other as if detected in conspiracy. Miss Naylor, who for an inscrutable reason had put on her best frock, a purple, relieved at the chest with bird's-eye blue, conveyed an impression of trying to count a chicken which ran about too fast. When Greta asked what she had lost she was heard to mutter: "Mr.—Needlecase."

Christian, with big circles round her eyes, sat silent at her little table. She had had no sleep. Herr Paul coming into the room about noon gave her a furtive look and went out again; after this he went to his bedroom, took off all his clothes, flung them passionately one by one into a footbath, and got into bed.

"I might be a criminal!" he muttered to himself, while the buttons of his garments rattled on the bath.

"Am I her father? Have I authority? Do I know the world? Bssss! I might be a frog!"

Mrs. Decie, having caused herself to be announced, found him smoking a cigar, and counting the flies on the ceiling.

"If you have really done this, Paul," she said in a restrained voice, "you have done a very unkind thing, and what is worse, you have made us all ridiculous. But perhaps you have not done it?"

"I have done it," cried Herr Paul, staring dreadfully: "I have done it, I tell you, I have done it—"

"Very well, you have done it—and why, pray? What conceivable good was there in it? I suppose you know that Nicholas has driven him to the frontier? Nicholas is probably more dead than alive by this time; you know his state of health."

Herr Paul's fingers ploughed up his beard.

"Nicholas is mad—and the girl is mad! Leave me alone! I will not be made angry; do you understand? I will not be worried—I am not fit for it." His prominent brown eyes stared round the room, as if looking for a way of escape.

"If I may prophesy, you will be worried a good deal," said Mrs. Decie coldly, "before you have finished with this affair."

The anxious, uncertain glance which Herr Paul gave her at these words roused an unwilling feeling of compunction in her.

"You are not made for the outraged father of the family," she said. "You had better give up the attitude, Paul; it does not suit you."

Herr Paul groaned.

"I suppose it is not your fault," she added.

Just then the door was opened, and Fritz, with an air of saying the right thing, announced:

"A gentleman of the police to see you, sir."

Herr Paul bounded.

"Keep him out!" he cried.

Mrs. Decie, covering her lips, disappeared with a rustling of silk; in her place stood a stiff man in blue....

Thus the morning dragged itself away without any one being able to settle to anything, except Herr Paul, who was settled in bed. As was fitting in a house that had lost its soul, meals were neglected, even by the dog.

About three o'clock a telegram came for Christian, containing these words: "All right; self returns to-morrow. Treffry." After reading it she put on her hat and went out, followed closely by Greta, who, when she thought that she would not be sent away, ran up from behind and pulled her by the sleeve.

"Let me come, Chris—I shall not talk."

The two girls walked on together. When they had gone some distance Christian said:

"I'm going to get his pictures, and take charge of them!"

"Oh!" said Greta timidly.

"If you are afraid," said Christian, "you had better go back home."

"I am not afraid, Chris," said Greta meekly.

Neither girl spoke again till they had taken the path along the wall. Over the tops of the vines the heat was dancing.

"The sun-fairies are on the vines!" murmured Greta to herself.

At the old house they stopped, and Christian, breathing quickly, pushed the door; it was immovable.

"Look!" said Greta, "they have screwed it!" She pointed out three screws with a rosy-tipped forefinger.

Christian stamped her foot.

"We mustn't stand here," she said; "let's sit on that bench and think."

"Yes," murmured Greta, "let us think." Dangling an end of hair, she regarded Christian with her wide blue eyes.

"I can't make any plan," Christian cried at last, "while you stare at me like that."

"I was thinking," said Greta humbly, "if they have screwed it up, perhaps we shall screw it down again; there is the big screw-driver of Fritz."

"It would take a long time; people are always passing."

"People do not pass in the evening," murmured Greta, "because the gate at our end is always shut."

Christian rose.

"We will come this evening, just before the gate is shut."

"But, Chris, how shall we get back again?"

"I don't know; I mean to have the pictures."

"It is not a high gate," murmured Greta.

After dinner the girls went to their room, Greta bearing with her the big screw-driver of Fritz. At dusk they slipped downstairs and out.

They arrived at the old house, and stood, listening, in the shadow of the doorway. The only sounds were those of distant barking dogs, and of the bugles at the barracks.

"Quick!" whispered Christian; and Greta, with all the strength of her small hands, began to turn the screws. It was some time before they yielded; the third was very obstinate, till Christian took the screw-driver and passionately gave the screw a starting twist.

"It is like a pig—that one," said Greta, rubbing her wrists mournfully.

The opened door revealed the gloom of the dank rooms and twisting staircase, then fell to behind them with a clatter.

Greta gave a little scream, and caught her sister's dress.

"It is dark," she gasped; "O Chris! it is dark!"

Christian groped for the bottom stair, and Greta felt her arm shaking.

"Suppose there is a man to keep guard! O Chris! suppose there are bats!"

"You are a baby!" Christian answered in a trembling voice. "You had better go home!"

Greta choked a little in the dark.

"I am—not—going home, but I'm afraid of bats. O Chris! aren't you afraid?"

"Yes," said Christian, "but I'm going to have the pictures."

Her cheeks were burning; she was trembling all over. Having found the bottom step she began to mount with Greta clinging to her skirts.

The haze above inspired a little courage in the child, who, of all things, hated darkness. The blanket across the doorway of the loft had been taken down, there was nothing to veil the empty room.

"Nobody here, you see," said Christian.

"No-o," whispered Greta, running to the window, and clinging to the wall, like one of the bats she dreaded.

"But they have been here!" cried Christian angrily. "They have broken this." She pointed to the fragments of a plaster cast that had been thrown down.

Out of the corner she began to pull the canvases set in rough, wooden frames, dragging them with all her strength.

"Help me!" she cried; "it will be dark directly."

They collected a heap of sketches and three large pictures, piling them before the window, and peering at them in the failing light.

Greta said ruefully:

"O Chris! they are heavy ones; we shall never carry them, and the gate is shut now!"

Christian took a pointed knife from the table.

"I shall cut them out of the frames," she said. "Listen! What's that?"

It was the sound of whistling, which stopped beneath the window. The girls, clasping each other's hands, dropped on their knees.

"Hallo!" cried a voice.

Greta crept to the window, and, placing her face level with the floor, peered over.

"It is only Dr. Edmund; he doesn't know, then," she whispered; "I shall call him; he is going away!" cried Christian catching her sister's—"Don't!" cried Christian catching her sister's dress.

"He would help us," Greta said reproachfully, "and it would not be so dark if he were here."

Christian's cheeks were burning.

"I don't choose," she said, and began handling the pictures, feeling their edges with her knife.

"Chris! Suppose anybody came?"

"The door is screwed," Christian answered absently.

"O Chris! We screwed it unscrewed; anybody who wishes shall come!"

Christian, leaning her chin in her hands, gazed at her thoughtfully.

"It will take a long time to cut these pictures out carefully; or, perhaps I can get them out without cutting. You must screw me up and go home. In the morning you must come early, when the gate is open, unscrew me again, and help carry the pictures."

Greta did not answer at once. At last she shook her head violently.

"I am afraid," she gasped.

"We can't both stay here all night," said Christian; "if any one comes to our room there will be nobody to answer. We can't lift these pictures over the gate. One of us must go back; you can climb over the gate—there is nothing to be afraid of."

Greta pressed her hands together.

"Do you want the pictures badly, Chris?"

Christian nodded.

"Very badly?"

"Yes—yes—yes!"

Greta remained sitting where she was, shivering violently, as a little animal shivers when it scents danger. At last she rose.

"I am going," she said in a despairing voice. At the doorway she turned.

"If Miss Naylor shall ask me where you are, Chris, I shall be telling her a story."

Christian started.

"I forgot that—O Greta, I am sorry! I will go instead."

Greta took another step—a quick one.

"I shall die if I stay here alone," she said; "I can tell her that you are in bed; you must go to bed here, Chris, so it shall be true after all."

Christian threw her arms about her.

"I am so sorry, darling; I wish I could go instead. But if you have to tell a lie, I would tell a straight one."

"Would you?" said Greta doubtfully.

"Yes."

"I think," said Greta to herself, beginning to descend the stairs, "I think I will tell it in my way." She shuddered and went on groping in the darkness.

Christian listened for the sound of the screws. It came slowly, threatening her with danger and solitude.

Sinking on her knees she began to work at freeing the canvas of a picture. Her heart throbbed distressfully; at the stir of wind-breath or any distant note of clamour she stopped, and held her breathing. No sounds came near. She toiled on, trying only to think that she was at the very spot where last night his arms had been round her. How long ago it seemed! She was full of vague terror, overmastered by the darkness, dreadfully alone. The new glow of resolution seemed suddenly to have died down in her heart, and left her cold.

She would never be fit to be his wife, if at the first test her courage failed! She set her teeth; and suddenly she felt a kind of exultation, as if she too were entering into life, were knowing something within herself that she had never known before. Her fingers hurt, and the pain even gave pleasure; her cheeks were burning; her breath came fast. They could not stop her now! This feverish task in darkness was her baptism into life. She finished; and rolling the pictures very carefully, tied them with cord. She had done something for him! Nobody could take that from her! She had a part of him! This night had made him hers! They might do their worst! She lay down on his mattress and soon fell asleep....

She was awakened by Scruff's tongue against her face. Greta was standing by her side.

"Wake up, Chris! The gate is open!"

In the cold early light the child seemed to glow with warmth and colour; her eyes were dancing.

"I am not afraid now; Scruff and I sat up all night, to catch the morning—I—think it was fun; and O Chris!" she ended with a rueful gleam in her eyes, "I told it."

Christian hugged her.

"Come—quick! There is nobody about. Are those the pictures?"

Each supporting an end, the girls carried the bundle downstairs, and set out with their corpse-like burden along the wall-path between the river and the vines.

XIX

Hidden by the shade of rose-bushes Greta lay stretched at length, cheek on arm, sleeping the sleep of the unrighteous. Through the flowers the sun flicked her parted lips with kisses, and spilled the withered petals on her. In a denser islet of shade, Scruff lay snapping at a fly. His head lolled drowsily in the middle of a snap, and snapped in the middle of a loll.

At three o'clock Miss Naylor too came out, carrying a basket and pair of scissors. Lifting her skirts to avoid the lakes of water left by the garden hose, she stopped in front of a rose-bush, and began to snip off the shrivelled flowers. The little lady's silvered head and thin, brown face sustained the shower of sunlight unprotected, and had a gentle dignity in their freedom.

Presently, as the scissors flittered in and out of the leaves, she, began talking to herself.

"If girls were more like what they used to be, this would not have happened. Perhaps we don't understand; it's very easy to forget." Burying her nose and lips in a rose, she sniffed. "Poor dear girl! It's such a pity his father is—a—"

"A farmer," said a sleepy voice behind the rosebush.

Miss Naylor leaped. "Greta! How you startled me! A farmer—that is—an— an agriculturalist!"

"A farmer with vineyards—he told us, and he is not ashamed. Why is it a pity, Miss Naylor?"

Miss Naylor's lips looked very thin.

"For many reasons, of which you know nothing."

"That is what you always say," pursued the sleepy voice; "and that is why, when I am to be married, there shall also be a pity."

"Greta!" Miss Naylor cried, "it is not proper for a girl of your age to talk like that."

"Why?" said Greta. "Because it is the truth?"

Miss Naylor made no reply to this, but vexedly cut off a sound rose, which she hastily picked up and regarded with contrition. Greta spoke again:

"Chris said: 'I have got the pictures, I shall tell her'. but I shall tell you instead, because it was I that told the story."

Miss Naylor stared, wrinkling her nose, and holding the scissors wide apart....

"Last night," said Greta slowly, "I and Chris went to his studio and took his pictures, and so, because the gate was shut, I came back to tell it; and when you asked me where Chris was, I told it; because she was in the studio all night, and I and Scruff sat up all night, and in the morning we brought the pictures, and hid them under our beds, and that is why—we—are—so—sleepy."

Over the rose-bush Miss Naylor peered down at her; and though she was obliged to stand on tiptoe this did not altogether destroy her dignity.

"I am surprised at you, Greta; I am surprised at Christian, more surprised at Christian. The world seems upside down."

Greta, a sunbeam entangled in her hair, regarded her with inscrutable, innocent eyes.

"When you were a girl, I think you would be sure to be in love," she murmured drowsily.

Miss Naylor, flushing deeply, snipped off a particularly healthy bud.

"And so, because you are not married, I think—"

The scissors hissed.

Greta nestled down again. "I think it is wicked to cut off all the good buds," she said, and shut her eyes.

Miss Naylor continued to peer across the rosebush; but her thin face, close to the glistening leaves, had become oddly soft, pink, and girlish. At a deeper breath from Greta, the little lady put down her basket, and began to pace the lawn, followed dubiously by Scruff. It was thus that Christian came on them.

Miss Naylor slipped her arm into the girl's and though she made no sound, her lips kept opening and shutting, like the beak of a bird contemplating a worm.

Christian spoke first:

"Miss Naylor, I want to tell you please—"

"Oh, my dear! I know; Greta has been in the confessional before you." She gave the girl's arm a squeeze. "Isn't it a lovely day? Did you ever see 'Five Fingers' look so beautiful?" And she pointed to the great peaks of the Funffingerspitze glittering in the sun like giant crystals.

"I like them better with clouds about them."

"Well," agreed Miss Naylor nervously, "they certainly are nicer with clouds about them. They look almost hot and greasy, don't they.... My dear!" she went on, giving Christian's arm a dozen little squeezes, "we all of us—that is, we all of us—"

Christian turned her eyes away.

"My dear," Miss Naylor tried again, "I am far—that is, I mean, to all of us at some time or another—and then you see—well—it is hard!"

Christian kissed the gloved hand resting on her arm. Miss Naylor bobbed her head; a tear trickled off her nose.

"Do let us wind your skein of woof!" she said with resounding gaiety.

Some half-hour later Mrs. Decie called Christian to her room.

"My dear!" she said; "come here a minute; I have a message for you."

Christian went with an odd, set look about her mouth.

Her aunt was sitting, back to the light, tapping a bowl of goldfish with the tip of a polished finger-nail; the room was very cool. She held a letter out. "Your uncle is not coming back tonight."

Christian took the letter. It was curtly worded, in a thin, toppling hand:

"DEAR CON—Can't get back to-night. Sending Dominique for things. Tell Christian to come over with him for night if possible.—Yr. aff. brother, NICLS. TREFFRY."

"Dominique has a carriage here," said Mrs. Decie. "You will have nice time to catch the train. Give my love to your uncle. You must take Barbi with you, I insist on that." She rose from her chair and held Christian's hand: "My dear! You look very tired—very! Almost ill. I don't like to see you look like that. Come!" She thrust her pale lips forward, and kissed the girl's paler cheek.

Then as Christian left the room she sank back in her chair, with creases in her forehead, and began languidly to cut a magazine. 'Poor Christian!' she thought, 'how hardly she does take it! I am sorry for her; but perhaps it's just as well, as things are turning out. Psychologically it is interesting!'

Christian found her things packed, and the two servants waiting. In a few minutes they were driving to the station. She made Dominique take the seat opposite.

"Well?" she asked him.

Dominique's eyebrows twitched, he smiled deprecatingly.

"M'mselle, Mr. Treffry told me to hold my tongue."

"But you can tell me, Dominique; Barbi can't understand."

"To you, then, M'mselle," said Dominique, as one who accepts his fate; "to you, then, who will doubtless forget all that I shall tell you—my master is not well; he has terrible pain here; he has a cough; he is not well at all; not well at all."

A feeling of dismay seized on the girl.

"We were a caravan for all that night," Dominique resumed. "In the morning by noon we ceased to be a caravan; Signor Harz took a mule path; he will be in Italy—certainly in Italy. As for us, we stayed at San Martino, and my master went to bed. It was time; I had much trouble with his clothes, his legs were swollen. In the afternoon came a signor of police, on horseback, red and hot; I persuaded him that we were at Paneveggio, but as we were not, he came back angry—Mon Die! as angry as a cat. It was not good to meet him—when he was with my master I was outside. There was much noise. I do not know what passed, but at last the signor came out through the door, and went away in a hurry." Dominique's features were fixed in a sardonic grin; he rubbed the palm of one hand with the finger of the other. "Mr. Treffry made me give him whisky afterwards, and he had no money to pay the bill—that I know because I paid it. Well, M'mselle, to-day he would be dressed and very slowly we came as far as Auer; there he could do no more, so went to bed. He is not well at all."

Christian was overwhelmed by forebodings; the rest of the journey was made in silence, except when Barbi, a country girl, filled with the delirium of railway travel, sighed: "Ach! gnadige Fraulein!" looking at Christian with pleasant eyes.

At once, on arriving at the little hostel, Christian went to see her uncle. His room was darkened, and smelt of beeswax.

"Ah! Chris," he said, "glad to see you."

In a blue flannel gown, with a rug over his feet, he was lying on a couch lengthened artificially by chairs; the arm he reached out issued many inches from its sleeve, and showed the corded veins of the wrist. Christian, settling his pillows, looked anxiously into his eyes.

"I'm not quite the thing, Chris," said Mr. Treffry. "Somehow, not quite the thing. I'll come back with you to-morrow."

"Let me send for Dr. Dawney, Uncle?"

"No—no! Plenty of him when I get home. Very good young fellow, as doctors go, but I can't stand his puddin's—slops and puddin's, and all that trumpery medicine on the top. Send me Dominique, my dear—I'll put myself to rights a bit!" He fingered his unshaven cheek, and clutched the gown together on his chest. "Got this from the landlord. When you come back we'll have a little talk!"

He was asleep when she came into the room an hour later. Watching his uneasy breathing, she wondered what it was that he was going to say.

He looked ill! And suddenly she realised that her thoughts were not of him.... When she was little he would take her on his back; he had built cocked hats for her and paper boats; had taught her to ride; slid her between his knees; given her things without number; and taken his payment in kisses. And now he was ill, and she was not thinking of him! He had been all that was most dear to her, yet before her eyes would only come the vision of another.

Mr. Treffry woke suddenly. "Not been asleep, have I? The beds here are infernal hard."

"Uncle Nic, won't you give me news of him?"

Mr. Treffry looked at her, and Christian could not bear that look.

"He's safe into Italy; they aren't very keen after him, it's so long ago; I squared 'em pretty easily. Now, look here, Chris!"

Christian came close; he took her hand.

"I'd like to see you pull yourself together. 'Tisn't so much the position; 'tisn't so much the money; because after all there's always mine—" Christian shook her head. "But," he went on with shaky emphasis, "there's the difference of blood, and that's a serious thing; and there's this anarch—this political affair; and there's the sort of life, an' that's a serious thing; but—what I'm coming to is this, Chris—there's the man!"

Christian drew away her hand. Mr. Treffry went on:

"Ah! yes. I'm an old chap and fond of you, but I must speak out what I think. He's got pluck, he's strong, he's in earnest; but he's got a damned hot temper, he's an egotist, and—he's not the man for you. If you marry him, as sure as I lie here, you'll be sorry for it. You're not your father's child for nothing; nice fellow as ever lived, but soft as butter. If you take this chap, it'll be like mixing earth and ironstone, and they don't blend!" He dropped his head back on the pillows, and stretching out his hand, repeated wistfully: "Take my word for it, my dear, he's not the man for you."

Christian, staring at the wall beyond, said quietly: "I can't take any one's word for that."

"Ah!" muttered Mr. Treffry, "you're obstinate enough, but obstinacy isn't strength.

"You'll give up everything to him, you'll lick his shoes; and you'll never play anything but second fiddle in his life. He'll always be first with himself, he and his work, or whatever he calls painting pictures; and some day you'll find that out. You won't like it, and I don't like it for you, Chris, and that's flat."

He wiped his brow where the perspiration stood in beads.

Christian said: "You don't understand; you don't believe in him; you don't see! If I do come after his work—if I do give him everything, and he can't give all back—I don't care! He'll give what he can; I don't want any more. If you're afraid of the life for me, uncle, if you think it'll be too hard—"

Mr. Treffry bowed his head. "I do, Chris."

"Well, then, I hate to be wrapped in cotton wool; I want to breathe. If I come to grief, it's my own affair; nobody need mind."

Mr. Treffry's fingers sought his beard. "Ah! yes. Just so!"

Christian sank on her knees.

"Oh! Uncle! I'm a selfish beast!"

Mr. Treffry laid his hand against her cheek. "I think I could do with a nap," he said.

Swallowing a lump in her throat, she stole out of the room.

XX

By a stroke of Fate Mr. Treffry's return to Villa Rubein befell at the psychological moment when Herr Paul, in a suit of rather too bright blue, was starting for Vienna.

As soon as he saw the carriage appear between the poplars he became as pensive as a boy caught in the act of stealing cherries. Pitching his hatbox to Fritz, he recovered himself, however, in time to whistle while Mr. Treffry was being assisted into the house. Having forgotten his anger, he was only anxious now to smooth out its after effects; in the glances he cast at Christian and his brother-in-law there was a kind of shamed entreaty which seemed to say: "For goodness' sake, don't worry me about that business again! Nothing's come of it, you see!"

He came forward: "Ah! Mon cher! So you return; I put off my departure, then. Vienna must wait for me—that poor Vienna!"

But noticing the extreme feebleness of Mr. Treffry's advance, he exclaimed with genuine concern:

"What is it? You're ill? My God!" After disappearing for five minutes, he came back with a whitish liquid in a glass.

"There!" he said, "good for the gout—for a cough—for everything!"

Mr. Treffry sniffed, drained the glass, and sucked his moustache.

"Ah!" he said. "No doubt! But it's uncommonly like gin, Paul." Then turning to Christian, he said: "Shake hands, you two!"

Christian looked from one to the other, and at last held out her hand to Herr Paul, who brushed it with his moustache, gazing after her as she left the room with a queer expression.

"My dear!" he began, "you support her in this execrable matter? You forget my position, you make me ridiculous. I have been obliged to go to bed in my own house, absolutely to go to bed, because I was in danger of becoming funny."

"Look here, Paul!" Mr. Treffry said gruffly, "if any one's to bully Chris, it's I."

"In that case," returned Herr Paul sarcastically, "I will go to Vienna."

"You may go to the devil!" said Mr. Treffry; "and I'll tell you what—in my opinion it was low to set the police on that young chap; a low, dirty trick."

Herr Paul divided his beard carefully in two, took his seat on the very edge of an arm-chair, and placing his hands on his parted knees, said:

"I have regretted it since—mais, que diable! He called me a coward—it is very hot weather!—there were drinks at the Kurhaus—I am her guardian—the affair is a very beastly one—there were more drinks—I was a little enfin!" He shrugged his shoulders. "Adieu, my dear; I shall be some time in Vienna; I need rest!" He rose and went to the door; then he turned, and waved his cigar. "Adieu! Be good; get well! I will buy you some cigars up there." And going out, he shut the door on any possibility of answer.

Mr. Treffry lay back amongst his cushions. The clock ticked; pigeons cooed on the veranda; a door opened in the distance, and for a moment a treble voice was heard. Mr. Treffry's head drooped forward; across his face, gloomy and rugged, fell a thin line of sunlight.

The clock suddenly stopped ticking, and outside, in mysterious accord, the pigeons rose with a great fluttering of wings, and flew off. Mr. Treffry made a startled, heavy movement. He tried to get on to his feet and reach the bell, but could not, and sat on the side of the couch with drops of sweat rolling off his forehead, and his hands clawing his chest. There was no sound at all throughout the house. He looked about him, and tried to call, but again could not. He tried once more to reach the bell, and, failing, sat still, with a thought that made him cold.

"I'm done for," he muttered. "By George! I believe I'm done for this time!" A voice behind him said:

"Can we have a look at you, sir?"

"Ah! Doctor, bear a hand, there's a good fellow."

Dawney propped him against the cushions, and loosened his shirt. Receiving no answer to his questions, he stepped alarmed towards the bell. Mr. Treffry stopped him with a sign.

"Let's hear what you make of me," he said.

When Dawney had examined him, he asked:

"Well?"

"Well," answered Dawney slowly, "there's trouble, of course."

Mr. Treffry broke out with a husky whisper: "Out with it, Doctor; don't humbug me."

Dawney bent down, and took his wrist.

"I don't know how you've got into this state, sir," he said with the brusqueness of emotion. "You're in a bad way. It's the old trouble; and you know what that means as well as I. All I can tell you is, I'm going to have a big fight with it. It shan't be my fault, there's my hand on that."

Mr. Treffry lay with his eyes fixed on the ceiling; at last he said:

"I want to live."

"Yes—yes."

"I feel better now; don't make a fuss about it. It'll be very awkward if I die just now. Patch me up, for the sake of my niece."

Dawney nodded. "One minute, there are a few things I want," and he went out.

A moment later Greta stole in on tiptoe. She bent over till her hair touched Mr. Treffry's face.

"Uncle Nic!" she whispered. He opened his eyes.

"Hallo, Greta!"

"I have come to bring you my love, Uncle Nic, and to say good-bye. Papa says that I and Scruff and Miss Naylor are going to Vienna with him; we have had to pack in half an hour; in five minutes we are going to Vienna, and it is my first visit there, Uncle Nic."

"To Vienna!" Mr. Treffry repeated slowly. "Don't have a guide, Greta; they're humbugs."

"No, Uncle Nic," said Greta solemnly.

"Draw the curtains, old girl, let's have a look at you. Why, you're as smart as ninepence!"

"Yes," said Greta with a sigh, touching the buttons of her cape, "because I am going to Vienna; but I am sorry to leave you, Uncle Nic."

"Are you, Greta?"

"But you will have Chris, and you are fonder of Chris than of me, Uncle Nic."

"I've known her longer."

"Perhaps when you've known me as long as Chris, you shall be as fond of me."

"When I've known you as long—may be."

"While I am gone, Uncle Nic, you are to get well, you are not very well, you know."

"What put that into your head?"

"If you were well you would be smoking a cigar—it is just three o'clock. This kiss is for myself, this is for Scruff, and this is for Miss Naylor."

She stood upright again; a tremulous, joyful gravity was in her eyes and on her lips.

"Good-bye, my dear; take care of yourselves; and don't you have a guide, they're humbugs."

"No, Uncle Nic. There is the carriage! To Vienna, Uncle Nic!" The dead gold of her hair gleamed in the doorway. Mr. Treffry raised himself upon his elbow.

"Give us one more, for luck!"

Greta ran back.

"I love you very much!" she said, and kissing him, backed slowly, then, turning, flew out like a bird.

Mr. Treffry fixed his eyes on the shut door.

XXI

After many days of hot, still weather, the wind had come, and whirled the dust along the parched roads. The leaves were all astir, like tiny wings. Round Villa Rubein the pigeons cooed uneasily, all the other birds were silent. Late in the afternoon Christian came out on the veranda, reading a letter:

"DEAR CHRIS,—We are here now six days, and it is a very large place with many churches. In the first place then we have been to a great many, but the nicest of them is not St. Stephan's Kirche, it is another, but I do not remember the name. Papa is out nearly all the night; he says he is resting here, so he is not able to come to the churches with us, but I do not think he rests very much. The day before yesterday we, that is, Papa, I, and Miss Naylor, went to an exhibition of pictures. It was quite beautiful and interesting (Miss Naylor says it is not right to say 'quite' beautiful, but I do not know what other word could mean 'quite' except the word 'quite,' because it is not exceedingly and not extremely). And O Chris! there was one picture painted by him; it was about a ship without masts—Miss Naylor says it is a barge, but I do not know what a barge is—on fire, and, floating down a river in a fog. I think it is extremely beautiful. Miss Naylor says it is very impressionistick—what is that? and Papa said 'Puh!' but he did not know it was painted by Herr Harz, so I did not tell him.

"There has also been staying at our hotel that Count Sarelli who came one evening to dinner at our house, but he is gone away now. He sat all day in the winter garden reading, and at night he went out with Papa. Miss Naylor says he is unhappy, but I think he does not take enough exercise; and O Chris! one day he said to me, 'That is your sister, Mademoiselle, that young lady in the white dress? Does she always wear white dresses?' and I said to him: 'It is not always a white dress; in the picture, it is green, because the picture is called 'Spring.' But I did not tell him the colours of all your dresses because he looked so tired. Then he said to me: 'She is very charming.' So I tell you this, Chris, because I think you shall like to know. Scruff' has a sore toe; it is because he has eaten too much meat.

"It is not nice without you, Chris, and Miss Naylor says I am improving my mind here, but I do not think it shall improve very much, because at night I like it always best, when the shops are lighted and the carriages are driving past; then I am wanting to dance. The first night Papa said he would take me to the theatre, but yesterday he said it was not good for me; perhaps to-morrow he shall think it good for me again.

"Yesterday we have been in the Prater, and saw many people, and some that Papa knew; and then came the most interesting part of all, sitting under the trees in the rain for two hours because we could not get a carriage (very exciting).

"There is one young lady here, only she is not any longer very young, who knew Papa when he was a boy. I like her very much; she shall soon know me quite to the bottom and is very kind.

"The ill husband of Cousin Teresa who went with us to Meran and lost her umbrella and Dr. Edmund was so sorry about it, has been very much worse, so she is not here but in Baden. I wrote to her but have no news, so I do not know whether he is still living or not, at any rate he can't get well again so soon (and I don't think he ever shall). I think as the weather is very warm you and Uncle Nic are sitting much out of doors. I am sending presents to you all in a wooden box and screwed very firm, so you shall have to use again the big screw-driver of Fritz. For Aunt Constance, photographs; for Uncle Nic, a green bird on a stand with a hole in the back of the bird to put his ashes in; it is a good green and not expensif please tell him, because he does not like expensif presents (Miss Naylor says the bird has an inquiring eye—it is a parrat); for you, a little brooch of turquoise because I like them best; for Dr. Edmund a machine to weigh medicines in because he said he could not get a good one in Botzen; this is a very good one, the shopman told me so, and is the most expensif of all the presents—so that is all my money, except two gulden. If Papa shall give me some more, I shall buy for Miss Naylor a parasol, because it is useful and the handle of hers is 'wobbley' (that is one of Dr. Edmund's words and I like it).

"Good-bye for this time. Greta sends you her kiss.

"P. S.—Miss Naylor has read all this letter (except about the parasol) and there are several things she did not want me to put, so I have copied it without the things, but at the last I have kept that copy myself, so that is why this is smudgy and several words are not spelt well, but all the things are here."

Christian read, smiling, but to finish it was like dropping a talisman, and her face clouded. A sudden draught blew her hair about, and from within, Mr. Treffry's cough mingled with the soughing of the wind; the sky was fast blackening. She went indoors, took a pen and began to write:

"MY FRIEND,—Why haven't you written to me? It is so, long to wait. Uncle says you are in Italy—it is dreadful not to know for certain. I feel you would have written if you could; and I can't help thinking of all the things that may have happened. I am unhappy. Uncle Nic is ill; he will not confess it, that is his way; but he is very ill. Though perhaps you will never see this, I must write down all my thoughts. Sometimes I feel that I am brutal to be always thinking about you, scheming how to be with you again, when he is lying there so ill. How good he has always been to me; it is terrible that love should pull one apart so. Surely love should be beautiful, and peaceful, instead of filling me with bitter, wicked thoughts. I love you—and I love him; I feel as if I were torn in two. Why should it be so? Why should the beginning of one life mean the ending of another, one love the destruction of another? I don't understand. The same spirit makes me love you and him, the same sympathy, the same trust—yet it sometimes seems as if I were a criminal in loving you. You know what he thinks—he is too honest not to have shown you. He has talked to me; he likes you in a way, but you are a foreigner—he says-your life is not my life. 'He is not the man for you!' Those were his words. And now he doesn't talk to me, but when I am in the room he looks at me—that's worse—a thousand times; when he talks it rouses me to fight—when it's his eyes only, I'm a coward at once; I feel I would do anything, anything, only not to hurt him. Why can't he see? Is it because he's old and we are young? He may consent, but he will never, never see; it will always hurt him.

"I want to tell you everything; I have had worse thoughts than these—sometimes I have thought that I should never have the courage to face the struggle which you have to face. Then I feel quite broken; it is like something giving way in me. Then I think of you, and it is over; but it has been there, and I am ashamed—I told you I was a coward. It's like the feeling one would have going out into a storm on a dark night, away from a warm fire—only of the spirit not the body—which makes it worse. I had to tell you this; you mustn't think of it again, I mean to fight it away and forget that it has ever been there. But Uncle Nic—what am I to do? I hate myself because I am young, and he is old and weak—sometimes I seem even to hate him. I have all sorts of thoughts, and always at the end of them, like a dark hole at the end of a passage, the thought that I ought to give you up. Ought I? Tell me. I want to know, I want to do what is right; I still want to do that, though sometimes I think I am all made of evil.

"Do you remember once when we were talking, you said: 'Nature always has an answer for every question; you cannot get an answer from laws, conventions, theories, words, only from Nature.' What do you say to me now; do you tell me it is Nature to come to you in spite of everything, and so, that it must be right? I think you would; but can it be Nature to do something which will hurt terribly one whom I love and who loves me? If it is—Nature is cruel. Is that one of the 'lessons of life'. Is that what Aunt Constance means when she says: 'If life were not a paradox, we could not get on at all'. I am beginning to see that everything has its dark side; I never believed that before.

"Uncle Nic dreads the life for me; he doesn't understand (how should he?—he has always had money) how life can be tolerable without money—it is horrible that the accident of money should make such difference in our lives. I am sometimes afraid myself, and I can't outface that fear in him; he sees the shadow of his fear in me—his eyes seem to see everything that is in me now; the eyes of old people are the saddest things in the world. I am writing like a wretched coward, but you will never see this letter I suppose, and so it doesn't matter; but if you do, and I pray that you may—well, if I am only worth taking at my best, I am not worth taking at all. I want you to know the worst of me—you, and no one else.

"With Uncle Nic it is not as with my stepfather; his opposition only makes me angry, mad, ready to do anything, but with Uncle Nic I feel so bruised—so sore. He said: 'It is not so much the money, because there is always mine.' I could never do a thing he cannot bear, and take his money, and you would never let me. One knows very little of anything in the world till trouble comes. You know how it is with flowers and trees; in the early spring they look so quiet and self-contained; then all in a moment they change—I think it must be like that with the heart. I used to think I knew a great deal, understood why and how things came about; I thought self-possession and reason so easy; now I know nothing. And nothing in the world matters but to see you and hide away from that look in Uncle Nic's eyes. Three months ago I did not know you, now I write like this. Whatever I look at, I try to see as you would see; I feel, now you are away even more than when you were with me, what your thoughts would be, how you would feel about this or that. Some things you have said seem always in my mind like lights—"

A slanting drift of rain was striking the veranda tiles with a cold, ceaseless hissing. Christian shut the window, and went into her uncle's room.

He was lying with closed eyes, growling at Dominique, who moved about noiselessly, putting the room ready for the night. When he had finished, and with a compassionate bow had left the room, Mr. Treffry opened his eyes, and said:

"This is beastly stuff of the doctor's, Chris, it puts my monkey up; I can't help swearing after I've taken it; it's as beastly as a vulgar woman's laugh, and I don't know anything beastlier than that!"

"I have a letter from Greta, Uncle Nic; shall I read it?"

He nodded, and Christian read the letter, leaving out the mention of Harz, and for some undefined reason the part about Sarelli.

"Ay!" said Mr. Treffry with a feeble laugh, "Greta and her money! Send her some more, Chris. Wish I were a youngster again; that's a beast of a proverb about a dog and his day. I'd like to go fishing again in the West Country! A fine time we had when we were youngsters. You don't get such times these days. 'Twasn't often the fishing-smacks went out without us. We'd watch their lights from our bedroom window; when they were swung aboard we were out and down to the quay before you could say 'knife.' They always waited for us; but your Uncle Dan was the favourite, he was the chap for luck. When I get on my legs, we might go down there, you and I? For a bit, just to see? What d'you say, old girl?"

Their eyes met.

"I'd like to look at the smack lights going to sea on a dark night; pity you're such a duffer in a boat—we might go out with them. Do you a power of good! You're not looking the thing, my dear."

His voice died wistfully, and his glance, sweeping her face, rested on her hands, which held and twisted Greta's letter. After a minute or two of silence he boomed out again with sudden energy:

"Your aunt'll want to come and sit with me, after dinner; don't let her, Chris, I can't stand it. Tell her I'm asleep—the doctor'll be here directly; ask him to make up some humbug for you—it's his business."

He was seized by a violent fit of pain which seemed to stab his breath away, and when it was over signed that he would be left alone. Christian went back to her letter in the other room, and had written these words, when the gong summoned her to dinner:

"I'm like a leaf in the wind, I put out my hand to one thing, and it's seized and twisted and flung aside. I want you—I want you; if I could see you I think I should know what to do—"

XXII

The rain drove with increasing fury. The night was very black. Nicholas Treffry slept heavily. By the side of his bed the night-lamp cast on to the opposite wall a bright disc festooned by the hanging shadow of the ceiling. Christian was leaning over him. For the moment he filled all her heart, lying there, so helpless. Fearful of waking him she slipped into the sitting-room. Outside the window stood a man with his face pressed to the pane. Her heart thumped; she went up and unlatched the window. It was Harz, with the rain dripping off him. He let fall his hat and cape.

"You!" she said, touching his sleeve. "You! You!"

He was sodden with wet, his face drawn and tired; a dark growth of beard covered his cheeks and chin.

"Where is your uncle?" he said; "I want to see him."

She put her hand up to his lips, but he caught it and covered it with kisses.

"He's asleep—ill—speak gently!"

"I came to him first," he muttered.

Christian lit the lamp; and he looked at her hungrily without a word.

"It's not possible to go on like this; I came to tell your uncle so. He is a man. As for the other, I want to have nothing to do with him! I came back on foot across the mountains. It's not possible to go on like this, Christian."

She handed him her letter. He held it to the light, clearing his brow of raindrops. When he had read to the last word he gave it her back, and whispered: "Come!"

Her lips moved, but she did not speak.

"While this goes on I can't work; I can do nothing. I can't—I won't bargain with my work; if it's to be that, we had better end it. What are we waiting for? Sooner or later we must come to this. I'm sorry that he's ill, God knows! But that changes nothing. To wait is tying me hand and foot—it's making me afraid! Fear kills! It will kill you! It kills work, and I must work, I can't waste time—I won't! I will sooner give you up." He put his hands on her shoulders. "I love you! I want you! Look in my eyes and see if you dare hold back!"

Christian stood with the grip of his strong hands on her shoulders, without a movement or sign. Her face was very white. And suddenly he began to kiss that pale, still face, to kiss its eyes and lips, to kiss it from its chin up to its hair; and it stayed pale, as a white flower, beneath those kisses—as a white flower, whose stalk the fingers bend back a little.

There was a sound of knocking on the wall; Mr. Treffry called feebly. Christian broke away from Harz.

"To-morrow!" he whispered, and picking up his hat and cloak, went out again into the rain.

XXIII

It was not till morning that Christian fell into a troubled sleep. She dreamed that a voice was calling her, and she was filled with a helpless, dumb dream terror.

When she woke the light was streaming in; it was Sunday, and the cathedral bells were chiming. Her first thought was of Harz. One step, one moment of courage! Why had she not told her uncle? If he had only asked! But why—why should she tell him? When it was over and she was gone, he would see that all was for the best.

Her eyes fell on Greta's empty bed. She sprang up, and bending over, kissed the pillow. 'She will mind at first; but she's so young! Nobody will really miss me, except Uncle Nic!' She stood along while in the window without moving. When she was dressed she called out to her maid:

"Bring me some milk, Barbi; I'm going to church."

"Ach! gnadiges Fraulein, will you no breakfast have?"

"No thank you, Barbi."

"Liebes Fraulein, what a beautiful morning after the rain it has become! How cool! It is for you good—for the colour in your cheeks; now they will bloom again!" and Barbi stroked her own well-coloured cheeks.

Dominique, sunning himself outside with a cloth across his arm, bowed as she passed, and smiled affectionately:

"He is better this morning, M'mselle. We march—we are getting on. Good news will put the heart into you."

Christian thought: 'How sweet every one is to-day!'

Even the Villa seemed to greet her, with the sun aslant on it; and the trees, trembling and weeping golden tears. At the cathedral she was early for the service, but here and there were figures on their knees; the faint, sickly odour of long-burnt incense clung in the air; a priest moved silently at the far end. She knelt, and when at last she rose the service had begun. With the sound of the intoning a sense of peace came to her—the peace of resolution. For good or bad she felt that she had faced her fate.

She went out with a look of quiet serenity and walked home along the dyke. Close to Harz's studio she sat down. Now—it was her own; all that had belonged to him, that had ever had a part in him.

An old beggar, who had been watching her, came gently from behind. "Gracious lady!" he said, peering at her eyes, "this is the lucky day for you. I have lost my luck."

Christian opened her purse, there was only one coin in it, a gold piece; the beggar's eyes sparkled.

She thought suddenly: 'It's no longer mine; I must begin to be careful,' but she felt ashamed when she looked at the old man.

"I am sorry," she said; "yesterday I would have given you this, but—but now it's already given."

He seemed so old and poor—what could she give him? She unhooked a little silver brooch at her throat. "You will get something for that," she said; "it's better than nothing. I am very sorry you are so old and poor."

The beggar crossed himself. "Gracious lady," he muttered, "may you never want!"

Christian hurried on; the rustling of leaves soon carried the words away. She did not feel inclined to go in, and crossing the bridge began to climb the hill. There was a gentle breeze, drifting the clouds across the sun; lizards darted out over the walls, looked at her, and whisked away.

The sunshine, dappling through the tops of trees, gashed down on a torrent. The earth smelt sweet, the vineyards round the white farms glistened; everything seemed to leap and dance with sap and life; it was a moment of Spring in midsummer. Christian walked on, wondering at her own happiness.

'Am I heartless?' she thought. 'I am going to leave him—I am going into life; I shall have to fight now, there'll be no looking back.'

The path broke away and wound down to the level of the torrent; on the other side it rose again, and was lost among trees. The woods were dank; she hastened home.

In her room she began to pack, sorting and tearing up old letters. 'Only one thing matters,' she thought; 'singleness of heart; to see your way, and keep to it with all your might.'

She looked up and saw Barbi standing before her with towels in her hands, and a scared face.

"Are you going a journey, gnadiges Fraulein?"

"I am going away to be married, Barbi," said Christian at last; "don't speak of it to any one, please."

Barbi leant a little forward with the towels clasped to the blue cotton bosom of her dress.

"No, no! I will not speak. But, dear Fraulein, that is a big matter; have you well thought?"

"Thought, Barbi? Have I not!"

"But, dear Fraulein, will you be rich?"

"No! I shall be as poor as you."

"Ach! dear God! that is terrible. Katrina, my sister, she is married; she tells me all her life; she tells me it is very hard, and but for the money in her stocking it would be harder. Dear Fraulein, think again! And is he good? Sometimes they are not good."

"He is good," said Christian, rising; "it is all settled!" and she kissed Barbi on the cheek.

"You are crying, liebes Fraulein! Think yet again, perhaps it is not quite all settled; it is not possible that a maiden should not a way out leave?"

Christian smiled. "I don't do things that way, Barbi."

Barbi hung the towels on the horse, and crossed herself.

XXIV

Mr. Treffry's gaze was fixed on a tortoise-shell butterfly fluttering round the ceiling. The insect seemed to fascinate him, as things which move quickly always fascinate the helpless. Christian came softly in.

"Couldn't stay in bed, Chris," he called out with an air of guilt. "The heat was something awful. The doctor piped off in a huff, just because o' this." He motioned towards a jug of claret-cup and a pipe on the table by his elbow. "I was only looking at 'em."

Christian, sitting down beside him, took up a fan.

"If I could get out of this heat—" he said, and closed his eyes.

'I must tell him,' she thought; 'I can't slink away.'

"Pour me out some of that stuff, Chris."

She reached for the jug. Yes! She must tell him! Her heart sank.

Mr. Treffry took a lengthy draught. "Broken my promise; don't matter—won't hurt any one but me." He took up the pipe and pressed tobacco into it. "I've been lying here with this pain going right through me, and never a smoke! D'you tell me anything the parsons say can do me half the good of this pipe?" He leaned back, steeped in a luxury of satisfaction. He went on, pursuing a private train of thought: "Things have changed a lot since my young days. When I was a youngster, a young fellow had to look out for peck and perch—he put the future in his pocket. He did well or not, according as he had stuff in him. Now he's not content with that, it seems—trades on his own opinion of himself; thinks he is what he says he's going to be."

"You are unjust," said Christian.

Mr. Treffry grunted. "Ah, well! I like to know where I am. If I lend money to a man, I like to know whether he's going to pay it back; I may not care whether he does or not, but I like to know. The same with other things. I don't care what a man has—though, mind you, Chris, it's not a bad rule that measures men by the balance at their banks; but when it comes to marriage, there's a very simple rule, What's not enough for one is not enough for two. You can't talk black white, or bread into your mouth. I don't care to speak about myself, as you know, Chris, but I tell you this—when I came to London I wanted to marry—I hadn't any money, and I had to want. When I had the money—but that's neither here nor there!" He frowned, fingering his pipe.

"I didn't ask her, Chris; I didn't think it the square thing; it seems that's out of fashion!"

Christian's cheeks were burning.

"I think a lot while I lie here," Mr. Treffry went on; "nothing much else to do. What I ask myself is this: What do you know about what's best for you? What do you know of life? Take it or leave it, life's not all you think; it's give and get all the way, a fair start is everything."

Christian thought: 'Will he never see?'

Mr. Treffry went on:

"I get better every day, but I can't last for ever. It's not pleasant to lie here and know that when I'm gone there'll be no one to keep a hand on the check string!"

"Don't talk like that, dear!" Christian murmured.

"It's no use blinking facts, Chris. I've lived a long time in the world; I've seen things pretty well as they are; and now there's not much left for me to think about but you."

"But, Uncle, if you loved him, as I do, you couldn't tell me to be afraid! It's cowardly and mean to be afraid. You must have forgotten!"

Mr. Treffry closed his eyes.

"Yes," he said; "I'm old."

The fan had dropped into Christian's lap; it rested on her white frock like a large crimson leaf; her eyes were fixed on it.

Mr. Treffry looked at her. "Have you heard from him?" he asked with sudden intuition.

"Last night, in that room, when you thought I was talking to Dominique—"

The pipe fell from his hand.

"What!" he stammered: "Back?"

Christian, without looking up, said:

"Yes, he's back; he wants me—I must go to him, Uncle."

There was a long silence.

"You must go to him?" he repeated.

She longed to fling herself down at his knees, but he was so still, that to move seemed impossible; she remained silent, with folded hands.

Mr. Treffry spoke:

"You'll let me know—before—you—go. Goodnight!"

Christian stole out into the passage. A bead curtain rustled in the draught; voices reached her.

"My honour is involved, or I would give the case up."

"He is very trying, poor Nicholas! He always had that peculiar quality of opposition; it has brought him to grief a hundred times. There is opposition in our blood; my family all have it. My eldest brother died of it; with my poor sister, who was as gentle as a lamb, it took the form of doing the right thing in the wrong place. It is a matter of temperament, you see. You must have patience."

"Patience," repeated Dawney's voice, "is one thing; patience where there is responsibility is another. I've not had a wink of sleep these last two nights."

There was a faint, shrill swish of silk.

"Is he so very ill?"

Christian held her breath. The answer came at last.

"Has he made his will? With this trouble in the side again, I tell you plainly, Mrs. Decie, there's little or no chance."

Christian put her hands up to her ears, and ran out into the air. What was she about to do, then—to leave him dying!

XXV

On the following day Harz was summoned to the Villa. Mr. Treffry had just risen, and was garbed in a dressing-suit, old and worn, which had a certain air of magnificence. His seamed cheeks were newly shaved.

"I hope I see you well," he said majestically.

Thinking of the drive and their last parting, Harz felt sorry and ashamed. Suddenly Christian came into the room; she stood for a moment looking at him; then sat down.

"Chris!" said Mr. Treffry reproachfully. She shook her head, and did not move; mournful and intent, her eyes seemed full of secret knowledge.

Mr. Treffry spoke:

"I've no right to blame you, Mr. Harz, and Chris tells me you came to see me first, which is what I would have expected of you; but you shouldn't have come back."

"I came back, sir, because I found I was obliged. I must speak out."

"I ask nothing better," Mr. Treffry replied.

Harz looked again at Christian; but she made no sign, sitting with her chin resting on her hands.

"I have come for her," he said; "I can make my living—enough for both of us. But I can't wait."

"Why?"

Harz made no answer.

Mr. Treffry boomed out again: "Why? Isn't she worth waiting for? Isn't she worth serving for?"

"I can't expect you to understand me," the painter said. "My art is my life to me. Do you suppose that if it wasn't I should ever have left my village; or gone through all that I've gone through, to get as far even as I am? You tell me to wait. If my thoughts and my will aren't free, how can I work? I shan't be worth my salt. You tell me to go back to England—knowing she is here, amongst you who hate me, a thousand miles away. I shall know that there's a death fight going on in her and outside her against me—you think that I can go on working under these conditions. Others may be able, I am not. That's the plain truth. If I loved her less—"

There was a silence, then Mr. Treffry said:

"It isn't fair to come here and ask what you're asking. You don't know what's in the future for you, you don't know that you can keep a wife. It isn't pleasant, either, to think you can't hold up your head in your own country."

Harz turned white.

"Ah! you bring that up again!" he broke out. "Seven years ago I was a boy and starving; if you had been in my place you would have done what I did. My country is as much to me as your country is to you. I've been an exile seven years, I suppose I shall always be I've had punishment enough; but if you think I am a rascal, I'll go and give myself up." He turned on his heel.

"Stop! I beg your pardon! I never meant to hurt you. It isn't easy for me to eat my words," Mr. Treffry said wistfully, "let that count for something." He held out his hand.

Harz came quickly back and took it. Christian's gaze was never for a moment withdrawn; she seemed trying to store up the sight of him within her. The light darting through the half-closed shutters gave her eyes a strange, bright intensity, and shone in the folds of her white dress like the sheen of birds' wings.

Mr. Treffry glanced uneasily about him. "God knows I don't want anything but her happiness," he said. "What is it to me if you'd murdered your mother? It's her I'm thinking of."

"How can you tell what is happiness to her? You have your own ideas of happiness—not hers, not mine. You can't dare to stop us, sir!"

"Dare?" said Mr. Treffry. "Her father gave her over to me when she was a mite of a little thing; I've known her all her life. I've—I've loved her—and you come here with your 'dare'." His hand dragged at his beard, and shook as though palsied.

A look of terror came into Christian's face.

"All right, Chris! I don't ask for quarter, and I don't give it!"

Harz made a gesture of despair.

"I've acted squarely by you, sir," Mr. Treffry went on, "I ask the same of you. I ask you to wait, and come like an honest man, when you can say, 'I see my way—here's this and that for her.' What makes this art you talk of different from any other call in life? It doesn't alter facts, or give you what other men have no right to expect. It doesn't put grit into you, or keep your hands clean, or prove that two and two make five."

Harz answered bitterly:

"You know as much of art as I know of money. If we live a thousand years we shall never understand each other. I am doing what I feel is best for both of us."

Mr. Treffry took hold of the painter's sleeve.

"I make you an offer," he said. "Your word not to see or write to her for a year! Then, position or not, money or no money, if she'll have you, I'll make it right for you."

"I could not take your money."

A kind of despair seemed suddenly to seize on Mr. Nicholas Treffry. He rose, and stood towering over them.

"All my life—" he said; but something seemed to click deep down in his throat, and he sank back in his seat.

"Go!" whispered Christian, "go!" But Mr. Treffry found his voice again: "It's for the child to say. Well, Chris!"

Christian did not speak.

It was Harz who broke the silence. He pointed to Mr. Treffry.

"You know I can't tell you to come with—that, there. Why did you send for me?" And, turning, he went out.

Christian sank on her knees, burying her face in her hands. Mr. Treffry pressed his handkerchief with a stealthy movement to his mouth. It was dyed crimson with the price of his victory.

XXVI

A telegram had summoned Herr Paul from Vienna. He had started forthwith, leaving several unpaid accounts to a more joyful opportunity, amongst them a chemist's bill, for a wonderful quack medicine of which he brought six bottles.

He came from Mr. Treffry's room with tears rolling down his cheeks, saying:

"Poor Nicholas! Poor Nicholas! Il n'a pas de chance!"

It was difficult to find any one to listen; the women were scared and silent, waiting for the orders that were now and then whispered through the door. Herr Paul could not bear this silence, and talked to his servant for half an hour, till Fritz also vanished to fetch something from the town. Then in despair Herr Paul went to his room.

It was hard not to be allowed to help—it was hard to wait! When the heart was suffering, it was frightful! He turned and, looking furtively about him, lighted a cigar. Yes, it came to every one—at some time or other; and what was it, that death they talked of? Was it any worse than life? That frightful jumble people made for themselves! Poor Nicholas! After all, it was he that had the luck!

His eyes filled with tears, and drawing a penknife from his pocket, he began to stab it into the stuffing of his chair. Scruff, who sat watching the chink of light under the door, turned his head, blinked at him, and began feebly tapping with a claw.

It was intolerable, this uncertainty—to be near, and yet so far, was not endurable!

Herr Paul stepped across the room. The dog, following, threw his black-marked muzzle upwards with a gruff noise, and went back to the door. His master was holding in his hand a bottle of champagne.

Poor Nicholas! He had chosen it. Herr Paul drained a glass.

Poor Nicholas! The prince of fellows, and of what use was one? They kept him away from Nicholas!

Herr Paul's eyes fell on the terrier. "Ach! my dear," he said, "you and I, we alone are kept away!"

He drained a second glass.

What was it? This life! Froth-like that! He tossed off a third glass. Forget! If one could not help, it was better to forget!

He put on his hat. Yes. There was no room for him there! He was not wanted!

He finished the bottle, and went out into the passage. Scruff ran and lay down at Mr. Treffry's door. Herr Paul looked at him. "Ach!" he said, tapping his chest, "ungrateful hound!" And opening the front door he went out on tiptoe....

Late that afternoon Greta stole hatless through the lilac bushes; she looked tired after her night journey, and sat idly on a chair in the speckled shadow of a lime-tree.

'It is not like home,' she thought; 'I am unhappy. Even the birds are silent, but perhaps that is because it is so hot. I have never been sad like this—for it is not fancy that I am sad this time, as it is sometimes. It is in my heart like the sound the wind makes through a wood, it feels quite empty in my heart. If it is always like this to be unhappy, then I am sorry for all the unhappy things in the world; I am sorrier than I ever was before.'

A shadow fell on the grass, she raised her eyes, and saw Dawney.

"Dr. Edmund!" she whispered.

Dawney turned to her; a heavy furrow showed between his brows. His eyes, always rather close together, stared painfully.

"Dr. Edmund," Greta whispered, "is it true?"

He took her hand, and spread his own palm over it.

"Perhaps," he said; "perhaps not. We must hope."

Greta looked up, awed.

"They say he is dying."

"We have sent for the best man in Vienna."

Greta shook her head.

"But you are clever, Dr. Edmund; and you are afraid."

"He is brave," said Dawney; "we must all be brave, you know. You too!"

"Brave?" repeated Greta; "what is it to be brave? If it is not to cry and make a fuss—that I can do. But if it is not to be sad in here," she touched her breast, "that I cannot do, and it shall not be any good for me to try."

"To be brave is to hope; don't give up hope, dear."

"No," said Greta, tracing the pattern of the sunlight on her skirt. "But I think that when we hope, we are not brave, because we are expecting something for ourselves. Chris says that hope is prayer, and if it is prayer, then all the time we are hoping, we are asking for something, and it is not brave to ask for things."

A smile curved Dawney's mouth.

"Go on, Philosopher!" he said. "Be brave in your own way, it will be just as good as anybody else's."

"What are you going to do to be brave, Dr. Edmund?"

"I? Fight! If only we had five years off his life!"

Greta watched him as he walked away.

"I shall never be brave," she mourned; "I shall always be wanting to be happy." And, kneeling down, she began to disentangle a fly, imprisoned in a cobweb. A plant of hemlock had sprung up in the long grass by her feet. Greta thought, dismayed: 'There are weeds!'

It seemed but another sign of the death of joy.

'But it's very beautiful,' she thought, 'the blossoms are like stars. I am not going to pull it up. I will leave it; perhaps it will spread all through the garden; and if it does I do not care, for now things are not like they used to be and I do not, think they ever shall be again.'

XXVII

The days went by; those long, hot days, when the heat haze swims up about ten of the forenoon, and, as the sun sinks level with the mountains, melts into golden ether which sets the world quivering with sparkles.

At the lighting of the stars those sparkles die, vanishing one by one off the hillsides; evening comes flying down the valleys, and life rests under her cool wings. The night falls; and the hundred little voices of the night arise.

It was near grape-gathering, and in the heat the fight for Nicholas Treffry's life went on, day in, day out, with gleams of hope and moments of despair. Doctors came, but after the first he refused to see them.

"No," he said to Dawney—"throwing away money. If I pull through it won't be because of them."

For days together he would allow no one but Dawney, Dominique, and the paid nurse in the room.

"I can stand it better," he said to Christian, "when I don't see any of you; keep away, old girl, and let me get on with it!"

To have been able to help would have eased the tension of her nerves, and the aching of her heart. At his own request they had moved his bed into a corner so that he might face the wall. There he would lie for hours together, not speaking a word, except to ask for drink.

Sometimes Christian crept in unnoticed, and sat watching, with her arms tightly folded across her breast. At night, after Greta was asleep, she would toss from side to side, muttering feverish prayers. She spent hours at her little table in the schoolroom, writing letters to Harz that were never sent. Once she wrote these words: "I am the most wicked of all creatures—I have even wished that he may die!" A few minutes afterwards Miss Naylor found her with her head buried on her arms. Christian sprang up; tears were streaming down her cheeks. "Don't touch me!" she cried, and rushed away. Later, she stole into her uncle's room, and sank down on the floor beside the bed. She sat there silently, unnoticed all the evening. When night came she could hardly be persuaded to leave the room.

One day Mr. Treffry expressed a wish to see Herr Paul; it was a long while before the latter could summon courage to go in.

"There's a few dozen of the Gordon sherry at my Chambers, in London, Paul," Mr. Treffry said; "I'd be glad to think you had 'em. And my man, Dominique, I've made him all right in my will, but keep your eye on him; he's a good sort for a foreigner, and no chicken, but sooner or later, the women'll get hold of him. That's all I had to say. Send Chris to me."

Herr Paul stood by the bedside speechless. Suddenly he blurted out.

"Ah! my dear! Courage! We are all mortal. You will get well!" All the morning he walked about quite inconsolable. "It was frightful to see him, you know, frightful! An iron man could not have borne it."

When Christian came to him, Mr. Treffry raised himself and looked at her a long while.

His wistful face was like an accusation. But that very afternoon the news came from the sickroom that he was better, having had no pain for several hours.

Every one went about with smiles lurking in their eyes, and ready to break forth at a word. In the kitchen Barbi burst out crying, and, forgetting to toss the pan, spoiled a Kaiser-Schmarn she was making. Dominique was observed draining a glass of Chianti, and solemnly casting forth the last drops in libation. An order was given for tea to be taken out under the acacias, where it was always cool; it was felt that something in the nature of high festival was being held. Even Herr Paul was present; but Christian did not come. Nobody spoke of illness; to mention it might break the spell.

Miss Naylor, who had gone into the house, came back, saying:

"There is a strange man standing over there by the corner of the house."

"Really!" asked Mrs. Decie; "what does he want?"

Miss Naylor reddened. "I did not ask him. I—don't—know—whether he is quite respectable. His coat is buttoned very close, and he—doesn't seem—to have a—collar."

"Go and see what he wants, dear child," Mrs. Decie said to Greta.

"I don't know—I really do not know—" began Miss Naylor; "he has very—high—boots," but Greta was already on her way, with hands clasped behind her, and demure eyes taking in the stranger's figure.

"Please?" she said, when she was close to him.

The stranger took his cap off with a jerk.

"This house has no bells," he said in a nasal voice; "it has a tendency to discourage one."

"Yes," said Greta gravely, "there is a bell, but it does not ring now, because my uncle is so ill."

"I am very sorry to hear that. I don't know the people here, but I am very sorry to hear that.

"I would be glad to speak a few words to your sister, if it is your sister that I want."

And the stranger's face grew very red.

"Is it," said Greta, "that you are a friend of Herr Harz? If you are a friend of his, you will please come and have some tea, and while you are having tea I will look for Chris."

Perspiration bedewed the stranger's forehead.

"Tea? Excuse me! I don't drink tea."

"There is also coffee," Greta said.

The stranger's progress towards the arbour was so slow that Greta arrived considerably before him.

"It is a friend of Herr Harz," she whispered; "he will drink coffee. I am going to find Chris."

"Greta!" gasped Miss Naylor.

Mrs. Decie put up her hand.

"Ah!" she said, "if it is so, we must be very nice to him for Christian's sake."

Miss Naylor's face grew soft.

"Ah, yes!" she said; "of course."

"Bah!" muttered Herr Paul, "that recommences.'

"Paul!" murmured Mrs. Decie, "you lack the elements of wisdom."

Herr Paul glared at the approaching stranger.

Mrs. Decie had risen, and smilingly held out her hand.

"We are so glad to know you; you are an artist too, perhaps? I take a great interest in art, and especially in that school which Mr. Harz represents."

The stranger smiled.

"He is the genuine article, ma'am," he said. "He represents no school, he is one of that kind whose corpses make schools."

"Ah!" murmured Mrs. Decie, "you are an American. That is so nice. Do sit down! My niece will soon be here."

Greta came running back.

"Will you come, please?" she said. "Chris is ready."

Gulping down his coffee, the stranger included them all in a single bow, and followed her.

"Ach!" said Herr Paul, "garcon tres chic, celui-la!"

Christian was standing by her little table. The stranger began.

"I am sending Mr. Harz's things to England; there are some pictures here. He would be glad to have them."

A flood of crimson swept over her face.

"I am sending them to London," the stranger repeated; "perhaps you could give them to me to-day."

"They are ready; my sister will show you."

Her eyes seemed to dart into his soul, and try to drag something from it. The words rushed from her lips:

"Is there any message for me?"

The stranger regarded her curiously.

"No," he stammered, "no! I guess not. He is well.... I wish...." He stopped; her white face seemed to flash scorn, despair, and entreaty on him all at once. And turning, she left him standing there.

XXVIII

When Christian went that evening to her uncle's room he was sitting up in bed, and at once began to talk. "Chris," he said, "I can't stand this dying by inches. I'm going to try what a journey'll do for me. I want to get back to the old country. The doctor's promised. There's a shot in the locker yet! I believe in that young chap; he's stuck to me like a man.... It'll be your birthday, on Tuesday, old girl, and you'll be twenty. Seventeen years since your father died. You've been a lot to me.... A parson came here today. That's a bad sign. Thought it his duty! Very civil of him! I wouldn't see him, though. If there's anything in what they tell you, I'm not going to sneak in at this time o' day. There's one thing that's rather badly on my mind. I took advantage of Mr. Harz with this damned pitifulness of mine. You've a right to look at me as I've seen you sometimes when you thought I was asleep. If I hadn't been ill he'd never have left you. I don't blame you, Chris—not I! You love me? I know that, my dear. But one's alone when it comes to the run-in. Don't cry! Our minds aren't Sunday-school books; you're finding it out, that's all!" He sighed and turned away.

The noise of sun-blinds being raised vibrated through the house. A feeling of terror seized on the girl; he lay so still, and yet the drawing of each breath was a fight. If she could only suffer in his place! She went close, and bent over him.

"It's air we want, both you and I!" he muttered. Christian beckoned to the nurse, and stole out through the window.

A regiment was passing in the road; she stood half-hidden amongst the lilac bushes watching. The poplar leaves drooped lifeless and almost black above her head, the dust raised by the soldiers' feet hung in the air; it seemed as if in all the world no freshness and no life were stirring. The tramp of feet died away. Suddenly within arm's length of her a man appeared, his stick shouldered like a sword. He raised his hat.

"Good-evening! You do not remember me? Sarelli. Pardon! You looked like a ghost standing there. How badly those fellows marched! We hang, you see, on the skirts of our profession and criticise; it is all we are fit for." His black eyes, restless and malevolent like a swan's, seemed to stab her face. "A fine evening! Too hot. The storm is wanted; you feel that? It is weary waiting for the storm; but after the storm, my dear young lady, comes peace." He smiled, gently, this time, and baring his head again, was lost to view in the shadow of the trees.

His figure had seemed to Christian like the sudden vision of a threatening, hidden force. She thrust out her hands, as though to keep it off.

No use; it was within her, nothing could keep it away! She went to Mrs. Decie's room, where her aunt and Miss Naylor were conversing in low tones. To hear their voices brought back the touch of this world of everyday which had no part or lot in the terrifying powers within her.

Dawney slept at the Villa now. In the dead of night he was awakened by a light flashed in his eyes. Christian was standing there, her face pale and wild with terror, her hair falling in dark masses on her shoulders.

"Save him! Save him!" she cried. "Quick! The bleeding!"

He saw her muffle her face in her white sleeves, and seizing the candle, leaped out of bed and rushed away.

The internal haemorrhage had come again, and Nicholas Treffry wavered between life and death. When it had ceased, he sank into a sort of stupor. About six o'clock he came back to consciousness; watching his eyes, they could see a mental struggle taking place within him. At last he singled Christian out from the others by a sign.

"I'm beat, Chris," he whispered. "Let him know, I want to see him."

His voice grew a little stronger. "I thought that I could see it through—but here's the end." He lifted his hand ever so little, and let it fall again. When told a little later that a telegram had been sent to Harz his eyes expressed satisfaction.

Herr Paul came down in ignorance of the night's events. He stopped in front of the barometer and tapped it, remarking to Miss Naylor: "The glass has gone downstairs; we shall have cool weather—it will still go well with him!"

When, with her brown face twisted by pity and concern, she told him that it was a question of hours, Herr Paul turned first purple, then pale, and sitting down, trembled violently. "I cannot believe it," he exclaimed almost angrily. "Yesterday he was so well! I cannot believe it! Poor Nicholas! Yesterday he spoke to me!" Taking Miss Naylor's hand, he clutched it in his own. "Ah!" he cried, letting it go suddenly, and striking at his forehead, "it is too terrible; only yesterday he spoke to me of sherry. Is there nobody, then, who can do good?"

"There is only God," replied Miss Naylor softly.

"God?" said Herr Paul in a scared voice.

"We—can—all—pray to Him," Miss Naylor murmured; little spots of colour came into her cheeks. "I am going to do it now."

Herr Paul raised her hand and kissed it.

"Are you?" he said; "good! I too." He passed through his study door, closed it carefully behind him, then for some unknown reason set his back against it. Ugh! Death! It came to all! Some day it would come to him. It might come tomorrow! One must pray!

The day dragged to its end. In the sky clouds had mustered, and, crowding close on one another, clung round the sun, soft, thick, greywhite, like the feathers on a pigeon's breast. Towards evening faint tremblings were felt at intervals, as from the shock of immensely distant earthquakes.

Nobody went to bed that night, but in the morning the report was the same: "Unconscious—a question of hours." Once only did he recover consciousness, and then asked for Harz. A telegram had come from him, he was on the way. Towards seven of the evening the long-expected storm broke in a sky like ink. Into the valleys and over the crests of mountains it seemed as though an unseen hand were spilling goblets of pale wine, darting a sword-blade zigzag over trees, roofs, spires, peaks, into the very firmament, which answered every thrust with great bursts of groaning. Just beyond the veranda Greta saw a glowworm shining, as it might be a tiny bead of the fallen lightning. Soon the rain covered everything. Sometimes a jet of light brought the hilltops, towering, dark, and hard, over the house, to disappear again behind the raindrops and shaken leaves. Each breath drawn by the storm was like the clash of a thousand cymbals; and in his room Mr. Treffry lay unconscious of its fury.

Greta had crept in unobserved; and sat curled in a corner, with Scruff in her arms, rocking slightly to and fro. When Christian passed, she caught her skirt, and whispered: "It is your birthday, Chris!"

Mr. Treffry stirred.

"What's that? Thunder?—it's cooler. Where am I? Chris!"

Dawney signed for her to take his place.

"Chris!" Mr. Treffry said. "It's near now." She bent across him, and her tears fell on his forehead.

"Forgive!" she whispered; "love me!"

He raised his finger, and touched her cheek.

For an hour or more he did not speak, though once or twice he moaned, and faintly tightened his pressure on her fingers. The storm had died away, but very far off the thunder was still muttering.

His eyes opened once more, rested on her, and passed beyond, into that abyss dividing youth from age, conviction from conviction, life from death.

At the foot of the bed Dawney stood covering his face; behind him Dominique knelt with hands held upwards; the sound of Greta's breathing, soft in sleep, rose and fell in the stillness.

XXIX

One afternoon in March, more than three years after Mr. Treffry's death, Christian was sitting at the window of a studio in St. John's Wood. The sky was covered with soft, high clouds, through which shone little gleams of blue. Now and then a bright shower fell, sprinkling the trees, where every twig was curling upwards as if waiting for the gift of its new leaves. And it seemed to her that the boughs thickened and budded under her very eyes; a great concourse of sparrows had gathered on those boughs, and kept raising a shrill chatter. Over at the far side of the room Harz was working at a picture.

On Christian's face was the quiet smile of one who knows that she has only to turn her eyes to see what she wishes to see; of one whose possessions are safe under her hand. She looked at Harz with that possessive smile. But as into the brain of one turning in his bed grim fancies will suddenly leap up out of warm nothingness, so there leaped into her mind the memory of that long ago dawn, when he had found her kneeling by Mr. Treffry's body. She seemed to see again the dead face, so gravely quiet, and furrowless. She seemed to see her lover and herself setting forth silently along the river wall where they had first met; sitting down, still silent, beneath the poplar-tree where the little bodies of the chafers had lain strewn in the Spring. To see the trees changing from black to grey, from grey to green, and in the dark sky long white lines of cloud, lighting to the south like birds; and, very far away, rosy peaks watching the awakening of the earth. And now once again, after all that time, she felt her spirit shrink away from his; as it had shrunk in that hour, when she had seemed hateful to herself. She remembered the words she had spoken: "I have no heart left. You've torn it in two between you. Love is all self—I wanted him to die." She remembered too the raindrops on the vines like a million tiny lamps, and the throstle that began singing. Then, as dreams die out into warm nothingness, recollection vanished, and the smile came back to her lips.

She took out a letter.

"....O Chris! We are really coming; I seem to be always telling it to myself, and I have told Scruff many times, but he does not care, because he is getting old. Miss Naylor says we shall arrive for breakfast, and that we shall be hungry, but perhaps she will not be very hungry, if it is rough. Papa said to me: 'Je serai inconsolable, mais inconsolable!' But I think he will not be, because he is going to Vienna. When we are come, there will be nobody at Villa Rubein; Aunt Constance has gone a fortnight ago to Florence. There is a young man at her hotel; she says he will be one of the greatest playwriters in England, and she sent me a play of his to read; it was only a little about love, I did not like it very much.... O Chris! I think I shall cry when I see you.

As I am quite grown up, Miss Naylor is not to come back with me; sometimes she is sad, but she will be glad to see you, Chris. She seems always sadder when it is Spring. Today I walked along the wall; the little green balls of wool are growing on the poplars already, and I saw one chafer; it will not be long before the cherry blossom comes; and I felt so funny, sad and happy together, and once I thought that I had wings and could fly away up the valley to Meran—but I had none, so I sat on the bench where we sat the day we took the pictures, and I thought and thought; there was nothing came to me in my thoughts, but all was sweet and a little noisy, and rather sad; it was like the buzzing of the chafer, in my head; and now I feel so tired and all my blood is running up and down me. I do not mind, because I know it is the Spring.

"Dominique came to see us the other day; he is very well, and is half the proprietor of the Adler Hotel, at Meran; he is not at all different, and he asked about you and about Alois—do you know, Chris, to myself I call him Herr Harz, but when I have seen him this time I shall call him Alois in my heart also.

"I have a letter from Dr. Edmund; he is in London, so perhaps you have seen him, only he has a great many patients and some that he has 'hopes of killing soon'. especially one old lady, because she is always wanting him to do things for her, and he is never saying 'No,' so he does not like her. He says that he is getting old. When I have finished this letter I am going to write and tell him that perhaps he shall see me soon, and then I think he will be very sad. Now that the Spring is come there are more flowers to take to Uncle Nic's grave, and every day, when I am gone, Barbi is to take them so that he shall not miss you, Chris, because all the flowers I put there are for you.

"I am buying some toys without paint on for my niece.

"O Chris! this will be the first baby that I have known.

"I am only to stay three weeks with you, but I think when I am once there I shall be staying longer. I send a kiss for my niece, and to Herr Harz, my love—that is the last time I shall call him Herr Harz; and to you, Chris, all the joy that is in my heart.—Your loving

"GRETA."

Christian rose, and, turning very softly, stood, leaning her elbows on the back of a high seat, looking at her husband.

In her eyes there was a slow, clear, faintly smiling, yet yearning look, as though this strenuous figure bent on its task were seen for a moment as something apart, and not all the world to her.

"Tired?" asked Harz, putting his lips to her hand.

"No, it's only—what Greta says about the Spring; it makes one want more than one has got."

Slipping her hand away, she went back to the window. Harz stood, looking after her; then, taking up his palette, again began painting.

In the world, outside, the high soft clouds flew by; the trees seemed thickening and budding.

And Christian thought:

'Can we never have quite enough?'

December 1890.

A MAN OF DEVON

I

"MOOR, 20th July.

.... It is quiet here, sleepy, rather—a farm is never quiet; the sea, too, is only a quarter of a mile away, and when it's windy, the sound of it travels up the combe; for distraction, you must go four miles to Brixham or five to Kingswear, and you won't find much then. The farm lies in a sheltered spot, scooped, so to speak, high up the combe side—behind is a rise of fields, and beyond, a sweep of down. You have the feeling of being able to see quite far, which is misleading, as you soon find out if you walk. It is true Devon country-hills, hollows, hedge-banks, lanes dipping down into the earth or going up like the sides of houses, coppices, cornfields, and little streams wherever there's a place for one; but the downs along the cliff, all gorse and ferns, are wild. The combe ends in a sandy cove with black rock on one side, pinkish cliffs away to the headland on the other, and a coastguard station. Just now, with the harvest coming on, everything looks its richest, the apples ripening, the trees almost too green. It's very hot, still weather; the country and the sea seem to sleep in the sun. In front of the farm are half-a-dozen pines that look as if they had stepped out of another land, but all round the back is orchard as lush, and gnarled, and orthodox as any one could wish. The house, a long, white building with three levels of roof, and splashes of brown all over it, looks as if it might be growing down into the earth. It was freshly thatched two years ago—and that's all the newness there is about it; they say the front door, oak, with iron knobs, is three hundred years old at least. You can touch the ceilings with your hand. The windows certainly might be larger—a heavenly old place, though, with a flavour of apples, smoke, sweetbriar, bacon, honeysuckle, and age, all over it.

The owner is a man called John Ford, about seventy, and seventeen stone in weight—very big, on long legs, with a grey, stubbly beard, grey, watery eyes, short neck and purplish complexion; he is asthmatic, and has a very courteous, autocratic manner. His clothes are made of Harris tweed—except on Sundays, when he puts on black—a seal ring, and a thick gold cable chain. There's nothing mean or small about John Ford; I suspect him of a warm heart, but he doesn't let you know much about him. He's a north-country man by birth, and has been out in New Zealand all his life. This little Devonshire farm is all he has now. He had a large "station" in the North Island, and was much looked up to, kept open house, did everything, as one would guess, in a narrow-minded, large-handed way. He came to grief suddenly; I don't quite know how. I believe his only son lost money on the turf, and then, unable to face his father, shot himself; if you had seen John Ford, you could imagine that. His wife died, too, that year. He paid up to the last penny, and came home, to live on this farm. He told me the other night that he had only one relation in the world, his granddaughter, who lives here with him. Pasiance Voisey—old spelling for Patience, but they pronounce, it Pash-yence—is sitting out here with me at this moment on a sort of rustic loggia that opens into the orchard. Her sleeves are rolled up, and she's stripping currants, ready for black currant tea. Now and then she rests her elbows on the table, eats a berry, pouts her lips, and, begins again. She has a round, little face; a long, slender body; cheeks like poppies; a bushy mass of black-brown hair, and dark-brown, almost black, eyes; her nose is snub; her lips quick, red, rather full; all her motions quick and soft. She loves bright colours. She's rather like a little cat; sometimes she seems all sympathy, then in a moment as hard as tortoise-shell. She's all impulse; yet she doesn't like to show her feelings; I sometimes wonder whether she has any. She plays the violin.

It's queer to see these two together, queer and rather sad. The old man has a fierce tenderness for her that strikes into the very roots of him. I see him torn between it, and his cold north-country horror of his feelings; his life with her is an unconscious torture to him. She's a restless, chafing thing, demure enough one moment, then flashing out into mocking speeches or hard little laughs. Yet she's fond of him in her fashion; I saw her kiss him once when he was asleep. She obeys him generally—in a way as if she couldn't breathe while she was doing it. She's had a queer sort of education—history, geography, elementary mathematics, and nothing else; never been to school; had a few lessons on the violin, but has taught herself most of what she knows. She is well up in the lore of birds, flowers, and insects; has three cats, who follow her about; and is full of pranks. The other day she called out to me, "I've something for you. Hold out your hand and shut your eyes!" It was a large, black slug! She's the child of the old fellow's only daughter, who was sent home for schooling at Torquay, and made a runaway match with one Richard Voisey, a yeoman farmer, whom she met in the hunting-field. John Ford was furious—his ancestors, it appears, used to lead ruffians on the Cumberland side of the Border—he looked on "Squire" Rick Voisey as a cut below him. He was called "Squire," as far as I can make out, because he used to play cards every evening with a parson in the neighbourhood who went by the name of "Devil" Hawkins. Not that the Voisey stock is to be despised. They have had this farm since it was granted to one Richard Voysey by copy dated 8th September, 13 Henry VIII. Mrs. Hopgood, the wife of the bailiff—a dear, quaint, serene old soul with cheeks like a rosy, withered apple, and an unbounded love of Pasiance—showed me the very document.

"I kape it," she said. "Mr. Ford be tu proud—but other folks be proud tu. 'Tis a pra-aper old fam'ly: all the women is Margery, Pasiance, or Mary; all the men's Richards an' Johns an' Rogers; old as they apple-trees."

Rick Voisey was a rackety, hunting fellow, and "dipped" the old farm up to its thatched roof. John Ford took his revenge by buying up the mortgages, foreclosing, and commanding his daughter and Voisey to go on living here rent free; this they dutifully did until they were both killed in a dog-cart accident, eight years ago. Old Ford's financial smash came a year later, and since then he's lived here with Pasiance. I fancy it's the cross in her blood that makes her so restless, and irresponsible: if she had been all a native she'd have been happy enough here, or all a stranger like John Ford himself, but the two strains struggling for mastery seem to give her no rest. You'll think this a far-fetched theory, but I believe it to be the true one. She'll stand with lips pressed together, her arms folded tight across her narrow chest, staring as if she could see beyond the things round her; then something catches her attention, her eyes will grow laughing, soft, or scornful all in a minute! She's eighteen, perfectly fearless in a boat, but you can't get her to mount a horse—a sore subject with her grandfather, who spends most of his day on a lean, half-bred pony, that carries him like a feather, for all his weight.

They put me up here as a favour to Dan Treffry; there's an arrangement of L. s. d. with Mrs. Hopgood in the background. They aren't at all well off; this is the largest farm about, but it doesn't bring them in much. To look at John Ford, it seems incredible he should be short of money—he's too large.

We have family prayers at eight, then, breakfast—after that freedom for writing or anything else till supper and evening prayers. At midday one forages for oneself. On Sundays, two miles to church twice, or you get into John Ford's black books.... Dan Treffry himself is staying at Kingswear. He says he's made his pile; it suits him down here—like a sleep after years of being too wide-awake; he had a rough time in New Zealand, until that mine made his fortune. You'd hardly remember him; he reminds me of his uncle, old Nicholas Treffry; the same slow way of speaking, with a hesitation, and a trick of repeating your name with everything he says; left-handed too, and the same slow twinkle in his eyes. He has a dark, short beard, and red-brown cheeks; is a little bald on the temples, and a bit grey, but hard as iron. He rides over nearly every day, attended by a black spaniel with a wonderful nose and a horror of petticoats. He has told me lots of good stories of John Ford in the early squatter's times; his feats with horses live to this day; and he was through the Maori wars; as Dan says, "a man after Uncle Nic's own heart."

They are very good friends, and respect each other; Dan has a great admiration for the old man, but the attraction is Pasiance. He talks very little when she's in the room, but looks at her in a sidelong, wistful sort of way. Pasiance's conduct to him would be cruel in any one else, but in her, one takes it with a pinch of salt. Dan goes off, but turns up again as quiet and dogged as you please.

Last night, for instance, we were sitting in the loggia after supper. Pasiance was fingering the strings of her violin, and suddenly Dan (a bold thing for him) asked her to play.

"What!" she said, "before men? No, thank you!"

"Why not?"

"Because I hate them."

Down came John Ford's hand on the wicker table: "You forget yourself! Go to bed!"

She gave Dan a look, and went; we could hear her playing in her bedroom; it sounded like a dance of spirits; and just when one thought she had finished, out it would break again like a burst of laughter. Presently, John Ford begged our pardons ceremoniously, and stumped off indoors. The violin ceased; we heard his voice growling at her; down he came again. Just as he was settled in his chair there was a soft swish, and something dark came falling through the apple boughs. The violin! You should have seen his face! Dan would have picked the violin up, but the old man stopped him. Later, from my bedroom window, I saw John Ford come out and stand looking at the violin. He raised his foot as if to stamp on it. At last he picked it up, wiped it carefully, and took it in....

My room is next to hers. I kept hearing her laugh, a noise too as if she were dragging things about the room. Then I fell asleep, but woke with a start, and went to the window for a breath of fresh air. Such a black, breathless night! Nothing to be seen but the twisted, blacker branches; not the faintest stir of leaves, no sound but muffled grunting from the cowhouse, and now and then a faint sigh. I had the queerest feeling of unrest and fear, the last thing to expect on such a night. There is something here that's disturbing; a sort of suppressed struggle. I've never in my life seen anything so irresponsible as this girl, or so uncompromising as the old man; I keep thinking of the way he wiped that violin. It's just as if a spark would set everything in a blaze. There's a menace of tragedy—or—perhaps it's only the heat, and too much of Mother Hopgood's crame....

II

"Tuesday.

.... I've made a new acquaintance. I was lying in the orchard, and presently, not seeing me, he came along—a man of middle height, with a singularly good balance, and no lumber—rather old blue clothes, a flannel shirt, a dull red necktie, brown shoes, a cap with a leather peak pushed up on the forehead. Face long and narrow, bronzed with a kind of pale burnt-in brownness; a good forehead. A brown moustache, beard rather pointed, blackening about the cheeks; his chin not visible, but from the beard's growth must be big; mouth I should judge sensuous. Nose straight and blunt; eyes grey, with an upward look, not exactly frank, because defiant; two parallel furrows down each cheek, one from the inner corner of the eye, one from the nostril; age perhaps thirty-five. About the face, attitude, movements, something immensely vital, adaptable, daring, and unprincipled.

He stood in front of the loggia, biting his fingers, a kind of nineteenth-century buccaneer, and I wondered what he was doing in this galley. They say you can tell a man of Kent or a Somersetshire man; certainly you can tell a Yorkshire man, and this fellow could only have been a man of Devon, one of the two main types found in this county. He whistled; and out came Pasiance in a geranium-coloured dress, looking like some tall poppy—you know the slight droop of a poppy's head, and the way the wind sways its stem.... She is a human poppy, her fuzzy dark hair is like a poppy's lustreless black heart, she has a poppy's tantalising attraction and repulsion, something fatal, or rather fateful. She came walking up to my new friend, then caught sight of me, and stopped dead.

"That," she said to me, "is Zachary Pearse. This," she said to him, "is our lodger." She said it with a wonderful soft malice. She wanted to scratch me, and she scratched. Half an hour later I was in the yard, when up came this fellow Pearse.

"Glad to know you," he said, looking thoughtfully at the pigs.

"You're a writer, aren't you?"

"A sort of one," I said.

"If by any chance," he said suddenly, "you're looking for a job, I could put something in your way. Walk down to the beach with me, and I'll tell you; my boat's at anchor, smartest little craft in these parts."

It was very hot, and I had no desire whatever to go down to the beach—I went, all the same. We had not gone far when John Ford and Dan Treffry came into the lane. Our friend seemed a little disconcerted, but soon recovered himself. We met in the middle of the lane, where there was hardly room to pass. John Ford, who looked very haughty, put on his pince-nez and stared at Pearse.

"Good-day!" said Pearse; "fine weather! I've been up to ask Pasiance to come for a sail. Wednesday we thought, weather permitting; this gentleman's coming. Perhaps you'll come too, Mr. Treffry. You've never seen my place. I'll give you lunch, and show you my father. He's worth a couple of hours' sail any day." It was said in such an odd way that one couldn't resent his impudence. John Ford was seized with a fit of wheezing, and seemed on the eve of an explosion; he glanced at me, and checked himself.

"You're very good," he said icily; "my granddaughter has other things to do. You, gentlemen, will please yourselves"; and, with a very slight bow, he went stumping on to the house. Dan looked at me, and I looked at him.

"You'll come?" said Pearse, rather wistfully. Dan stammered: "Thank you, Mr. Pearse; I'm a better man on a horse than in a boat, but—thank you." Cornered in this way, he's a shy, soft-hearted being. Pearse smiled his thanks. "Wednesday, then, at ten o'clock; you shan't regret it."

"Pertinacious beggar!" I heard Dan mutter in his beard; and found myself marching down the lane again by Pearse's side. I asked him what he was good enough to mean by saying I was coming, without having asked me. He answered, unabashed:

"You see, I'm not friends with the old man; but I knew he'd not be impolite to you, so I took the liberty."

He has certainly a knack of turning one's anger to curiosity. We were down in the combe now; the tide was running out, and the sand all little, wet, shining ridges. About a quarter of a mile out lay a cutter, with her tan sail half down, swinging to the swell. The sunlight was making the pink cliffs glow in the most wonderful way; and shifting in bright patches over the sea like moving shoals of goldfish. Pearse perched himself on his dinghy, and looked out under his hand. He seemed lost in admiration.

"If we could only net some of those spangles," he said, "an' make gold of 'em! No more work then."

"It's a big job I've got on," he said presently; "I'll tell you about it on Wednesday. I want a journalist."

"But I don't write for the papers," I said; "I do other sort of work. My game is archaeology."

"It doesn't matter," he said, "the more imagination the better. It'd be a thundering good thing for you."

His assurance was amazing, but it was past supper-time, and hunger getting the better of my curiosity, I bade him good-night. When I looked back, he was still there, on the edge of his boat, gazing at the sea. A queer sort of bird altogether, but attractive somehow.

Nobody mentioned him that evening; but once old Ford, after staring a long time at Pasiance, muttered a propos of nothing, "Undutiful children!" She was softer than usual; listening quietly to our talk, and smiling when spoken to. At bedtime she went up to her grand-father, without waiting for the usual command, "Come and kiss me, child."

Dan did not stay to supper, and he has not been here since. This morning I asked Mother Hopgood who Zachary Pearse was. She's a true Devonian; if there's anything she hates, it is to be committed to a definite statement. She ambled round her answer, and at last told me that he was "son of old Cap'en Jan Pearse to Black Mill. 'Tes an old family to Dartymouth an' Plymouth," she went on in a communicative outburst. "They du say Francis Drake tuke five o' they Pearses with 'en to fight the Spaniards. At least that's what I've heard Mr. Zachary zay; but Ha-apgood can tell yu." Poor Hopgood, the amount of information she saddles him with in the course of the day! Having given me thus to understand that she had run dry, she at once went on:

"Cap'en Jan Pearse made a dale of ventures. He's old now—they du say nigh an 'undred. Ha-apgood can tell yu."

"But the son, Mrs. Hopgood?"

Her eyes twinkled with sudden shrewdness: She hugged herself placidly.

"An' what would yu take for dinner to-day? There's duck; or yu might like 'toad in the hole,' with an apple tart; or then, there's—Well! we'll see what we can du like." And off she went, without waiting for my answer.

To-morrow is Wednesday. I shan't be sorry to get another look at this fellow Pearse....

III

"Friday, 29th July.

.... Why do you ask me so many questions, and egg me on to write about these people instead of minding my business? If you really want to hear, I'll tell you of Wednesday's doings.

It was a splendid morning; and Dan turned up, to my surprise—though I might have known that when he says a thing, he does it. John Ford came out to shake hands with him, then, remembering why he had come, breathed loudly, said nothing, and went in again. Nothing was to be seen of Pasiance, and we went down to the beach together.

"I don't like this fellow Pearse, George," Dan said to me on the way; "I was fool enough to say I'd go, and so I must, but what's he after? Not the man to do things without a reason, mind you."

I remarked that we should soon know.

"I'm not so sure—queer beggar; I never look at him without thinking of a pirate."

The cutter lay in the cove as if she had never moved. There too was Zachary Pearse seated on the edge of his dinghy.

"A five-knot breeze," he said, "I'll run you down in a couple of hours." He made no inquiry about Pasiance, but put us into his cockleshell and pulled for the cutter. A lantern-jawed fellow, named Prawle, with a spiky, prominent beard, long, clean-shaven upper lip, and tanned complexion—a regular hard-weather bird—received us.

The cutter was beautifully clean; built for a Brixham trawler, she still had her number—DH 113—uneffaced. We dived into a sort of cabin, airy, but dark, fitted with two bunks and a small table, on which stood some bottles of stout; there were lockers, too, and pegs for clothes. Prawle, who showed us round, seemed very proud of a steam contrivance for hoisting sails. It was some minutes before we came on deck again; and there, in the dinghy, being pulled towards the cutter, sat Pasiance.

"If I'd known this," stammered Dan, getting red, "I wouldn't have come." She had outwitted us, and there was nothing to be done.

It was a very pleasant sail. The breeze was light from the south-east, the sun warm, the air soft. Presently Pasiance began singing:

"Columbus is dead and laid in his grave, Oh! heigh-ho! and laid in his grave; Over his head the apple-trees wave Oh! heigh-ho! the apple-trees wave....

"The apples are ripe and ready to fall, Oh! heigh-ho! and ready to fall; There came an old woman and gathered them all, Oh! heigh-ho! and gathered them all....

"The apples are gathered, and laid on the shelf, Oh! heigh-ho! and laid on the shelf; If you want any more, you must sing for yourself, Oh! heigh-ho! and sing for yourself."

Her small, high voice came to us in trills and spurts, as the wind let it, like the singing of a skylark lost in the sky. Pearse went up to her and whispered something. I caught a glimpse of her face like a startled wild creature's; shrinking, tossing her hair, laughing, all in the same breath. She wouldn't sing again, but crouched in the bows with her chin on her hands, and the sun falling on one cheek, round, velvety, red as a peach....

We passed Dartmouth, and half an hour later put into a little wooded bay. On a low reddish cliff was a house hedged round by pine-trees. A bit of broken jetty ran out from the bottom of the cliff. We hooked on to this, and landed. An ancient, fish-like man came slouching down and took charge of the cutter. Pearse led us towards the house, Pasiance following mortally shy all of a sudden.

The house had a dark, overhanging thatch of the rush reeds that grow in the marshes hereabouts; I remember nothing else remarkable. It was neither old, nor new; neither beautiful, nor exactly ugly; neither clean, nor entirely squalid; it perched there with all its windows over the sea, turning its back contemptuously on the land.

Seated in a kind of porch, beside an immense telescope, was a very old man in a panama hat, with a rattan cane. His pure-white beard and moustache, and almost black eyebrows, gave a very singular, piercing look to his little, restless, dark-grey eyes; all over his mahogany cheeks and neck was a network of fine wrinkles. He sat quite upright, in the full sun, hardly blinking.

"Dad!" said Zachary, "this is Pasiance Voisey." The old man turned his eyes on her and muttered, "How do you do, ma'am?" then took no further notice. And Pasiance, who seemed to resent this, soon slipped away and went wandering about amongst the pines. An old woman brought some plates and bottles and laid them casually on a table; and we sat round the figure of old Captain Pearse without a word, as if we were all under a spell.

Before lunch there was a little scene between Zachary Pearse and Dan, as to which of them should summon Pasiance. It ended in both going, and coming back without her. She did not want any lunch, would stay where she was amongst the pines.

For lunch we had chops, wood-pigeons, mushrooms, and mulberry preserve, and drank wonderful Madeira out of common wine-glasses. I asked the old man where he got it; he gave me a queer look, and answered with a little bow:

"Stood me in tu shillin' the bottle, an' the country got nothing out of it, sir. In the early Thirties; tu shillin' the bottle; there's no such wine nowadays and," he added, looking at Zachary, "no such men."

Zachary smiled and said: "You did nothing so big, dad, as what I'm after, now!"

The old man's eyes had a sort of disdain in them.

"You're going far, then, in the Pied Witch, Zack?"

"I am," said Zachary.

"And where might yu be goin' in that old trampin' smut factory?"

"Morocco."

"Heu!" said the old man, "there's nothing there; I know that coast, as I know the back o' my hand." He stretched out a hand covered with veins and hair.

Zachary began suddenly to pour out a flood of words:

"Below Mogador—a fellow there—friend of mine—two years ago now. Concessions—trade-gunpowder—cruisers—feuds—money— chiefs—Gatling guns—Sultan—rifles—rebellion—gold." He detailed a reckless, sordid, bold scheme, which, on the pivot of a trading venture, was intended to spin a whole wheel of political convulsions.

"They'll never let you get there," said old Pearse.

"Won't they?" returned Zachary. "Oh yes, they will, an' when I leave, there'll be another dynasty, and I'll be a rich man."

"Yu'll never leave," answered the old man.

Zachary took out a sheet of paper covered with figures. He had worked the whole thing out. So much—equipment, so much—trade, so much—concessions, so much—emergencies. "My last mag!" he ended, "a thousand short; the ship's ready, and if I'm not there within a month my chance is as good as gone."

This was the pith of his confidences—an appeal for money, and we all looked as men will when that crops up.

"Mad!" muttered the old man, looking at the sea.

"No," said Zachary. That one word was more eloquent than all the rest of his words put together. This fellow is no visionary. His scheme may be daring, and unprincipled, but—he knows very well what he's about.

"Well!" said old Pearse, "you shall have five 'undred of my money, if it's only to learn what yu're made of. Wheel me in!" Zachary wheeled him into the house, but soon came back.

"The old man's cheque for five hundred pounds!" he said, holding it up. "Mr. Treffry, give me another, and you shall have a third of the profits."

I expected Dan to give a point-blank refusal. But he only asked:

"Would that clear you for starting?"

"With that," said Zachary, "I can get to sea in a fortnight."

"Good!" Dan said slowly. "Give me a written promise! To sea in fourteen days and my fair share on the five hundred pounds—no more—no less."

Again I thought Pearse would have jumped at this, but he leaned his chin on his hand, and looked at Dan, and Dan looked at him. While they were staring at each other like this, Pasiance came up with a kitten.

"See!" she said, "isn't it a darling?" The kitten crawled and clawed its way up behind her neck. I saw both men's eyes as they looked at Pasiance, and suddenly understood what they were at. The kitten rubbed itself against Pasiance's cheek, overbalanced, and fell, clawing, down her dress. She caught it up and walked away. Some one, I don't know which of us, sighed, and Pearse cried "Done!"

The bargain had been driven.

"Good-bye, Mr. Pearse," said Dan; "I guess that's all I'm wanted for. I'll find my pony waiting in the village. George, you'll see Pasiance home?"

We heard the hoofs of his pony galloping down the road; Pearse suddenly excused himself, and disappeared.

This venture of his may sound romantic and absurd, but it's matter-of-fact enough. He's after L. s. d.! Shades of Drake, Raleigh, Hawkins, Oxenham! The worm of suspicion gnaws at the rose of romance. What if those fellows, too, were only after L. s. d....?

I strolled into the pine-wood. The earth there was covered like a bee's body with black and gold stripes; there was the blue sea below, and white, sleepy clouds, and bumble-bees booming above the heather; it was all softness, a summer's day in Devon. Suddenly I came on Pearse standing at the edge of the cliff with Pasiance sitting in a little hollow below, looking up at him. I heard him say:

"Pasiance—Pasiance!" The sound of his voice, and the sight of her soft, wondering face made me furious. What business has she with love, at her age? What business have they with each other?

He told me presently that she had started off for home, and drove me to the ferry, behind an old grey pony. On the way he came back to his offer of the other day.

"Come with me," he said. "It doesn't do to neglect the Press; you can see the possibilities. It's one of the few countries left. If I once get this business started you don't know where it's going to stop. You'd have free passage everywhere, and whatever you like in reason."

I answered as rudely as I could—but by no means as rudely as I wanted—that his scheme was mad. As a matter of fact, it's much too sane for me; for, whatever the body of a scheme, its soul is the fibre of the schemer.

"Think of it," he urged, as if he could see into me. "You can make what you like of it. Press paragraphs, of course. But that's mechanical; why, even I could do it, if I had time. As for the rest, you'll be as free—as free as a man."

There, in five words of one syllable, is the kernel of this fellow Pearse—"As free as a man!" No rule, no law, not even the mysterious shackles that bind men to their own self-respects! "As free as a man!" No ideals; no principles; no fixed star for his worship; no coil he can't slide out of! But the fellow has the tenacity of one of the old Devon mastiffs, too. He wouldn't take "No" for an answer.

"Think of it," he said; "any day will do—I've got a fortnight.... Look! there she is!" I thought that he meant Pasiance; but it was an old steamer, sluggish and black in the blazing sun of mid-stream, with a yellow-and-white funnel, and no sign of life on her decks.

"That's her—the Pied Witch! Do her twelve knots; you wouldn't think it! Well! good-evening! You'd better come. A word to me at any time. I'm going aboard now."

As I was being ferried across I saw him lolling in the stern-sheets of a little boat, the sun crowning his straw hat with glory.

I came on Pasiance, about a mile up the road, sitting in the hedge. We walked on together between the banks—Devonshire banks, as high as houses, thick with ivy and ferns, bramble and hazel boughs, and honeysuckle.

"Do you believe in a God?" she said suddenly.

"Grandfather's God is simply awful. When I'm playing the fiddle, I can feel God; but grandfather's is such a stuffy God—you know what I mean: the sea, the wind, the trees, colours too—they make one feel. But I don't believe that life was meant to 'be good' in. Isn't there anything better than being good? When I'm 'good,' I simply feel wicked." She reached up, caught a flower from the hedge, and slowly tore its petals.

"What would you do," she muttered, "if you wanted a thing, but were afraid of it? But I suppose you're never afraid!" she added, mocking me. I admitted that I was sometimes afraid, and often afraid of being afraid.

"That's nice! I'm not afraid of illness, nor of grandfather, nor of his God; but—I want to be free. If you want a thing badly, you're afraid about it."

I thought of Zachary Pearse's words, "free as a man."

"Why are you looking at me like that?" she said.

I stammered: "What do you mean by freedom?"

"Do you know what I shall do to-night?" she answered. "Get out of my window by the apple-tree, and go to the woods, and play!"

We were going down a steep lane, along the side of a wood, where there's always a smell of sappy leaves, and the breath of the cows that come close to the hedge to get the shade.

There was a cottage in the bottom, and a small boy sat outside playing with a heap of dust.

"Hallo, Johnny!" said Pasiance. "Hold your leg out and show this man your bad place!" The small boy undid a bandage round his bare and dirty little leg, and proudly revealed a sore.

"Isn't it nasty?" cried Pasiance ruefully, tying up the bandage again; "poor little feller! Johnny, see what I've brought you!" She produced from her pocket a stick of chocolate, the semblance of a soldier made of sealing-wax and worsted, and a crooked sixpence.

It was a new glimpse of her. All the way home she was telling me the story of little Johnny's family; when she came to his mother's death, she burst out: "A beastly shame, wasn't it, and they're so poor; it might just as well have been somebody else. I like poor people, but I hate rich ones—stuck-up beasts."

Mrs. Hopgood was looking over the gate, with her cap on one side, and one of Pasiance's cats rubbing itself against her skirts. At the sight of us she hugged herself.

"Where's grandfather?" asked Pasiance. The old lady shook her head.

"Is it a row?" Mrs. Hopgood wriggled, and wriggled, and out came:

"Did you get yure tay, my pretty? No? Well, that's a pity; yu'll be falin' low-like."

Pasiance tossed her head, snatched up the cat, and ran indoors. I remained staring at Mrs. Hopgood.

"Dear-dear," she clucked, "poor lamb. So to spake it's—" and she blurted out suddenly, "chuckin' full of wra-ath, he is. Well, there!"

My courage failed that evening. I spent it at the coastguard station, where they gave me bread and cheese and some awful cider. I passed the kitchen as I came back. A fire was still burning there, and two figures, misty in the darkness, flitted about with stealthy laughter like spirits afraid of being detected in a carnal-meal. They were Pasiance and Mrs. Hopgood; and so charming was the smell of eggs and bacon, and they had such an air of tender enjoyment of this dark revel, that I stifled many pangs, as I crept hungry up to bed.

In the middle of the night I woke and heard what I thought was screaming; then it sounded like wind in trees, then like the distant shaking of a tambourine, with the high singing of a human voice. Suddenly it stopped—two long notes came wailing out like sobs—then utter stillness; and though I listened for an hour or more there was no other sound ....

IV

"4th August.

.... For three days after I wrote last, nothing at all happened here. I spent the mornings on the cliff reading, and watching the sun-sparks raining on the sea. It's grand up there with the gorse all round, the gulls basking on the rocks, the partridges calling in the corn, and now and then a young hawk overhead. The afternoons I spent out in the orchard. The usual routine goes on at the farm all the time—cow-milking, bread-baking, John Ford riding in and out, Pasiance in her garden stripping lavender, talking to the farm hands; and the smell of clover, and cows and hay; the sound of hens and pigs and pigeons, the soft drawl of voices, the dull thud of the farm carts; and day by day the apples getting redder. Then, last Monday, Pasiance was away from sunrise till sunset—nobody saw her go—nobody knew where she had gone. It was a wonderful, strange day, a sky of silver-grey and blue, with a drift of wind-clouds, all the trees sighing a little, the sea heaving in a long, low swell, the animals restless, the birds silent, except the gulls with their old man's laughter and kitten's mewing.

A something wild was in the air; it seemed to sweep across the downs and combe, into the very house, like a passionate tune that comes drifting to your ears when you're sleepy. But who would have thought the absence of that girl for a few hours could have wrought such havoc! We were like uneasy spirits; Mrs. Hopgood's apple cheeks seemed positively to wither before one's eyes. I came across a dairymaid and farm hand discussing it stolidly with very downcast faces. Even Hopgood, a hard-bitten fellow with immense shoulders, forgot his imperturbability so far as to harness his horse, and depart on what he assured me was "just a wild-guse chaace." It was long before John Ford gave signs of noticing that anything was wrong, but late in the afternoon I found him sitting with his hands on his knees, staring straight before him. He rose heavily when he saw me, and stalked out. In the evening, as I was starting for the coastguard station to ask for help to search the cliff, Pasiance appeared, walking as if she could hardly drag one leg after the other. Her cheeks were crimson; she was biting her lips to keep tears of sheer fatigue out of her eyes. She passed me in the doorway without a word. The anxiety he had gone through seemed to forbid the old man from speaking. He just came forward, took her face in his hands, gave it a great kiss, and walked away. Pasiance dropped on the floor in the dark passage, and buried her face on her arms. "Leave me alone!" was all she would say. After a bit she dragged herself upstairs. Presently Mrs. Hopgood came to me.

"Not a word out of her—an' not a bite will she ate, an' I had a pie all ready— scrumptious. The good Lord knows the truth—she asked for brandy; have you any brandy, sir? Ha-apgood'e don't drink it, an' Mister Ford 'e don't allaow for anything but caowslip wine."

I had whisky.

The good soul seized the flask, and went off hugging it. She returned it to me half empty.

"Lapped it like a kitten laps milk. I misdaoubt it's straong, poor lamb, it lusened 'er tongue praaperly. 'I've a-done it,' she says to me, 'Mums-I've a-done it,' an' she laughed like a mad thing; and then, sir, she cried, an' kissed me, an' pusshed me thru the door. Gude Lard! What is 't she's a-done...?"

It rained all the next day and the day after. About five o'clock yesterday the rain ceased; I started off to Kingswear on Hopgood's nag to see Dan Treffry. Every tree, bramble, and fern in the lanes was dripping water; and every bird singing from the bottom of his heart. I thought of Pasiance all the time. Her absence that day was still a mystery; one never ceased asking oneself what she had done. There are people who never grow up—they have no right to do things. Actions have consequences—and children have no business with consequences.

Dan was out. I had supper at the hotel, and rode slowly home. In the twilight stretches of the road, where I could touch either bank of the lane with my whip, I thought of nothing but Pasiance and her grandfather; there was something in the half light suited to wonder and uncertainty. It had fallen dark before I rode into the straw-yard. Two young bullocks snuffled at me, a sleepy hen got up and ran off with a tremendous shrieking. I stabled the horse, and walked round to the back. It was pitch black under the apple-trees, and the windows were all darkened. I stood there a little, everything smelled so delicious after the rain; suddenly I had the uncomfortable feeling that I was being watched. Have you ever felt like that on a dark night? I called out at last: "Is any one there?" Not a sound! I walked to the gate-nothing! The trees still dripped with tiny, soft, hissing sounds, but that was all. I slipped round to the front, went in, barricaded the door, and groped up to bed. But I couldn't sleep. I lay awake a long while; dozed at last, and woke with a jump. A stealthy murmur of smothered voices was going on quite close somewhere. It stopped. A minute passed; suddenly came the soft thud as of something falling. I sprang out of bed and rushed to the window. Nothing—but in the distance something that sounded like footsteps. An owl hooted; then clear as crystal, but quite low, I heard Pasiance singing in her room:

"The apples are ripe and ready to fall. Oh! heigh-ho! and ready to fall."

I ran to her door and knocked.

"What is it?" she cried.

"Is anything the matter?"

"Matter?"

"Is anything the matter?"

"Ha-ha-ha-ha! Good-night!" then quite low, I heard her catch her breath, hard, sharply. No other answer, no other sound.

I went to bed and lay awake for hours....

This evening Dan came; during supper he handed Pasiance a roll of music; he had got it in Torquay. The shopman, he said, had told him that it was a "corker."

It was Bach's "Chaconne." You should have seen her eyes shine, her fingers actually tremble while she turned over the pages. Seems odd to think of her worshipping at the shrine of Bach as odd as to think of a wild colt running of its free will into the shafts; but that's just it with her you can never tell. "Heavenly!" she kept saying.

John Ford put down his knife and fork.

"Heathenish stuff!" he muttered, and suddenly thundered out, "Pasiance!"

She looked up with a start, threw the music from her, and resumed her place.

During evening prayers, which follow every night immediately on food, her face was a study of mutiny. She went to bed early. It was rather late when we broke up—for once old Ford had been talking of his squatter's life. As we came out, Dan held up his hand. A dog was barking. "It's Lass," he said. "She'll wake Pasiance."

The spaniel yelped furiously. Dan ran out to stop her. He was soon back.

"Somebody's been in the orchard, and gone off down to the cove." He ran on down the path. I, too, ran, horribly uneasy. In front, through the darkness, came the spaniel's bark; the lights of the coastguard station faintly showed. I was first on the beach; the dog came to me at once, her tail almost in her mouth from apology. There was the sound of oars working in rowlocks; nothing visible but the feathery edges of the waves. Dan said behind, "No use! He's gone." His voice sounded hoarse, like that of a man choking with passion.

"George," he stammered, "it's that blackguard. I wish I'd put a bullet in him." Suddenly a light burned up in the darkness on the sea, seemed to swing gently, and vanished. Without another word we went back up the hill. John Ford stood at the gate motionless, indifferent—nothing had dawned on him as yet. I whispered to Dan, "Let it alone!"

"No," he said, "I'm going to show you." He struck a match, and slowly hunted the footsteps in the wet grass of the orchard. "Look—here!"

He stopped under Pasiance's window and swayed the match over the ground. Clear as daylight were the marks of some one who had jumped or fallen. Dan held the match over his head.

"And look there!" he said. The bough of an apple-tree below the window was broken. He blew the match out.

I could see the whites of his eyes, like an angry animal's.

"Drop it, Dan!" I said.

He turned on his heel suddenly, and stammered out, "You're right."

But he had turned into John Ford's arms.

The old man stood there like some great force, darker than the darkness, staring up at the window, as though stupefied. We had not a word to say. He seemed unconscious of our presence. He turned round, and left us standing there.

"Follow him!" said Dan. "Follow him—by God! it's not safe."

We followed. Bending, and treading heavily, he went upstairs. He struck a blow on Pasiance's door. "Let me in!" he said. I drew Dan into my bedroom. The key was slowly turned, her door was flung open, and there she stood in her dressing-gown, a candle in her hand, her face crimson, and oh! so young, with its short, crisp hair and round cheeks. The old man—like a giant in front of her—raised his hands, and laid them on her shoulders.

"What's this? You—you've had a man in your room?"

Her eyes did not drop.

"Yes," she said. Dan gave a groan.

"Who?"

"Zachary Pearse," she answered in a voice like a bell.

He gave her one awful shake, dropped his hands, then raised them as though to strike her. She looked him in the eyes; his hands dropped, and he too groaned. As far as I could see, her face never moved.

"I'm married to him," she said, "d' you hear? Married to him. Go out of my room!" She dropped the candle on the floor at his feet, and slammed the door in his face. The old man stood for a minute as though stunned, then groped his way downstairs.

"Dan," I said, "is it true?"

"Ah!" he answered, "it's true; didn't you hear her?"

I was glad I couldn't see his face.

"That ends it," he said at last; "there's the old man to think of."

"What will he do?"

"Go to the fellow this very night." He seemed to have no doubt. Trust one man of action to know another.

I muttered something about being an outsider—wondered if there was anything I could do to help.

"Well," he said slowly, "I don't know that I'm anything but an outsider now; but I'll go along with him, if he'll have me."

He went downstairs. A few minutes later they rode out from the straw-yard. I watched them past the line of hayricks, into the blacker shadows of the pines, then the tramp of hoofs began to fail in the darkness, and at last died away.

I've been sitting here in my bedroom writing to you ever since, till my candle's almost gone. I keep thinking what the end of it is to be; and reproaching myself for doing nothing. And yet, what could I have done? I'm sorry for her—sorrier than I can say. The night is so quiet—I haven't heard a sound; is she asleep, awake, crying, triumphant?

It's four o'clock; I've been asleep.

They're back. Dan is lying on my bed. I'll try and tell you his story as near as I can, in his own words.

"We rode," he said, "round the upper way, keeping out of the lanes, and got to Kingswear by half-past eleven. The horse-ferry had stopped running, and we had a job to find any one to put us over. We hired the fellow to wait for us, and took a carriage at the 'Castle.' Before we got to Black Mill it was nearly one, pitch-dark. With the breeze from the southeast, I made out he should have been in an hour or more. The old man had never spoken to me once: and before we got there I had begun to hope we shouldn't find the fellow after all. We made the driver pull up in the road, and walked round and round, trying to find the door. Then some one cried, 'Who are you?'

"'John Ford.'

"'What do you want?' It was old Pearse.

"'To see Zachary Pearse.'

"The long window out of the porch where we sat the other day was open, and in we went. There was a door at the end of the room, and a light coming through. John Ford went towards it; I stayed out in the dark.

"'Who's that with you?'

"'Mr. Treffry.'

"'Let him come in!' I went in. The old fellow was in bed, quite still on his pillows, a candle by his side; to look at him you'd think nothing of him but his eyes were alive. It was queer being there with those two old men!"

Dan paused, seemed to listen, then went on doggedly.

"'Sit down, gentleman,' said old Pearse. 'What may you want to see my son for?' John Ford begged his pardon, he had something to say, he said, that wouldn't wait.

"They were very polite to one another," muttered Dan ....

"'Will you leave your message with me?' said Pearse.

"'What I have to say to your son is private.'

"'I'm his father.'

"'I'm my girl's grandfather; and her only stand-by.'

"'Ah!' muttered old Pearse, 'Rick Voisey's daughter?'

"'I mean to see your son.'

"Old Pearse smiled. Queer smile he's got, sort of sneering sweet.

"'You can never tell where Zack may be,' he said. 'You think I want to shield him. You're wrong; Zack can take care of himself.'

"'Your son's here!' said John Ford. 'I know.' Old Pearse gave us a very queer look.

"'You come into my house like thieves in the night,' he said, 'and give me the lie, do you?'

"'Your son came to my child's room like a thief in the night; it's for that I want to see him,' and then," said Dan, "there was a long silence. At last Pearse said:

"'I don't understand; has he played the blackguard?'

"John Ford answered, 'He's married her, or, before God, I'd kill him.'

"Old Pearse seemed to think this over, never moving on his pillows. 'You don't know Zack,' he said; 'I'm sorry for you, and I'm sorry for Rick Voisey's daughter; but you don't know Zack.'

"'Sorry!' groaned out John Ford; 'he's stolen my child, and I'll punish him.'

"'Punish!' cried old Pearse, 'we don't take punishment, not in my family.'

"'Captain Jan Pearse, as sure as I stand here, you and your breed will get your punishment of God.' Old Pearse smiled.

"'Mr. John Ford, that's as may be; but sure as I lie here we won't take it of you. You can't punish unless you make to feel, and that you can't du.'"

And that is truth!

Dan went on again:

"'You won't tell me where your son is!' but old Pearse never blinked.

"'I won't,' he said, 'and now you may get out. I lie here an old man alone, with no use to my legs, night on night, an' the house open; any rapscallion could get in; d' ye think I'm afraid of you?'

"We were beat; and walked out without a word. But that old man; I've thought of him a lot—ninety-two, and lying there. Whatever he's been, and they tell you rum things of him, whatever his son may be, he's a man. It's not what he said, nor that there was anything to be afraid of just then, but somehow it's the idea of the old chap lying there. I don't ever wish to see a better plucked one...."

We sat silent after that; out of doors the light began to stir among the leaves. There were all kinds of rustling sounds, as if the world were turning over in bed.

Suddenly Dan said:

"He's cheated me. I paid him to clear out and leave her alone. D' you think she's asleep?" He's made no appeal for sympathy, he'd take pity for an insult; but he feels it badly.

"I'm tired as a cat," he said at last, and went to sleep on my bed.

It's broad daylight now; I too am tired as a cat....

V

"Saturday, 6th August.

.... I take up my tale where I left off yesterday.... Dan and I started as soon as we could get Mrs. Hopgood to give us coffee. The old lady was more tentative, more undecided, more pouncing, than I had ever seen her. She was manifestly uneasy: Ha-apgood—who "don't slape" don't he, if snores are any criterion—had called out in the night, "Hark to th' 'arses' 'oofs!" Had we heard them? And where might we be going then? 'Twas very earrly to start, an' no breakfast. Haapgood had said it was goin' to shaowerr. Miss Pasiance was not to 'er violin yet, an' Mister Ford 'e kept 'is room. Was it?—would there be—? "Well, an' therr's an 'arvest bug; 'tis some earrly for they!" Wonderful how she pounces on all such creatures, when I can't even see them. She pressed it absently between finger and thumb, and began manoeuvring round another way. Long before she had reached her point, we had gulped down our coffee, and departed. But as we rode out she came at a run, holding her skirts high with either hand, raised her old eyes bright and anxious in their setting of fine wrinkles, and said:

"'Tidden sorrow for her?"

A shrug of the shoulders was all the answer she got. We rode by the lanes; through sloping farmyards, all mud and pigs, and dirty straw, and farmers with clean-shaven upper lips and whiskers under the chin; past fields of corn, where larks were singing. Up or down, we didn't draw rein till we came to Dan's hotel.

There was the river gleaming before us under a rainbow mist that hallowed every shape. There seemed affinity between the earth and the sky. I've never seen that particular soft unity out of Devon. And every ship, however black or modern, on those pale waters, had the look of a dream ship. The tall green woods, the red earth, the white houses, were all melted into one opal haze. It was raining, but the sun was shining behind. Gulls swooped by us—ghosts of the old greedy wanderers of the sea.

We had told our two boatmen to pull us out to the Pied Witch! They started with great resolution, then rested on their oars.

"The Pied Witch, zurr?" asked one politely; "an' which may her be?"

That's the West countryman all over! Never say you "nay," never lose an opportunity, never own he doesn't know, or can't do anything—independence, amiability, and an eye to the main chance. We mentioned Pearse's name.

"Capt'n Zach'ry Pearse!" They exchanged a look half-amused, half-admiring.

"The Zunflaower, yu mane. That's her. Zunflaower, ahoy!" As we mounted the steamer's black side I heard one say:

"Pied Witch! A pra-aper name that—a dandy name for her!" They laughed as they made fast.

The mate of the Sunflower, or Pied Witch, or whatever she was called, met us—a tall young fellow in his shirtsleeves, tanned to the roots of his hair, with sinewy, tattooed arms, and grey eyes, charred round the rims from staring at weather.

"The skipper is on board," he said. "We're rather busy, as you see. Get on with that, you sea-cooks," he bawled at two fellows who were doing nothing. All over the ship, men were hauling, splicing, and stowing cargo.

"To-day's Friday: we're off on Wednesday with any luck. Will you come this way?" He led us down the companion to a dark hole which he called the saloon. "Names? What! are you Mr. Treffry? Then we're partners!" A schoolboy's glee came on his face.

"Look here!" he said; "I can show you something," and he unlocked the door of a cabin. There appeared to be nothing in it but a huge piece of tarpaulin, which depended, bulging, from the topmost bunk. He pulled it up. The lower bunk had been removed, and in its place was the ugly body of a dismounted Gatling gun.

"Got six of them," he whispered, with unholy mystery, through which his native frankness gaped out. "Worth their weight in gold out there just now, the skipper says. Got a heap of rifles, too, and lots of ammunition. He's given me a share. This is better than the P. and O., and playing deck cricket with the passengers. I'd made up my mind already to chuck that, and go in for plantin' sugar, when I ran across the skipper. Wonderful chap, the skipper! I'll go and tell him. He's been out all night; only came aboard at four bells; having a nap now, but he won't mind that for you."

Off he went. I wondered what there was in Zachary Pearse to attract a youngster of this sort; one of the customary twelve children of some country parson, no doubt-burning to shoot a few niggers, and for ever frank and youthful.

He came back with his hands full of bottles.

"What'll you drink? The skipper'll be here in a jiffy. Excuse my goin' on deck. We're so busy."

And in five minutes Zachary Pearse did come. He made no attempt to shake hands, for which I respected him. His face looked worn, and more defiant than usual.

"Well, gentlemen?" he said.

"We've come to ask what you're going to do?" said Dan.

"I don't know," answered Pearse, "that that's any of your business."

Dan's little eyes were like the eyes of an angry pig.

"You've got five hundred pounds of mine," he said; "why do you think I gave it you?"

Zachary bit his fingers.

"That's no concern of mine," he said. "I sail on Wednesday. Your money's safe."

"Do you know what I think of you?" said Dan.

"No, and you'd better not tell me!" Then, with one of his peculiar changes, he smiled: "As you like, though."

Dan's face grew very dark. "Give me a plain answer," he said: "What are you going to do about her?"

Zachary looked up at him from under his brows.

"Nothing."

"Are you cur enough to deny that you've married her?"

Zachary looked at him coolly. "Not at all," he said.

"What in God's name did you do it for?"

"You've no monopoly in the post of husband, Mr. Treffry."

"To put a child in that position! Haven't you the heart of a man? What d' ye come sneaking in at night for? By Gad! Don't you know you've done a beastly thing?"

Zachary's face darkened, he clenched his fists. Then he seemed to shut his anger into himself.

"You wanted me to leave her to you," he sneered. "I gave her my promise that I'd take her out there, and we'd have gone off on Wednesday quietly enough, if you hadn't come and nosed the whole thing out with your infernal dog. The fat's in the fire! There's no reason why I should take her now. I'll come back to her a rich man, or not at all."

"And in the meantime?" I slipped in.

He turned to me, in an ingratiating way.

"I would have taken her to save the fuss—I really would—it's not my fault the thing's come out. I'm on a risky job. To have her with me might ruin the whole thing; it would affect my nerve. It isn't safe for her."

"And what's her position to be," I said, "while you're away? Do you think she'd have married you if she'd known you were going to leave her like this? You ought to give up this business.

"You stole her. Her life's in your hands; she's only a child!"

A quiver passed over his face; it showed that he was suffering.

"Give it up!" I urged.

"My last farthing's in it," he sighed; "the chance of a lifetime."

He looked at me doubtfully, appealingly, as if for the first time in his life he had been given a glimpse of that dilemma of consequences which his nature never recognises. I thought he was going to give in. Suddenly, to my horror, Dan growled, "Play the man!"

Pearse turned his head. "I don't want your advice anyway," he said; "I'll not be dictated to."

"To your last day," said Dan, "you shall answer to me for the way you treat her."

Zachary smiled.

"Do you see that fly?" he said. "Wel—I care for you as little as this," and he flicked the fly off his white trousers. "Good-morning...!"

The noble mariners who manned our boat pulled lustily for the shore, but we had hardly shoved off when a storm of rain burst over the ship, and she seemed to vanish, leaving a picture on my eyes of the mate waving his cap above the rail, with his tanned young face bent down at us, smiling, keen, and friendly.

.... We reached the shore drenched, angry with ourselves, and with each other; I started sulkily for home.

As I rode past an orchard, an apple, loosened by the rainstorm, came down with a thud.

"The apples were ripe and ready to fall, Oh! heigh-ho! and ready to fall."

I made up my mind to pack, and go away. But there's a strangeness, a sort of haunting fascination in it all. To you, who don't know the people, it may only seem a piece of rather sordid folly. But it isn't the good, the obvious, the useful that puts a spell on us in life. It's the bizarre, the dimly seen, the mysterious for good or evil.

The sun was out again when I rode up to the farm; its yellow thatch shone through the trees as if sheltering a store of gladness and good news. John Ford himself opened the door to me.

He began with an apology, which made me feel more than ever an intruder; then he said:

"I have not spoken to my granddaughter—I waited to see Dan Treffry."

He was stern and sad-eyed, like a man with a great weight of grief on his shoulders. He looked as if he had not slept; his dress was out of order, he had not taken his clothes off, I think. He isn't a man whom you can pity. I felt I had taken a liberty in knowing of the matter at all. When I told him where we had been, he said:

"It was good of you to take this trouble. That you should have had to! But since such things have come to pass—" He made a gesture full of horror. He gave one the impression of a man whose pride was struggling against a mortal hurt. Presently he asked:

"You saw him, you say? He admitted this marriage? Did he give an explanation?"

I tried to make Pearse's point of view clear. Before this old man, with his inflexible will and sense of duty, I felt as if I held a brief for Zachary, and must try to do him justice.

"Let me understand," he said at last. "He stole her, you say, to make sure; and deserts her within a fortnight."

"He says he meant to take her—"

"Do you believe that?"

Before I could answer, I saw Pasiance standing at the window. How long she had been there I don't know.

"Is it true that he is going to leave me behind?" she cried out.

I could only nod.

"Did you hear him your own self?"

"Yes."

She stamped her foot.

"But he promised! He promised!"

John Ford went towards her.

"Don't touch me, grandfather! I hate every one! Let him do what he likes, I don't care."

John Ford's face turned quite grey.

"Pasiance," he said, "did you want to leave me so much?"

She looked straight at us, and said sharply:

"What's the good of telling stories. I can't help its hurting you."

"What did you think you would find away from here?"

She laughed.

"Find? I don't know—nothing; I wouldn't be stifled anyway. Now I suppose you'll shut me up because I'm a weak girl, not strong like men!"

"Silence!" said John Ford; "I will make him take you."

"You shan't!" she cried; "I won't let you. He's free to do as he likes. He's free—I tell you all, everybody—free!"

She ran through the window, and vanished.

John Ford made a movement as if the bottom had dropped out of his world. I left him there.

I went to the kitchen, where Hopgood was sitting at the table, eating bread and cheese. He got up on seeing me, and very kindly brought me some cold bacon and a pint of ale.

"I thart I shude be seeing yu, zurr," he said between his bites; "Therr's no thart to 'atin' 'bout the 'ouse to-day. The old wumman's puzzivantin' over Miss Pasiance. Young girls are skeery critters"—he brushed his sleeve over his broad, hard jaws, and filled a pipe "specially when it's in the blood of 'em. Squire Rick Voisey werr a dandy; an' Mistress Voisey—well, she werr a nice lady tu, but"—rolling the stem of his pipe from corner to corner of his mouth—"she werr a pra-aper vixen."

Hopgood's a good fellow, and I believe as soft as he looks hard, but he's not quite the sort with whom one chooses to talk over a matter like this. I went upstairs, and began to pack, but after a bit dropped it for a book, and somehow or other fell asleep.

I woke, and looked at my watch; it was five o'clock. I had been asleep four hours. A single sunbeam was slanting across from one of my windows to the other, and there was the cool sound of milk dropping into pails; then, all at once, a stir as of alarm, and heavy footsteps.

I opened my door. Hopgood and a coast-guardsman were carrying Pasiance slowly up the stairs. She lay in their arms without moving, her face whiter than her dress, a scratch across the forehead, and two or three drops there of dried blood. Her hands were clasped, and she slowly crooked and stiffened out her fingers. When they turned with her at the stair top, she opened her lips, and gasped, "All right, don't put me down. I can bear it." They passed, and, with a half-smile in her eyes, she said something to me that I couldn't catch; the door was shut, and the excited whispering began again below. I waited for the men to come out, and caught hold of Hopgood. He wiped the sweat off his forehead.

"Poor young thing!" he said. "She fell—down the cliffs—'tis her back—coastguard saw her 'twerr they fetched her in. The Lord 'elp her mebbe she's not broken up much! An' Mister Ford don't know! I'm gwine for the doctor."

There was an hour or more to wait before he came; a young fellow; almost a boy. He looked very grave, when he came out of her room.

"The old woman there fond of her? nurse her well...? Fond as a dog!—good! Don't know—can't tell for certain! Afraid it's the spine, must have another opinion! What a plucky girl! Tell Mr. Ford to have the best man he can get in Torquay—there's C——. I'll be round the first thing in the morning. Keep her dead quiet. I've left a sleeping draught; she'll have fever tonight."

John Ford came in at last. Poor old man! What it must have cost him not to go to her for fear of the excitement! How many times in the next few hours didn't I hear him come to the bottom of the stairs; his heavy wheezing, and sighing; and the forlorn tread of his feet going back! About eleven, just as I was going to bed, Mrs. Hopgood came to my door.

"Will yu come, sir," she said; "she's asking for yu. Naowt I can zay but what she will see yu; zeems crazy, don't it?" A tear trickled down the old lady's cheek. "Du 'ee come; 'twill du 'err 'arm mebbe, but I dunno—she'll fret else."

I slipped into the room. Lying back on her pillows, she was breathing quickly with half-closed eyes. There was nothing to show that she had wanted me, or even knew that I was there. The wick of the candle, set by the bedside, had been snuffed too short, and gave but a faint light; both window and door stood open, still there was no draught, and the feeble little flame burned quite still, casting a faint yellow stain on the ceiling like the refection from a buttercup held beneath a chin. These ceilings are far too low! Across the wide, squat window the apple branches fell in black stripes which never stirred. It was too dark to see things clearly. At the foot of the bed was a chest, and there Mrs. Hopgood had sat down, moving her lips as if in speech. Mingled with the half-musty smell of age; there were other scents, of mignonette, apples, and some sweet-smelling soap. The floor had no carpet, and there was not one single dark object except the violin, hanging from a nail over the bed. A little, round clock ticked solemnly.

"Why won't you give me that stuff, Mums?" Pasiance said in a faint, sharp voice. "I want to sleep."

"Have you much pain?" I asked.

"Of course I have; it's everywhere."

She turned her face towards me.

"You thought I did it on purpose, but you're wrong. If I had, I'd have done it better than this. I wouldn't have this brutal pain." She put her fingers over her eyes. "It's horrible to complain! Only it's so bad! But I won't again—promise."

She took the sleeping draught gratefully, making a face, like a child after a powder.

"How long do you think it'll be before I can play again? Oh! I forgot—there are other things to think about." She held out her hand to me. "Look at my ring. Married—isn't it funny? Ha, ha! Nobody will ever understand—that's funny too! Poor Gran! You see, there wasn't any reason—only me. That's the only reason I'm telling you now; Mums is there—but she doesn't count; why don't you count, Mums?"

The fever was fighting against the draught; she had tossed the clothes back from her throat, and now and then raised one thin arm a little, as if it eased her; her eyes had grown large, and innocent like a child's; the candle, too, had flared, and was burning clearly.

"Nobody is to tell him—nobody at all; promise...! If I hadn't slipped, it would have been different. What would have happened then? You can't tell; and I can't—that's funny! Do you think I loved him? Nobody marries without love, do they? Not quite without love, I mean. But you see I wanted to be free, he said he'd take me; and now he's left me after all! I won't be left, I can't! When I came to the cliff—that bit where the ivy grows right down—there was just the sea there, underneath; so I thought I would throw myself over and it would be all quiet; and I climbed on a ledge, it looked easier from there, but it was so high, I wanted to get back; and then my foot slipped; and now it's all pain. You can't think much, when you're in pain."

From her eyes I saw that she was dropping off.

"Nobody can take you away from-yourself. He's not to be told—not even—I don't—want you—to go away, because—" But her eyes closed, and she dropped off to sleep.

They don't seem to know this morning whether she is better or worse....

VI

"Tuesday, 9th August.

.... It seems more like three weeks than three days since I wrote. The time passes slowly in a sickhouse...! The doctors were here this morning, they give her forty hours. Not a word of complaint has passed her lips since she knew. To see her you would hardly think her ill; her cheeks have not had time to waste or lose their colour. There is not much pain, but a slow, creeping numbness.... It was John Ford's wish that she should be told. She just turned her head to the wall and sighed; then to poor old Mrs. Hopgood, who was crying her heart out: "Don't cry, Mums, I don't care."

When they had gone, she asked for her violin. She made them hold it for her, and drew the bow across the strings; but the notes that came out were so trembling and uncertain that she dropped the bow and broke into a passion of sobbing. Since then, no complaint or moan of any kind....

But to go back. On Sunday, the day after I wrote, as I was coming from a walk, I met a little boy making mournful sounds on a tin whistle.

"Coom ahn!" he said, "the Miss wahnts t' zee yu."

I went to her room. In the morning she had seemed better, but now looked utterly exhausted. She had a letter in her hand.

"It's this," she said. "I don't seem to understand it. He wants me to do something—but I can't think, and my eyes feel funny. Read it to me, please."

The letter was from Zachary. I read it to her in a low voice, for Mrs. Hopgood was in the room, her eyes always fixed on Pasiance above her knitting. When I'd finished, she made me read it again, and yet again. At first she seemed pleased, almost excited, then came a weary, scornful look, and before I'd finished the third time she was asleep. It was a remarkable letter, that seemed to bring the man right before one's eyes. I slipped it under her fingers on the bed-clothes, and went out. Fancy took me to the cliff where she had fallen. I found the point of rock where the cascade of ivy flows down the cliff; the ledge on which she had climbed was a little to my right—a mad place. It showed plainly what wild emotions must have been driving her! Behind was a half-cut cornfield with a fringe of poppies, and swarms of harvest insects creeping and flying; in the uncut corn a landrail kept up a continual charring. The sky was blue to the very horizon, and the sea wonderful, under that black wild cliff stained here and there with red. Over the dips and hollows of the fields great white clouds hung low down above the land. There are no brassy, east-coast skies here; but always sleepy, soft-shaped clouds, full of subtle stir and change. Passages of Zachary's Pearse's letter kept rising to my lips. After all he's the man that his native place, and life, and blood have made him. It is useless to expect idealists where the air is soft and things good to look on (the idealist grows where he must create beauty or comfort for himself); useless to expect a man of law and order, in one whose fathers have stared at the sea day and night for a thousand years—the sea, full of its promises of unknown things, never quite the same, a slave to its own impulses. Man is an imitative animal....

"Life's hard enough," he wrote, "without tying yourself down. Don't think too hardly of me! Shall I make you happier by taking you into danger? If I succeed you'll be a rich woman; but I shall fail if you're with me. To look at you makes me soft. At sea a man dreams of all the good things on land, he'll dream of the heather, and honey—you're like that; and he'll dream of the apple-trees, and the grass of the orchards—you're like that; sometimes he only lies on his back and wishes—and you're like that, most of all like that...."

When I was reading those words I remember a strange, soft, half-scornful look came over Pasiance's face; and once she said, "But that's all nonsense, isn't it...?"

Then followed a long passage about what he would gain if he succeeded, about all that he was risking, the impossibility of failure, if he kept his wits about him. "It's only a matter of two months or so," he went on; "stay where you are, dear, or go to my Dad. He'll be glad to have you. There's my mother's room. There's no one to say 'No' to your fiddle there; you can play it by the sea; and on dark nights you'll have the stars dancing to you over the water as thick as bees. I've looked at them often, thinking of you...."

Pasiance had whispered to me, "Don't read that bit," and afterwards I left it out.... Then the sensuous side of him shows up: "When I've brought this off, there's the whole world before us. There are places I can take you to. There's one I know, not too warm and not too cold, where you can sit all day in the shade and watch the creepers, and the cocoa-palms, still as still; nothing to do or care about; all the fruits you can think of; no noise but the parrots and the streams, and a splash when a nigger dives into a water-hole. Pasiance, we'll go there! With an eighty-ton craft there's no sea we couldn't know. The world's a fine place for those who go out to take it; there's lots of unknown stuff in it yet. I'll fill your lap, my pretty, so full of treasures that you shan't know yourself. A man wasn't meant to sit at home...."

Throughout this letter—for all its real passion—one could feel how the man was holding to his purpose—the rather sordid purpose of this venture. He's unconscious of it; for he is in love with her; but he must be furthering his own ends. He is vital—horribly vital! I wonder less now that she should have yielded.

What visions hasn't he dangled before her. There was physical attraction, too—I haven't forgotten the look I saw on her face at Black Mill. But when all's said and done, she married him, because she's Pasiance Voisey, who does things and wants "to get back." And she lies there dying; not he nor any other man will ever take her away. It's pitiful to think of him tingling with passion, writing that letter to this doomed girl in that dark hole of a saloon. "I've wanted money," he wrote, "ever since I was a little chap sitting in the fields among the cows.... I want it for you now, and I mean to have it. I've studied the thing two years; I know what I know....

"The moment this is in the post I leave for London. There are a hundred things to look after still; I can't trust myself within reach of you again till the anchor's weighed. When I re-christened her the Pied Witch, I thought of you—you witch to me...."

There followed a solemn entreaty to her to be on the path leading to the cove at seven o'clock on Wednesday evening (that is, to-morrow) when he would come ashore and bid her good-bye. It was signed, "Your loving husband, Zachary Pearse...."

I lay at the edge of that cornfield a long time; it was very peaceful. The church bells had begun to ring. The long shadows came stealing out from the sheaves; woodpigeons rose one by one, and flapped off to roost; the western sky was streaked with red, and all the downs and combe bathed in the last sunlight. Perfect harvest weather; but oppressively still, the stillness of suspense....

Life at the farm goes on as usual. We have morning and evening prayers. John Ford reads them fiercely, as though he were on the eve of a revolt against his God. Morning and evening he visits her, comes out wheezing heavily, and goes to his own room; I believe, to pray. Since this morning I haven't dared meet him. He is a strong old man—but this will break him up....

VII

"KINGSWEAR, Saturday, 13th August.

.... It's over—I leave here to-morrow, and go abroad.

A quiet afternoon—not a breath up in the churchyard! I was there quite half an hour before they came. Some red cows had strayed into the adjoining orchard, and were rubbing their heads against the railing. While I stood there an old woman came and drove them away; afterwards, she stooped and picked up the apples that had fallen before their time.

"The apples are ripe and ready to fall, Oh! heigh-ho! and ready to fall; There came an old woman and gathered them all, Oh! heigh-ho! and gathered them all."

.... They brought Pasiance very simply—no hideous funeral trappings, thank God—the farm hands carried her, and there was no one there but John Ford, the Hopgoods, myself, and that young doctor. They read the service over her grave. I can hear John Ford's "Amen!" now. When it was over he walked away bareheaded in the sun, without a word. I went up there again this evening, and wandered amongst the tombstones. "Richard Voisey," "John, the son of Richard and Constance Voisey," "Margery Voisey," so many generations of them in that corner; then "Richard Voisey and Agnes his wife," and next to it that new mound on which a sparrow was strutting and the shadows of the apple-trees already hovering.

I will tell you the little left to tell....

On Wednesday afternoon she asked for me again.

"It's only till seven," she whispered. "He's certain to come then. But if I—were to die first—then tell him—I'm sorry for him. They keep saying: 'Don't talk—don't talk!' Isn't it stupid? As if I should have any other chance! There'll be no more talking after to-night! Make everybody come, please—I want to see them all. When you're dying you're freer than any other time—nobody wants you to do things, nobody cares what you say.... He promised me I should do what I liked if I married him—I never believed that really—but now I can do what I like; and say all the things I want to." She lay back silent; she could not after all speak the inmost thoughts that are in each of us, so sacred that they melt away at the approach of words.

I shall remember her like that—with the gleam of a smile in her half-closed eyes, her red lips parted—such a quaint look of mockery, pleasure, regret, on her little round, upturned face; the room white, and fresh with flowers, the breeze guttering the apple-leaves against the window. In the night they had unhooked the violin and taken it away; she had not missed it.... When Dan came, I gave up my place to him. He took her hand gently in his great paw, without speaking.

"How small my hand looks there," she said, "too small." Dan put it softly back on the bedclothes and wiped his forehead. Pasiance cried in a sharp whisper: "Is it so hot in here? I didn't know." Dan bent down, put his lips to her fingers and left the room.

The afternoon was long, the longest I've ever spent. Sometimes she seemed to sleep, sometimes whispered to herself about her mother, her grandfather, the garden, or her cats—all sorts of inconsequent, trivial, even ludicrous memories seemed to throng her mind—never once, I think, did she speak of Zachary, but, now and then, she asked the time.... Each hour she grew visibly weaker. John Ford sat by her without moving, his heavy breathing was often the only sound; sometimes she rubbed her fingers on his hand, without speaking. It was a summary of their lives together. Once he prayed aloud for her in a hoarse voice; then her pitiful, impatient eyes signed to me.

"Quick," she whispered, "I want him; it's all so—cold."

I went out and ran down the path towards the cove.

Leaning on a gate stood Zachary, an hour before his time; dressed in the same old blue clothes and leather-peaked cap as on the day when I saw him first. He knew nothing of what had happened. But at a quarter of the truth, I'm sure he divined the whole, though he would not admit it to himself. He kept saying, "It can't be. She'll be well in a few days—a sprain! D' you think the sea-voyage.... Is she strong enough to be moved now at once?"

It was painful to see his face, so twisted by the struggle between his instinct and his vitality. The sweat poured down his forehead. He turned round as we walked up the path, and pointed out to sea. There was his steamer. "I could get her on board in no time. Impossible! What is it, then? Spine? Good God! The doctors.... Sometimes they'll do wonders!" It was pitiful to see his efforts to blind himself to the reality.

"It can't be, she's too young. We're walking very slow." I told him she was dying.

For a second I thought he was going to run away. Then he jerked up his head, and rushed on towards the house. At the foot of the staircase he gripped me by the shoulder.

"It's not true!" he said; "she'll get better now I'm here. I'll stay. Let everything go. I'll stay."

"Now's the time," I said, "to show you loved her. Pull yourself together, man!" He shook all over.

"Yes!" was all he answered. We went into her room. It seemed impossible she was going to die; the colour was bright in her cheeks, her lips trembling and pouted as if she had just been kissed, her eyes gleaming, her hair so dark and crisp, her face so young....

Half an hour later I stole to the open door of her room. She was still and white as the sheets of her bed. John Ford stood at the foot; and, bowed to the level of the pillows, his head on his clenched fists, sat Zachary. It was utterly quiet. The guttering of the leaves had ceased. When things have come to a crisis, how little one feels—no fear, no pity, no sorrow, rather the sense, as when a play is over, of anxiety to get away!

Suddenly Zachary rose, brushed past me without seeing, and ran downstairs.

Some hours later I went out on the path leading to the cove. It was pitch-black; the riding light of the Pied Witch was still there, looking no bigger than a firefly. Then from in front I heard sobbing—a man's sobs; no sound is quite so dreadful. Zachary Pearse got up out of the bank not ten paces off.

I had no heart to go after him, and sat down in the hedge. There was something subtly akin to her in the fresh darkness of the young night; the soft bank, the scent of honeysuckle, the touch of the ferns and brambles. Death comes to all of us, and when it's over it's over; but this blind business—of those left behind!

A little later the ship whistled twice; her starboard light gleamed faintly—and that was all....

VIII

"TORQUAY, 30th October.

.... Do you remember the letters I wrote you from Moor Farm nearly three years ago? To-day I rode over there. I stopped at Brixham on the way for lunch, and walked down to the quay. There had been a shower—but the sun was out again, shining on the sea, the brown-red sails, and the rampart of slate roofs.

A trawler was lying there, which had evidently been in a collision. The spiky-bearded, thin-lipped fellow in torn blue jersey and sea-boots who was superintending the repairs, said to me a little proudly:

"Bane in collision, zurr; like to zee over her?" Then suddenly screwing up his little blue eyes, he added:

"Why, I remembers yu. Steered yu along o' the young lady in this yer very craft."

It was Prawle, Zachary Pearse's henchman.

"Yes," he went on, "that's the cutter."

"And Captain Pearse?"

He leant his back against the quay, and spat. "He was a pra-aper man; I never zane none like 'en."

"Did you do any good out there?"

Prawle gave me a sharp glance.

"Gude? No, t'was arrm we done, vrom ztart to finish—had trouble all the time. What a man cude du, the skipper did. When yu caan't du right, zome calls it 'Providence'. 'Tis all my eye an' Betty Martin! What I zay es, 'tis these times, there's such a dale o' folk, a dale of puzzivantin' fellers; the world's to small."

With these words there flashed across me a vision of Drake crushed into our modern life by the shrinkage of the world; Drake caught in the meshes of red tape, electric wires, and all the lofty appliances of our civilization. Does a type survive its age; live on into times that have no room for it? The blood is there—and sometimes there's a throw-back.... All fancy! Eh?

"So," I said, "you failed?"

Prawle wriggled.

"I wudden' goo for to zay that, zurr—'tis an ugly word. Da-am!" he added, staring at his boots, "'twas thru me tu. We were along among the haythen, and I mus' nades goo for to break me leg. The capt'n he wudden' lave me. 'One Devon man,' he says to me, 'don' lave anotherr.' We werr six days where we shuld ha' been tu; when we got back to the ship a cruiser had got her for gun-runnin'."

"And what has become of Captain Pearse?"

Prawle answered, "Zurr, I belave 'e went to China, 'tis onsartin."

"He's not dead?"

Prawle looked at me with a kind of uneasy anger.

"Yu cudden' kell 'en! 'Tis true, mun 'll die zome day. But therr's not a one that'll show better zport than Capt'n Zach'ry Pearse."

I believe that; he will be hard to kill. The vision of him comes up, with his perfect balance, defiant eyes, and sweetish smile; the way the hair of his beard crisped a little, and got blacker on the cheeks; the sort of desperate feeling he gave, that one would never get the better of him, that he would never get the better of himself.

I took leave of Prawle and half a crown. Before I was off the quay I heard him saying to a lady, "Bane in collision, marm! Like to zee over her?"

After lunch I rode on to Moor. The old place looked much the same; but the apple-trees were stripped of fruit, and their leaves beginning to go yellow and fall. One of Pasiance's cats passed me in the orchard hunting a bird, still with a ribbon round its neck. John Ford showed me all his latest improvements, but never by word or sign alluded to the past. He inquired after Dan, back in New Zealand now, without much interest; his stubbly beard and hair have whitened; he has grown very stout, and I noticed that his legs are not well under control; he often stops to lean on his stick. He was very ill last winter; and sometimes, they say, will go straight off to sleep in the middle of a sentence.

I managed to get a few minutes with the Hopgoods. We talked of Pasiance sitting in the kitchen under a row of plates, with that clinging smell of wood-smoke, bacon, and age bringing up memories, as nothing but scents can. The dear old lady's hair, drawn so nicely down her forehead on each side from the centre of her cap, has a few thin silver lines; and her face is a thought more wrinkled. The tears still come into her eyes when she talks of her "lamb."

Of Zachary I heard nothing, but she told me of old Pearse's death.

"Therr they found 'en, zo to spake, dead—in th' sun; but Ha-apgood can tell yu," and Hopgood, ever rolling his pipe, muttered something, and smiled his wooden smile.

He came to see me off from the straw-yard. "'Tis like death to the varrm, zurr," he said, putting all the play of his vast shoulders into the buckling of my girths. "Mister Ford—well! And not one of th' old stock to take it when 'e's garn.... Ah! it werr cruel; my old woman's never been hersel' since. Tell 'ee what 'tis—don't du t' think to much."

I went out of my way to pass the churchyard. There were flowers, quite fresh, chrysanthemums, and asters; above them the white stone, already stained:

"PASIANCE

"WIFE OF ZACHARY PEARSE

"'The Lord hath given, and the Lord hath taken away.'"

The red cows were there too; the sky full of great white clouds, some birds whistling a little mournfully, and in the air the scent of fallen leaves....

May, 1900.

A KNIGHT

I

At Monte Carlo, in the spring of the year 189-, I used to notice an old fellow in a grey suit and sunburnt straw hat with a black ribbon. Every morning at eleven o'clock, he would come down to the Place, followed by a brindled German boarhound, walk once or twice round it, and seat himself on a bench facing the casino. There he would remain in the sun, with his straw hat tilted forward, his thin legs apart, his brown hands crossed between them, and the dog's nose resting on his knee. After an hour or more he would get up, and, stooping a little from the waist, walk slowly round the Place and return up hill. Just before three, he would come down again in the same clothes and go into the casino, leaving the dog outside.

One afternoon, moved by curiosity, I followed him. He passed through the hall without looking at the gambling-rooms, and went into the concert. It became my habit after that to watch for him. When he sat in the Place I could see him from the window of my room. The chief puzzle to me was the matter of his nationality.

His lean, short face had a skin so burnt that it looked like leather; his jaw was long and prominent, his chin pointed, and he had hollows in his cheeks. There were wrinkles across his forehead; his eyes were brown; and little white moustaches were brushed up from the corners of his lips. The back of his head bulged out above the lines of his lean neck and high, sharp shoulders; his grey hair was cropped quite close. In the Marseilles buffet, on the journey out, I had met an Englishman, almost his counterpart in features—but somehow very different! This old fellow had nothing of the other's alert, autocratic self-sufficiency. He was quiet and undemonstrative, without looking, as it were, insulated against shocks and foreign substances. He was certainly no Frenchman. His eyes, indeed, were brown, but hazel-brown, and gentle—not the red-brown sensual eye of the Frenchman. An American? But was ever an American so passive? A German? His moustache was certainly brushed up, but in a modest, almost pathetic way, not in the least Teutonic. Nothing seemed to fit him. I gave him up, and named him "the Cosmopolitan."

Leaving at the end of April, I forgot him altogether. In the same month, however, of the following year I was again at Monte Carlo, and going one day to the concert found myself seated next this same old fellow. The orchestra was playing Meyerbeer's "Prophete," and my neighbour was asleep, snoring softly. He was dressed in the same grey suit, with the same straw hat (or one exactly like it) on his knees, and his hands crossed above it. Sleep had not disfigured him—his little white moustache was still brushed up, his lips closed; a very good and gentle expression hovered on his face. A curved mark showed on his right temple, the scar of a cut on the side of his neck, and his left hand was covered by an old glove, the little finger of which was empty. He woke up when the march was over and brisked up his moustache.

The next thing on the programme was a little thing by Poise from Le joli Gilles, played by Mons. Corsanego on the violin. Happening to glance at my old neighbour, I saw a tear caught in the hollow of his cheek, and another just leaving the corner of his eye; there was a faint smile on his lips. Then came an interval; and while orchestra and audience were resting, I asked him if he were fond of music. He looked up without distrust, bowed, and answered in a thin, gentle voice: "Certainly. I know nothing about it, play no instrument, could never sing a note; but fond of it! Who would not be?" His English was correct enough, but with an emphasis not quite American nor quite foreign. I ventured to remark that he did not care for Meyerbeer. He smiled.

"Ah!" he said, "I was asleep? Too bad of me. He is a little noisy—I know so little about music. There is Bach, for instance. Would you believe it, he gives me no pleasure? A great misfortune to be no musician!" He shook his head.

I murmured, "Bach is too elevating for you perhaps."

"To me," he answered, "any music I like is elevating. People say some music has a bad effect on them. I never found any music that gave me a bad thought—no—no—quite the opposite; only sometimes, as you see, I go to sleep. But what a lovely instrument the violin!" A faint flush came on his parched cheeks. "The human soul that has left the body. A curious thing, distant bugles at night have given me the same feeling." The orchestra was now coming back, and, folding his hands, my neighbour turned his eyes towards them. When the concert was over we came out together. Waiting at the entrance was his dog.

"You have a beautiful dog!"

"Ah! yes, Freda, mia cara, da su mano!" The dog squatted on her haunches, and lifted her paw in the vague, bored way of big dogs when requested to perform civilities. She was a lovely creature—the purest brindle, without a speck of white, and free from the unbalanced look of most dogs of her breed.

"Basta! basta!" He turned to me apologetically. "We have agreed to speak Italian; in that way I keep up the language; astonishing the number of things that dog will understand!" I was about to take my leave, when he asked if I would walk a little way with him—"If you are free, that is." We went up the street with Freda on the far side of her master.

"Do you never 'play' here?" I asked him.

"Play? No. It must be very interesting; most exciting, but as a matter of fact, I can't afford it. If one has very little, one is too nervous."

He had stopped in front of a small hairdresser's shop. "I live here," he said, raising his hat again. "Au revoir!—unless I can offer you a glass of tea. It's all ready. Come! I've brought you out of your way; give me the pleasure!"

I have never met a man so free from all self-consciousness, and yet so delicate and diffident the combination is a rare one. We went up a steep staircase to a room on the second floor. My companion threw the shutters open, setting all the flies buzzing. The top of a plane-tree was on a level with the window, and all its little brown balls were dancing, quite close, in the wind. As he had promised, an urn was hissing on a table; there was also a small brown teapot, some sugar, slices of lemon, and glasses. A bed, washstand, cupboard, tin trunk, two chairs, and a small rug were all the furniture. Above the bed a sword in a leather sheath was suspended from two nails. The photograph of a girl stood on the closed stove. My host went to the cupboard and produced a bottle, a glass, and a second spoon. When the cork was drawn, the scent of rum escaped into the air. He sniffed at it and dropped a teaspoonful into both glasses.

"This is a trick I learned from the Russians after Plevna; they had my little finger, so I deserved something in exchange." He looked round; his eyes, his whole face, seemed to twinkle. "I assure you it was worth it—makes all the difference. Try!" He poured off the tea.

"Had you a sympathy with the Turks?"

"The weaker side—" He paused abruptly, then added: "But it was not that." Over his face innumerable crow's-feet had suddenly appeared, his eyes twitched; he went on hurriedly, "I had to find something to do just then—it was necessary." He stared into his glass; and it was some time before I ventured to ask if he had seen much fighting.

"Yes," he replied gravely, "nearly twenty years altogether; I was one of Garibaldi's Mille in '60."

"Surely you are not Italian?"

He leaned forward with his hands on his knees. "I was in Genoa at that time learning banking; Garibaldi was a wonderful man! One could not help it." He spoke quite simply. "You might say it was like seeing a little man stand up to a ring of great hulking fellows; I went, just as you would have gone, if you'd been there. I was not long with them—our war began; I had to go back home." He said this as if there had been but one war since the world began. "In '60," he mused, "till '65. Just think of it! The poor country. Why, in my

State, South Carolina—I was through it all—nobody could be spared there—we were one to three."

"I suppose you have a love of fighting?"

"H'm!" he said, as if considering the idea for the first time. "Sometimes I fought for a living, and sometimes—because I was obliged; one must try to be a gentleman. But won't you have some more?"

I refused more tea and took my leave, carrying away with me a picture of the old fellow looking down from the top of the steep staircase, one hand pressed to his back, the other twisting up those little white moustaches, and murmuring, "Take care, my dear sir, there's a step there at the corner."

"To be a gentleman!" I repeated in the street, causing an old French lady to drop her parasol, so that for about two minutes we stood bowing and smiling to each other, then separated full of the best feeling.

II

A week later I found myself again seated next him at a concert. In the meantime I had seen him now and then, but only in passing. He seemed depressed. The corners of his lips were tightened, his tanned cheeks had a greyish tinge, his eyes were restless; and, between two numbers of the programme, he murmured, tapping his fingers on his hat, "Do you ever have bad days? Yes? Not pleasant, are they?"

Then something occurred from which all that I have to tell you followed. There came into the concert-hall the heroine of one of those romances, crimes, follies, or irregularities, call it what you will, which had just attracted the "world's" stare. She passed us with her partner, and sat down in a chair a few rows to our right. She kept turning her head round, and at every turn I caught the gleam of her uneasy eyes. Some one behind us said: "The brazen baggage!"

My companion turned full round, and glared at whoever it was who had spoken. The change in him was quite remarkable. His lips were drawn back from his teeth; he frowned; the scar on his temple had reddened.

"Ah!" he said to me. "The hue and cry! Contemptible! How I hate it! But you wouldn't understand—!" he broke off, and slowly regained his usual air of self-obliteration; he even seemed ashamed, and began trying to brush his moustaches higher than ever, as if aware that his heat had robbed them of neatness.

"I'm not myself, when I speak of such matters," he said suddenly; and began reading his programme, holding it upside down. A minute later, however, he said in a peculiar voice: "There are people to be found who object to vivisecting animals; but the vivisection of a woman, who minds that? Will you tell me it's right, that because of some tragedy like this—believe me, it is always a tragedy—we should hunt down a woman? That her fellow-women should make an outcast of her? That we, who are men, should make a prey of her? If I thought that...." Again he broke off, staring very hard in front of him. "It is we who make them what they are; and even if that is not so—why! if I thought there was a woman in the world I could not take my hat off to—I—I—couldn't sleep at night." He got up from his seat, put on his old straw hat with trembling fingers, and, without a glance back, went out, stumbling over the chair-legs.

I sat there, horribly disturbed; the words, "One must try to be a gentleman!" haunting me. When I came out, he was standing by the entrance with one hand on his hip and the other on his dog. In that attitude of waiting he was such a patient figure; the sun glared down and showed the threadbare nature of his clothes and the thinness of his brown hands, with their long fingers and nails yellow from tobacco. Seeing me he came up the steps again, and raised his hat.

"I am glad to have caught you; please forget all that." I asked if he would do me the honour of dining at my hotel.

"Dine?" he repeated with the sort of smile a child gives if you offer him a box of soldiers; "with the greatest pleasure. I seldom dine out, but I think I can muster up a coat. Yes—yes—and at what time shall I come? At half-past seven, and your hotel is—? Good! I shall be there. Freda, mia cara, you will be alone this evening. You do not smoke caporal, I fear. I find it fairly good; though it has too much bite." He walked off with Freda, puffing at his thin roll of caporal.

Once or twice he stopped, as if bewildered or beset by some sudden doubt or memory; and every time he stopped, Freda licked his hand. They disappeared round the corner of the street, and I went to my hotel to see about dinner. On the way I met Jules le Ferrier, and asked him to come too.

"My faith, yes!" he said, with the rosy pessimism characteristic of the French editor. "Man must dine!"

At half-past six we assembled. My "Cosmopolitan" was in an old frock-coat braided round the edges, buttoned high and tight, defining more than ever the sharp lines of his shoulders and the slight kink of his back; he had brought with him, too, a dark-peaked cap of military shape, which he had evidently selected as more fitting to the coat than a straw hat. He smelled slightly of some herb.

We sat down to dinner, and did not rise for two hours. He was a charming guest, praised everything he ate—not with commonplaces, but in words that made you feel it had given him real pleasure. At first, whenever Jules made one of his caustic remarks, he looked quite pained, but suddenly seemed to make up his mind that it was bark, not bite; and then at each of them he would turn to me and say, "Aha! that's good—isn't it?" With every glass of wine he became more gentle and more genial, sitting very upright, and tightly buttoned-in; while the little white wings of his moustache seemed about to leave him for a better world.

In spite of the most leading questions, however, we could not get him to talk about himself, for even Jules, most cynical of men, had recognised that he was a hero of romance. He would answer gently and precisely, and then sit twisting his moustaches, perfectly unconscious that we wanted more. Presently, as the wine went a little to his head, his thin, high voice grew thinner, his cheeks became flushed, his eyes brighter; at the end of dinner he said: "I hope I have not been noisy."

We assured him that he had not been noisy enough. "You're laughing at me," he answered. "Surely I've been talking all the time!"

"Mon Dieu!" said Jules, "we have been looking for some fables of your wars; but nothing—nothing, not enough to feed a frog!"

The old fellow looked troubled.

"To be sure!" he mused. "Let me think! there is that about Colhoun at Gettysburg; and there's the story of Garibaldi and the Miller." He plunged into a tale, not at all about himself, which would have been extremely dull, but for the conviction in his eyes, and the way he stopped and commented. "So you see," he ended, "that's the sort of man Garibaldi was! I could tell you another tale of him." Catching an introspective look in Jules's eye, however, I proposed taking our cigars over to the cafe opposite.

"Delightful!" the old fellow said: "We shall have a band and the fresh air, and clear consciences for our cigars. I cannot like this smoking in a room where there are ladies dining."

He walked out in front of us, smoking with an air of great enjoyment. Jules, glowing above his candid shirt and waistcoat, whispered to me, "Mon cher Georges, how he is good!" then sighed, and added darkly: "The poor man!"

We sat down at a little table. Close by, the branches of a plane-tree rustled faintly; their leaves hung lifeless, speckled like the breasts of birds, or black against the sky; then, caught by the breeze, fluttered suddenly.

The old fellow sat, with head thrown back, a smile on his face, coming now and then out of his enchanted dreams to drink coffee, answer our questions, or hum the tune that the band was playing. The ash of his cigar grew very long. One of those bizarre figures in Oriental garb, who, night after night, offer their doubtful wares at a great price, appeared in the white glare of a lamp, looked with a furtive smile at his face, and glided back, discomfited by its unconsciousness. It was a night for dreams! A faint, half-eastern scent in the air, of black tobacco and spice; few people as yet at the little tables, the waiters leisurely, the band soft! What was he dreaming of, that old fellow, whose cigar-ash grew so long? Of youth, of his battles, of those things that must be done by those who try to be gentlemen; perhaps only of his dinner; anyway of something gilded in vague fashion as the light was gilding the branches of the plane-tree.

Jules pulled my sleeve: "He sleeps." He had smilingly dropped off; the cigar-ash—that feathery tower of his dreams—had broken and fallen on his sleeve. He awoke, and fell to dusting it.

The little tables round us began to fill. One of the bandsmen played a czardas on the czymbal. Two young Frenchmen, talking loudly, sat down at the adjoining table. They were discussing the lady who had been at the concert that afternoon.

"It's a bet," said one of them, "but there's the present man. I take three weeks, that's enough 'elle est declassee; ce n'est que le premier pas—'"

My old friend's cigar fell on the table. "Monsieur," he stammered, "you speak of a lady so, in a public place?"

The young man stared at him. "Who is this person?" he said to his companion.

My guest took up Jules's glove that lay on the table; before either of us could raise a finger, he had swung it in the speaker's face. "Enough!" he said, and, dropping the glove, walked away.

We all jumped to our feet. I left Jules and hurried after him. His face was grim, his eyes those of a creature who has been struck on a raw place. He made a movement of his fingers which said plainly. "Leave me, if you please!"

I went back to the cafe. The two young men had disappeared, so had Jules, but everything else was going on just as before; the bandsman still twanging out his czardas; the waiters serving drinks; the orientals trying to sell their carpets. I paid the bill, sought out the manager, and apologised. He shrugged his shoulders, smiled and said: "An eccentric, your friend, nicht wahr?" Could he tell me where M. Le Ferrier was? He could not. I left to look for Jules; could not find him, and returned to my hotel disgusted. I was sorry for my old guest, but vexed with him too; what business had he to carry his Quixotism to such an unpleasant length? I tried to read. Eleven o'clock struck; the casino disgorged a stream of people; the Place seemed fuller of life than ever; then slowly it grew empty and quite dark. The whim seized me to go out. It was a still night, very warm, very black. On one of the seats a man and woman sat embraced, on another a girl was sobbing, on a third—strange sight—a priest dozed. I became aware of some one at my side; it was my old guest.

"If you are not too tired," he said, "can you give me ten minutes?"

"Certainly; will you come in?"

"No, no; let us go down to the Terrace. I shan't keep you long."

He did not speak again till we reached a seat above the pigeon-shooting grounds; there, in a darkness denser for the string of lights still burning in the town, we sat down.

"I owe you an apology," he said; "first in the afternoon, then again this evening—your guest—your friend's glove! I have behaved as no gentleman should." He was leaning forward with his hands on the handle of a stick. His voice sounded broken and disturbed.

"Oh!" I muttered. "It's nothing!"

"You are very good," he sighed; "but I feel that I must explain. I consider I owe this to you, but I must tell you I should not have the courage if it were not for another reason. You see I have no friend." He looked at me with an uncertain smile. I bowed, and a minute or two later he began....

III

"You will excuse me if I go back rather far. It was in '74, when I had been ill with Cuban fever. To keep me alive they had put me on board a ship at Santiago, and at the end of the voyage I found myself in London. I had very little money; I knew nobody. I tell you, sir, there are times when it's hard for a fighting man to get anything to do. People would say to me: 'Afraid we've nothing for a man like you in our business.' I tried people of all sorts; but it was true—I had been fighting here and there since '60, I wasn't fit for anything—" He shook his head. "In the South, before the war, they had a saying, I remember, about a dog and a soldier having the same value. But all this has nothing to do with what I have to tell you." He sighed again and went on, moistening his lips: "I was walking along the Strand one day, very disheartened, when I heard my name called. It's a queer thing, that, in a strange street. By the way," he put in with dry ceremony, "you don't know my name, I think: it is Brune—Roger Brune. At first I did not recognise the person who called me. He had just got off an omnibus—a square-shouldered man with heavy moustaches, and round spectacles. But when he shook my hand I knew him at once. He was a man called Dalton, who was taken prisoner at Gettysburg; one of you Englishmen who came to fight with us— a major in the regiment where I was captain. We were comrades during two campaigns. If I had been his brother he couldn't have seemed more pleased to see me. He took me into a bar for the sake of old times. The drink went to my head, and by the time we reached Trafalgar Square I was quite unable to walk. He made me sit down on a bench. I was in fact—drunk. It's disgraceful to be drunk, but there was some excuse. Now I tell you, sir" (all through his story he was always making use of that expression, it seemed to infuse fresh spirit into him, to help his memory in obscure places, to give him the mastery of his emotions; it was like the piece of paper a nervous man holds in his hand to help him through a speech), "there never was a man with a finer soul than my friend Dalton. He was not clever, though he had read much; and sometimes perhaps he was too fond of talking. But he was a gentleman; he listened to me as if I had been a child; he was not ashamed of me—and it takes a gentleman not to be ashamed of a drunken man in the streets of London; God knows what things I said to him while we were sitting there! He took me to his home and put me to bed himself; for I was down again with fever." He stopped, turned slightly from me, and put his hand up to his brow. "Well, then it was, sir, that I first saw her. I am not a poet and I cannot tell you what she seemed to me. I was delirious, but I always knew when she was there. I had dreams of sunshine and cornfields, of dancing waves at sea, young trees—never the same dreams, never anything for long together; and when I had my senses I was afraid to say so for fear she would go away. She'd be in the corner of the room, with her hair hanging about her neck, a bright gold colour; she never worked and never read, but sat and talked to herself in a whisper, or looked at me for a long time together out of her blue eyes, a little frown between them, and her upper lip closed firm on her lower lip, where she had an uneven tooth. When her father came, she'd jump up and hang on to his neck until he groaned, then run away, but presently come stealing back on tiptoe. I used to listen for her footsteps on the stairs, then the knock, the door flung back or opened quietly—you never could tell which; and her voice, with a little lisp, 'Are you better today, Mr. Brune? What funny things you say when you're delirious! Father says you've been in heaps of battles!'"

He got up, paced restlessly to and fro, and sat down again. "I remember every word as if it were yesterday, all the things she said, and did; I've had a long time to think them over, you see. Well, I must tell you, the first morning that I was able to get up, I missed her. Dalton came in her place, and I asked him where she was. 'My dear fellow,' he answered, 'I've sent Eilie away to her old nurse's inn down on the river; she's better there at this time of year.' We looked at each other, and I saw that he had sent her away because he didn't trust me. I was hurt by this. Illness spoils one. He was right, he was quite right, for all he knew about me was that I could fight and had got drunk; but I am very quick-tempered. I made up my mind at once to leave him. But I was too weak—he had to put me to bed again. The very next morning he came and proposed that I should go into partnership with him. He kept a fencing-school and pistol-gallery. It seemed like the finger of God; and perhaps it was—who knows?" He fell into a reverie, and taking out his caporal, rolled himself a cigarette; having lighted it, he went on suddenly: "There, in the room above the school, we used to sit in the evenings, one on each side of the grate. The room was on the second floor, I remember, with two windows, and a view of nothing but the houses opposite. The furniture was covered up with chintz. The things on the bookshelf were never disturbed, they were Eilie's—half-broken cases with butterflies, a dead frog in a bottle, a horse-shoe covered with tinfoil, some shells too, and a cardboard box with three speckled eggs in it, and these words written on the lid: 'Missel-thrush from Lucy's tree—second family, only one blown.'" He smoked fiercely, with puffs that were like sharp sighs.

"Dalton was wrapped up in her. He was never tired of talking to me about her, and I was never tired of hearing. We had a number of pupils; but in the evening when we sat there, smoking—our talk would sooner or later—come round to her. Her bedroom opened out of that sitting—room; he took me in once and showed me a narrow little room the width of a passage, fresh and white, with a photograph of her mother above the bed, and an empty basket for a dog or cat." He broke off with a vexed air, and resumed sternly, as if trying to bind himself to the narration of his more important facts: "She was then fifteen—her mother had been dead twelve years—a beautiful, face, her mother's; it had been her death that sent Dalton to fight with us. Well, sir, one day in August, very hot weather, he proposed a run into the country, and who should meet us on the platform when we arrived but Eilie, in a blue sun-bonnet and frock—flax blue, her favourite colour. I was angry with Dalton for not telling me that we should see her; my clothes were not quite—my hair wanted cutting. It was black then, sir," he added, tracing a pattern in the darkness with his stick. "She had a little donkey-cart; she drove, and, while we walked one on each side, she kept looking at me from under her sunbonnet. I must tell you that she never laughed—her eyes danced, her cheeks would go pink, and her hair shake about on her neck, but she never laughed. Her old nurse, Lucy, a very broad, good woman, had married the proprietor of the inn in the village there. I have never seen anything like that inn: sweetbriar up to the roof! And the scent—I am very susceptible to scents!" His head drooped, and the cigarette fell from his hand. A train passing beneath sent up a shower of sparks. He started, and went on: "We had our lunch in the parlour—I remember that room very well, for I spent the happiest days of my life afterwards in that inn.... We went into a meadow after lunch, and my friend Dalton fell asleep. A wonderful thing happened then. Eilie whispered to me, 'Let's have a jolly time.' She took me for the most glorious walk. The river was close by. A lovely stream, your river Thames, so calm and broad; it is like the spirit of your people. I was bewitched; I forgot my friend, I thought of nothing but how to keep her to myself. It was such a day! There are days that are the devil's, but that was truly one of God's. She took me to a little pond under an elm-tree, and we dragged it, we two, an hour, for a kind of tiny red worm to feed some creature that she had. We found them in the mud, and while she was bending over, the curls got in her eyes. If you could have seen her then, I think, sir, you would have said she was like the first sight of spring.... We had tea afterwards, all together, in the long grass under some fruit-trees. If I had the knack of words, there are things that I could say." He bent, as though in deference to those unspoken memories. "Twilight came on while we were sitting there. A wonderful thing is twilight in the country! It became time for us to go. There was an avenue of trees close by—like a church with a window at the end, where golden light came through. I walked up and down it with her. 'Will you come again?' she whispered, and suddenly she lifted up her face to be kissed. I kissed her as if she were a little child. And when we said good-bye, her eyes were looking at me across her father's shoulder, with surprise and sorrow in them. 'Why do you go away?' they seemed to say.... But I must tell you," he went on hurriedly, "of a thing that happened before we had gone a hundred yards. We were smoking our pipes, and I, thinking of her—when out she sprang from the hedge and stood in front of us. Dalton cried out, 'What are you here for again, you mad girl?' She rushed up to him and hugged him; but when she looked at me, her face was quite different—careless, defiant, as one might say—it hurt me. I couldn't understand it, and what one doesn't understand frightens one."

IV

"Time went on. There was no swordsman, or pistol-shot like me in London, they said. We had as many pupils as we liked—it was the only part of my life when I have been able to save money. I had no chance to spend it. We gave lessons all day, and in the evening were too tired to go out. That year I had the misfortune to lose my dear mother. I became a rich man—yes, sir, at that time I must have had not less than six hundred a year.

"It was a long time before I saw Eilie again. She went abroad to Dresden with her father's sister to learn French and German. It was in the autumn of 1875 when she came back to us. She was seventeen then—a beautiful young creature." He paused, as if to gather his forces for description, and went on.

"Tall, as a young tree, with eyes like the sky. I would not say she was perfect, but her imperfections were beautiful to me. What is it makes you love—ah! sir, that is very hidden and mysterious. She had never lost the trick of closing her lips tightly when she remembered her uneven tooth. You may say that was vanity, but in a young girl—and which of us is not vain, eh? 'Old men and maidens, young men and children!'

"As I said, she came back to London to her little room, and in the evenings was always ready with our tea. You mustn't suppose she was housewifely; there is something in me that never admired housewifeliness—a fine quality, no doubt, still—" He sighed.

"No," he resumed, "Eilie was not like that, for she was never quite the same two days together. I told you her eyes were like the sky—that was true of all of her. In one thing, however, at that time, she always seemed the same—in love for her father. For me! I don't know what I should have expected; but my presence seemed to have the effect of making her dumb; I would catch her looking at me with a frown, and then, as if to make up to her own nature—and a more loving nature never came into this world, that I shall maintain to my dying day—she would go to her father and kiss him. When I talked with him she pretended not to notice, but I could see her face grow cold and stubborn. I am not quick; and it was a long time before I understood that she was jealous, she wanted him all to herself. I've often wondered how she could be his daughter, for he was the very soul of justice and a slow man too—and she was as quick as a bird. For a long time after I saw her dislike of me, I refused to believe it—if one does not want to believe a thing there are always reasons why it should not seem true, at least so it is with me, and I suppose with all selfish men.

"I spent evening after evening there, when, if I had not thought only of myself, I should have kept away. But one day I could no longer be blind.

"It was a Sunday in February. I always had an invitation on Sundays to dine with them in the middle of the day. There was no one in the sitting-room; but the door of Eilie's bedroom was open. I heard her voice: 'That man, always that man!' It was enough for me, I went down again without coming in, and walked about all day.

"For three weeks I kept away. To the school of course I came as usual, but not upstairs. I don't know what I told Dalton—it did not signify what you told him, he always had a theory of his own, and was persuaded of its truth—a very single-minded man, sir.

"But now I come to the most wonderful days of my life. It was an early spring that year. I had fallen away already from my resolution, and used to slink up—seldom, it's true—and spend the evening with them as before. One afternoon I came up to the sitting-room; the light was failing—it was warm, and the windows were open. In the air was that feeling which comes to you once a year, in the spring, no matter where you may be, in a crowded street, or alone in a forest; only once—a feeling like—but I cannot describe it.

"Eilie was sitting there. If you don't know, sir, I can't tell you what it means to be near the woman one loves. She was leaning on the windowsill, staring down into the street. It was as though she might be looking out for some one. I stood, hardly breathing. She turned her head, and saw me. Her eyes were strange. They seemed to ask me a question. But I couldn't have spoken for the world. I can't tell you what I felt—I dared not speak, or think, or hope. I have been in nineteen battles—several times in positions of some danger, when the lifting of a finger perhaps meant death; but I have never felt what I was feeling at that moment. I knew something was coming; and I was paralysed with terror lest it should not come!" He drew a long breath.

"The servant came in with a light and broke the spell. All that night I lay awake and thought of how she had looked at me, with the colour coming slowly up in her cheeks—

"It was three days before I plucked up courage to go again; and then I felt her eyes on me at once—she was making a 'cat's cradle' with a bit of string, but I could see them stealing up from her hands to my face. And she went wandering about the room, fingering at everything. When her father called out: 'What's the matter with you, Elie?' she stared at him like a child caught doing wrong. I looked straight at her then, she tried to look at me, but she couldn't; and a minute later she went out of the room. God knows what sort of nonsense I talked—I was too happy.

"Then began our love. I can't tell you of that time. Often and often Dalton said to me: 'What's come to the child? Nothing I can do pleases her.' All the love she had given him was now for me; but he was too simple and straight to see what was going on. How many times haven't I felt criminal towards him! But when you're happy, with the tide in your favour, you become a coward at once...."

V

"Well, sir," he went on, "we were married on her eighteenth birthday. It was a long time before Dalton became aware of our love. But one day he said to me with a very grave look:

"'Eilie has told me, Brune; I forbid it. She's too young, and you're—too old!' I was then forty-five, my hair as black and thick as a rook's feathers, and I was strong and active. I answered him: 'We shall be married within a month!' We parted in anger. It was a May night, and I walked out far into the country. There's no remedy for anger, or, indeed, for anything, so fine as walking. Once I stopped—it was on a common, without a house or light, and the stars shining like jewels. I was hot from walking, I could feel the blood boiling in my veins—I said to myself 'Old, are you?' And I laughed like a fool. It was the thought of losing her—I wished to believe myself angry, but really I was afraid; fear and anger in me are very much the same. A friend of mine, a bit of a poet, sir, once called them 'the two black wings of self.' And so they are, so they are...! The next morning I went to Dalton again, and somehow I made him yield. I'm not a philosopher, but it has often seemed to me that no benefit can come to us in this life without an equal loss somewhere, but does that stop us? No, sir, not often....

"We were married on the 30th of June 1876, in the parish church. The only people present were Dalton, Lucy, and Lucy's husband—a big, red-faced fellow, with blue eyes and a golden beard parted in two. It had been arranged that we should spend the honeymoon down at their inn on the river. My wife, Dalton and I, went to a restaurant for lunch. She was dressed in grey, the colour of a pigeon's feathers." He paused, leaning forward over the crutch handle of his stick; trying to conjure up, no doubt, that long-ago image of his young bride in her dress "the colour of a pigeon's feathers," with her blue eyes and yellow hair, the little frown between her brows, the firmly shut red lips, opening to speak the words, "For better, for worse, for richer, for poorer, in sickness and in health."

"At that time, sir," he went on suddenly, "I was a bit of a dandy. I wore, I remember, a blue frock-coat, with white trousers, and a grey top hat. Even now I should always prefer to be well dressed....

"We had an excellent lunch, and drank Veuve Clicquot, a wine that you cannot get in these days! Dalton came with us to the railway station. I can't bear partings; and yet, they must come.

"That evening we walked out in the cool under the aspen-trees. What should I remember in all my life if not that night—the young bullocks snuffling in the gateways—the campion flowers all lighted up along the hedges—the moon with a halo-bats, too, in and out among the stems, and the shadows of the cottages as black and soft as that sea down there. For a long time we stood on the river-bank beneath a lime-tree. The scent of the lime flowers! A man can only endure about half his joy; about half his sorrow. Lucy and her husband," he went on, presently, "his name was Frank Tor—a man like an old Viking, who ate nothing but milk, bread, and fruit—were very good to us! It was like Paradise in that inn—though the commissariat, I am bound to say, was limited. The sweetbriar grew round our bedroom windows; when the breeze blew the leaves across the opening—it was like a bath of perfume. Eilie grew as brown as a gipsy while we were there. I don't think any man could have loved her more than I did. But there were times when my heart stood still; it didn't seem as if she understood how much I loved her. One day, I remember, she coaxed me to take her camping. We drifted downstream all the afternoon, and in the evening pulled into the reeds under the willow-boughs and lit a fire for her to cook by—though, as a matter of fact, our provisions were cooked already—but you know how it is; all the romance was in having a real fire. 'We won't pretend,' she kept saying. While we were eating our supper a hare came to our clearing—a big fellow—how surprised he looked! 'The tall hare,' Eilie called him. After that we sat by the ashes and watched the shadows, till at last she roamed away from me. The time went very slowly; I got up to look for her. It was past sundown. I called and called. It was a long time before I found her—and she was like a wild thing, hot and flushed, her pretty frock torn, her hands and face scratched, her hair down, like some beautiful creature of the woods. If one loves, a little thing will scare one. I didn't think she had noticed my fright; but when we got back to the boat she threw her arms round my neck, and said, 'I won't ever leave you again!'

"Once in the night I woke—a water-hen was crying, and in the moonlight a kingfisher flew across. The wonder on the river—the wonder of the moon and trees, the soft bright mist, the stillness! It was like another world, peaceful, enchanted, far holier than ours. It seemed like a vision of the thoughts that come to one—how seldom! and go if one tries to grasp them. Magic—poetry-sacred!" He was silent a minute, then went on in a wistful voice: "I looked at her, sleeping like a child, with her hair loose, and her lips apart, and I thought: 'God do so to me, if ever I bring her pain!' How was I to understand her? the mystery and innocence of her soul! The river has had all my light and all my darkness, the happiest days, and the hours when I've despaired; and I like to think of it, for, you know, in time bitter memories fade, only the good remain.... Yet the good have their own pain, a different kind of aching, for we shall never get them back. Sir," he said, turning to me with a faint smile, "it's no use crying over spilt milk.... In the neighbourhood of Lucy's inn, the Rose and Maybush—Can you imagine a prettier name? I have been all over the world, and nowhere found names so pretty as in the

English country. There, too, every blade of grass; and flower, has a kind of pride about it; knows it will be cared for; and all the roads, trees, and cottages, seem to be certain that they will live for ever.... But I was going to tell you: Half a mile from the inn was a quiet old house which we used to call the 'Convent'—though I believe it was a farm. We spent many afternoons there, trespassing in the orchard—Eilie was fond of trespassing; if there were a long way round across somebody else's property, she would always take it. We spent our last afternoon in that orchard, lying in the long grass. I was reading Childe Harold for the first time—a wonderful, a memorable poem! I was at that passage—the bull-fight—you remember:

"Thrice sounds the clarion; lo! the signal falls,

The din expands, and expectation mute'

—"when suddenly Eilie said: 'Suppose I were to leave off loving you?' It was as if some one had struck me in the face. I jumped up, and tried to take her in my arms, but she slipped away; then she turned, and began laughing softly. I laughed too. I don't know why...."

VI

"We went back to London the next day; we lived quite close to the school, and about five days a week Dalton came to dine with us. He would have come every day, if he had not been the sort of man who refuses to consult his own pleasure. We had more pupils than ever. In my leisure I taught my wife to fence. I have never seen any one so lithe and quick; or so beautiful as she looked in her fencing dress, with embroidered shoes.

"I was completely happy. When a man has obtained his desire he becomes careless and self-satisfied; I was watchful, however, for I knew that I was naturally a selfish man. I studied to arrange my time and save my money, to give her as much pleasure as I could. What she loved best in the world just then was riding. I bought a horse for her, and in the evenings of the spring and summer we rode together; but when it was too dark to go out late, she would ride alone, great distances, sometimes spend the whole day in the saddle, and come back so tired she could hardly walk upstairs—I can't say that I liked that. It made me nervous, she was so headlong—but I didn't think it right to interfere with her. I had a good deal of anxiety about money, for though I worked hard and made more than ever, there never seemed enough. I was anxious to save—I hoped, of course—but we had no child, and this was a trouble to me. She grew more beautiful than ever, and I think was happy. Has it ever struck you that each one of us lives on the edge of a volcano? There is, I imagine, no one who has not some affection or interest so strong that he counts the rest for nothing, beside it. No doubt a man may live his life through without discovering that. But some of us—! I am not complaining; what is—is." He pulled the cap lower over his eyes, and clutched his hands firmly on the top of his stick. He was like a man who rushes his horse at some hopeless fence, unwilling to give himself time, for fear of craning at the last moment. "In the spring of '78, a new pupil came to me, a young man of twenty-one who was destined for the army. I took a fancy to him, and did my best to turn him into a good swordsman; but there was a kind of perverse recklessness in him; for a few minutes one would make a great impression, then he would grow utterly careless. 'Francis,' I would say, 'if I were you I should be ashamed.' 'Mr. Brune,' he would answer, 'why should I be ashamed? I didn't make myself.' God knows, I wish to do him justice, he had a heart—one day he drove up in a cab, and brought in his poor dog, who had been run over, and was dying: For half an hour he shut himself up with its body, we could hear him sobbing like a child; he came out with his eyes all red, and cried: 'I know where to find the brute who drove over him,' and off he rushed. He had beautiful Italian eyes; a slight figure, not very tall; dark hair, a little dark moustache; and his lips were always a trifle parted—it was that, and his walk, and the way he drooped his eyelids, which gave him a peculiar, soft, proud look. I used to tell him that he'd never make a soldier! 'Oh!' he'd answer, 'that'll be all right when the time comes!' He believed in a kind of luck that was to do everything for him, when the time came. One day he came in as I was giving Eilie her lesson. This was the first time they saw each other. After that he came more often, and sometimes stayed to dinner with us. I won't deny, sir, that I was glad to welcome him; I thought it good for Eilie. Can there be anything more odious," he burst out, "than such a self-complacent blindness? There are people who say, 'Poor man, he had such faith!' Faith, sir! Conceit! I was a fool—in this world one pays for folly....

"The summer came; and one Saturday in early June, Eilie, I, and Francis—I won't tell you his other name—went riding. The night had been wet; there was no dust, and presently the sun came out—a glorious day! We rode a long way. About seven o'clock we started back-slowly, for it was still hot, and there was all the cool of night before us. It was nine o'clock when we came to Richmond Park. A grand place, Richmond Park; and in that half-light wonderful, the deer moving so softly, you might have thought they were spirits. We were silent too—great trees have that effect on me....

"Who can say when changes come? Like a shift of the wind, the old passes, the new is on you. I am telling you now of a change like that. Without a sign of warning, Eilie put her horse into a gallop. 'What are you doing?' I shouted. She looked back with a smile, then he dashed past me too. A hornet might have stung them both: they galloped over fallen trees, under low hanging branches, up hill and down. I had to watch that madness! My horse was not so fast. I rode like a demon; but fell far behind. I am not a man who takes things quietly. When I came up with them at last, I could not speak for rage. They were riding side by side, the reins on the horses' necks, looking in each other's faces. 'You should take care,' I said. 'Care!' she cried; 'life is not all taking care!' My anger left me. I dropped behind, as grooms ride behind their mistresses... Jealousy! No torture is so ceaseless or so black.... In those minutes a hundred things came up in me—a hundred memories, true, untrue, what do I know? My soul was poisoned. I tried to reason with myself. It was absurd to think such things! It was unmanly.... Even if it were true, one should try to be a gentleman! But I found myself laughing; yes, sir, laughing at that word." He spoke faster, as if pouring his heart out not to a live listener, but to the night. "I could not sleep that night. To lie near her with those thoughts in my brain was impossible! I made an excuse, and sat up with some papers. The hardest thing in life is to see a thing coming and be able to do nothing to prevent it. What could I do? Have you noticed how people may become utter strangers without a word? It only needs a thought.... The very next day she said: 'I want to go to Lucy's.' 'Alone?' 'Yes.' I had made up my mind by then that she must do just as she wished. Perhaps I acted wrongly;

I do not know what one ought to do in such a case; but before she went I said to her: 'Eilie, what is it?' 'I don't know,' she answered; and I kissed her—that was all.... A month passed; I wrote to her nearly every day, and I had short letters from her, telling me very little of herself. Dalton was a torture to me, for I could not tell him; he had a conviction that she was going to become a mother. 'Ah, Brune!' he said, 'my poor wife was just like that.' Life, sir, is a somewhat ironical affair...! He—I find it hard to speak his name—came to the school two or three times a week. I used to think I saw a change, a purpose growing up through his recklessness; there seemed a violence in him as if he chafed against my blade. I had a kind of joy in feeling I had the mastery, and could toss the iron out of his hand any minute like a straw. I was ashamed, and yet I gloried in it. Jealousy is a low thing, sir—a low, base thing! When he asked me where my wife was, I told him; I was too proud to hide it. Soon after that he came no more to the school.

"One morning, when I could bear it no longer, I wrote, and said I was coming down. I would not force myself on her, but I asked her to meet me in the orchard of the old house we called the Convent. I asked her to be there at four o'clock. It has always been my belief that a man must neither beg anything of a woman, nor force anything from her. Women are generous—they will give you what they can. I sealed my letter, and posted it myself. All the way down I kept on saying to myself, 'She must come—surely she will come!'"

VII

"I was in high spirits, but the next moment trembled like a man with ague. I reached the orchard before my time. She was not there. You know what it is like to wait? I stood still and listened; I went to the point whence I could see farthest; I said to myself, 'A watched pot never boils; if I don't look for her she will come.' I walked up and down with my eyes on the ground. The sickness of it! A hundred times I took out my watch.... Perhaps it was fast, perhaps hers was slow—I can't tell you a thousandth part of my hopes and fears. There was a spring of water, in one corner. I sat beside it, and thought of the last time I had been there—and something seemed to burst in me. It was five o'clock before I lost all hope; there comes a time when you're glad that hope is dead, it means rest. 'That's over,' you say, 'now I can act.' But what was I to do? I lay down with my face to the ground; when one's in trouble, it's the only thing that helps—something to press against and cling to that can't give way. I lay there for two hours, knowing all the time that I should play the coward. At seven o'clock I left the orchard and went towards the inn; I had broken my word, but I felt happy.... I should see her—and, sir, nothing—nothing seemed to matter beside that. Tor was in the garden snipping at his roses. He came up, and I could see that he couldn't look me in the face. 'Where's my wife?' I said. He answered, 'Let's get Lucy.' I ran indoors. Lucy met me with two letters; the first—my own—unopened; and the second, this:

"'I have left you. You were good to me, but now—it is no use.

"EILIE.'"

"She told me that a boy had brought a letter for my wife the day before, from a young gentleman in a boat. When Lucy delivered it she asked, 'Who is he, Miss Eilie? What will Mr. Brune say?' My wife looked at her angrily, but gave her no answer—and all that day she never spoke. In the evening she was gone, leaving this note on the bed.... Lucy cried as if her heart would break. I took her by the shoulders and put her from the room; I couldn't bear the noise. I sat down and tried to think. While I was sitting there Tor came in with a letter. It was written on the notepaper of an inn twelve miles up the river: these were the words.

"'Eilie is mine. I am ready to meet you where you like.'"

He went on with a painful evenness of speech. "When I read those words, I had only one thought—to reach them; I ran down to the river, and chose out the lightest boat. Just as I was starting, Tor came running. 'You dropped this letter, sir,' he said. 'Two pair of arms are better than one.' He came into the boat. I took the sculls and I pulled out into the stream. I pulled like a madman; and that great man, with his bare arms crossed, was like a huge, tawny bull sitting there opposite me. Presently he took my place, and I took the rudder lines. I could see his chest, covered with hair, heaving up and down, it gave me a sort of comfort—it meant that we were getting nearer. Then it grew dark, there was no moon, I could barely see the bank; there's something in the dark which drives one into oneself. People tell you there comes a moment when your nature is decided—'saved' or 'lost' as they call it—for good or evil. That is not true, your self is always with you, and cannot be altered; but, sir, I believe that in a time of agony one finds out what are the things one can do, and what are those one cannot. You get to know yourself, that's all. And so it was with me. Every thought and memory and passion was so clear and strong! I wanted to kill him. I wanted to kill myself. But her—no! We are taught that we possess our wives, body and soul, we are brought up in that faith, we are commanded to believe it—but when I was face to face with it, those words had no meaning; that belief, those commands, they were without meaning to me, they were—vile. Oh yes, I wanted to find comfort in them, I wanted to hold on to them—but I couldn't. You may force a body; how can you force a soul? No, no—cowardly! But I wanted to—I wanted to kill him and force her to come back to me! And then, suddenly, I felt as if I were pressing right on the most secret nerve of my heart. I seemed to see her face, white and quivering, as if I'd stamped my heel on it. They say this world is ruled by force; it may be true—I know I have a weak spot in me.... I couldn't bear it. At last I Jumped to my feet and shouted out, 'Turn the boat round!' Tor looked up at me as if I had gone mad. And I had gone mad. I seized the boat-hook and threatened him; I called him fearful names. 'Sir,' he said, 'I don't take such names from any one!' 'You'll take them from me,' I shouted; 'turn the boat round, you idiot, you hound, you fish!...' I have a terrible temper, a perfect curse to me. He seemed amazed, even frightened; he sat down again suddenly and pulled the boat round. I fell on the seat, and hid my face. I believe the moon came up; there must have been a mist too, for I was cold as death. In this life, sir, we cannot hide our faces—but by degrees the pain of wounds grows less. Some will have it that such blows are mortal; it is not so. Time is merciful.

"In the early morning I went back to London. I had fever on me—and was delirious. I dare say I should have killed myself if I had not been so used to weapons—they and I were too old friends, I suppose—I can't explain. It was a long while before I was up and about. Dalton nursed me through it; his great heavy moustache had grown quite white. We never mentioned her; what was the good? There were things to settle of course, the lawyer—this was unspeakably distasteful to me. I told him it was to be as she wished, but the fellow would come to me, with his—there, I don't want to be unkind. I wished him to say it was my fault, but he said—I remember his smile now—he said, that was impossible, would be seen through, talked of collusion—I don't understand these things, and what's more, I can't bear them, they are—dirty.

"Two years later, when I had come back to London, after the Russo-Turkish war, I received a letter from her. I have it here." He took an old, yellow sheet of paper out of a leathern pocketbook, spread it in his fingers, and sat staring at it. For some minutes he did not speak.

"In the autumn of that same year she died in childbirth. He had deserted her. Fortunately for him, he was killed on the Indian frontier, that very year. If she had lived she would have been thirty-two next June; not a great age.... I know I am what they call a crank; doctors will tell you that you can't be cured of a bad illness, and be the same man again. If you are bent, to force yourself straight must leave you weak in another place. I must and will think well of women—everything done, and everything said against them is a stone on her dead body. Could you sit, and listen to it?" As though driven by his own question, he rose, and paced up and down. He came back to the seat at last.

"That, sir, is the reason of my behaviour this afternoon, and again this evening. You have been so kind, I wanted!—wanted to tell you. She had a little daughter—Lucy has her now. My friend Dalton is dead; there would have been no difficulty about money, but, I am sorry to say, that he was swindled—disgracefully. It fell to me to administer his affairs—he never knew it, but he died penniless; he had trusted some wretched fellows—had an idea they would make his fortune. As I very soon found, they had ruined him. It was impossible to let Lucy—such a dear woman—bear that burden. I have tried to make provision; but, you see," he took hold of my sleeve, "I, too, have not been fortunate; in fact, it's difficult to save a great deal out of L 190 a year; but the capital is perfectly safe—and I get L 47, 10s. a quarter, paid on the nail. I have often been tempted to reinvest at a greater rate of interest, but I've never dared. Anyway, there are no debts—I've been obliged to make a rule not to buy what I couldn't pay for on the spot.... Now I am really plaguing you—but I wanted to tell you—in case—anything should happen to me." He seemed to take a sudden scare, stiffened, twisted his moustache, and muttering, "Your great kindness! Shall never forget!" turned hurriedly away.

He vanished; his footsteps, and the tap of his stick grew fainter and fainter. They died out. He was gone. Suddenly I got up and hastened after him. I soon stopped—what was there to say?

VIII

The following day I was obliged to go to Nice, and did not return till midnight. The porter told me that Jules le Ferrier had been to see me. The next morning, while I was still in bed, the door was opened, and Jules appeared. His face was very pale; and the moment he stood still drops of perspiration began coursing down his cheeks.

"Georges!" he said, "he is dead. There, there! How stupid you look! My man is packing. I have half an hour before the train; my evidence shall come from Italy. I have done my part, the rest is for you. Why did you have that dinner? The Don Quixote! The idiot! The poor man! Don't move! Have you a cigar? Listen! When you followed him, I followed the other two. My infernal curiosity! Can you conceive a greater folly? How fast they walked, those two! feeling their cheeks, as if he had struck them both, you know; it was funny. They soon saw me, for their eyes were all round about their heads; they had the mark of a glove on their cheeks." The colour began to come back, into Jules's face; he gesticulated with his cigar and became more and more dramatic. "They waited for me. 'Tiens!' said one, 'this gentleman was with him. My friend's name is M. Le Baron de——. The man who struck him was an odd-looking person; kindly inform me whether it is possible for my friend to meet him?' Eh!" commented Jules, "he was offensive! Was it for me to give our dignity away? 'Perfectly, monsieur!' I answered. 'In that case,' he said, 'please give me his name and address.... I could not remember his name, and as for the address, I never knew it...! I reflected. 'That,' I said, 'I am unable to do, for special reasons.' 'Aha!' he said, 'reasons that will prevent our fighting him, I suppose? 'On the contrary,' I said. 'I will convey your request to him; I may mention that I have heard he is the best swordsman and pistol-shot in Europe. Good-night!' I wished to give them something to dream of, you understand.... Patience, my dear! Patience! I was, coming to you, but I thought I would let them sleep on it—there was plenty of time! But yesterday morning I came into the Place, and there he was on the bench, with a big dog. I declare to you he blushed like a young girl. 'Sir,' he said, 'I was hoping to meet you; last evening I made a great disturbance. I took an unpardonable liberty'—and he put in my hand an envelope. My friend, what do you suppose it contained—a pair of gloves! Senor Don Punctilioso, hein? He was the devil, this friend of yours; he fascinated me with his gentle eyes and his white moustachettes, his humility, his flames—poor man...! I told him I had been asked to take him a challenge. 'If anything comes of it,' I said, 'make use of me!' 'Is that so?' he said. 'I am most grateful for your kind offer. Let me see—it is so long since I fought a duel. The sooner it's over the better. Could you arrange to-morrow morning? Weapons? Yes; let them choose.' You see, my friend, there was no hanging back here; nous voila en train."

Jules took out his watch. "I have sixteen minutes. It is lucky for you that you were away yesterday, or you would be in my shoes now. I fixed the place, right hand of the road to Roquebrune, just by the railway cutting, and the time—five-thirty of the morning. It was arranged that I should call for him. Disgusting hour; I have not been up so early since I fought Jacques Tirbaut in '85. At five o'clock I found him ready and drinking tea with rum in it—singular man! he made me have some too, brrr! He was shaved, and dressed in that old frock-coat. His great dog jumped into the carriage, but he bade her get out, took her paws on his shoulders, and whispered in her ear some Italian words; a charm, hein! and back she went, the tail between the legs. We drove slowly, so as not to shake his arm. He was more gay than I. All the way he talked to me of you: how kind you were! how good you had been to him! 'You do not speak of yourself!' I said. 'Have you no friends, nothing to say? Sometimes an accident will happen!' 'Oh!' he answered, 'there is no danger; but if by any chance—well, there is a letter in my pocket.' 'And if you should kill him?' I said. 'But I shall not,' he answered slyly: 'do you think I am going to fire at him? No, no; he is too young.' 'But,' I said, 'I—'I am not going to stand that!' 'Yes,' he replied, 'I owe him a shot; but there is no danger—not the least danger.' We had arrived; already they were there. Ah bah! You know the preliminaries, the politeness—this duelling, you know, it is absurd, after all. We placed them at twenty paces. It is not a bad place. There are pine-trees round, and rocks; at that hour it was cool and grey as a church. I handed him the pistol. How can I describe him to you, standing there, smoothing the barrel with his fingers! 'What a beautiful thing a good pistol!' he said. 'Only a fool or a madman throws away his life,' I said. 'Certainly,' he replied, 'certainly; but there is no danger,' and he regarded me, raising his moustachette.

"There they stood then, back to back, with the mouths of their pistols to the sky. 'Un!' I cried, 'deux! tirez!' They turned, I saw the smoke of his shot go straight up like a prayer; his pistol dropped. I ran to him. He looked surprised, put out his hand, and fell into my arms. He was dead. Those fools came running up. 'What is it?' cried one. I made him a bow. 'As you see,' I said; 'you have made a pretty shot. My friend fired in the air. Messieurs, you had better breakfast in Italy.' We carried him to the carriage, and covered him with a rug; the others drove for the frontier. I brought him to his room. Here is his letter." Jules stopped; tears were running down his face. "He is dead; I have closed his eyes. Look here, you know, we are all of us cads—it is the rule; but this—this, perhaps, was the exception." And without another word he rushed away....

Outside the old fellow's lodging a dismounted cocher was standing disconsolate in the sun. "How was I to know they were going to fight a duel?" he burst out on seeing me. "He had white hair—I call you to witness he had white hair. This is bad for me: they will ravish my licence. Aha! you will see—this is bad for me!" I gave him the slip and found my way upstairs. The old fellow was alone, lying on the bed, his feet covered with a rug as if he might feel cold; his eyes were closed, but in this sleep of death, he still had that air of faint surprise. At full length, watching the bed intently, Freda lay, as she lay nightly when he was really asleep. The shutters were half open; the room still smelt slightly of rum. I stood for a long time looking at the face: the little white fans of moustache brushed upwards even in death, the hollows in his cheeks, the quiet of his figure; he was like some old knight.... The dog broke the spell. She sat up, and resting her paws on the bed, licked his face. I went downstairs—I couldn't bear to hear her howl. This was his letter to me, written in a pointed handwriting:

"MY DEAR SIR,—Should you read this, I shall be gone. I am ashamed to trouble you—a man should surely manage so as not to give trouble; and yet I believe you will not consider me importunate. If, then, you will pick up the pieces of an old fellow, I ask you to have my sword, the letter enclosed in this, and the photograph that stands on the stove buried with me. My will and the acknowledgments of my property are between the leaves of the Byron in my tin chest; they should go to Lucy Tor—address thereon. Perhaps you will do me the honour to retain for yourself any of my books that may give you pleasure. In the Pilgrim's Progress you will find some excellent recipes for Turkish coffee, Italian and Spanish dishes, and washing wounds. The landlady's daughter speaks Italian, and she would, I know, like to have Freda; the poor dog will miss me. I have read of old Indian warriors taking their horses and dogs with them to the happy hunting-grounds. Freda would come—noble animals are dogs! She eats once a day—a good large meal—and requires much salt. If you have animals of your own, sir, don't forget—all animals require salt. I have no debts, thank God! The money in my pockets would bury me decently—not that there is any danger. And I am ashamed to weary you with details—the least a man can do is not to make a fuss—and yet he must be found ready.—Sir, with profound gratitude, your servant,

"ROGER BRUNE."

Everything was as he had said. The photograph on the stove was that of a young girl of nineteen or twenty, dressed in an old-fashioned style, with hair gathered backward in a knot. The eyes gazed at you with a little frown, the lips were tightly closed; the expression of the face was eager, quick, wilful, and, above all, young.

The tin trunk was scented with dry fragments of some herb, the history of which in that trunk man knoweth not.... There were a few clothes, but very few, all older than those he usually wore. Besides the Byron and Pilgrim's Progress were Scott's Quentin Durward, Captain Marryat's Midshipman

Easy, a pocket Testament, and a long and frightfully stiff book on the art of fortifying towns, much thumbed, and bearing date 1863. By far the most interesting thing I found, however, was a diary, kept down to the preceding Christmas. It was a pathetic document, full of calculations of the price of meals; resolutions to be careful over this or that; doubts whether he must not give up smoking; sentences of fear that Freda had not enough to eat. It appeared that he had tried to live on ninety pounds a year, and send the other hundred pounds home to Lucy for the child; in this struggle he was always failing, having to send less than the amount—the entries showed that this was a nightmare to him. The last words, written on Christmas Day, were these "What is the use of writing this, since it records nothing but failure!"

The landlady's daughter and myself were at the funeral. The same afternoon I went into the concert-room, where I had spoken to him first. When I came out Freda was lying at the entrance, looking into the faces of every one that passed, and sniffing idly at their heels. Close by the landlady's daughter hovered, a biscuit in her hand, and a puzzled, sorry look on her face.

September 1900.

SALVATION OF A FORSYTE

I

Swithin Forsyte lay in bed. The corners of his mouth under his white moustache drooped towards his double chin. He panted:

"My doctor says I'm in a bad way, James."

His twin-brother placed his hand behind his ear. "I can't hear you. They tell me I ought to take a cure. There's always a cure wanted for something. Emily had a cure."

Swithin replied: "You mumble so. I hear my man, Adolph. I trained him.... You ought to have an ear-trumpet. You're getting very shaky, James."

There was silence; then James Forsyte, as if galvanised, remarked: "I s'pose you've made your will. I s'pose you've left your money to the family; you've nobody else to leave it to. There was Danson died the other day, and left his money to a hospital."

The hairs of Swithin's white moustache bristled. "My fool of a doctor told me to make my will," he said, "I hate a fellow who tells you to make your will. My appetite's good; I ate a partridge last night. I'm all the better for eating. He told me to leave off champagne! I eat a good breakfast. I'm not eighty. You're the same age, James. You look very shaky."

James Forsyte said: "You ought to have another opinion. Have Blank; he's the first man now. I had him for Emily; cost me two hundred guineas. He sent her to Homburg; that's the first place now. The Prince was there—everybody goes there."

Swithin Forsyte answered: "I don't get any sleep at night, now I can't get out; and I've bought a new carriage—gave a pot of money for it. D' you ever have bronchitis? They tell me champagne's dangerous; it's my belief I couldn't take a better thing."

James Forsyte rose.

"You ought to have another opinion. Emily sent her love; she would have come in, but she had to go to Niagara. Everybody goes there; it's the place now. Rachel goes every morning: she overdoes it—she'll be laid up one of these days. There's a fancy ball there to-night; the Duke gives the prizes."

Swithin Forsyte said angrily: "I can't get things properly cooked here; at the club I get spinach decently done." The bed-clothes jerked at the tremor of his legs.

James Forsyte replied: "You must have done well with Tintos; you must have made a lot of money by them. Your ground-rents must be falling in, too. You must have any amount you don't know what to do with." He mouthed the words, as if his lips were watering.

Swithin Forsyte glared. "Money!" he said; "my doctor's bill's enormous."

James Forsyte stretched out a cold, damp hand "Goodbye! You ought to have another opinion. I can't keep the horses waiting: they're a new pair—stood me in three hundred. You ought to take care of yourself. I shall speak to Blank about you. You ought to have him—everybody says he's the first man. Good-bye!"

Swithin Forsyte continued to stare at the ceiling. He thought: 'A poor thing, James! a selfish beggar! Must be worth a couple of hundred thousand!' He wheezed, meditating on life....

He was ill and lonely. For many years he had been lonely, and for two years ill; but as he had smoked his first cigar, so he would live his life-stoutly, to its predestined end. Every day he was driven to the club; sitting forward on the spring cushions of a single brougham, his hands on his knees, swaying a little, strangely solemn. He ascended the steps into that marble hall—the folds of his chin wedged into the aperture of his collar—walking squarely with a stick. Later he would dine, eating majestically, and savouring his food, behind a bottle of champagne set in an ice-pail—his waistcoat defended by a napkin, his eyes rolling a little or glued in a stare on the waiter. Never did he suffer his head or back to droop, for it was not distinguished so to do.

Because he was old and deaf, he spoke to no one; and no one spoke to him. The club gossip, an Irishman, said to each newcomer: "Old Forsyte! Look at 'um! Must ha' had something in his life to sour 'um!" But Swithin had had nothing in his life to sour him.

For many days now he had lain in bed in a room exuding silver, crimson, and electric light, smelling of opopanax and of cigars. The curtains were drawn, the firelight gleamed; on a table by his bed were a jug of barley-water and the Times. He made an attempt to read, failed, and fell again to thinking. His face with its square chin, looked like a block of pale leather bedded in the pillow. It was lonely! A woman in the room would have made all the difference! Why had he never married? He breathed hard, staring froglike at the ceiling; a memory had come into his mind. It was a long time ago—forty odd years—but it seemed like yesterday....

It happened when he was thirty-eight, for the first and only time in his life travelling on the Continent, with his twin-brother James and a man named Traquair. On the way from Germany to Venice, he had found himself at the Hotel Goldene Alp at Salzburg. It was late August, and weather for the gods: sunshine on the walls and the shadows of the vine-leaves, and at night, the moonlight, and again on the walls the shadows of the vine-leaves. Averse to the suggestions of other people, Swithin had refused to visit the Citadel; he had spent the day alone in the window of his bedroom, smoking a succession of cigars, and disparaging the appearance of the passers-by. After dinner he was driven by boredom into the streets. His chest puffed out like a pigeon's, and with something of a pigeon's cold and inquiring eye, he strutted, annoyed at the frequency of uniforms, which seemed to him both needless and offensive. His spleen rose at this crowd of foreigners, who spoke an unintelligible language, wore hair on their faces, and smoked bad tobacco. 'A queer lot!' he thought. The sound of music from a cafe attracted him; he walked in, vaguely moved by a wish for the distinction of adventure, without the trouble which adventure usually brought with it; spurred too, perhaps, by an after-dinner demon. The cafe was the bier-halle of the 'Fifties, with a door at either end, and lighted by a large wooden lantern. On a small dais three musicians were fiddling. Solitary men, or groups, sat at some dozen tables, and the waiters hurried about replenishing glasses; the air was thick with smoke. Swithin sat down. "Wine!" he said sternly. The astonished waiter brought him wine. Swithin pointed to a beer glass on the table. "Here!" he said, with the same ferocity. The waiter poured out the wine. 'Ah!' thought Swithin, 'they can understand if they like.' A group of officers close by were laughing; Swithin stared at them uneasily. A hollow cough sounded almost in his ear. To his left a man sat reading, with his elbows on the corners of a journal, and his gaunt shoulders raised almost to his eyes. He had a thin, long nose, broadening suddenly at the nostrils; a black-brown beard, spread in a savage fan over his chest; what was visible of the face was the colour of old parchment. A strange, wild, haughty-looking creature! Swithin observed his clothes with some displeasure—they were the clothes of a journalist or strolling actor. And yet he was impressed. This was singular. How could he be impressed by a fellow in such clothes! The man reached out a hand, covered with black hairs, and took up a tumbler that contained a dark-coloured fluid. 'Brandy!' thought Swithin. The crash of a falling chair startled him—his neighbour had risen. He was of immense height, and very thin; his great beard seemed to splash away from his mouth; he was glaring at the group of officers, and speaking. Swithin made out two words: "Hunde! Deutsche Hunde!" 'Hounds! Dutch hounds!' he thought: 'Rather strong!' One of the officers had jumped up, and now drew his sword. The tall man swung his chair up, and brought it down with a thud. Everybody round started up and closed on him. The tall man cried out, "To me, Magyars!"

Swithin grinned. The tall man fighting such odds excited his unwilling admiration; he had a momentary impulse to go to his assistance. 'Only get a broken nose!' he thought, and looked for a safe corner. But at that moment a thrown lemon struck him on the jaw. He jumped out of his chair and rushed at the officers. The Hungarian, swinging his chair, threw him a look of gratitude—Swithin glowed with momentary admiration of himself. A sword blade grazed his—arm; he felt a sudden dislike of the Hungarian. 'This is too much,' he thought, and, catching up a chair, flung it at the wooden lantern. There was a crash—faces and swords vanished. He struck a match, and by the light of it bolted for the door. A second later he was in the street.

II

A voice said in English, "God bless you, brother!"

Swithin looked round, and saw the tall Hungarian holding out his hand. He took it, thinking, 'What a fool I've been!' There was something in the Hungarian's gesture which said, "You are worthy of me!"

It was annoying, but rather impressive. The man seemed even taller than before; there was a cut on his cheek, the blood from which was trickling down his beard. "You English!" he said. "I saw you stone Haynau—I saw you cheer Kossuth. The free blood of your people cries out to us." He looked at Swithin. "You are a big man, you have a big soul—and strong, how you flung them down! Ha!" Swithin had an impulse to take to his heels. "My name," said the Hungarian, "is Boleskey. You are my friend." His English was good.

'Bulsh-kai-ee, Burlsh-kai-ee,' thought Swithin; 'what a devil of a name!' "Mine," he said sulkily, "is Forsyte."

The Hungarian repeated it.

"You've had a nasty jab on the cheek," said Swithin; the sight of the matted beard was making him feel sick. The Hungarian put his fingers to his cheek, brought them away wet, stared at them, then with an indifferent air gathered a wisp of his beard and crammed it against the cut.

"Ugh!" said Swithin. "Here! Take my handkerchief!"

The Hungarian bowed. "Thank you!" he said; "I couldn't think of it! Thank you a thousand times!"

"Take it!" growled Swithin; it seemed to him suddenly of the first importance. He thrust the handkerchief into the Hungarian's hand, and felt a pain in his arm. 'There!' he thought, 'I've strained a muscle.'

The Hungarian kept muttering, regardless of passers-by, "Swine! How you threw them over! Two or three cracked heads, anyway—the cowardly swine!"

"Look here!" said Swithin suddenly; "which is my way to the Goldene Alp?"

The Hungarian replied, "But you are coming with me, for a glass of wine?"

Swithin looked at the ground. 'Not if I know it!' he thought.

"Ah!" said the Hungarian with dignity, "you do not wish for my friendship!"

'Touchy beggar!' thought Swithin. "Of course," he stammered, "if you put it in that way—"

The Hungarian bowed, murmuring, "Forgive me!"

They had not gone a dozen steps before a youth, with a beardless face and hollow cheeks, accosted them. "For the love of Christ, gentlemen," he said, "help me!"

"Are you a German?" asked Boleskey.

"Yes," said the youth.

"Then you may rot!"

"Master, look here!" Tearing open his coat, the youth displayed his skin, and a leather belt drawn tight round it. Again Swithin felt that desire to take to his heels. He was filled with horrid forebodings—a sense of perpending intimacy with things such as no gentleman had dealings with.

The Hungarian crossed himself. "Brother," he said to the youth, "come you in!"

Swithin looked at them askance, and followed. By a dim light they groped their way up some stairs into a large room, into which the moon was shining through a window bulging over the street. A lamp burned low; there was a smell of spirits and tobacco, with a faint, peculiar scent, as of rose leaves. In one corner stood a czymbal, in another a great pile of newspapers. On the wall hung some old-fashioned pistols, and a rosary of yellow beads. Everything was tidily arranged, but dusty. Near an open fireplace was a table with the remains of a meal. The ceiling, floor, and walls were all of dark wood. In spite of the strange disharmony, the room had a sort of refinement. The Hungarian took a bottle out of a cupboard and, filling some glasses, handed one to Swithin. Swithin put it gingerly to his nose. 'You never know your luck! Come!' he thought, tilting it slowly into his mouth. It was thick, too sweet, but of a fine flavour.

"Brothers!" said the Hungarian, refilling, "your healths!"

The youth tossed off his wine. And Swithin this time did the same; he pitied this poor devil of a youth now. "Come round to-morrow!" he said, "I'll give you a shirt or two." When the youth was gone, however, he remembered with relief that he had not given his address.

'Better so,' he reflected. 'A humbug, no doubt.'

"What was that you said to him?" he asked of the Hungarian.

"I said," answered Boleskey, "'You have eaten and drunk; and now you are my enemy!'"

"Quite right!" said Swithin, "quite right! A beggar is every man's enemy."

"You do not understand," the Hungarian replied politely. "While he was a beggar—I, too, have had to beg" (Swithin thought, 'Good God! this is awful!'., "but now that he is no longer hungry, what is he but a German? No Austrian dog soils my floors!"

His nostrils, as it seemed to Swithin, had distended in an unpleasant fashion; and a wholly unnecessary raucousness invaded his voice. "I am an exile—all of my blood are exiles. Those Godless dogs!" Swithin hurriedly assented.

As he spoke, a face peeped in at the door.

"Rozsi!" said the Hungarian. A young girl came in. She was rather short, with a deliciously round figure and a thick plait of hair. She smiled, and showed her even teeth; her little, bright, wide-set grey eyes glanced from one man to the other. Her face was round, too, high in the cheekbones, the colour of wild roses, with brows that had a twist-up at the corners. With a gesture of alarm, she put her hand to her cheek, and called, "Margit!" An older girl appeared, taller, with fine shoulders, large eyes, a pretty mouth, and what Swithin described to himself afterwards as a "pudding" nose. Both girls, with little cooing sounds, began attending to their father's face.

Swithin turned his back to them. His arm pained him.

'This is what comes of interfering,' he thought sulkily; 'I might have had my neck broken!' Suddenly a soft palm was placed in his, two eyes, half-fascinated, half-shy, looked at him; then a voice called, "Rozsi!" the door was slammed, he was alone again with the Hungarian, harassed by a sense of soft disturbance.

"Your daughter's name is Rosy?" he said; "we have it in England—from rose, a flower."

"Rozsi (Rozgi)," the Hungarian replied; "your English is a hard tongue, harder than French, German, or Czechish, harder than Russian, or Roumanian—I know no more."

"What?" said Swithin, "six languages?" Privately he thought, 'He knows how to lie, anyway.'

"If you lived in a country like mine," muttered the Hungarian, "with all men's hands against you! A free people—dying—but not dead!"

Swithin could not imagine what he was talking of. This man's face, with its linen bandage, gloomy eyes, and great black wisps of beard, his fierce mutterings, and hollow cough, were all most unpleasant. He seemed to be suffering from some kind of mental dog-bite. His emotion indeed appeared so indecent, so uncontrolled and open, that its obvious sincerity produced a sort of awe in Swithin. It was like being forced to look into a furnace. Boleskey stopped roaming up and down. "You think it's over?" he said; "I tell you, in the breast of each one of us Magyars there is a hell. What is sweeter than life? What is more sacred than each breath we draw? Ah! my country!" These words were uttered so slowly, with such intense mournfulness, that Swithin's jaw relaxed; he converted the movement to a yawn.

"Tell me," said Boleskey, "what would you do if the French conquered you?"

Swithin smiled. Then suddenly, as though something had hurt him, he grunted, "The 'Froggies'. Let 'em try!"

"Drink!" said Boleskey—"there is nothing like it"; he filled Swithin's glass. "I will tell you my story."

Swithin rose hurriedly. "It's late," he said. "This is good stuff, though; have you much of it?"

"It is the last bottle."

"What?" said Swithin; "and you gave it to a beggar?"

"My name is Boleskey—Stefan," the Hungarian said, raising his head; "of the Komorn Boleskeys." The simplicity of this phrase—as who shall say: What need of further description?—made an impression on Swithin; he stopped to listen. Boleskey's story went on and on. "There were many abuses," boomed his deep voice, "much wrong done—much cowardice. I could see clouds gathering—rolling over our plains. The Austrian wished to strangle the breath of our mouths—to take from us the shadow of our liberty—the shadow—all we had. Two years ago—the year of '48, when every man and boy answered the great voice—brother, a dog's life!—to use a pen when all of your blood are fighting, but it was decreed for me! My son was killed; my brothers taken—and myself was thrown out like a dog—I had written out my heart, I had written out all the blood that was in my body!" He seemed to tower, a gaunt shadow of a man, with gloomy, flickering eyes staring at the wall.

Swithin rose, and stammered, "Much obliged—very interesting." Boleskey made no effort to detain him, but continued staring at the wall. "Good-night!" said Swithin, and stamped heavily downstairs.

III

When at last Swithin reached the Goldene Alp, he found his brother and friend standing uneasily at the door. Traquair, a prematurely dried-up man, with whiskers and a Scotch accent, remarked, "Ye're airly, man!" Swithin growled something unintelligible, and swung up to bed. He discovered a slight cut on his arm. He was in a savage temper—the elements had conspired to show him things he did not want to see; yet now and then a memory of Rozsi, of her soft palm in his, a sense of having been stroked and flattered, came over him. During breakfast next morning his brother and Traquair announced their intention of moving on. James Forsyte, indeed, remarked that it was no place for a "collector," since all the "old" shops were in the hands of Jews or very grasping persons—he had discovered this at once. Swithin pushed his cup aside. "You may do what you like," he said, "I'm staying here."

James Forsyte replied, tumbling over his own words: "Why! what do you want to stay here for? There's nothing for you to do here—there's nothing to see here, unless you go up the Citadel, an' you won't do that."

Swithin growled, "Who says so?" Having gratified his perversity, he felt in a better temper. He had slung his arm in a silk sash, and accounted for it by saying he had slipped. Later he went out and walked on to the bridge. In the brilliant sunshine spires were glistening against the pearly background of the hills; the town had a clean, joyous air. Swithin glanced at the Citadel and thought, 'Looks a strong place! Shouldn't wonder if it were impregnable!' And this for some occult reason gave him pleasure. It occurred to him suddenly to go and look for the Hungarian's house.

About noon, after a hunt of two hours, he was gazing about him blankly, pale with heat, but more obstinate than ever, when a voice above him called, "Mister!" He looked up and saw Rozsi. She was leaning her round chin on her round hand, gazing down at him with her deepset, clever eyes. When Swithin removed his hat, she clapped her hands. Again he had the sense of being admired, caressed. With a careless air, that sat grotesquely on his tall square person, he walked up to the door; both girls stood in the passage. Swithin felt a confused desire to speak in some foreign tongue. "Maam'selles," he began, "er—bong jour-er, your father—pare, comment?"

"We also speak English," said the elder girl; "will you come in, please?"

Swithin swallowed a misgiving, and entered. The room had a worn appearance by daylight, as if it had always been the nest of tragic or vivid lives. He sat down, and his eyes said: "I am a stranger, but don't try to get the better of me, please—that is impossible." The girls looked at him in silence.

Rozsi wore a rather short skirt of black stuff, a white shirt, and across her shoulders an embroidered yoke; her sister was dressed in dark green, with a coral necklace; both girls had their hair in plaits. After a minute Rozsi touched the sleeve of his hurt arm.

"It's nothing!" muttered Swithin.

"Father fought with a chair, but you had no chair," she said in a wondering voice.

He doubled the fist of his sound arm and struck a blow at space. To his amazement she began to laugh. Nettled at this, he put his hand beneath the heavy table and lifted it. Rozsi clapped her hands. "Ah I now I see—how strong you are!" She made him a curtsey and whisked round to the window. He found the quick intelligence of her eyes confusing; sometimes they seemed to look beyond him at something invisible—this, too, confused him. From Margit he learned that they had been two years in England, where their father had made his living by teaching languages; they had now been a year in Salzburg.

"We wait," suddenly said Rozsi; and Margit, with a solemn face, repeated, "We wait."

Swithin's eyes swelled a little with his desire to see what they were waiting for. How queer they were, with their eyes that gazed beyond him! He looked at their figures. 'She would pay for dressing,' he thought, and he tried to imagine Rozsi in a skirt with proper flounces, a thin waist, and hair drawn back over her ears. She would pay for dressing, with that supple figure, fluffy hair, and little hands! And instantly his own hands, face, and clothes disturbed him. He got up, examined the pistols on the wall, and felt resentment at the faded, dusty room. 'Smells like a pot-house!' he thought. He sat down again close to Rozsi.

"Do you love to dance?" she asked; "to dance is to live. First you hear the music—how your feet itch! It is wonderful! You begin slow, quick—quicker; you fly—you know nothing—your feet are in the air. It is wonderful!"

A slow flush had mounted into Swithin's face.

"Ah!" continued Rozsi, her eyes fixed on him, "when I am dancing—out there I see the plains—your feet go one—two—three—quick, quick, quick, quicker—you fly."

She stretched herself, a shiver seemed to pass all down her. "Margit! dance!" and, to Swithin's consternation, the two girls—their hands on each other's shoulders—began shuffling their feet and swaying to and fro. Their heads were thrown back, their eyes half-closed; suddenly the step quickened, they swung to one side, then to the other, and began whirling round in front of him. The sudden fragrance of rose leaves enveloped him. Round they flew again. While they were still dancing, Boleskey came into the room. He caught Swithin by both hands.

"Brother, welcome! Ah! your arm is hurt! I do not forget." His yellow face and deep-set eyes expressed a dignified gratitude. "Let me introduce to you my friend Baron Kasteliz."

Swithin bowed to a man with a small forehead, who had appeared softly, and stood with his gloved hands touching his waist. Swithin conceived a sudden aversion for this catlike man. About Boleskey there was that which made contempt impossible—the sense of comradeship begotten in the fight; the man's height; something lofty and savage in his face; and an obscure instinct that it would not pay to show distaste; but this Kasteliz, with his neat jaw, low brow, and velvety, volcanic look, excited his proper English animosity. "Your friends are mine," murmured Kasteliz. He spoke with suavity, and hissed his s's. A long, vibrating twang quavered through the room. Swithin turned and saw Rozsi sitting at the czymbal; the notes rang under the little hammers in her hands, incessant, metallic, rising and falling with that strange melody. Kasteliz had fixed his glowing eyes on her; Boleskey, nodding his head, was staring at the floor; Margit, with a pale face, stood like a statue.

'What can they see in it?' thought Swithin; 'it's not a tune.' He took up his hat. Rozsi saw him and stopped; her lips had parted with a faintly dismayed expression. His sense of personal injury diminished; he even felt a little sorry for her. She jumped up from her seat and twirled round with a pout. An inspiration seized on Swithin. "Come and dine with me," he said to Boleskey, "to-morrow—the Goldene Alp—bring your friend." He felt the eyes of the whole room on him—the Hungarian's fine eyes; Margit's wide glance; the narrow, hot gaze of Kasteliz; and lastly—Rozsi's. A glow of satisfaction ran down his spine. When he emerged into the street he thought gloomily, 'Now I've done it!' And not for some paces did he look round; then, with a forced smile, turned and removed his hat to the faces at the window.

Notwithstanding this moment of gloom, however, he was in an exalted state all day, and at dinner kept looking at his brother and Traquair enigmatically. 'What do they know of life?' he thought; 'they might be here a year and get no farther.' He made jokes, and pinned the menu to the waiter's coat-tails. "I like this place," he said, "I shall spend three weeks here." James, whose lips were on the point of taking in a plum, looked at him uneasily.

IV

On the day of the dinner Swithin suffered a good deal. He reflected gloomily on Boleskey's clothes. He had fixed an early hour—there would be fewer people to see them. When the time approached he attired himself with a certain neat splendour, and though his arm was still sore, left off the sling....

Nearly three hours afterwards he left the Goldene Alp between his guests. It was sunset, and along the riverbank the houses stood out, unsoftened by the dusk; the streets were full of people hurrying home. Swithin had a hazy vision of empty bottles, of the ground before his feet, and the accessibility of all the world. Dim recollections of the good things he had said, of his brother and Traquair seated in the background eating ordinary meals with inquiring, acid visages, caused perpetual smiles to break out on his face, and he steered himself stubbornly, to prove that he was a better man than either of his guests. He knew, vaguely, that he was going somewhere with an object; Rozsi's face kept dancing before him, like a promise. Once or twice he gave Kasteliz a glassy stare. Towards Boleskey, on the other hand, he felt quite warm, and recalled with admiration the way he had set his glass down empty, time after time. 'I like to see him take his liquor,' he thought; 'the fellow's a gentleman, after all.' Boleskey strode on, savagely inattentive to everything; and Kasteliz had become more like a cat than ever. It was nearly dark when they reached a narrow street close to the cathedral. They stopped at a door held open by an old woman. The change from the fresh air to a heated corridor, the noise of the door closed behind him, the old woman's anxious glances, sobered Swithin.

"I tell her," said Boleskey, "that I reply for you as for my son."

Swithin was angry. What business had this man to reply for him!

They passed into a large room, crowded with men and women; Swithin noticed that they all looked at him. He stared at them in turn—they seemed of all classes, some in black coats or silk dresses, others in the clothes of work-people; one man, a cobbler, still wore his leather apron, as if he had rushed there straight from his work. Laying his hand on Swithin's arm, Boleskey evidently began explaining who he was; hands were extended, people beyond reach bowed to him. Swithin acknowledged the greetings with a stiff motion of his head; then seeing other people dropping into seats, he, too, sat down. Some one whispered his name—Margit and Rozsi were just behind him.

"Welcome!" said Margit; but Swithin was looking at Rozsi. Her face was so alive and quivering! 'What's the excitement all about?' he thought. 'How pretty she looks!' She blushed, drew in her hands with a quick tense movement, and gazed again beyond him into the room. 'What is it?' thought Swithin; he had a longing to lean back and kiss her lips. He tried angrily to see what she was seeing in those faces turned all one way.

Boleskey rose to speak. No one moved; not a sound could be heard but the tone of his deep voice. On and on he went, fierce and solemn, and with the rise of his voice, all those faces—fair or swarthy—seemed to be glowing with one and the same feeling. Swithin felt the white heat in those faces—it was not decent! In that whole speech he only understood the one word—"Magyar" which came again and again. He almost dozed off at last. The twang of a czymbal woke him. 'What?' he thought, 'more of that infernal music!' Margit, leaning over him, whispered: "Listen! Racoczy! It is forbidden!" Swithin saw that Rozsi was no longer in her seat; it was she who was striking those forbidden notes. He looked round—everywhere the same unmoving faces, the same entrancement, and fierce stillness. The music sounded muffled, as if it, too, were bursting its heart in silence. Swithin felt within him a touch of panic. Was this a den of tigers? The way these people listened, the ferocity of their stillness, was frightful...! He gripped his chair and broke into a perspiration; was there no chance to get away? 'When it stops,' he thought, 'there'll be a rush!' But there was only a greater silence. It flashed across him that any hostile person coming in then would be torn to pieces. A woman sobbed. The whole thing was beyond words unpleasant. He rose, and edged his way furtively towards the doorway. There was a cry of "Police!" The whole crowd came pressing after him. Swithin would soon have been out, but a little behind he caught sight of Rozsi swept off her feet. Her frightened eyes angered him. 'She doesn't deserve it,' he thought sulkily; 'letting all this loose!' and forced his way back to her. She clung to him, and a fever went stealing through his veins; he butted forward at the crowd, holding her tight. When they were outside he let her go.

"I was afraid," she said.

"Afraid!" muttered Swithin; "I should think so." No longer touching her, he felt his grievance revive.

"But you are so strong," she murmured.

"This is no place for you," growled Swithin, "I'm going to see you home."

"Oh!" cried Rozsi; "but papa and—Margit!"

"That's their look-out!" and he hurried her away.

She slid her hand under his arm; the soft curves of her form brushed him gently, each touch only augmented his ill-humour. He burned with a perverse rage, as if all the passions in him were simmering and ready to boil over; it was as if a poison were trying to work its way out of him, through the layers of his stolid flesh. He maintained a dogged silence; Rozsi, too, said nothing, but when they reached the door, she drew her hand away.

"You are angry!" she said.

"Angry," muttered Swithin; "no! How d'you make that out?" He had a torturing desire to kiss her.

"Yes, you are angry," she repeated; "I wait here for papa and Margit."

Swithin also waited, wedged against the wall. Once or twice, for his sight was sharp, he saw her steal a look at him, a beseeching look, and hardened his heart with a kind of pleasure. After five minutes Boleskey, Margit, and Kasteliz appeared. Seeing Rozsi they broke into exclamations of relief, and Kasteliz, with a glance at Swithin, put his lips to her hand. Rozsi's look said, "Wouldn't you like to do that?" Swithin turned short on his heel, and walked away.

V

All night he hardly slept, suffering from fever, for the first time in his life. Once he jumped out of bed, lighted a candle, and going to the glass, scrutinised himself long and anxiously. After this he fell asleep, but had frightful dreams. His first thought when he woke was, 'My liver's out of order!' and, thrusting his head into cold water, he dressed hastily and went out. He soon left the house behind. Dew covered everything; blackbirds whistled in the bushes; the air was fresh and sweet. He had not been up so early since he was a boy. Why was he walking through a damp wood at this hour of the morning? Something intolerable and unfamiliar must have sent him out. No fellow in his senses would do such a thing! He came to a dead stop, and began unsteadily to walk back. Regaining the hotel, he went to bed again, and dreamed that in some wild country he was living in a room full of insects, where a housemaid—Rozsi—holding a broom, looked at him with mournful eyes. There seemed an unexplained need for immediate departure; he begged her to forward his things; and shake them out carefully before she put them into the trunk. He understood that the charge for sending would be twenty-two shillings, thought it a great deal, and had the horrors of indecision. "No," he muttered, "pack, and take them myself." The housemaid turned suddenly into a lean creature; and he awoke with a sore feeling in his heart.

His eye fell on his wet boots. The whole thing was scaring, and jumping up, he began to throw his clothes into his trunks. It was twelve o'clock before he went down, and found his brother and Traquair still at the table arranging an itinerary; he surprised them by saying that he too was coming; and without further explanation set to work to eat. James had heard that there were salt-mines in the neighbourhood—his proposal was to start, and halt an hour or so on the road for their inspection; he said: "Everybody'll ask you if you've seen the salt-mines: I shouldn't like to say I hadn't seen the salt-mines. What's the good, they'd say, of your going there if you haven't seen the salt-mines?" He wondered, too, if they need fee the second waiter—an idle chap!

A discussion followed; but Swithin ate on glumly, conscious that his mind was set on larger affairs. Suddenly on the far side of the street Rozsi and her sister passed, with little baskets on their arms. He started up, and at that moment Rozsi looked round—her face was the incarnation of enticement, the chin tilted, the lower lip thrust a little forward, her round neck curving back over her shoulder. Swithin muttered, "Make your own arrangements—leave me out!" and hurried from the room, leaving James beside himself with interest and alarm.

When he reached the street, however, the girls had disappeared. He hailed a carriage. "Drive!" he called to the man, with a flourish of his stick, and as soon as the wheels had begun to clatter on the stones he leaned back, looking sharply to right and left. He soon had to give up thought of finding them, but made the coachman turn round and round again. All day he drove about, far into the country, and kept urging the driver to use greater speed. He was in a strange state of hurry and elation. Finally, he dined at a little country inn; and this gave the measure of his disturbance—the dinner was atrocious.

Returning late in the evening he found a note written by Traquair. "Are you in your senses, man?" it asked; "we have no more time to waste idling about here. If you want to rejoin us, come on to Danielli's Hotel, Venice." Swithin chuckled when he read it, and feeling frightfully tired, went to bed and slept like a log.

VI

Three weeks later he was still in Salzburg, no longer at the Goldene Alp, but in rooms over a shop near the Boleskeys'. He had spent a small fortune in the purchase of flowers. Margit would croon over them, but Rozsi, with a sober "Many tanks!" as if they were her right, would look long at herself in the glass, and pin one into her hair. Swithin ceased to wonder; he ceased to wonder at anything they did. One evening he found Boleskey deep in conversation with a pale, dishevelled-looking person.

"Our friend Mr. Forsyte—Count D....," said Boleskey.

Swithin experienced a faint, unavoidable emotion; but looking at the Count's trousers, he thought: 'Doesn't look much like one!' And with an ironic bow to the silent girls, he turned, and took his hat. But when he had reached the bottom of the dark stairs he heard footsteps. Rozsi came running down, looked out at the door, and put her hands up to her breast as if disappointed; suddenly with a quick glance round she saw him. Swithin caught her arm. She slipped away, and her face seemed to bubble with defiance or laughter; she ran up three steps, stopped, looked at him across her shoulder, and fled on up the stairs. Swithin went out bewildered and annoyed.

'What was she going to say to me?' he kept thinking. During these three weeks he had asked himself all sorts of questions: whether he were being made a fool of; whether she were in love with him; what he was doing there, and sometimes at night, with all his candles burning as if he wanted light, the breeze blowing on him through the window, his cigar, half-smoked, in his hand, he sat, an hour or more, staring at the wall. 'Enough of this!' he thought every morning. Twice he packed fully—once he ordered his travelling carriage, but countermanded it the following day. What definitely he hoped, intended, resolved, he could not have said. He was always thinking of Rozsi, he could not read the riddle in her face—she held him in a vice, notwithstanding that everything about her threatened the very fetishes of his existence. And Boleskey! Whenever he looked at him he thought, 'If he were only clean?' and mechanically fingered his own well-tied cravatte. To talk with the fellow, too, was like being forced to look at things which had no place in the light of day. Freedom, equality, self-sacrifice!

'Why can't he settle down at some business,' he thought, 'instead of all this talk?' Boleskey's sudden diffidences, self-depreciation, fits of despair, irritated him. "Morbid beggar!" he would mutter; "thank God I haven't a thin skin." And proud too! Extraordinary! An impecunious fellow like that! One evening, moreover, Boleskey had returned home drunk. Swithin had hustled him away into his bedroom, helped him to undress, and stayed until he was asleep. 'Too much of a good thing!' he thought, 'before his own daughters, too!' It was after this that he ordered his travelling carriage. The other occasion on which he packed was one evening, when not only Boleskey, but Rozsi herself had picked chicken bones with her fingers.

Often in the mornings he would go to the Mirabell Garden to smoke his cigar; there, in stolid contemplation of the statues—rows of half-heroic men carrying off half-distressful females—he would spend an hour pleasantly, his hat tilted to keep the sun off his nose. The day after Rozsi had fled from him on the stairs, he came there as usual. It was a morning of blue sky and sunlight glowing on the old prim garden, on its yew-trees, and serio-comic statues, and walls covered with apricots and plums. When Swithin approached his usual seat, who should be sitting there but Rozsi—"Good-morning," he stammered; "you knew this was my seat then?"

Rozsi looked at the ground. "Yes," she answered.

Swithin felt bewildered. "Do you know," he said, "you treat me very funnily?"

To his surprise Rozsi put her little soft hand down and touched his; then, without a word, sprang up and rushed away. It took him a minute to recover. There were people present; he did not like to run, but overtook her on the bridge, and slipped her hand beneath his arm.

"You shouldn't have done that," he said; "you shouldn't have run away from me, you know."

Rozsi laughed. Swithin withdrew his arm; a desire to shake her seized him. He walked some way before he said, "Will you have the goodness to tell me what you came to that seat for?"

Rozsi flashed a look at him. "To-morrow is the fete," she answered.

Swithin muttered, "Is that all?"

"If you do not take us, we cannot go."

"Suppose I refuse," he said sullenly, "there are plenty of others."

Rozsi bent her head, scurrying along. "No," she murmured, "if you do not go—I do not wish."

Swithin drew her hand back within his arm. How round and soft it was! He tried to see her face. When she was nearly home he said goodbye, not wishing, for some dark reason, to be seen with her. He watched till she had disappeared; then slowly retraced his steps to the Mirabell Garden. When he came to where she had been sitting, he slowly lighted his cigar, and for a long time after it was smoked out remained there in the silent presence of the statues.

VII

A crowd of people wandered round the booths, and Swithin found himself obliged to give the girls his arms. 'Like a little Cockney clerk!' he thought. His indignation passed unnoticed; they talked, they laughed, each sight and sound in all the hurly-burly seemed to go straight into their hearts. He eyed them ironically—their eager voices, and little coos of sympathy seemed to him vulgar. In the thick of the crowd he slipped his arm out of Margit's, but, just as he thought that he was free, the unwelcome hand slid up again. He tried again, but again Margit reappeared, serene, and full of pleasant humour; and his failure this time appeared to him in a comic light. But when Rozsi leaned across him, the glow of her round cheek, her curving lip, the inscrutable grey gleam of her eyes, sent a thrill of longing through him. He was obliged to stand by while they parleyed with a gipsy, whose matted locks and skinny hands inspired him with a not unwarranted disgust. "Folly!" he muttered, as Rozsi held out her palm. The old woman mumbled, and shot a malignant look at him. Rozsi drew back her hand, and crossed herself. 'Folly!' Swithin thought again; and seizing the girls' arms, he hurried them away.

"What did the old hag say?" he asked.

Rozsi shook her head.

"You don't mean that you believe?"

Her eyes were full of tears. "The gipsies are wise," she murmured.

"Come, what did she tell you?"

This time Rozsi looked hurriedly round, and slipped away into the crowd. After a hunt they found her, and Swithin, who was scared, growled: "You shouldn't do such things—it's not respectable."

On higher ground, in the centre of a clear space, a military band was playing. For the privilege of entering this charmed circle Swithin paid three kronen, choosing naturally the best seats. He ordered wine, too, watching Rozsi out of the corner of his eye as he poured it out. The protecting tenderness of yesterday was all lost in this medley. It was every man for himself, after all! The colour had deepened again in her cheeks, she laughed, pouting her lips. Suddenly she put her glass aside. "Thank you, very much," she said, "it is enough!"

Margit, whose pretty mouth was all smiles, cried, "Lieber Gott! is it not good-life?" It was not a question Swithin could undertake to answer. The band began to play a waltz. "Now they will dance. Lieber Gott! and are the lights not wonderful?" Lamps were flickering beneath the trees like a swarm of fireflies. There was a hum as from a gigantic beehive. Passers-by lifted their faces, then vanished into the crowd; Rozsi stood gazing at them spellbound, as if their very going and coming were a delight.

The space was soon full of whirling couples. Rozsi's head began to beat time. "O Margit!" she whispered.

Swithin's face had assumed a solemn, uneasy expression. A man raising his hat, offered his arm to Margit. She glanced back across her shoulder to reassure Swithin. "It is a friend," she said.

Swithin looked at Rozsi—her eyes were bright, her lips tremulous. He slipped his hand along the table and touched her fingers. Then she flashed a look at him—appeal, reproach, tenderness, all were expressed in it. Was she expecting him to dance? Did she want to mix with the rift-raff there; wish him to make an exhibition of himself in this hurly-burly? A voice said, "Good-evening!" Before them stood Kasteliz, in a dark coat tightly buttoned at the waist.

"You are not dancing, Rozsi Kozsanony?" (Miss Rozsi). "Let me, then, have the pleasure." He held out his arm. Swithin stared in front of him. In the very act of going she gave him a look that said as plain as words: "Will you not?" But for answer he turned his eyes away, and when he looked again she was gone. He paid the score and made his way into the crowd. But as he went she danced by close to him, all flushed and panting. She hung back as if to stop him, and he caught the glistening of tears. Then he lost sight of her again. To be deserted the first minute he was alone with her, and for that jackanapes with the small head and the volcanic glances! It was too much! And suddenly it occurred to him that she was alone with Kasteliz—alone at night, and far from home. 'Well,' he thought, 'what do I care?' and shouldered his way on through the crowd. It served him right for mixing with such people here. He left the fair, but the further he went, the more he nursed his rage, the more heinous seemed her offence, the sharper grew his jealousy. "A beggarly baron!" was his thought.

A figure came alongside—it was Boleskey. One look showed Swithin his condition. Drunk again! This was the last straw!

Unfortunately Boleskey had recognised him. He seemed violently excited. "Where—where are my daughters?" he began.

Swithin brushed past, but Boleskey caught his arm. "Listen—brother!" he said; "news of my country! After to-morrow...."

"Keep it to yourself!" growled Swithin, wrenching his arm free. He went straight to his lodgings, and, lying on the hard sofa of his unlighted sitting-room, gave himself up to bitter thoughts. But in spite of all his anger, Rozsi's supply-moving figure, with its pouting lips, and roguish appealing eyes, still haunted him.

VIII

Next morning there was not a carriage to be had, and Swithin was compelled to put off his departure till the morrow. The day was grey and misty; he wandered about with the strained, inquiring look of a lost dog in his eyes.

Late in the afternoon he went back to his lodgings. In a corner of the sitting-room stood Rozsi. The thrill of triumph, the sense of appeasement, the emotion, that seized on him, crept through to his lips in a faint smile. Rozsi made no sound, her face was hidden by her hands. And this silence of hers weighed on Swithin. She was forcing him to break it. What was behind her hands? His own face was visible! Why didn't she speak? Why was she here? Alone? That was not right surely.

Suddenly Rozsi dropped her hands; her flushed face was quivering—it seemed as though a word, a sign, even, might bring a burst of tears.

He walked over to the window. 'I must give her time!' he thought; then seized by unreasoning terror at this silence, spun round, and caught her by the arms. Rozsi held back from him, swayed forward and buried her face on his breast....

Half an hour later Swithin was pacing up and down his room. The scent of rose leaves had not yet died away. A glove lay on the floor; he picked it up, and for a long time stood weighing it in his hand. All sorts of confused thoughts and feelings haunted him. It was the purest and least selfish moment of his life, this moment after she had yielded. But that pure gratitude at her fiery, simple abnegation did not last; it was followed by a petty sense of triumph, and by uneasiness. He was still weighing the little glove in his hand, when he had another visitor. It was Kasteliz.

"What can I do for you?" Swithin asked ironically.

The Hungarian seemed suffering from excitement. Why had Swithin left his charges the night before? What excuse had he to make? What sort of conduct did he call this?

Swithin, very like a bull-dog at that moment, answered: What business was it of his?

The business of a gentleman! What right had the Englishman to pursue a young girl?

"Pursue?" said Swithin; "you've been spying, then?"

"Spying—I—Kasteliz—Maurus Johann—an insult!"

"Insult!" sneered Swithin; "d'you mean to tell me you weren't in the street just now?"

Kasteliz answered with a hiss, "If you do not leave the city I will make you, with my sword—do you understand?"

"And if you do not leave my room I will throw you out of the window!"

For some minutes Kasteliz spoke in pure Hungarian while Swithin waited, with a forced smile and a fixed look in his eye. He did not understand Hungarian.

"If you are still in the city to-morrow evening," said Kasteliz at last in English, "I will spit you in the street."

Swithin turned to the window and watched his visitor's retiring back with a queer mixture of amusement, stubbornness, and anxiety. 'Well,' he thought, 'I suppose he'll run me through!' The thought was unpleasant; and it kept recurring, but it only served to harden his determination. His head was busy with plans for seeing Rozsi; his blood on fire with the kisses she had given him.

IX

Swithin was long in deciding to go forth next day. He had made up his mind not to go to Rozsi till five o'clock. 'Mustn't make myself too cheap,' he thought. It was a little past that hour when he at last sallied out, and with a beating heart walked towards Boleskey's. He looked up at the window, more than half expecting to see Rozsi there; but she was not, and he noticed with faint surprise that the window was not open; the plants, too, outside, looked singularly arid. He knocked. No one came. He beat a fierce tattoo. At last the door was opened by a man with a reddish beard, and one of those sardonic faces only to be seen on shoemakers of Teutonic origin.

"What do you want, making all this noise?" he asked in German.

Swithin pointed up the stairs. The man grinned, and shook his head.

"I want to go up," said Swithin.

The cobbler shrugged his shoulders, and Swithin rushed upstairs. The rooms were empty. The furniture remained, but all signs of life were gone. One of his own bouquets, faded, stood in a glass; the ashes of a fire were barely cold; little scraps of paper strewed the hearth; already the room smelt musty. He went into the bedrooms, and with a feeling of stupefaction stood staring at the girls' beds, side by side against the wall. A bit of ribbon caught his eye; he picked it up and put it in his pocket—it was a piece of evidence that she had once existed. By the mirror some pins were dropped about; a little powder had been spilled. He looked at his own disquiet face and thought, 'I've been cheated!'

The shoemaker's voice aroused him. "Tausend Teufel! Eilen Sie, nur! Zeit is Geld! Kann nich' Langer warten!" Slowly he descended.

"Where have they gone?" asked Swithin painfully. "A pound for every English word you speak. A pound!" and he made an O with his fingers.

The corners of the shoemaker's lips curled. "Geld! Mf! Eilen Sie, nur!"

But in Swithin a sullen anger had begun to burn. "If you don't tell me," he said, "it'll be the worse for you."

"Sind ein komischer Kerl!" remarked the shoemaker. "Hier ist meine Frau!"

A battered-looking woman came hurrying down the passage, calling out in German, "Don't let him go!"

With a snarling sound the shoemaker turned his back, and shambled off.

The woman furtively thrust a letter into Swithin's hand, and furtively waited.

The letter was from Rozsi.

"Forgive me"—it ran—"that I leave you and do not say goodbye. To-day our father had the call from our dear Father-town so long awaited. In two hours we are ready. I pray to the Virgin to keep you ever safe, and that you do not quite forget me.—Your unforgetting good friend, ROZSI."

When Swithin read it his first sensation was that of a man sinking in a bog; then his obstinacy stiffened. 'I won't be done,' he thought. Taking out a sovereign he tried to make the woman comprehend that she could earn it, by telling him where they had gone. He got her finally to write the words out in his pocket-book, gave her the sovereign, and hurried to the Goldene Alp, where there was a waiter who spoke English. The translation given him was this:

"At three o'clock they start in a carriage on the road to Linz—they have bad horses—the Herr also rides a white horse."

Swithin at once hailed a carriage and started at full gallop on the road to Linz. Outside the Mirabell Garden he caught sight of Kasteliz and grinned at him. 'I've sold him anyway,' he thought; 'for all their talk, they're no good, these foreigners!'

His spirits rose, but soon fell again. What chance had he of catching them? They had three hours' start! Still, the roads were heavy from the rain of the last two nights—they had luggage and bad horses; his own were good, his driver bribed—he might overtake them by ten o'clock! But did he want to? What a fool he had been not to bring his luggage; he would then have had a respectable position. What a brute he would look without a change of shirt, or anything to shave with! He saw himself with horror, all bristly, and in soiled linen. People would think him mad. 'I've given myself away,' flashed across him, 'what the devil can I say to them?' and he stared sullenly at the driver's back. He read Rozsi's letter again; it had a scent of her. And in the growing darkness, jolted by the swinging of the carriage, he suffered tortures from his prudence, tortures from his passion.

It grew colder and dark. He turned the collar of his coat up to his ears. He had visions of Piccadilly. This wild-goose chase appeared suddenly a dangerous, unfathomable business. Lights, fellowship, security! 'Never again!' he brooded; 'why won't they let me alone?' But it was not clear whether by 'they' he meant the conventions, the Boleskeys, his passions, or those haunting memories of Rozsi. If he had only had a bag with him! What was he going to say? What was he going to get by this? He received no answer to these questions. The darkness itself was less obscure than his sensations. From time to time he took out his watch. At each village the driver made inquiries. It was past ten when he stopped the carriage with a jerk. The stars were bright as steel, and by the side of the road a reedy lake showed in the moonlight. Swithin shivered. A man on a horse had halted in the centre of the road. "Drive on!" called Swithin, with a stolid face. It turned out to be Boleskey, who, on a gaunt white horse, looked like some winged creature. He stood where he could bar the progress of the carriage, holding out a pistol.

'Theatrical beggar!' thought Swithin, with a nervous smile. He made no sign of recognition. Slowly Boleskey brought his lean horse up to the carriage. When he saw who was within he showed astonishment and joy.

"You?" he cried, slapping his hand on his attenuated thigh, and leaning over till his beard touched Swithin. "You have come? You followed us?"

"It seems so," Swithin grunted out.

"You throw in your lot with us. Is it possible? You—you are a knight-errant then!"

"Good God!" said Swithin. Boleskey, flogging his dejected steed, cantered forward in the moonlight. He came back, bringing an old cloak, which he insisted on wrapping round Swithin's shoulders. He handed him, too, a capacious flask.

"How cold you look!" he said. "Wonderful! Wonderful! you English!" His grateful eyes never left Swithin for a moment. They had come up to the heels of the other carriage now, but Swithin, hunched in the cloak, did not try to see what was in front of him. To the bottom of his soul he resented the Hungarian's gratitude. He remarked at last, with wasted irony:

"You're in a hurry, it seems!"

"If we had wings," Boleskey answered, "we would use them."

"Wings!" muttered Swithin thickly; "legs are good enough for me."

X

Arrived at the inn where they were to pass the night, Swithin waited, hoping to get into the house without a "scene," but when at last he alighted the girls were in the doorway, and Margit greeted him with an admiring murmur, in which, however, he seemed to detect irony. Rozsi, pale and tremulous, with a half-scared look, gave him her hand, and, quickly withdrawing it, shrank behind her sister. When they had gone up to their room Swithin sought Boleskey. His spirits had risen remarkably. "Tell the landlord to get us supper," he said; "we'll crack a bottle to our luck." He hurried on the landlord's preparations. The window of the room faced a wood, so near that he could almost touch the trees. The scent from the pines blew in on him. He turned away from that scented darkness, and began to draw the corks of winebottles. The sound seemed to conjure up Boleskey. He came in, splashed all over, smelling slightly of stables; soon after, Margit appeared, fresh and serene, but Rozsi did not come.

"Where is your sister?" Swithin said. Rozsi, it seemed, was tired. "It will do her good to eat," said Swithin. And Boleskey, murmuring, "She must drink to our country," went out to summon her, Margit followed him, while Swithin cut up a chicken. They came back without her. She had "a megrim of the spirit."

Swithin's face fell. "Look here!" he said, "I'll go and try. Don't wait for me."

"Yes," answered Boleskey, sinking mournfully into a chair; "try, brother, try—by all means, try."

Swithin walked down the corridor with an odd, sweet, sinking sensation in his chest; and tapped on Rozsi's door. In a minute, she peeped forth, with her hair loose, and wondering eyes.

"Rozsi," he stammered, "what makes you afraid of me, now?"

She stared at him, but did not answer.

"Why won't you come?"

Still she did not speak, but suddenly stretched out to him her bare arm. Swithin pressed his face to it. With a shiver, she whispered above him, "I will come," and gently shut the door.

Swithin stealthily retraced his steps, and paused a minute outside the sitting-room to regain his self-control.

The sight of Boleskey with a bottle in his hand steadied him.

"She is coming," he said. And very soon she did come, her thick hair roughly twisted in a plait.

Swithin sat between the girls; but did not talk, for he was really hungry. Boleskey too was silent, plunged in gloom; Rozsi was dumb; Margit alone chattered.

"You will come to our Father-town? We shall have things to show you. Rozsi, what things we will show him!" Rozsi, with a little appealing movement of her hands, repeated, "What things we will show you!" She seemed suddenly to find her voice, and with glowing cheeks, mouths full, and eyes bright as squirrels', they chattered reminiscences of the "dear Father-town," of "dear friends," of the "dear home."

'A poor place!' Swithin could not help thinking. This enthusiasm seemed to him common; but he was careful to assume a look of interest, feeding on the glances flashed at him from Rozsi's restless eyes.

As the wine waned Boleskey grew more and more gloomy, but now and then a sort of gleaming flicker passed over his face. He rose to his feet at last.

"Let us not forget," he said, "that we go perhaps to ruin, to death; in the face of all this we go, because our country needs—in this there is no credit, neither to me nor to you, my daughters; but for this noble Englishman, what shall we say? Give thanks to God for a great heart. He comes—not for country, not for fame, not for money, but to help the weak and the oppressed. Let us drink, then, to him; let us drink again and again to heroic Forsyte!" In the midst of the dead silence, Swithin caught the look of suppliant mockery in Rozsi's eyes. He glanced at the Hungarian. Was he laughing at him? But Boleskey, after drinking up his wine, had sunk again into his seat; and there suddenly, to the surprise of all, he began to snore. Margit rose and, bending over him like a mother, murmured: "He is tired—it is the ride!" She raised him in her strong arms, and leaning on her shoulder Boleskey staggered from the room. Swithin and Rozsi were left alone. He slid his hand towards her hand that lay so close, on the rough table-cloth. It seemed to await his touch. Something gave way in him, and words came welling up; for the moment he forgot himself, forgot everything but that he was near her. Her head dropped on his shoulder, he breathed the perfume of her hair. "Good-night!" she whispered, and the whisper was like a kiss; yet before he could stop her she was gone. Her footsteps died away in the passage, but Swithin sat gazing intently at a single bright drop of spilt wine quivering on the table's edge. In that moment she, in her helplessness and emotion, was all in all to him—his life nothing; all the real things—his conventions, convictions, training, and himself—all seemed remote, behind a mist of passion and strange chivalry. Carefully with a bit of bread he soaked up the bright drop; and suddenly he thought: 'This is tremendous!' For a long time he stood there in the window, close to the dark pine-trees.

XI

In the early morning he awoke, full of the discomfort of this strange place and the medley of his dreams. Lying, with his nose peeping over the quilt, he was visited by a horrible suspicion. When he could bear it no longer, he started up in bed. What if it were all a plot to get him to marry her? The thought was treacherous, and inspired in him a faint disgust. Still, she might be ignorant of it! But was she so innocent? What innocent girl would have come to his room like that? What innocent girl? Her father, who pretended to be caring only for his country? It was not probable that any man was such a fool; it was all part of the game—a scheming rascal! Kasteliz, too—his threats! They intended him to marry her! And the horrid idea was strengthened by his reverence for marriage. It was the proper, the respectable condition; he was genuinely afraid of this other sort of liaison—it was somehow too primitive! And yet the thought of that marriage made his blood run cold. Considering that she had already yielded, it would be all the more monstrous! With the cold, fatal clearness of the morning light he now for the first time saw his position in its full bearings. And, like a fish pulled out of water, he gasped at what was disclosed. Sullen resentment against this attempt to force him settled deep into his soul.

He seated himself on the bed, holding his head in his hands, solemnly thinking out what such marriage meant. In the first place it meant ridicule, in the next place ridicule, in the last place ridicule. She would eat chicken bones with her fingers—those fingers his lips still burned to kiss. She would dance wildly with other men. She would talk of her "dear Father-town," and all the time her eyes would look beyond him, some where or other into some d—d place he knew nothing of. He sprang up and paced the room, and for a moment thought he would go mad.

They meant him to marry her! Even she—she meant him to marry her! Her tantalising inscrutability; her sudden little tendernesses; her quick laughter; her swift, burning kisses; even the movements of her hands; her tears—all were evidence against her. Not one of these things that Nature made her do counted on her side, but how they fanned his longing, his desire, and distress! He went to the glass and tried to part his hair with his fingers, but being rather fine, it fell into lank streaks. There was no comfort to be got from it. He drew his muddy boots on. Suddenly he thought: 'If I could see her alone, I could arrive at some arrangement!' Then, with a sense of stupefaction, he made the discovery that no arrangement could possibly be made that would not be dangerous, even desperate. He seized his hat, and, like a rabbit that has been fired at, bolted from the room. He plodded along amongst the damp woods with his head down, and resentment and dismay in his heart. But, as the sun rose, and the air grew sweet with pine scent, he slowly regained a sort of equability. After all, she had already yielded; it was not as if...! And the tramp of his own footsteps lulled him into feeling that it would all come right.

'Look at the thing practically,' he thought. The faster he walked the firmer became his conviction that he could still see it through. He took out his watch—it was past seven—he began to hasten back. In the yard of the inn his driver was harnessing the horses; Swithin went up to him.

"Who told you to put them in?" he asked.

The driver answered, "Der Herr."

Swithin turned away. 'In ten minutes,' he thought, 'I shall be in that carriage again, with this going on in my head! Driving away from England, from all I'm used to—driving to—what?' Could he face it? Could he face all that he had been through that morning; face it day after day, night after night? Looking up, he saw Rozsi at her open window gazing down at him; never had she looked sweeter, more roguish. An inexplicable terror seized on him; he ran across the yard and jumped into his carriage. "To Salzburg!" he cried; "drive on!" And rattling out of the yard without a look behind, he flung a sovereign at the hostler. Flying back along the road faster even than he had come, with pale face, and eyes blank and staring like a pug-dog's, Swithin spoke no single word; nor, till he had reached the door of his lodgings, did he suffer the driver to draw rein.

XII

Towards evening, five days later, Swithin, yellow and travel-worn, was ferried in a gondola to Danielli's Hotel. His brother, who was on the steps, looked at him with an apprehensive curiosity.

"Why, it's you!" he mumbled. "So you've got here safe?"

"Safe?" growled Swithin.

James replied, "I thought you wouldn't leave your friends!" Then, with a jerk of suspicion, "You haven't brought your friends?"

"What friends?" growled Swithin.

James changed the subject. "You don't look the thing," he said.

"Really!" muttered Swithin; "what's that to you?"

He appeared at dinner that night, but fell asleep over his coffee. Neither Traquair nor James asked him any further question, nor did they allude to Salzburg; and during the four days which concluded the stay in Venice Swithin went about with his head up, but his eyes half-closed like a dazed man. Only after they had taken ship at Genoa did he show signs of any healthy interest in life, when, finding that a man on board was perpetually strumming, he locked the piano up and pitched the key into the sea.

That winter in London he behaved much as usual, but fits of moroseness would seize on him, during which he was not pleasant to approach.

One evening when he was walking with a friend in Piccadilly, a girl coming from a side-street accosted him in German. Swithin, after staring at her in silence for some seconds, handed her a five-pound note, to the great amazement of his friend; nor could he himself have explained the meaning of this freak of generosity.

Of Rozsi he never heard again....

This, then, was the substance of what he remembered as he lay ill in bed. Stretching out his hand he pressed the bell. His valet appeared, crossing the room like a cat; a Swede, who had been with Swithin many years; a little man with a dried face and fierce moustache, morbidly sharp nerves, and a queer devotion to his master.

Swithin made a feeble gesture. "Adolf," he said, "I'm very bad."

"Yes, sir!"

"Why do you stand there like a cow?" asked Swithin; "can't you see I'm very bad?"

"Yes, sir!" The valet's face twitched as though it masked the dance of obscure emotions.

"I shall feel better after dinner. What time is it?"

"Five o'clock."

"I thought it was more. The afternoons are very long."

"Yes, sir!" Swithin sighed, as though he had expected the consolation of denial.

"Very likely I shall have a nap. Bring up hot water at half-past six and shave me before dinner."

The valet moved towards the door. Swithin raised himself.

"What did Mr. James say to you?"

"He said you ought to have another doctor; two doctors, he said, better than one. He said, also, he would look in again on his way 'home.'"

Swithin grunted, "Umph! What else did he say?"

"He said you didn't take care of yourself."

Swithin glared.

"Has anybody else been to see me?"

The valet turned away his eyes. "Mrs. Thomas Forsyte came last Monday fortnight."

"How long have I been ill?"

"Five weeks on Saturday."

"Do you think I'm very bad?"

Adolf's face was covered suddenly with crow's-feet. "You have no business to ask me question like that! I am not paid, sir, to answer question like that."

Swithin said faintly: "You're a peppery fool! Open a bottle of champagne!"

Adolf took a bottle of champagne—from a cupboard and held nippers to it. He fixed his eyes on Swithin. "The doctor said—"

"Open the bottle!"

"It is not—"

"Open the bottle—or I give you warning."

Adolf removed the cork. He wiped a glass elaborately, filled it, and bore it scrupulously to the bedside. Suddenly twirling his moustaches, he wrung his hands, and burst out: "It is poison."

Swithin grinned faintly. "You foreign fool!" he said. "Get out!"

The valet vanished.

'He forgot himself!' thought Swithin. Slowly he raised the glass, slowly put it back, and sank gasping on his pillows. Almost at once he fell asleep.

He dreamed that he was at his club, sitting after dinner in the crowded smoking-room, with its bright walls and trefoils of light. It was there that he sat every evening, patient, solemn, lonely, and sometimes fell asleep, his square, pale old face nodding to one side. He dreamed that he was gazing at the picture over the fireplace, of an old statesman with a high collar, supremely finished face, and sceptical eyebrows—the picture, smooth, and reticent as sealing-wax, of one who seemed for ever exhaling the narrow wisdom of final judgments. All round him, his fellow members were chattering. Only he himself, the old sick member, was silent. If fellows only knew what it was like to sit by yourself and feel ill all the time! What they were saying he had heard a hundred times. They were talking of investments, of cigars, horses, actresses, machinery. What was that? A foreign patent for cleaning boilers? There was no such thing; boilers couldn't be cleaned, any fool knew that! If an Englishman couldn't clean a boiler, no foreigner could clean one. He appealed to the old statesman's eyes. But for once those eyes seemed hesitating, blurred, wanting in finality. They vanished. In their place were Rozsi's little deep-set eyes, with their wide and far-off look; and as he gazed they seemed to grow bright as steel, and to speak to him. Slowly the whole face grew to be there, floating on the dark background of the picture; it was pink, aloof, unfathomable, enticing, with its fluffy hair and quick lips, just as he had last seen it. "Are you looking for something?" she seemed to say: "I could show you."

"I have everything safe enough," answered Swithin, and in his sleep he groaned.

He felt the touch of fingers on his forehead. 'I'm dreaming,' he thought in his dream.

She had vanished; and far away, from behind the picture, came a sound of footsteps.

Aloud, in his sleep, Swithin muttered: "I've missed it."

Again he heard the rustling of those light footsteps, and close in his ear a sound, like a sob. He awoke; the sob was his own. Great drops of perspiration stood on his forehead. 'What is it?' he thought; 'what have I lost?' Slowly his mind travelled over his investments; he could not think of any single one that was unsafe. What was it, then, that he had lost? Struggling on his pillows, he clutched the wine-glass. His lips touched the wine. 'This isn't the "Heidseck"!' he thought angrily, and before the reality of that displeasure all the dim vision passed away. But as he bent to drink, something snapped, and, with a sigh, Swithin Forsyte died above the bubbles....

When James Forsyte came in again on his way home, the valet, trembling took his hat and stick.

"How's your master?"

"My master is dead, sir!"

"Dead! He can't be! I left him safe an hour ago."

On the bed Swithin's body was doubled like a sack; his hand still grasped the glass.

James Forsyte paused. "Swithin!" he said, and with his hand to his ear he waited for an answer; but none came, and slowly in the glass a last bubble rose and burst.

December 1900.

THE SILENCE

I

In a car of the Naples express a mining expert was diving into a bag for papers. The strong sunlight showed the fine wrinkles on his brown face and the shabbiness of his short, rough beard. A newspaper cutting slipped from his fingers; he picked it up, thinking: 'How the dickens did that get in here?' It was from a colonial print of three years back; and he sat staring, as if in that forlorn slip of yellow paper he had encountered some ghost from his past.

These were the words he read: "We hope that the setback to civilisation, the check to commerce and development, in this promising centre of our colony may be but temporary; and that capital may again come to the rescue. Where one man was successful, others should surely not fail? We are convinced that it only needs...." And the last words: "For what can be sadder than to see the forest spreading its lengthening shadows, like symbols of defeat, over the untenanted dwellings of men; and where was once the merry chatter of human voices, to pass by in the silence...."

On an afternoon, thirteen years before, he had been in the city of London, at one of those emporiums where mining experts perch, before fresh flights, like sea-gulls on some favourite rock. A clerk said to him: "Mr. Scorrier, they are asking for you downstairs—Mr. Hemmings of the New Colliery Company."

Scorrier took up the speaking tube. "Is that you, Mr. Scorrier? I hope you are very well, sir, I am—Hemmings—I am—coming up."

In two minutes he appeared, Christopher Hemmings, secretary of the New Colliery Company, known in the City—behind his back—as "Down-by-the-starn" Hemmings. He grasped Scorrier's hand—the gesture was deferential, yet distinguished. Too handsome, too capable, too important, his figure, the cut of his iron-grey beard, and his intrusively fine eyes, conveyed a continual courteous invitation to inspect their infallibilities. He stood, like a City "Atlas," with his legs apart, his coat-tails gathered in his hands, a whole globe of financial matters deftly balanced on his nose. "Look at me!" he seemed to say. "It's heavy, but how easily I carry it. Not the man to let it down, Sir!"

"I hope I see you well, Mr. Scorrier," he began. "I have come round about our mine. There is a question of a fresh field being opened up—between ourselves, not before it's wanted. I find it difficult to get my Board to take a comprehensive view. In short, the question is: Are you prepared to go out for us, and report on it? The fees will be all right." His left eye closed. "Things have been very—er—dicky; we are going to change our superintendent. I have got little Pippin—you know little Pippin?"

Scorrier murmured, with a feeling of vague resentment: "Oh yes. He's not a mining man!"

Hemmings replied: "We think that he will do." 'Do you?' thought Scorrier; 'that's good of you!'

He had not altogether shaken off a worship he had felt for Pippin—"King" Pippin he was always called, when they had been boys at the Camborne Grammar-school. "King" Pippin! the boy with the bright colour, very bright hair, bright, subtle, elusive eyes, broad shoulders, little stoop in the neck, and a way of moving it quickly like a bird; the boy who was always at the top of everything, and held his head as if looking for something further to be the top of. He remembered how one day "King" Pippin had said to him in his soft way, "Young Scorrie, I'll do your sums for you"; and in answer to his dubious, "Is that all right?" had replied, "Of course—I don't want you to get behind that beast Blake, he's not a Cornishman" (the beast Blake was an Irishman not yet twelve). He remembered, too, an occasion when "King" Pippin with two other boys fought six louts and got a licking, and how Pippin sat for half an hour afterwards, all bloody, his head in his hands, rocking to and fro, and weeping tears of mortification; and how the next day he had sneaked off by himself, and, attacking the same gang, got frightfully mauled a second time.

Thinking of these things he answered curtly: "When shall I start?"

"Down-by-the-starn" Hemmings replied with a sort of fearful sprightliness: "There's a good fellow! I will send instructions; so glad to see you well." Conferring on Scorrier a look—fine to the verge of vulgarity—he withdrew. Scorrier remained, seated; heavy with insignificance and vague oppression, as if he had drunk a tumbler of sweet port.

A week later, in company with Pippin, he was on board a liner.

The "King" Pippin of his school-days was now a man of forty-four. He awakened in Scorrier the uncertain wonder with which men look backward at their uncomplicated teens; and staggering up and down the decks in the long Atlantic roll, he would steal glances at his companion, as if he expected to find out from them something about himself. Pippin had still "King" Pippin's bright, fine hair, and dazzling streaks in his short beard; he had still a bright colour and suave voice, and what there were of wrinkles suggested only subtleties of humour and ironic sympathy. From the first, and apparently without negotiation, he had his seat at the captain's table, to which on the second day Scorrier too found himself translated, and had to sit, as he expressed it ruefully, "among the big-wigs."

During the voyage only one incident impressed itself on Scorrier's memory, and that for a disconcerting reason. In the forecastle were the usual complement of emigrants. One evening, leaning across the rail to watch them, he felt a touch on his arm; and, looking round, saw Pippin's face and beard quivering in the lamplight. "Poor people!" he said. The idea flashed on Scorrier that he was like some fine wire sound-recording instrument.

'Suppose he were to snap!' he thought. Impelled to justify this fancy, he blurted out: "You're a nervous chap. The way you look at those poor devils!"

Pippin hustled him along the deck. "Come, come, you took me off my guard," he murmured, with a sly, gentle smile, "that's not fair."

He found it a continual source of wonder that Pippin, at his age, should cut himself adrift from the associations and security of London life to begin a new career in a new country with dubious prospect of success. 'I always heard he was doing well all round,' he thought; 'thinks he'll better himself, perhaps. He's a true Cornishman.'

The morning of arrival at the mines was grey and cheerless; a cloud of smoke, beaten down by drizzle, clung above the forest; the wooden houses straggled dismally in the unkempt semblance of a street, against a background of endless, silent woods. An air of blank discouragement brooded over everything; cranes jutted idly over empty trucks; the long jetty oozed black slime; miners with listless faces stood in the rain; dogs fought under their very legs. On the way to the hotel they met no one busy or serene except a Chinee who was polishing a dish-cover.

The late superintendent, a cowed man, regaled them at lunch with his forebodings; his attitude toward the situation was like the food, which was greasy and uninspiring. Alone together once more, the two newcomers eyed each other sadly.

"Oh dear!" sighed Pippin. "We must change all this, Scorrier; it will never do to go back beaten. I shall not go back beaten; you will have to carry me on my shield;" and slyly: "Too heavy, eh? Poor fellow!" Then for a long time he was silent, moving his lips as if adding up the cost. Suddenly he sighed, and grasping Scorrier's arm, said: "Dull, aren't I? What will you do? Put me in your report, 'New Superintendent—sad, dull dog—not a word to throw at a cat!'" And as if the new task were too much for him, he sank back in thought. The last words he said to Scorrier that night were: "Very silent here. It's hard to believe one's here for life. But I feel I am. Mustn't be a coward, though!" and brushing his forehead, as though to clear from it a cobweb of faint thoughts, he hurried off.

Scorrier stayed on the veranda smoking. The rain had ceased, a few stars were burning dimly; even above the squalor of the township the scent of the forests, the interminable forests, brooded. There sprang into his mind the memory of a picture from one of his children's fairy books—the picture of a little bearded man on tiptoe, with poised head and a great sword, slashing at the castle of a giant. It reminded him of Pippin. And suddenly, even to Scorrier—whose existence was one long encounter with strange places—the unseen presence of those woods, their heavy, healthy scent, the little sounds, like squeaks from tiny toys, issuing out of the gloomy silence, seemed intolerable, to be shunned, from the mere instinct of self-preservation. He thought of the evening he had spent in the bosom of "Down-by-the-starn" Hemmings' family, receiving his last instructions—the security of that suburban villa, its discouraging gentility; the superior acidity of the Miss Hemmings; the noble names of large contractors, of company promoters, of a peer, dragged with the lightness of gun-carriages across the conversation; the autocracy of Hemmings, rasped up here and there, by some domestic contradiction. It was all so nice and safe—as if the whole thing had been fastened to an anchor sunk beneath the pink cabbages of the drawing-room carpet! Hemmings, seeing him off the premises, had said with secrecy: "Little Pippin will have a good thing. We shall make his salary L——. He'll be a great man—quite a king. Ha-ha!"

Scorrier shook the ashes from his pipe. 'Salary!' he thought, straining his ears; 'I wouldn't take the place for five thousand pounds a year. And yet it's a fine country,' and with ironic violence he repeated, 'a dashed fine country!'

Ten days later, having finished his report on the new mine, he stood on the jetty waiting to go abroad the steamer for home.

"God bless you!" said Pippin. "Tell them they needn't be afraid; and sometimes when you're at home think of me, eh?"

Scorrier, scrambling on board, had a confused memory of tears in his eyes, and a convulsive handshake.

II

It was eight years before the wheels of life carried Scorrier back to that disenchanted spot, and this time not on the business of the New Colliery Company. He went for another company with a mine some thirty miles away. Before starting, however, he visited Hemmings. The secretary was surrounded by pigeon-holes and finer than ever; Scorrier blinked in the full radiance of his courtesy. A little man with eyebrows full of questions, and a grizzled beard, was seated in an arm-chair by the fire.

"You know Mr. Booker," said Hemmings—"one of my directors. This is Mr. Scorrier, sir—who went out for us."

These sentences were murmured in a way suggestive of their uncommon value. The director uncrossed his legs, and bowed. Scorrier also bowed, and Hemmings, leaning back, slowly developed the full resources of his waistcoat.

"So you are going out again, Scorrier, for the other side? I tell Mr. Scorrier, sir, that he is going out for the enemy. Don't find them a mine as good as you found us, there's a good man."

The little director asked explosively: "See our last dividend? Twenty per cent; eh, what?"

Hemmings moved a finger, as if reproving his director. "I will not disguise from you," he murmured, "that there is friction between us and—the enemy; you know our position too well—just a little too well, eh? 'A nod's as good as a wink.'"

His diplomatic eyes flattered Scorrier, who passed a hand over his brow—and said: "Of course."

"Pippin doesn't hit it off with them. Between ourselves, he's a leetle too big for his boots. You know what it is when a man in his position gets a sudden rise!"

Scorrier caught himself searching on the floor for a sight of Hemmings' boots; he raised his eyes guiltily. The secretary continued: "We don't hear from him quite as often as we should like, in fact."

To his own surprise Scorrier murmured: "It's a silent place!"

The secretary smiled. "Very good! Mr. Scorrier says, sir, it's a silent place; ha-ha! I call that very good!" But suddenly a secret irritation seemed to bubble in him; he burst forth almost violently: "He's no business to let it affect him; now, has he? I put it to you, Mr. Scorrier, I put it to you, sir!"

But Scorrier made no reply, and soon after took his leave: he had been asked to convey a friendly hint to Pippin that more frequent letters would be welcomed. Standing in the shadow of the Royal Exchange, waiting to thread his way across, he thought: 'So you must have noise, must you—you've got some here, and to spare....'

On his arrival in the new world he wired to Pippin asking if he might stay with him on the way up country, and received the answer: "Be sure and come."

A week later he arrived (there was now a railway) and found Pippin waiting for him in a phaeton. Scorrier would not have known the place again; there was a glitter over everything, as if some one had touched it with a wand. The tracks had given place to roads, running firm, straight, and black between the trees under brilliant sunshine; the wooden houses were all painted; out in the gleaming harbour amongst the green of islands lay three steamers, each with a fleet of busy boats; and here and there a tiny yacht floated, like a sea-bird on the water. Pippin drove his long-tailed horses furiously; his eyes brimmed with subtle kindness, as if according Scorrier a continual welcome. During the two days of his stay Scorrier never lost that sense of glamour. He had every opportunity for observing the grip Pippin had over everything. The wooden doors and walls of his bungalow kept out no sounds. He listened to interviews between his host and all kinds and conditions of men. The voices of the visitors would rise at first—angry, discontented, matter-of-fact, with nasal twang, or guttural drawl; then would come the soft patter of the superintendent's feet crossing and recrossing the room. Then a pause, the sound of hard breathing, and quick questions—the visitor's voice again, again the patter, and Pippin's ingratiating but decisive murmurs. Presently out would come the visitor with an expression on his face which Scorrier soon began to know by heart, a kind of pleased, puzzled, helpless look, which seemed to say, "I've been done, I know—I'll give it to myself when I'm round the corner."

Pippin was full of wistful questions about "home." He wanted to talk of music, pictures, plays, of how London looked, what new streets there were, and, above all, whether Scorrier had been lately in the West Country. He talked of getting leave next winter, asked whether Scorrier thought they would "put up with him at home"; then, with the agitation which had alarmed Scorrier before, he added: "Ah! but I'm not fit for home now. One gets spoiled; it's big and silent here. What should I go back to? I don't seem to realise."

Scorrier thought of Hemmings. "'Tis a bit cramped there, certainly," he muttered.

Pippin went on as if divining his thoughts. "I suppose our friend Hemmings would call me foolish; he's above the little weaknesses of imagination, eh? Yes; it's silent here. Sometimes in the evening I would give my head for somebody to talk to—Hemmings would never give his head for anything, I think. But all the same, I couldn't face them at home. Spoiled!" And slyly he murmured: "What would the Board say if they could hear that?"

Scorrier blurted out: "To tell you the truth, they complain a little of not hearing from you."

Pippin put out a hand, as if to push something away. "Let them try the life here!" he broke out; "it's like sitting on a live volcano—what with our friends, 'the enemy,' over there; the men; the American competition. I keep it going, Scorrier, but at what a cost—at what a cost!"

"But surely—letters?"

Pippin only answered: "I try—I try!"

Scorrier felt with remorse and wonder that he had spoken the truth. The following day he left for his inspection, and while in the camp of "the enemy" much was the talk he heard of Pippin.

"Why!" said his host, the superintendent, a little man with a face somewhat like an owl's, "d'you know the name they've given him down in the capital— 'the King'—good, eh? He's made them 'sit up' all along this coast. I like him well enough—good-hearted man, shocking nervous; but my people down there can't stand him at any price. Sir, he runs this colony. You'd think butter wouldn't melt in that mouth of his; but he always gets his way; that's what riles 'em so; that and the success he's making of his mine. It puzzles me; you'd think he'd only be too glad of a quiet life, a man with his nerves. But no, he's never happy unless he's fighting, something where he's got a chance to score a victory. I won't say he likes it, but, by Jove, it seems he's got to do it. Now that's funny! I'll tell you one thing, though shouldn't be a bit surprised if he broke down some day; and I'll tell you another," he added darkly, "he's sailing very near the wind, with those large contracts that he makes. I wouldn't care to take his risks. Just let them have a strike, or something that shuts them down for a spell—and mark my words, sir—it'll be all up with them. But," he concluded confidentially, "I wish I had his hold on the men; it's a great thing in this country. Not like home, where you can go round a corner and get another gang. You have to make the best you can out of the lot you have; you won't get another man for love or money without you ship him a few hundred miles." And with a frown he waved his arm over the forests to indicate the barrenness of the land.

III

Scorrier finished his inspection and went on a shooting trip into the forest. His host met him on his return. "Just look at this!" he said, holding out a telegram. "Awful, isn't it?" His face expressed a profound commiseration, almost ludicrously mixed with the ashamed contentment that men experience at the misfortunes of an enemy.

The telegram, dated the day before, ran thus "Frightful explosion New Colliery this morning, great loss of life feared."

Scorrier had the bewildered thought: 'Pippin will want me now.'

He took leave of his host, who called after him: "You'd better wait for a steamer! It's a beastly drive!"

Scorrier shook his head. All night, jolting along a rough track cut through the forest, he thought of Pippin. The other miseries of this calamity at present left him cold; he barely thought of the smothered men; but Pippin's struggle, his lonely struggle with this hydra-headed monster, touched him very nearly. He fell asleep and dreamed of watching Pippin slowly strangled by a snake; the agonised, kindly, ironic face peeping out between two gleaming coils was so horribly real, that he awoke. It was the moment before dawn: pitch-black branches barred the sky; with every jolt of the wheels the gleams from the lamps danced, fantastic and intrusive, round ferns and tree-stems, into the cold heart of the forest. For an hour or more Scorrier tried to feign sleep, and hide from the stillness, and overmastering gloom of these great woods. Then softly a whisper of noises stole forth, a stir of light, and the whole slow radiance of the morning glory. But it brought no warmth; and Scorrier wrapped himself closer in his cloak, feeling as though old age had touched him.

Close on noon he reached the township. Glamour seemed still to hover over it. He drove on to the mine. The winding-engine was turning, the pulley at the top of the head-gear whizzing round; nothing looked unusual. 'Some mistake!' he thought. He drove to the mine buildings, alighted, and climbed to the shaft head. Instead of the usual rumbling of the trolleys, the rattle of coal discharged over the screens, there was silence. Close by, Pippin himself was standing, smirched with dirt. The cage, coming swift and silent from below, shot open its doors with a sharp rattle. Scorrier bent forward to look. There lay a dead man, with a smile on his face.

"How many?" he whispered.

Pippin answered: "Eighty-four brought up—forty-seven still below," and entered the man's name in a pocket-book.

An older man was taken out next; he too was smiling—there had been vouchsafed to him, it seemed, a taste of more than earthly joy. The sight of those strange smiles affected Scorrier more than all the anguish or despair he had seen scored on the faces of other dead men. He asked an old miner how long Pippin had been at work.

"Thirty hours. Yesterday he wer' below; we had to nigh carry mun up at last. He's for goin' down again, but the chaps won't lower mun;" the old man gave a sigh. "I'm waiting for my boy to come up, I am."

Scorrier waited too—there was fascination about those dead, smiling faces. The rescuing of these men who would never again breathe went on and on. Scorrier grew sleepy in the sun. The old miner woke him, saying: "Rummy stuff this here chokedamp; see, they all dies drunk!" The very next to be brought up was the chief engineer. Scorrier had known him quite well, one of those Scotsmen who are born at the age of forty and remain so all their lives. His face—the only one that wore no smile—seemed grieving that duty had deprived it of that last luxury. With wide eyes and drawn lips he had died protesting.

Late in the afternoon the old miner touched Scorrier's arm, and said: "There he is—there's my boy!" And he departed slowly, wheeling the body on a trolley.

As the sun set, the gang below came up. No further search was possible till the fumes had cleared. Scorrier heard one man say: "There's some we'll never get; they've had sure burial."

Another answered him: "'Tis a gude enough bag for me!" They passed him, the whites of their eyes gleaming out of faces black as ink.

Pippin drove him home at a furious pace, not uttering a single word. As they turned into the main street, a young woman starting out before the horses obliged Pippin to pull up. The glance he bent on Scorrier was ludicrously prescient of suffering. The woman asked for her husband. Several times they were stopped thus by women asking for their husbands or sons. "This is what I have to go through," Pippin whispered.

When they had eaten, he said to Scorrier: "It was kind of you to come and stand by me! They take me for a god, poor creature that I am. But shall I ever get the men down again? Their nerve's shaken. I wish I were one of those poor lads, to die with a smile like that!"

Scorrier felt the futility of his presence. On Pippin alone must be the heat and burden. Would he stand under it, or would the whole thing come crashing to the ground? He urged him again and again to rest, but Pippin only gave him one of his queer smiles. "You don't know how strong I am!" he said.

IV

He himself slept heavily; and, waking at dawn, went down. Pippin was still at his desk; his pen had dropped; he was asleep. The ink was wet; Scorrier's eye caught the opening words:

"GENTLEMEN,—Since this happened I have not slept...."

He stole away again with a sense of indignation that no one could be dragged in to share that fight. The London Board-room rose before his mind. He imagined the portentous gravity of Hemmings; his face and voice and manner conveying the impression that he alone could save the situation; the six directors, all men of commonsense and certainly humane, seated behind large turret-shaped inkpots; the concern and irritation in their voices, asking how it could have happened; their comments: "An awful thing!" "I suppose Pippin is doing the best he can!" "Wire him on no account to leave the mine idle!" "Poor devils!" "A fund? Of course, what ought we to give?" He had a strong conviction that nothing of all this would disturb the commonsense with which they would go home and eat their mutton. A good thing too; the less it was taken to heart the better! But Scorrier felt angry. The fight was so unfair! A fellow all nerves—with not a soul to help him! Well, it was his own lookout! He had chosen to centre it all in himself, to make himself its very soul. If he gave way now, the ship must go down! By a thin thread, Scorrier's hero-worship still held. 'Man against nature,' he thought, 'I back the man.' The struggle in which he was so powerless to give aid, became intensely personal to him, as if he had engaged his own good faith therein.

The next day they went down again to the pit-head; and Scorrier himself descended. The fumes had almost cleared, but there were some places which would never be reached. At the end of the day all but four bodies had been recovered. "In the day o' judgment," a miner said, "they four'll come out of here." Those unclaimed bodies haunted Scorrier. He came on sentences of writing, where men waiting to be suffocated had written down their feelings. In one place, the hour, the word "Sleepy," and a signature. In another, "A. F.—done for." When he came up at last Pippin was still waiting, pocket-book in hand; they again departed at a furious pace.

Two days later Scorrier, visiting the shaft, found its neighbourhood deserted—not a living thing of any sort was there except one Chinaman poking his stick into the rubbish. Pippin was away down the coast engaging an engineer; and on his return, Scorrier had not the heart to tell him of the desertion. He was spared the effort, for Pippin said: "Don't be afraid—you've got bad news? The men have gone on strike."

Scorrier sighed. "Lock, stock, and barrel"

"I thought so—see what I have here!" He put before Scorrier a telegram:

"At all costs keep working—fatal to stop—manage this somehow.—HEMMINGS."

Breathing quickly, he added: "As if I didn't know! 'Manage this somehow'—a little hard!"

"What's to be done?" asked Scorrier.

"You see I am commanded!" Pippin answered bitterly. "And they're quite right; we must keep working—our contracts! Now I'm down—not a soul will spare me!"

The miners' meeting was held the following day on the outskirts of the town. Pippin had cleared the place to make a public recreation-ground—a sort of feather in the company's cap; it was now to be the spot whereon should be decided the question of the company's life or death.

The sky to the west was crossed by a single line of cloud like a bar of beaten gold; tree shadows crept towards the groups of men; the evening savour, that strong fragrance of the forest, sweetened the air. The miners stood all round amongst the burnt tree-stumps, cowed and sullen. They looked incapable of movement or expression. It was this dumb paralysis that frightened Scorrier. He watched Pippin speaking from his phaeton, the butt of all those sullen, restless eyes. Would he last out? Would the wires hold? It was like the finish of a race. He caught a baffled look on Pippin's face, as if he despaired of piercing that terrible paralysis. The men's eyes had begun to wander. 'He's lost his hold,' thought Scorrier; 'it's all up!'

A miner close beside him muttered: "Look out!"

Pippin was leaning forward, his voice had risen, the words fell like a whiplash on the faces of the crowd: "You shan't throw me over; do you think I'll give up all I've done for you? I'll make you the first power in the colony! Are you turning tail at the first shot? You're a set of cowards, my lads!"

Each man round Scorrier was listening with a different motion of the hands—one rubbed them, one clenched them, another moved his closed fist, as if stabbing some one in the back. A grisly-bearded, beetle-browed, twinkling-eyed old Cornishman muttered: "A'hm not troublin' about that." It seemed almost as if Pippin's object was to get the men to kill him; they had gathered closer, crouching for a rush. Suddenly Pippin's voice dropped to a whisper: "I'm disgraced Men, are you going back on me?"

The old miner next Scorrier called out suddenly: "Anny that's Cornishmen here to stand by the superintendent?" A group drew together, and with murmurs and gesticulation the meeting broke up.

In the evening a deputation came to visit Pippin; and all night long their voices and the superintendent's footsteps could be heard. In the morning, Pippin went early to the mine. Before supper the deputation came again; and again Scorrier had to listen hour after hour to the sound of voices and footsteps till he fell asleep. Just before dawn he was awakened by a light. Pippin stood at his bedside. "The men go down to-morrow," he said: "What did I tell you? Carry me home on my shield, eh?"

In a week the mine was in full work.

V

Two years later, Scorrier heard once more of Pippin. A note from Hemmings reached him asking if he could make it convenient to attend their Board meeting the following Thursday. He arrived rather before the appointed time. The secretary received him, and, in answer to inquiry, said: "Thank you, we are doing well—between ourselves, we are doing very well."

"And Pippin?"

The secretary frowned. "Ah, Pippin! We asked you to come on his account. Pippin is giving us a lot of trouble. We have not had a single line from him for just two years!" He spoke with such a sense of personal grievance that Scorrier felt quite sorry for him. "Not a single line," said Hemmings, "since that explosion—you were there at the time, I remember! It makes it very awkward; I call it personal to me."

"But how—" Scorrier began.

"We get—telegrams. He writes to no one, not even to his family. And why? Just tell me why? We hear of him; he's a great nob out there. Nothing's done in the colony without his finger being in the pie. He turned out the last Government because they wouldn't grant us an extension for our railway—shows he can't be a fool. Besides, look at our balance-sheet!"

It turned out that the question on which Scorrier's opinion was desired was, whether Hemmings should be sent out to see what was the matter with the superintendent. During the discussion which ensued, he was an unwilling listener to strictures on Pippin's silence. "The explosion," he muttered at last, "a very trying time!"

Mr. Booker pounced on him. "A very trying time! So it was—to all of us. But what excuse is that—now, Mr. Scorrier, what excuse is that?"

Scorrier was obliged to admit that it was none.

"Business is business—eh, what?"

Scorrier, gazing round that neat Board-room, nodded. A deaf director, who had not spoken for some months, said with sudden fierceness: "It's disgraceful!" He was obviously letting off the fume of long-unuttered disapprovals. One perfectly neat, benevolent old fellow, however, who had kept his hat on, and had a single vice—that of coming to the Board-room with a brown paper parcel tied up with string—murmured: "We must make all allowances," and started an anecdote about his youth. He was gently called to order by his secretary. Scorrier was asked for his opinion. He looked at Hemmings. "My importance is concerned," was written all over the secretary's face. Moved by an impulse of loyalty to Pippin, Scorrier answered, as if it were all settled: "Well, let me know when you are starting, Hemmings—I should like the trip myself."

As he was going out, the chairman, old Jolyon Forsyte, with a grave, twinkling look at Hemmings, took him aside. "Glad to hear you say that about going too, Mr. Scorrier; we must be careful—Pippin's such a good fellow, and so sensitive; and our friend there—a bit heavy in the hand, um?"

Scorrier did in fact go out with Hemmings. The secretary was sea-sick, and his prostration, dignified but noisy, remained a memory for ever; it was sonorous and fine—the prostration of superiority; and the way in which he spoke of it, taking casual acquaintances into the caves of his experience, was truly interesting.

Pippin came down to the capital to escort them, provided for their comforts as if they had been royalty, and had a special train to take them to the mines.

He was a little stouter, brighter of colour, greyer of beard, more nervous perhaps in voice and breathing. His manner to Hemmings was full of flattering courtesy; but his sly, ironical glances played on the secretary's armour like a fountain on a hippopotamus. To Scorrier, however, he could not show enough affection:

The first evening, when Hemmings had gone to his room, he jumped up like a boy out of school. "So I'm going to get a wigging," he said; "I suppose I deserve it; but if you knew—if you only knew...! Out here they've nicknamed me 'the King'—they say I rule the colony. It's myself that I can't rule"; and with a sudden burst of passion such as Scorrier had never seen in him: "Why did they send this man here? What can he know about the things that I've been through?" In a moment he calmed down again. "There! this is very stupid; worrying you like this!" and with a long, kind look into Scorrier's face, he hustled him off to bed.

Pippin did not break out again, though fire seemed to smoulder behind the bars of his courteous irony. Intuition of danger had evidently smitten Hemmings, for he made no allusion to the object of his visit. There were moments when Scorrier's common-sense sided with Hemmings—these were moments when the secretary was not present.

'After all,' he told himself, 'it's a little thing to ask—one letter a month. I never heard of such a case.' It was wonderful indeed how they stood it! It showed how much they valued Pippin! What was the matter with him? What was the nature of his trouble? One glimpse Scorrier had when even Hemmings, as he phrased it, received "quite a turn." It was during a drive back from the most outlying of the company's trial mines, eight miles through the forest. The track led through a belt of trees blackened by a forest fire. Pippin was driving. The secretary seated beside him wore an expression of faint alarm, such as

Pippin's driving was warranted to evoke from almost any face. The sky had darkened strangely, but pale streaks of light, coming from one knew not where, filtered through the trees. No breath was stirring; the wheels and horses' hoofs made no sound on the deep fern mould. All around, the burnt tree-trunks, leafless and jagged, rose like withered giants, the passages between them were black, the sky black, and black the silence. No one spoke, and literally the only sound was Pippin's breathing. What was it that was so terrifying? Scorrier had a feeling of entombment; that nobody could help him; the feeling of being face to face with Nature; a sensation as if all the comfort and security of words and rules had dropped away from him. And-nothing happened. They reached home and dined.

During dinner he had again that old remembrance of a little man chopping at a castle with his sword. It came at a moment when Pippin had raised his hand with the carving-knife grasped in it to answer some remark of Hemmings' about the future of the company. The optimism in his uplifted chin, the strenuous energy in his whispering voice, gave Scorrier a more vivid glimpse of Pippin's nature than he had perhaps ever had before. This new country, where nothing but himself could help a man—that was the castle! No wonder Pippin was impatient of control, no wonder he was out of hand, no wonder he was silent—chopping away at that! And suddenly he thought: 'Yes, and all the time one knows, Nature must beat him in the end!'

That very evening Hemmings delivered himself of his reproof. He had sat unusually silent; Scorrier, indeed, had thought him a little drunk, so portentous was his gravity; suddenly, however he rose. It was hard on a man, he said, in his position, with a Board (he spoke as of a family of small children), to be kept so short of information. He was actually compelled to use his imagination to answer the shareholders' questions. This was painful and humiliating; he had never heard of any secretary having to use his imagination! He went further—it was insulting! He had grown grey in the service of the company. Mr. Scorrier would bear him out when he said he had a position to maintain—his name in the City was a high one; and, by George! he was going to keep it a high one; he would allow nobody to drag it in the dust—that ought clearly to be understood. His directors felt they were being treated like children; however that might be, it was absurd to suppose that he (Hemmings) could be treated like a child...! The secretary paused; his eyes seemed to bully the room.

"If there were no London office," murmured Pippin, "the shareholders would get the same dividends."

Hemmings gasped. "Come!" he said, "this is monstrous!"

"What help did I get from London when I first came here? What help have I ever had?"

Hemmings swayed, recovered, and with a forced smile replied that, if this were true, he had been standing on his head for years; he did not believe the attitude possible for such a length of time; personally he would have thought that he too had had a little something to say to the company's position, but no matter...! His irony was crushing.... It was possible that Mr. Pippin hoped to reverse the existing laws of the universe with regard to limited companies; he would merely say that he must not begin with a company of which he (Hemmings) happened to be secretary. Mr. Scorrier had hinted at excuses; for his part, with the best intentions in the world, he had great difficulty in seeing them. He would go further—he did not see them! The explosion...! Pippin shrank so visibly that Hemmings seemed troubled by a suspicion that he had gone too far.

"We know," he said, "that it was trying for you...."

"Trying!" "burst out Pippin.

"No one can say," Hemmings resumed soothingly, "that we have not dealt liberally." Pippin made a motion of the head. "We think we have a good superintendent; I go further, an excellent superintendent. What I say is: Let's be pleasant! I am not making an unreasonable request!" He ended on a fitting note of jocularity; and, as if by consent, all three withdrew, each to his own room, without another word.

In the course of the next day Pippin said to Scorrier: "It seems I have been very wicked. I must try to do better"; and with a touch of bitter humour, "They are kind enough to think me a good superintendent, you see! After that I must try hard."

Scorrier broke in: "No man could have done so much for them;" and, carried away by an impulse to put things absolutely straight, went on "But, after all, a letter now and then—what does it amount to?"

Pippin besieged him with a subtle glance. "You too?" he said—"I must indeed have been a wicked man!" and turned away.

Scorrier felt as if he had been guilty of brutality; sorry for Pippin, angry with himself; angry with Pippin, sorry for himself. He earnestly desired to see the back of Hemmings. The secretary gratified the wish a few days later, departing by steamer with ponderous expressions of regard and the assurance of his goodwill.

Pippin gave vent to no outburst of relief, maintaining a courteous silence, making only one allusion to his late guest, in answer to a remark of Scorrier:

"Ah! don't tempt me! mustn't speak behind his back."

VI

A month passed, and Scorrier still—remained Pippin's guest. As each mail-day approached he experienced a queer suppressed excitement. On one of these occasions Pippin had withdrawn to his room; and when Scorrier went to fetch him to dinner he found him with his head leaning on his hands, amid a perfect fitter of torn paper. He looked up at Scorrier.

"I can't do it," he said, "I feel such a hypocrite; I can't put myself into leading-strings again. Why should I ask these people, when I've settled everything already? If it were a vital matter they wouldn't want to hear—they'd simply wire, 'Manage this somehow!'"

Scorrier said nothing, but thought privately 'This is a mad business!' What was a letter? Why make a fuss about a letter? The approach of mail-day seemed like a nightmare to the superintendent; he became feverishly nervous like a man under a spell; and, when the mail had gone, behaved like a respited criminal. And this had been going on two years! Ever since that explosion. Why, it was monomania!

One day, a month after Hemmings' departure, Pippin rose early from dinner; his face was flushed, he had been drinking wine. "I won't be beaten this time," he said, as he passed Scorrier. The latter could hear him writing in the next room, and looked in presently to say that he was going for a walk. Pippin gave him a kindly nod.

It was a cool, still evening: innumerable stars swarmed in clusters over the forests, forming bright hieroglyphics in the middle heavens, showering over the dark harbour into the sea. Scorrier walked slowly. A weight seemed lifted from his mind, so entangled had he become in that uncanny silence. At last Pippin had broken through the spell. To get that, letter sent would be the laying of a phantom, the rehabilitation of commonsense. Now that this silence was in the throes of being broken, he felt curiously tender towards Pippin, without the hero-worship of old days, but with a queer protective feeling. After all, he was different from other men. In spite of his feverish, tenacious energy, in spite of his ironic humour, there was something of the woman in him! And as for this silence, this horror of control—all geniuses had "bees in their bonnets," and Pippin was a genius in his way!

He looked back at the town. Brilliantly lighted it had a thriving air—difficult to believe of the place he remembered ten years back; the sounds of drinking, gambling, laughter, and dancing floated to his ears. 'Quite a city!' he thought.

With this queer elation on him he walked slowly back along the street, forgetting that he was simply an oldish mining expert, with a look of shabbiness, such as clings to men who are always travelling, as if their "nap" were for ever being rubbed off. And he thought of Pippin, creator of this glory.

He had passed the boundaries of the town, and had entered the forest. A feeling of discouragement instantly beset him. The scents and silence, after the festive cries and odours of the town, were undefinably oppressive. Notwithstanding, he walked a long time, saying to himself that he would give the letter every chance. At last, when he thought that Pippin must have finished, he went back to the house.

Pippin had finished. His forehead rested on the table, his arms hung at his sides; he was stone-dead! His face wore a smile, and by his side lay an empty laudanum bottle.

The letter, closely, beautifully written, lay before him. It was a fine document, clear, masterly, detailed, nothing slurred, nothing concealed, nothing omitted; a complete review of the company's position; it ended with the words: "Your humble servant, RICHARD PIPPIN."

Scorrier took possession of it. He dimly understood that with those last words a wire had snapped. The border-line had been overpassed; the point reached where that sense of proportion, which alone makes life possible, is lost. He was certain that at the moment of his death Pippin could have discussed bimetallism, or any intellectual problem, except the one problem of his own heart; that, for some mysterious reason, had been too much for him. His death had been the work of a moment of supreme revolt—a single instant of madness on a single subject! He found on the blotting-paper, scrawled across the impress of the signature, "Can't stand it!" The completion of that letter had been to him a struggle ungraspable by Scorrier. Slavery? Defeat? A violation of Nature? The death of justice? It were better not to think of it! Pippin could have told—but he would never speak again. Nature, at whom, unaided, he had dealt so many blows, had taken her revenge...!

In the night Scorrier stole down, and, with an ashamed face, cut off a lock of the fine grey hair. 'His daughter might like it!' he thought....

He waited till Pippin was buried, then, with the letter in his pocket, started for England.

He arrived at Liverpool on a Thursday morning, and travelling to town, drove straight to the office of the company. The Board were sitting. Pippin's successor was already being interviewed. He passed out as Scorrier came in, a middle-aged man with a large, red beard, and a foxy, compromising face. He also was a Cornishman. Scorrier wished him luck with a very heavy heart.

As an unsentimental man, who had a proper horror of emotion, whose living depended on his good sense, to look back on that interview with the Board was painful. It had excited in him a rage of which he was now heartily ashamed. Old Jolyon Forsyte, the chairman, was not there for once, guessing perhaps that the Board's view of this death would be too small for him; and little Mr. Booker sat in his place. Every one had risen, shaken hands with Scorrier, and expressed themselves indebted for his coming. Scorrier placed Pippin's letter on the table, and gravely the secretary read out to his Board the last words of their superintendent. When he had finished, a director said, "That's not the letter of a madman!" Another answered: "Mad as a hatter; nobody but a madman would have thrown up such a post." Scorrier suddenly withdrew. He heard Hemmings calling after him. "Aren't you well, Mr. Scorrier? aren't you well, sir?"

He shouted back: "Quite sane, I thank you...."

The Naples "express" rolled round the outskirts of the town. Vesuvius shone in the sun, uncrowned by smoke. But even as Scorrier looked, a white puff went soaring up. It was the footnote to his memories.

February 1901. February 1901.